Praise for *Shelter in the Storm*

"With lovely, evocative writing, Laurel Blount brings to life a tender story of two wounded hearts healing and finding lasting love in the wake of tragedy."

—Marta Perry, national bestselling
author of *A Springtime Heart*

"Laurel Blount's *Shelter in the Storm* is the perfect mixture of sweet romance and family drama. Naomi is a fully fleshed[-out] character who will win your heart with her sincerity and wisdom as she and Joseph face an unthinkable tragedy. Their Amish world is as fascinating as their struggle to remain grounded in their faith. Readers will relate to their unflagging efforts to hold on through a season of storms. As Joseph's father says, 'When our world goes dark, then we must hold hard to the rope of our faith, and trust Gott to lead us out.' This is the kind of hope-filled story that readers are hungry for."

—Dana Mentink, national bestselling
author of *Secrets Resurfaced*

"I couldn't stop reading *Shelter in the Storm*. Laurel Blount mixes comforting, homey Amish romance with exciting suspense and cliffhanger chapter endings. Her characters are real and appealing, and I was rooting for them from start to finish. I'm so glad there will be more books in the Johns Mill series. It is off to a wonderful start!"

—Lee Tobin McClain, *USA Today*
bestselling author of *Cottage at the Beach*

"Two very different worlds clash in this heartfelt story of faith, family, forgiveness, and love. Endearing characters warm the heart in this hopeful love story."

—Tina Radcliffe, author of *Ready to Trust*

"This is a very good book. Laurel Blount's *Shelter in the Storm* had me hooked from the first line. . . . This sweet, tragic story is touching and honest and beautiful. I highly recommend this book, and I can't wait for the next book in the Johns Mill Amish series by the amazing Laurel Blount."

—Lenora Worth, *New York Times* bestselling
author of *Seeking Refuge*

SHELTER IN THE STORM

Laurel Blount

JOVE
New York

A JOVE BOOK
Published by Berkley
An imprint of Penguin Random House LLC
penguinrandomhouse.com

Copyright © 2021 by Laurel Blount
Penguin Random House supports copyright. Copyright fuels creativity, encourages
diverse voices, promotes free speech, and creates a vibrant culture. Thank you for buying
an authorized edition of this book and for complying with copyright laws by not
reproducing, scanning, or distributing any part of it in any form without permission.
You are supporting writers and allowing Penguin Random House to continue to
publish books for every reader.

A JOVE BOOK, BERKLEY, and the BERKLEY & B colophon are registered
trademarks of Penguin Random House LLC.

ISBN: 9780593200209

First Edition: May 2021

Printed in the United States of America
1   3   5   7   9   10   8   6   4   2

Book design by George Towne

In memory of my beloved grandmother
Helen Beasley Russell,
who sheltered her own family through the storms of
war, widowhood, poverty, illness, and loss.
Her unflagging faith in her Lord,
her grace, and her grit
saw her through—and she did it
all laughing and dressed to the nines.

I have never seen her equal,
and she inspires me even today.

Oodles of love, Memama. Until we meet again.

CHAPTER ONE

❧

THERE WOULD BE NO MORE GENTLE DAYS.

Joseph Hochstedler knew it the minute he stepped out of his parents' Tennessee farmhouse into the predawn darkness. December had been showing on *Mamm*'s kitchen calendar for almost a week, but today was the first time he'd felt the bite of winter. And at twenty-six, he'd spent enough seasons working outside to sense that this sullen chill had hunkered down to stay.

His mind on the weather, Joseph walked halfway across the side yard before he realized his mistake. Before him lay the stone dairy, his automatic destination every morning up until about a month ago. He stood for a few heartbeats, studying the silent building that until recently had loomed so large in all their lives.

For six generations the habits of the Hochstedler men had been regulated by the unyielding discipline of twice-daily milkings. Dairy farming was regarded as one of the hardest ways for Amish men to earn a living, but that had never mattered to the Hochstedlers. They'd never been afraid of hard work.

Ever since he'd been old enough to follow *Daed* outside in the early mornings, Joseph had considered himself a dairyman. He'd grown up with the baritone lowing of the cows, the smell of the barn, the rich tradition of hanging his own hat on the same worn peg his great-grandfather had used. *Grossdaddi* had done this from necessity because he could milk faster bareheaded, pressing his forehead close to the Jersey's warm flank. Joseph's father had been allowed to use surge milkers in the dairy, but he had trained Joseph and his brother Caleb to hang up their hats in the barn, just the same.

Traditions died hard with the Hochstedlers.

At least *Grossdaddi* hadn't lived long enough to witness the death of the Hochstedler Dairy. Joseph was thankful for that.

He exhaled, his breath fogging the sharp air. Then he turned toward the smaller wooden barn, already glowing with the light from *Daed*'s lanterns.

"You're almost too late." Caleb, Joseph's younger brother, sat hunched in a stall, milking their last remaining Jersey. Sure enough, the steel pail was almost full; each hissing stream of milk sent splashes over the sides. "With only Daisy to milk, the chores go fast. Wouldn't you know? Not until I marry and leave home does *Daed* decide to sell the herd and take up the lazy life of a shopkeeper!"

Their father barked a laugh from the feed room, where he was measuring scratch for *Mamm*'s hens. "No time for laziness here, cows or not. Plenty of hard work yet, building up the store business."

"From what I hear, you already have plenty customers coming by. That's *gut*. A lot easier to spend your mornings adding up sales behind a shop counter instead of mucking out after two dozen cows, ain't so, Joseph?"

Joseph didn't answer. Keeping his back to his brother, he

forked the morning's ration of hay into the stalls of the family's buggy horses. His favorite gelding nickered appreciatively, and Joseph paused to stroke Titus's muscled neck.

He'd found nothing easy about any of the mornings he'd spent working in his parents' new store, selling jams and quilts and faceless dolls to *Englischers*. This particular morning, though, was turning into the hardest yet.

Yesterday, Caleb and Rhoda had returned to Johns Mill after their monthlong wedding trip visiting family in Kentucky and Ohio. Joseph had braced himself for that, and he thought he'd been prepared. Then last night Caleb had pointed out there was more room at the Hochstedlers' than with Rhoda's folks, and he'd asked if they could stay on for a few weeks while they looked around for a place of their own.

Joseph had caught the quick glance his parents had exchanged. They suspected, as he did, that Caleb's request had little to do with space and more to do with his headstrong brother's reluctance to live under the roof of the local bishop. Nonetheless, the request had been promptly granted. It was their way to take in family whenever needed, and *Mamm* was pleased to have the chance to spend more time with Caleb and her new daughter-in-law. The arrangement had been accepted matter-of-factly by everybody involved—except for Joseph.

He'd said nothing, of course, although the prospect of living elbow-to-elbow with the happy couple chafed him. The idea of seeing Rhoda every day, passing her in the hallways, seeing her seated at the family table as his brother's wife . . .

That was pain he could have done without.

Caleb started his new job on Samuel Christner's construction crew this morning. Joseph had hoped for a break from his brother, but Caleb had risen early and headed to the barn for chores, as if nothing had changed.

Joseph had lingered in the kitchen after *Daed* and Caleb

had gone out. The less Joseph saw of his brother with that scruff of new-married beard on his face, the easier it would be to hold his tongue. That was exactly what he had to do, until his stubborn heart fell in line with the faith he'd been born and baptized into—a faith that required forgiveness, regardless of the offense. Seeing Caleb wreathed in smiles, shooting possessive glances at Rhoda as she moved quietly around the kitchen helping *Mamm*, was testing Joseph's determination to its limit.

Joseph leaned the pitchfork against the weathered wall with the other tools just as Caleb clanged the lid on the milk pail.

"Are we about ready to head in for breakfast, *Daed*?" Caleb asked. "Rhoda's frying up that venison sausage we brought from Melvin's. Wait until you taste it!"

"*Ja*," their father answered. "I heard my brother was happy with his sausages this year."

"And that was the only thing he was happy about," Caleb replied. "It is hard to believe Melvin's your brother, *Daed*. Our *onkel* is the sourest man I have ever met."

Daed sighed. "*Ach*, well. He's had his share of sorrows, has Melvin. To have only the one son and then to have him crippled in an accident, not just in body but in his mind as well . . . that would be a hard blow for any man to bear without bitterness."

"Henry needs a lot of looking after, for sure. Rhoda helped Nella all she could while we were there, and I pitched in with the dairy work. There was more work than hands to do it, even so."

"It's hard for Nella and Melvin since their girls married into different districts," *Daed* agreed.

"I don't blame the *kossins* for leaving. Oak Point is stricter than most. Rhoda was spoken to for wearing a dress in too light a color. Can you believe that? Rhoda's never been in trouble in her life, and she was only a visitor there. It shamed her, and it made me mad."

"That does seem harsh. The both of you can count your blessings now you're back home, *ja?* You can go on to the house, Caleb. You'd best get that milk in and get ready for work. Your *bruder* and I will finish up."

"I've time yet before my driver comes. Rhoda and I want to do our share of the work while we're here." Caleb darted a look in Joseph's direction, but Joseph turned his head, focusing on the grain he was scooping into the horse's bucket.

Daed shooed his younger son away. "Right now, your share is to get that milk to your *mamm* for straining. If you don't, Melvin's sausage won't be the only thing frying in the kitchen this morning. She'll have your hindquarters up on the griddle, married man or not."

"She might at that." Chuckling, Caleb picked up the milk pail and started for the house. Joseph's glance strayed after his brother, then caught on the scene framed by the wide kitchen windows.

Rhoda stood at *Mamm*'s stove, a spatula poised in her hand. His heart thudded hard at the sight of her. It always did, ever since the afternoon he'd come home from the fields and found Rhoda Lambright and his sister Emma frying cherry pies to sell at the annual horse auction.

She'd worn a plum-colored dress that day, and her cheeks had matched it, flushed bright from the heat of the bubbling oil. Rhoda and Caleb's twin, Emma, had been friends since their schooldays. Joseph had never paid much attention to her before, but when she'd glanced up at him, Joseph had suddenly realized that little Rhoda wasn't so little anymore.

And that she was the prettiest thing he'd seen in all his life.

He'd set his heart on her in that moment, but she was only sixteen, barely old enough to think about courting. He was twenty-one, a bumbler when it came to talking with the girls, and the dairy was in its death throes. There was time enough, he'd figured. He'd wait for Rhoda to grow up some, wait until he had more than a pile of unpaid bills to offer a wife before he spoke.

He'd waited too long, and his brother had spoken first. Nobody had seen that coming. Headstrong Caleb, the Hochstedler who'd had more trouble with the deacons than all the rest of them combined, had somehow won the heart of the bishop's only daughter.

It would have been funny, that, if things had been different.

Joseph pulled his gaze away from the window. Rhoda was Caleb's *fraw* now, and she would be until death parted them. Somehow Joseph had to find a way to think of her exactly as he did Emma and Miriam, as a sister. Nothing less and certainly nothing more.

As impossible as that seemed right now, Joseph had a feeling it would be easier than coming to love Caleb as a brother again.

"Chicken feed is mixed. Are you done with the horses?"

Joseph jumped. Lost in his thoughts, he hadn't noticed *Daed* standing beside him on the hard-packed earthen floor of the barn. His father was dressed in his chore clothes, so soiled that they were no good for regular wear. He smelled like all the mornings of Joseph's memory—better mornings—of grain and manure, of horses and cows, and the warm sweetness of fresh milk.

Joseph missed those days, but it was clear enough that his parents did not. Years of relentless work and financial strain had taken a heavy toll. As the dairy and other local farms failed, Elijah Hochstedler's brothers and sisters had relocated to different communities, one by one, and each time, the lines in *Daed*'s face had deepened. Family, Elijah believed, was second only to *Gott*.

At least he seemed happier now that the difficulty of closing the dairy was behind him. He appeared to like the store work well enough, and he enjoyed spending his days busy with *Mamm*, interacting with folks. *Mamm* was happier, too. Since the herd had been sold off, she looked ten years younger.

It was *gut* for his parents, this change, and although Joseph would never be happy about the decision, he was thankful for that.

It made what he needed to say easier.

"*Daed*, I have been thinking. The store is running fine, and you've not much need of me here. Maybe I should go to Melvin's for a while, help him with his dairying. If you think he'd be agreeable, that is."

His father shot him a measuring look. "I think my brother would jump at such a chance. I also think he'd work you into the ground and give you little in return for your labor. And what of your woodworking? Don't you have projects to finish that folks have put money down on?"

"A few. I'll get them done before I leave."

"How long would you plan to stay?"

"I don't know." *Until this pain ebbs off. Until I can look at my brother's wife and not see only the woman I wanted for myself.* "A good while, likely."

His father sighed. "Is it so bad here, then? That you'd go to such a place as your brother described? I'll not stand in your way if you're bound to leave, but we've other family. You could go to Pennsylvania, maybe, and help Norman with his grocery store, if you're looking to spend time away."

"I'm no storekeeper, *Daed*. I'm a dairyman. You heard for yourself that Melvin needs the help."

"*Ja*, maybe that is true, but I don't think it's what's driving this buggy. It is a hard thing for you, seeing your brother married to the girl you'd chosen for yourself. I am sorry for that, but you should not let it push you into making a rash decision."

Joseph glanced up sharply. He'd never spoken to *Daed* about his feelings for Rhoda. In their community, such things weren't discussed until relationships were firmed up and headed for marriage. "You knew?"

"Ja." His father's lips twitched above his salt-and-pepper beard. "I have eyes, son, and I was once a young man myself. I knew. Just as I know that you are struggling now to set aside your own feelings for the good of the family, like you did when it came time to sell the herd. Two such hard blows back-to-back are not so easy to bear, but you must keep trusting in the Lord. When our world goes dark, then we must hold hard to the rope of our faith, and trust *Gott* to lead us out. He is merciful and will bring the good out of our troubles, in His own time."

Joseph blew out a slow breath. "I am not seeing so much *gut* right now."

"That will get easier. In time I believe you will join the rest of the family in thanking *Gott* for the blessing of this marriage. I was worried about Caleb and so was your *mamm.* He was born muleheaded, and he only got more stubborn as he got older. *Gott* knows His business, Joseph. He knew it would take strong ties to keep such a heart here among us. Rhoda's life is steeped in our faith. She and the *kinder* they will have together will steady Caleb's faith as well. It is a *gut* match."

"Ja. For Caleb." Joseph couldn't keep the bitterness out of his voice.

"For Rhoda, too. She's too serious, that one, but Caleb will liven her up. Before long, she'll be laughing as easily as our Emma." His father frowned suddenly. "Speaking of Emma, I've asked her to stay home and help Rhoda get settled in. *Mamm* and I will be taking Miriam with us at the store today."

Joseph lifted his eyebrows. Even at twenty, Miriam was painfully shy, and unlike her friendly older sister, she always went tongue-tied and red-faced around strangers. She'd be even more miserable working at the store than he was himself.

He hadn't asked his question aloud, but *Daed* answered it anyway. "An *Englisch* boy's been coming around since we started work on the store building back in October. His father's that lawyer who has the office in town. Abbott is the name. You and Caleb did some work for the family some time back, *ja?*"

Joseph nodded. "Two or three years ago, some cabinetry work in the kitchen." He remembered it well. It had been his most profitable job to date, even though Abbott had conveniently forgotten to pay for the upgraded cabinet pulls he'd added on at the last minute. "Trevor is their only child. Caleb and I didn't see much of him. He stayed in his room, mostly. Slept late. His *mamm* wouldn't let us make noise until after eleven in the morning." He and Caleb had marveled privately over a healthy boy being allowed to hold up men's work because of such laziness. *Daed* would have put a quick stop to that, certain sure. "Is he causing trouble?"

"He likes to talk to our Emma. At first, we thought little of it. The boy seemed lonesome and awkward, and you know your sister. Any wounded thing she sees, she wants to help. Since we opened the store, she takes her lunch break first, down at Miller's Café. It seems he's been coming to sit with her, bringing her things. Gifts that are not appropriate for her to accept, some very costly. So *Mamm* and I talked it over last night, and we think it best for Emma to be away from the store for a bit. You didn't know about any of this?"

"I did not. Emma told you about it?"

"She told Caleb. She did not know how to discourage the boy without hurting his feelings, and she wanted his advice. Caleb thought it best to tell me."

If Emma had wanted *Daed* to know, she'd have gone to him herself. Still, in spite of everything, Joseph couldn't fault his brother's decision. He'd have done the same. Sometimes Emma was too kindhearted for her own good.

"Like most *Englischers*, the Abbotts don't understand

much about our way of living. I can have a word with Trevor, if you want." Talking wasn't Joseph's strong suit, but he could make himself clear enough to get this job done.

His father gave him a knowing glance. "*Nee*, best I handle that. I just wanted to hear your thoughts on the matter, see what you knew of this boy."

"Not much. He wasn't so cocky as a lot of *Englisch youngies*, I remember that. He had the look of a whipped dog, never said too much. I'm not surprised Emma felt sorry for him or that he took to her. He'd likely take to anybody who showed him attention. Once Emma's gone from the store, I doubt he'll cause any more trouble."

"*Gut*." His father nodded. "Then this will be easily remedied. In any case, it will do Miriam good to spend time in town. We have coddled her too much, her being the youngest. She must make the effort to get past her shyness when it's necessary."

"Well, one thing's certain sure. You won't have to worry about Miriam striking up any friendships with *Englisch* boys. They scare her to death."

Just then *Mamm* stuck one arm out and clanged the large dinner bell mounted beside the back door. The sound echoed against the surrounding hills, Levonia Hochstedler's earsplitting warning that her menfolk were late for breakfast.

"We are coming!" his father called.

"*Gut!*" *Mamm* answered shortly. She disappeared, banging the door shut.

His father chuckled. "Nothing riles your *Mamm* like seeing her good food going cold. We'd best get ourselves inside."

"You can go on in. I've no time to eat this morning. I'm taking a crib next door to Aaron Lapp's. Katie's *boppli* is six weeks old already, and I just finished the thing last night. I'll head to the store after."

"*Nee*. You'll come back here after and work on finishing

your carpentry projects. If you're sure Ohio is where you want to go, I'll write a letter to Melvin this evening, and we'll get your visit arranged. Who knows? Maybe this is *Gott*'s plan. Likely you'll find yourself a nice girl while you're up there, and all this trouble will be forgotten." His father clapped him hard on the shoulder and winked. "But maybe you learn something from your old *Daed*, and you don't give your *fraw* such a loud bell by the back door, *ja?*"

CHAPTER TWO

❧

HUMMING SOFTLY, NAOMI SCHROCK WASHED THE breakfast dishes as slowly as she could. Her humming and the gentle sloshing of the sudsy water were the only sounds in the house. For the first time in all of her twenty-four years, Naomi was alone, and she was determined to enjoy every second of it.

She'd better. It would end soon enough.

She'd realized that an hour ago, when her *kossin* Katie had appeared in the kitchen with her second-best dress on and a look of purpose on her face.

"I can't stay cooped up in this house another minute!" she'd announced. "Let's hitch up the buggy and take little Sarah to see Aaron's *grossdaddi*. He's been doing poorly, and some of Aaron's cousins have come down to visit him. I haven't seen those girls since our wedding, and I want to show them the baby."

Naomi's heart had fallen to her sensible shoes. "Are you sure you're feeling up to it? And it's so chilly today. Do you really want to take Sarah out?"

Katie had flapped an impatient hand. "It's been six weeks since my C-section. I feel fine, and I've been fussed over enough. Not," she'd added quickly, "that I haven't appreciated your help! I didn't know what I was going to do when *Mamm* put her back out after only two weeks. You've been such a blessing, Naomi! But I'm truly all better now, and we can bundle Sarah up to her little nose. She'll be all right."

A few minutes ago, Katie and Sarah had clopped off down the road, but Naomi had decided to stay behind. Once she finished these breakfast dishes, she'd walk to the call shack and arrange her trip home. Then she'd come back here and do some serious scrubbing. Leaving Katie with a sparkling clean house was the least Naomi could do in exchange for the happiest four weeks of her life.

She hated to leave, but if Katie was well enough to go jaunting around for visits, she certainly didn't need Naomi underfoot anymore. Time to head home to Kentucky, to go back to being shuttled from one brother's home to another's, as she'd been since her mother had joined her father in heaven last year. The thought made silly tears spring to her eyes, and she impatiently dashed them away with the rolled-up sleeve of her dark green dress.

Schtupid to be crying when she should be on her knees thanking *Gott* for all He had given her. After everything she'd been through, just standing here healthy and energetic wasn't something she should take for granted. Besides, having family to go back to was a blessing some poor folks went their whole lives without—and Naomi had five brothers, all married and with growing families of their own.

Naomi rinsed a coffee cup and upended it neatly on the dish drainer. She *was* thankful, truly. It had just been so—nice—here with Katie and Aaron. Nice to have important work to do, nursing Katie and helping tend to baby Sarah, and finally trying her hand at some real cooking. Nice to have her own room and not be wedged in a corner of the children's bedroom, attempting to find ways to be a blessing to whatever overburdened sister-in-law was sheltering her at the moment.

It had been good to feel welcome for a change, to be useful and needed.

Naomi dunked the sticky oatmeal pot into the dishwater and scrubbed industriously. Well, she was done here with Katie, and maybe now her brothers and their wives would look at Naomi differently. They'd see that she was able-bodied, capable of being a help instead of a burden.

And if they didn't . . . well, *Gott* might send her other folks to help. Other new *mamms* or people recovering from operations. She knew plenty about that.

One thing was for sure and certain about the Plain life, there was no shortage of hard work. Now that Naomi was finally, wonderfully well, she could pitch in and start repaying the community that had helped her so much since she was diagnosed with Wolff-Parkinson-White syndrome at age two.

Before that, none of them had even heard of this congenital heart disorder, and any illness involving the heart was spiritually tricky for the Amish. Her church leaders had pored over the information sheets the pediatric cardiologist had provided, trying their best to understand how two separate areas of Naomi's heart were doing battle over its rhythm. They'd also dug deep in their collective pockets to pay for medications and expensive specialists while everyone waited to see if Naomi would be one of the children who simply outgrew the problem.

She hadn't been. She'd never forget the sacrifices her community had then made just so she could be standing at this sink washing dishes, her heart beating in a blessedly normal cadence. Naomi's health had been bought at a price, and she planned to make up for lost time, working hard and doing all the good she could.

A low rumbling noise distracted Naomi from her thoughts, and she tiptoed to peek through the kitchen window over the sink. A pickup carriage was lumbering up the drive toward the house. Joseph Hochstedler must finally be stopping by to deliver Sarah's crib.

Naomi's heartbeat sped up, and she froze and frowned, pressing one damp hand hard against her breast. Then she relaxed and shook her head ruefully.

She'd had her operation over three years ago. When would she start remembering that she no longer had to worry about heart flutters?

Anyway, these were no mystery. She was excited to see her old friend again. They'd missed each other at church, and she'd worried he wouldn't get around to delivering the crib until after she'd gone home.

She watched Joseph climb out of the carriage, noting that he still wore no beard. That wasn't entirely a surprise. The whole of Johns Mill had been buzzing about Caleb Hochstedler's recent marriage, and Naomi certainly would have heard if Joseph had also found himself a wife.

But for some reason, seeing his clean-shaven cheeks for herself made her heart do a second series of funny jumps.

Surprising, really, that Joseph was still unmarried. He'd always been the nicest boy. When *Mamm* had brought the family to Tennessee for visits, Joseph had always been the one who'd lingered behind the pack of *youngies*, shortening his long strides to match Naomi's slow pace, making sure that she was all right. Even her brothers had raced away with the others, relieved to pass off Naomi's care to somebody else for a change.

Joseph hadn't made Naomi feel like a trouble, even though she doubtlessly was. He'd always offered her his hand when the going was rough, and he'd never seemed to mind stopping to rest when she'd run out of breath.

Ja, she'd always liked Joseph Hochstedler, and it would

be *gut* to see him again. Maybe he could stay for a cup of tea, and she'd have the chance to share her wonderful news. He would be happy for her, of that she was sure.

Quickly Naomi filled the teakettle, set it to heat on the stove, and dropped four bags of Lady Grey into Katie's smallest teapot. She set out a plate of the cinnamon buns leftover from breakfast and two mugs and spoons. She'd best have everything ready if she hoped to get Joseph to linger a minute. By all accounts, he was a busy man these days, and he wouldn't have time to waste waiting for tea to brew.

She tucked a few wayward strands of her blond hair back under her *kapp* and smoothed down the front of the apron covering her dress. So silly how her hands were trembling, as if the man now knocking on Katie's door were a stranger instead of kindhearted Joseph Hochstedler, who'd once carried her for a full mile when she'd given out on a trek down to the Millers' pond.

Naomi pulled the back door open wide and offered a warm smile.

"*Guder mariye*, Joseph!"

He hesitated, his dark eyes startled. "Naomi! I didn't know you were visiting."

Naomi felt her smile sag. She'd been here for a month, and Johns Mill was a tiny, close-knit Plain community. She'd missed the last church meeting because Katie hadn't been up to attending services quite yet, but even so—how in the world hadn't he heard that she was in town? "I've been helping Katie with her new *boppli*."

"You came down by yourself?"

"I did."

She could tell from his expression that Joseph was confused. Small wonder. During her illness, Naomi had never been allowed far from her family's watchful eyes.

Ask me about it, she urged him silently.

Instead he glanced around the empty room. "Is Katie here? I've brought the crib she ordered."

"She's taken the baby and gone to see Aaron's family for the day, but she's had your money sitting ready for weeks now. Come in, and I'll get it for you."

He nodded shortly and stepped inside the kitchen.

She shut the door against the damp chill of the morning and turned to get a better look at him. Joseph had changed some over the years, but not so much that she wouldn't have recognized him.

His straight nose, the moss green flecks in his brown eyes, that single unruly lock of dark hair on the right side of his forehead that always curled up against the brim of his hat. All of that was just the same as she'd remembered.

But there was a firmer set to Joseph's jaw now, and he wasn't so gangly. He'd always been tall, but in his manhood he'd broadened enough to balance out his height. The kitchen seemed smaller with him standing in it, and as he reached to remove his hat, muscles flexed under his blue shirt. He smelled of newly sawed lumber—a scent Naomi particularly loved. It made her think of fresh starts.

She did love a nice, fresh start.

Oh, it was good to see him again! She drew in a happy breath. "*Vi bisht du*, Joseph?"

"Well enough, *denki*."

"And your family? How are they?"

"Do you know where Katie wants this crib put?" He glanced out the window at the lowering clouds. "I need to bring it in. The sky's brewing up to rain."

Naomi blinked. Joseph's tone was impatient—not quite rude, but awfully close. He'd never been one for soft talking, but he'd certainly never spoken to her like that before.

Ever.

Gathering her flustered wits, she nodded. "Of course! It would be a shame for it to get wet after all your hard work. Wait just a second."

She hurried to retrieve the envelope her *kossin* had tucked behind the earthenware crock holding her cooking spoons. "Here's the money Katie left. She's been so excited about this crib. It'll be such a nice surprise for her when she gets back from her visit."

He didn't open the envelope to check the amount. *"Denki."*

"Do you need help bringing it in? I could—"

"Nee." The teakettle purred, and he nodded toward the stove. "Your water's boiling. You'd best see to it." Without waiting for her response, he went back outside, leaving her alone in the kitchen.

Naomi went to the propane stove and turned off the burner. As she carried the steaming kettle to the table, hurt and disappointment swelled inside her.

Well, one thing was for sure. Joseph might look most the same as always, but he'd changed—and not for the better. The gentle boy she remembered had sometimes stumbled with his words, but he'd never spoken to her unkindly. All the other boys had either treated her like a nuisance, or ignored her altogether, but not Joseph. He'd made her feel . . . special.

Now those sweet memories were spoiled. She wished he hadn't come by after all, and she hoped he'd hurry up, get Sarah's crib in the house, and leave.

She lifted the ceramic lid off the teapot and filled it, watching the hot water coax rich brown swirls from the dangling tea bags. She was brewing enough for two, and today was the first really cold day of the season, a good reason to offer an old friend a warm drink.

Now she wasn't so sure she wanted to.

Naomi squared her thin shoulders. She was being silly and selfish. Joseph wasn't a carefree *youngie* anymore. He was a busy man with work to do and not so much time to pass pleasantries.

Maybe there was a *gut* reason Joseph wasn't acting much like the softhearted boy she remembered so fondly.

He could be genuinely worried about the crib he'd lavished so many hours on, or perhaps he wasn't feeling well.

She should certainly be able to understand that. She'd encountered plenty of grumpy people during her hospital stays. All too often, she'd been one of those grouchy folks herself, although she'd always been sorry later. She'd appreciated the nurses who didn't take her irritability personally—the ones who understood that her mood really wasn't about them at all. It was only a by-product of her pain and sometimes—her fear.

Now that she was finally well, she couldn't in good conscience pass up the chance to practice that sort of tolerance herself, could she? Especially toward a man who'd shown her so much kindness in the past.

She settled the lid back on top of the pot. Leaving the tea to steep, she set the kettle on a cool stove burner, just as she heard Joseph thumping onto the back porch.

She opened the door wide and propped it with the cast-iron doorstop Katie kept handy. Joseph had set the crib on the porch and was lining it up into position to bring it through the door.

He might lack some manners these days, but his reputation as a woodworker was well justified. The piece was a thing of beauty, and Naomi leaned down to examine it more closely

"Oh, Joseph!" She stroked an admiring hand along the golden wood. "Look at the spindles! And the carving up the side. Such fine work, and sturdy enough for a dozen babies to use in their turn. Katie will be so pleased!"

Joseph didn't look up. "I hope so. She waited long enough for me to finish it." He shifted the crib a bit more. "This is a tight fit," he muttered. "I don't want to scratch the sides."

Naomi tilted her head, considering. "*Ja*, you'll have to be careful. The metal lock-catch is sticking out on this side of the doorframe, right where the crib is widest. Here. Let me help."

"*Nee*, Naomi, *denki*. I can manage."

"I don't mind giving a hand. We need to shift it up and to the left. My left, that is. Grab your end. If we lift it just a bit." Naomi took a firm grip on her side of the crib and heaved it up an inch. "I think—"

"*Du naett!*"

Joseph's sharp command hit her like a slap. Naomi dropped the crib, which thumped solidly down on the floor, and she took a quick step backward.

"*Ich binn sorry*," she whispered, then immediately wished she hadn't. What did she have to apologize for? She'd only been trying to help. He was the one who was being rude.

There was a tense second or two of silence. Then Joseph spoke without meeting her eyes. "The crib is heavy, and it's too wide to go through the door without damage. I have some tools in the carriage. I will take it apart here on the porch and put it back together in the *boppli*'s room."

Naomi's cheeks stung, and she knew they must be red as tomatoes. Her good intentions to be kind and understanding disintegrated into annoyance.

She nodded shortly. "Fine."

She waited until he'd edged the crib fully back onto the porch, then shut the kitchen door with a bit more force than was absolutely necessary. Returning to the table, she poured herself a steaming mug of tea. She plunked down in a chair, chose the best-looking cinnamon roll on the plate, and took an enormous bite.

Eating, it turned out, wasn't the smartest idea. The bite of spiced bread grew so big in her mouth that it took two sips of the scalding tea to wash it down. After that, she didn't eat any more. She just sat, trying her best to ignore the sounds coming from the porch.

She worried a small piece off the soft roll and mashed it

flat on the plate. Joseph Hochstedler was surly and short-tempered, and she'd be glad to see the last of him. In fact, if she never laid eyes on him again, that would suit her just fine.

There was a soft knock on the door.

"*Kumm*," Naomi called without getting up. He didn't want her help? Fine. He could manage by himself. That included opening the door.

Joseph leaned into the kitchen. "Will you show me where Katie wants this?"

Naomi didn't stir from her seat. "Up the stairs, second room on the right. She'd like it put against the wall without windows, so there'll be no draft blowing over the baby."

"*Denki*." He stepped inside, carrying the delicately carved head- and footboards. He nodded at her, then headed through the open doorway to the staircase.

He had to make three trips. She could certainly have helped him carry the pieces, but she stayed right where she was, drinking her tea and paying absolutely no attention to him.

Or pretending not to.

Fifteen minutes after he'd carried his last load upstairs, he reappeared in the kitchen.

"It's done," he said. "I saw the crib mattress leaning against the wall, so I went ahead and put that in, too."

"*Gut.*" The short word sounded so harsh that her conscience pricked her. His rudeness was no excuse for hers. "It really is a *wunderbaar* crib, Joseph. I'm sure Katie and Aaron will be very pleased."

Now leave, she added silently.

Instead he hesitated, shifting his weight from one scuffed work boot to the other. "Naomi, I'm sorry."

"You should be." The sharp words slipped out before she could stop them. "I was only trying to help, and you nearly bit my head off."

"I know. I was irritated with myself for not realizing the

crib would be too wide to fit through the door. I should have taken it apart back at the shop, but I've been so scatter-brained lately, I—" He broke off. "When you tried to lift it, I thought you would hurt yourself. That scared me, but I should never have spoken to you like I did. Please forgive me."

A warm ripple of understanding tickled its way through Naomi's bruised heart. Of course Joseph would've been concerned to see her trying to pick up something so heavy. He'd no idea how her circumstances had changed.

"Never mind. You are forgiven. It's a raw day outside. Would you like some tea before you go?"

He glanced at the door, then back at her. "That would be nice."

"Sit, then." She poured the second mug full and set it in front of him. She collected a clean plate from the dish drainer, plopped a cinnamon roll on it, and slid that in his direction, too.

He thanked her politely, before lifting the roll and taking a bite. "Katie's cooking is as good as ever," he said when he could speak again.

The thread of warmth expanded. "It is, *ja*, but I made those."

"You did?"

She laughed at his surprise and picked her own roll up for a bite. It was much easier to chew now that they were back in harmony with each other. "Is that so hard to believe?"

He shook his head. "Not really. You always could do more than folks thought you could."

"And you always were one of the few who believed that. But now"—she took a deep breath—"it's true. I really can do whatever other people can do—or at least, I'm learning to. To tell you the truth, this was the first batch of my cinnamon rolls that didn't get fed to the pig, but I finally got them right." Her smile widened at his uncomprehending expression. "I had an operation a few years ago, Joseph. That's why I was able to come here by myself to help Katie, and that's why I tried to help you pick up the crib. I can do those things now."

He studied her, the half-eaten treat forgotten in his hand. "It fixed your heart, this operation? You're all better?"

"So the doctor says."

His eyes moved over her face. "*Ja*, I can see it now. Your color is much brighter. Your cheeks are red, even."

"Well, right now that's mostly because you made me mad. But I'm not as pale as I used to be, for sure."

He smiled then, really smiled, for the first time since he'd knocked on the door. "I'm glad for you, Naomi."

She smiled back. "I'm glad for you, too! So much good has happened for your folks. Your carpentry hobby is turning into a business, ain't so? Katie says that she could barely get on your worklist at all, it's so long these days. And Caleb has made such a *gut* marriage. I was sorry I wasn't here in time to go to the wedding. Everybody's talking about it. The most mischievous boy in the community marrying the bishop's only daughter! They say it is proof that *Gott* has a sense of humor, but they also say it is a *wunderbaar* match and that the two of them are very sweet together. Then there is your parents' new store. I have been in it twice already, and both times it was so busy! Your family has been very blessed. I know you are thankful."

"*Ja*. Of course." Joseph's smile faded. He set the last bite of cinnamon roll on his plate and picked up the mug of tea.

His words were all right, but there was something in his voice . . . Naomi frowned. Maybe Joseph hadn't been so quick to notice the new spring in her step or the pink in her cheeks, but he wasn't the only person not paying close attention. Until this second, she hadn't noticed those new, tight lines around his mouth or the purplish shadows under his eyes.

Something was wrong. She couldn't imagine what it

could be. She'd heard nothing but good news about the Hochstedlers. Whatever Joseph's problem was, it must be something private.

He toyed with the scrap of cinnamon roll he'd left on his plate. "I guess you heard that *Daed*'s leasing our pastures to Aaron next year. We've no use for them, now that the herd's sold."

Was that what was troubling Joseph? The fact that his father had shut down the family dairy? That change must have come hard. Folks in Johns Mill joked that Hochstedler men were born with milk instead of blood running through their veins, and even as a *youngie*, Joseph had been more traditional than most.

Naomi nodded. "*Ja*, Aaron mentioned that. He's thankful for it. There's such good soil there. He'd rather have bought them outright, but—"

"They're not for sale," Joseph interrupted.

"That's what your father said." Actually, what Elijah Hochstedler had said was, *They are not for sale this year. Maybe next, once we are sure that the store is going to work out.*

She decided not to mention that part. "At least now you'll have more time for your woodworking. That's a good thing, ain't so?"

"I am a dairyman. Woodworking is just a hobby."

"Hobbies can become businesses. You could sell some of your pieces in your father's store, maybe. The *Englisch* tourists would go crazy for them, I bet."

"Maybe."

Naomi poured another measure of tea into his near-empty mug. "You don't sound too enthusiastic about that idea."

"I am not sure that catering to the *Englisch* is how I want to make my living."

Naomi laughed. "Why not? Their money spends just as well as anybody else's, doesn't it?"

"I've made pieces for our *Englisch* neighbors when they ask, and we've done carpentry jobs for local folks sometimes. But luring people into the community by making a spectacle of ourselves seems wrong to me, especially when we only want to part them from their cash."

"That's just business, though. Your family sold milk to *Englischers* for years. Besides, I don't think we're only a spectacle to them. I spent a lot of time among the *Englisch* when I was in and out of the hospital, and most are nice enough. They're just curious, and that's understandable. We're so different from what they're used to."

"We're supposed to be different. We're called to be separate, not that you'd know it around here lately."

Naomi frowned. "Are we still talking about your father's store?"

"Not just that. I saw Donald Stoltzfus taking money for buggy rides last Saturday. He had so many customers that his horse was in a lather, and he had to stop at his house to switch animals. His *mamm* sold the *Englischers* cookies and lemonade and let them wait in her kitchen while he swapped horses. That does not seem so separate."

"It sounds like simple neighborliness to me."

"We should be kind, surely, but a line is getting blurred in Johns Mill. I'm thinking of relocating to a more conservative district."

Naomi's heart gave a quick, hard pang. "Oh? Whereabouts?"

"Up in Ohio, where my father's brother lives. I'm going there soon to help Melvin with his dairy and see how I like it. If it works out, I might stay on. Find myself a wife, get settled in. I'd rather raise my family in a place that's sticking closer to the old ways of doing things."

"Oh." Naomi swallowed hard. "That seems like a big decision, moving so far." Especially for Joseph, who'd always loved his home more than most. She'd never see him again, likely. She had no close kin in Ohio, nobody to visit there. The thought made her sad. "Aaron says Isaac is a pretty strict bishop. I don't think he'll let the community get far from the straight and narrow, do you? He's Caleb's father-in-law now, so he's family to you. Maybe you should talk to him about this. He might set your mind at ease about what's happening at Johns Mill."

"Isaac sees the money that's to be made with tourism, and he knows that we can't make our livings by farming alone anymore, not around here. Almost all of *Daed*'s family has already moved on, so I'll not be the first." He scraped his chair back and stood, settling his hat on his head. Naomi rose, too.

"*Denki-shay*, Naomi, for the food and the tea. I went without my breakfast this morning, and it hit the spot."

"*Du bisht welcome.*"

"I'm sorry again for snapping at you like I did."

She waved a hand. "That is forgotten."

"I'll be thanking *Gott* in my prayers for your good health." A smile tilted up the corners of his lips but only barely touched his eyes. "A blessing, for sure. I'm happy for you."

Naomi started to thank him, but a noise distracted her. She tilted her head, listening. "Katie's back. I didn't expect her until after lunch, but I'm glad she came before you left. She's been so excited about the crib. I know she'll want to thank you in person."

Joseph glanced out the window, and his expression shifted. "That's not Katie. It's Rhoda."

Naomi tiptoed to peer outside. Sure enough, Caleb's Rhoda was barreling up the drive in a pony cart. Two things registered in Naomi's mind at the same time.

The first was that Rhoda was driving far too fast. The cart was bouncing so hard that she flew off the seat with every jolt of the wheels.

The second was that Joseph looked at his brother's wife

with such soft, intense concern that Naomi's stomach twisted into a throbbing knot.

She suddenly had a pretty good idea what was really behind Joseph's decision to leave his beloved farm.

"Something's wrong. Emma's not with her." Joseph was outside and down the porch steps in a flash. Naomi hurried behind him.

The sullen gray sky was spitting rain. Icy drops chilled the back of her neck as she watched Rhoda yank the horse to a wheeling stop.

"Joseph!" The other woman leapt out of the cart so quickly that she nearly fell. Joseph reached forward to catch her arm.

"*Vass hot gevva?*" he asked.

"We need to go to town!" Rhoda was as wild-eyed as the heaving horse. Her breath came in gasps, and her face was white as milk. "A policeman came and took Emma away. I came as fast as I could to get you." She tugged at Joseph's sleeve. "We have to go now!"

Naomi blinked. She'd never seen the bishop's sedate, sensible daughter flustered, not once. Now the other woman seemed nearly witless, almost past talking sense.

This was bad, whatever it was, to have upset Rhoda so much. Naomi cut a worried glance at Joseph.

"What is wrong, Rhoda? Is somebody hurt?" Joseph's voice was calm, but his face had gone pale. "Is it Caleb? Did something happen at his work?"

"*Nee!*" Her face crumpled. "It's your *mamm* and *daed*, Joseph. He shot them, that *Englisch* boy, this morning at the store. Miriam's been taken to the hospital. I don't know if he shot her, too. The policeman didn't say, or if he did, I don't remember. Why can't I remember?" Rhoda balled up a fist and scrubbed feebly at her forehead.

Naomi, who'd been frozen with shock, suddenly came to her senses. Rhoda's voice had a hysterical shrillness to it, and she looked as if she was on the verge of collapsing right there in Katie's yard.

Naomi went to the other woman's side and put a steadying arm around her waist. "Come in the house, Rhoda, and sit down. You need to catch your breath."

"Nee." Rhoda shook her head. "There is no time! We have to go, Joseph. We have to be with Emma. And we must find Caleb, too. He doesn't know. We'll have to tell him." Her voice shook. "But how? How can I tell him such a thing?"

Joseph's lips had gone white. *"Mamm and Daed,* Rhoda. What did the policeman say about them? Are they bad hurt?"

"Ja." Rhoda began to cry in earnest, helpless, wracking sobs that made the whole of her slight body shake against Naomi's side. "Bad hurt. They're dead, Joseph. He's killed them both."

Chapter Three

❧

GENTLE HANDS REACHED OUT TO PAT HIS SHOUL-
ders and back as Joseph threaded slowly through the crowd
filling his parents' home. He kept his head down and
avoided eye contact, edging his way toward the front door.

Emma had slipped upstairs to take her turn sitting with
Miriam in her darkened bedroom, and Rhoda seemed to
have her grief-crazed husband safely corralled, at least for
the moment. Joseph's head ached, and he felt bone-weary.
None of them had slept much these past few days, and
though people were talking quietly, the noise level in the
house was unbearable. He needed to get outside where he
could breathe and try to gather his wits.

Of course, there was no way he'd be left alone for long.
This afternoon the Hochstedler siblings had buried both of
their parents, and their community had stood beside them,
shoulder to shoulder, as was their habit in times of tragedy.
Over seven hundred people had come to the funeral, he'd
heard, and it felt like nearly that many were jam-packed
into the house.

They meant well, but for the last few hours, Joseph had felt as if he was suffocating.

He walked onto the front porch, and the twenty or so men congregated there turned to look at him. Samuel Christner had been leaning against the porch rail, but the bulky man moved to stand between Joseph and the steps.

"Better you keep to the house, Joseph."

"I'll go back inside in a minute. I need some air, Sam, and a minute of peace."

"No peace to be had out here," Samuel said quietly. "Not right now, anyhow."

Joseph looked over his friend's wide shoulder. Carriages and buggies were parked neatly over the large expanse of lawn, but the two-lane country road running in front of the farm was lined with vans, most emblazed with letters and logos. At least a dozen men with cameras were striding up and down the road, filming the house and the scene. One woman with a waterfall of curly blond hair and a short skirt stood facing a cameraman, talking and gesturing to the Hochstedler farm behind her.

Four tan sheriff's cars, blue lights swirling silently, were parked among the other vehicles. The Walton County deputies had stationed themselves at various intervals and stood cross-armed, guns holstered on their belts, monitoring the situation. The black-garbed line of Amish men standing along the Hochstedler property line faced the milling crowd and formed a different, but no less effective, kind of guard.

As Joseph watched, one of the cameramen tried to slip past David Miller. The elderly Amish man edged over to stand in front of the intruder and spoke softly. When the cameraman sidestepped him, David moved to block him again, both hands held up in an appeasing gesture. The frustrated *Englischer* began arguing, pointing emphatically toward the house with his free hand.

Joseph's stomach tightened. The Amish had clear-cut

ideas about violence that outsiders often didn't understand. David wouldn't defend himself, no matter what the angry cameraman did. Instead, David would reason, pointing out that the Hochstedlers were grieving a great loss and needed their privacy. He would do his best to appeal to the man's better nature.

But David would not budge. The *Englischer* would have to physically push the old man down to get into the yard. And if he did, other men would step forward to be knocked down in their turn.

That was why so many men were standing around on the porch, Joseph realized. They watched the altercation with him, as tense as hounds on the scent of a rabbit, poised to step in if needed, to use their bodies as shields for him and what remained of his family.

Joseph's heart had gone numb the instant he'd arrived at his father's store and seen the blood smeared across the scarred wooden floor. Since that moment he hadn't wept, not even today when he'd watched his friends shoveling dirt on the pine caskets of his parents. But for some inexplicable reason, the sight of stoop-shouldered David standing stubborn vigil in the front yard came nearer to bringing Joseph to tears than anything else so far.

To his relief, a deputy stepped forward and herded the pushy cameraman back toward the highway. The men surrounding Joseph relaxed, and their quiet conversations about businesses and livestock resumed.

"If you need a moment in the fresh air, go around the porch, and down the side steps," Samuel suggested. "Take some time for yourself behind the house. Keep your back to the road if you don't want your face splashed all over the news. They tell me those cameras can take pictures from a quarter mile that look like you weren't standing more than two feet away from them."

Joseph nodded shortly. Without looking directly into Samuel's eyes, he reached out and clasped the man's fore-

arm, hard. Samuel covered Joseph's hand with the calloused warmth of his own. Neither man spoke. Then Joseph
walked around the L-shaped corner of the porch, leaving
his friends behind.

The boldest younger folks had congregated in knots
throughout the yard, staring at the chaos on the road and
whispering. This was exciting, and although they were
keeping a cautious distance, they didn't want to miss anything. They shot guilty glances at Joseph, but none of them
approached him.

That suited him fine. If he could make it around the back
corner of the house, he'd seek some solitude in the aban-
doned dairy building. Nobody would look for him there.

As he passed the kitchen door, it swung open.

"Joseph!" Naomi smiled at him. "There you are!" She
pattered down the five concrete steps. "Isaac and your uncle
are asking for you."

So much for stealing a few minutes of solitude. "All
right."

"Were you trying to escape?" Naomi's gray-green eyes
warmed with sympathetic understanding. "I can't say as I
blame you. You can't turn around in the house without
knocking over half a dozen folks, we're that packed in
there. Come." She tugged his sleeve, pulling him behind
Mamm's wash shed, out of view of the kitchen windows.
"Nobody will see you here, and you can stand for a minute
and catch your breath." Her lips curved into a rueful smile.
"You used to tell me that all the time, remember? *Just
stand here for a minute and catch your breath*."

"I remember."

"Then you'd wait with me until I could go on, no matter
how many times I told you to run ahead and catch up to the
others. You were always kind to me, Joseph. I've never forgotten."

"I did nothing special."

"Not for you, maybe, but for me that was plenty special."

She chuckled softly. "I had five older brothers who got awful tired of me holding them up. I was left behind a lot, but never by you. You were a *gut* friend, always." She paused, her smile fading. "I'm not being such a good friend though, am I? Here I stand blathering on when you need some time to yourself. I'll go back inside. Don't worry. I'll ask Aaron to stall Melvin and the bishop for you."

"Nee." The protest came out before he thought better of it. "You can stay a minute more, can't you?"

Her eyebrows arched, but she answered readily. *"Of koors,* if you want me to."

He did want her to. He didn't quite know why, and he was too tired to try to figure it out. But he did.

When they'd arrived back from the funeral, a group of women had already been bustling about the house. They'd come to prepare the meal and to stay with Miriam. His youngest sister hadn't been injured—at least, not physically. They were all thankful to *Gott* for sparing her life. Emotionally she was so shattered that her worried siblings had talked it over and decided it best if she didn't attend the funeral.

As he'd come through the front door, Naomi had walked out of the kitchen to place a tray of sandwiches on the table set up in the living room. She'd glanced over, and for a second or two, their gazes had connected. She hadn't smiled or said a word; her eyes had only crinkled just a little in the corners. Then she had put down the sandwiches and disappeared into the kitchen.

Something about that moment, of seeing her gentle face, had brought him an unexpected scrap of comfort. He'd looked hungrily for Naomi after that, catching glimpses of her moving quietly through the throngs with the other women, refilling pitchers and platters, carrying dirty dishes back to the kitchen. He didn't know why, but while he was watching her, he'd found it a little easier to breathe.

Maybe it was because of what she'd told him just before

Rhoda had come, about the operation and how she was all better now, miraculously freed from a lifetime of disability. Nobody had expected such a blessing for Naomi, but still, it had happened.

He glanced sideways at her. She'd followed his lead and was leaning against the dusty wall of the shed. She'd dirty her dress, likely, but she didn't seem to mind. She stared over the empty, winter brown fields, toying absently with the strings of her *kapp*.

She did look a lot better than she used to. Growing up, Naomi had been so scrawny, all wispy hair and huge eyes, with a pale, pointed face. She'd looked like a stiff breeze would blow her right out of the county, and Joseph had never understood how her older brothers could traipse off and leave her gasping behind.

Now, the sharpness of the December afternoon had pinched a healthy drift of pink in Naomi's cheeks, and there was a new energy in the way she stood and walked. She was still delicately built—always would be. But she was filling out; her face wasn't nearly so peaked, and even the light hair smoothed under her *kapp* seemed glossier and thicker.

Likely Naomi would go on and live a happy life. Maybe she'd even get married, have some *kinder* of her own. Joseph couldn't manage to feel good about much right now, but he felt good about that, for her sake.

Ja, that was probably why he felt a little better when he looked at her. Right now, Naomi's story was the one pinprick of shining hope in the pitch-black darkness of his world.

She turned her head and caught him studying her. She smiled but didn't speak. He was grateful for that. So many people had been talking to him today, asking questions, waiting for his answers. He could barely put one foot in front of the other, and he found conversation exhausting. Naomi's easy silence was a balm to his battered soul.

She understands, he realized suddenly. Naomi had walked her whole life in the shadow of death. She'd know better than most what comfort this kind of quiet companionship could be.

His mind flickered to his younger sister, huddled upstairs in her darkened bedroom, not eating, barely speaking. Miriam was his responsibility now, and he had little idea how to help her. Some well-meaning women had already advised that she should be forced to get up. It was wrong, they said, to let her hide herself away in her grief and fear. She must learn to accept from *Gott*'s hand sorrows as well as blessings, and to lean on her faith and her community.

Joseph had listened to them patiently, but so far, he had let Miriam be. His farm-bred instincts instructed him to be gentle, warned him that right now his sister needed soft, quiet care, like a calf that had been born too soon. An idea occurred to him, and he cleared his throat.

"I've a kindness to ask of you, Naomi, if you are willing."

She nodded without hesitation. "Of course."

"Could you come back tomorrow to sit with Miriam? They say she shouldn't be left alone, but I don't want her worried or bothered. We take our turns sitting with her, but—"

"You've other matters to tend to as well. I understand. I will be happy to stay with her."

"Tomorrow?"

"Tomorrow, *ja*, and every day after until you tell me different. I will see to it that nobody worries or bothers Miriam."

Naomi spoke simply, but he had no doubt she'd keep her word. A small portion of the immense weight on his heart broke loose and fell away.

"*Denki*. I'll see to it that you are paid for your time."

"*Nee*, you will not. It is my blessing to help you and your family, Joseph." She laid a gentle hand on his forearm and looked up at him earnestly. "Please don't rob me of that by offering me money."

"Joseph! There you are." Isaac rounded the corner of the small building, Melvin shuffling behind. Naomi looked down and withdrew her hand. His uncle's hooded eyes caught the movement, and the older man tightened his lips.

What did Melvin have against Naomi? No telling, but Melvin liked few people, so it was no surprise to see that sour look on his face. He looked at his own nieces and nephews in much the same way.

Isaac's ruddy face was somber. "I'm sorry to trouble you, but we have a situation that must be dealt with. Could we speak with you for a moment, your uncle and I?" The bishop's eyes darted to Naomi. "Privately?"

"*Excuse mich*," Naomi murmured. "I should be getting back to the kitchen." She gave Joseph one last smile, then walked toward the house.

Joseph's gaze trailed her. When he looked back, his uncle was frowning at him.

"*'Sis en shand*, Joseph! Courting on the day of your parents' funerals. You have been raised to know better."

"I was not courting, Melvin. Naomi is a friend, staying at our neighbors' home, and I was speaking with her about sitting with Miriam while she recovers."

His uncle continued as if he hadn't spoken. "*Of koors*, after spending time with that brother of yours, this is no surprise to me. I had to speak to him several times while he stayed at my home about unseemly behaviors. You *youngies* have lost all sense of decency."

There was little point arguing with Melvin. The old man was stubborn as a goat and about as reasonable. Joseph turned to the bishop instead. "What did you need to speak to me about, Isaac?"

Isaac Lambright combed his fingers through the gray-streaked waterfall of his beard, his eyes fixed compassionately on Joseph's face. "The sheriff has come to the house.

You could not be found, so your uncle and I took the liberty of talking with him ourselves."

"*Gut*." Joseph nodded, relieved. "Has he found some way to make the reporters leave?"

"I'm afraid not. He was here about something else. He—"

"Those *Englischers* are coming," Melvin interrupted. "The boy's parents. As if they have not caused enough trouble for this family, they must also push themselves in here where they are not wanted nor needed."

"The Abbotts are coming here?" Joseph's heart thumped hard, then went still. "Why?"

"They would like to pay their respects. Sheriff Townsend said he could prevent this, if you requested it." Isaac shot a sideways glance at Melvin. "Your uncle felt this might be best, but I told the sheriff to allow them to come. He has gone to get them now."

Joseph had no idea what he should say. He didn't like the idea of any *Englischers* coming here, not now when he felt so raw, but the idea of facing the Abbotts, of hearing their fumbling expressions of sympathy . . . the thought made him feel sick. He stood silently, waiting for the bishop to speak again.

"There is no real choice to make here, Joseph. Our faith requires us to offer forgiveness to those who harm us."

"To offer forgiveness, *ja*. We will seek no revenge against them or their son. But for them to look for a welcome here in this house on this day when our grief is still fresh?" Melvin shook his head. "That is too much to ask."

For once, Joseph found himself in agreement with his dour uncle, but Isaac shot the older man a hard look. "I disagree. One could reason that the Abbotts have more claim on our sympathies even than Joseph here. He has his faith to sustain him." The bishop turned entreatingly to Joseph. "Your parents are with *Gott* now, but the Abbotts' only son has committed murder and run away like a coward. Me, I would far rather be Elijah Hochstedler than Stephen Abbott this day."

Melvin made a disgruntled noise, but Joseph understood what Isaac was saying. And he agreed. He'd rather be grieving as he was today than be in the *Englischer's* shoes.

"They can come, if they wish. I won't ask the sheriff to prevent it. But you know I'm not so good with words, and I don't want to make a muddle of this. Will you speak to them for me, Isaac, on behalf of the family?"

Isaac Lambright was known as an upright man who never shied away from doing what needed doing. Joseph expected a quick agreement to his request.

Instead, he got an uncomfortable silence.

"That is not my place," the bishop protested gently. "This farm and this sorrow belong to you, Joseph. The welcome and the forgiveness are your blessings to give. This is a hard counsel, I know, but I believe this is what your *daed* would tell you to do, if he were standing here in my place."

Joseph's mind flashed to that last morning in the barn, recalling the weight of his father's hand on his shoulder.

When our world goes dark, then we must hold hard to the rope of our faith, and trust Gott to lead us out.

Whatever the *Englischers* wanted to achieve by coming here, it did not matter. He was Plain, and so he would do what his faith expected of him. "I'll speak with them."

"Gut." The other man clapped him firmly on the back. "I will be standing right beside you."

"Ja, at least while the *Englischers* with cameras are everywhere taking pictures," Melvin muttered.

Isaac turned sharply toward the older man, but before the bishop could speak, Joseph interrupted.

"What about the rest of my family? Miriam is not able."

"Nee," Melvin agreed immediately. "The *maidel* has gone feeble-headed. Nobody can expect such a thing of her."

"But Caleb and Emma . . . should someone go and find them?"

Isaac shook his head. "I'm afraid Emma has become a person of interest to the *Englisch*. Apparently, there is a great price set on a photograph of her, and the men with the cameras are being very persistent. Our folks had quite a time keeping them back during the funeral. Best to keep Emma out of sight, I think."

"That girl should have kept herself out of sight to start with," Melvin said. "Then maybe we wouldn't be standing here."

"Emma's not the one to blame for this, Melvin." Joseph didn't bother to veil his own impatience. He'd heard enough of his uncle's opinions. "What about Caleb?"

The bishop looked uneasy at the mention of his new son-in-law. "I don't think that would be wise, either. Your *bruder* is grieving too hard to be trusted. I won't lie to you, Joseph. I fear for Caleb if he can't rein in his anger."

What was it *Daed* called Caleb? *Muleheaded.* Joseph squared his shoulders. So, this unpleasant task was to fall to him alone. So be it, then. "All right."

The warning whoop of a siren sounded from the road, and the bishop craned his neck to peer over his shoulder. "They are arriving. Melvin, maybe you should wait inside."

The old man's eyes flashed. "That," he said, "was my intention." He shuffled toward the house.

Joseph and the bishop walked side by side across the yard, toward the crowd lining the road. Joseph fixed his eyes on the sheriff's car that had pulled into the drive, lights strobing. A black sedan pulled in after it and parked. The cameramen descended like a swarm of frenzied ants, jostling each other for prime positions as the driver's side door opened. The deputies hurried to stand between the vehicle and the reporters, barking orders, herding the mass of eager bodies back.

Joseph felt a guilty relief that the pushy *Englischers* were so focused on the Abbotts that they were paying no attention to him. He and Isaac made their long walk unnoticed, except by the watchful men standing on the front porch. As Joseph and Isaac passed the front of the house, the men filed down the steps and silently fell in step behind them.

Halfway up the drive, Isaac placed a restraining hand on Joseph's arm. "*Shtobb*," he said quietly. "We will wait here. The sheriff will bring them to us."

Joseph watched as Mr. Abbott battled his way around the front of the car to open the passenger's side door. The *Englischer* helped his wife out. She wore a jet-black skirt and jacket, her eyes hidden behind dark glasses. Her husband put a protective arm around her narrow shoulders and shepherded her forward.

Cameras clicked and the reporters shouted questions, no doubt trying to get the Abbotts to turn their heads so better pictures could be snapped.

"Have you heard from Trevor? Do you know where he is?"

"How are you feeling?"

"Is there anything you'd like to say to America today?"

The Abbotts ducked their heads and moved silently forward, encircled by the deputies.

Joseph frowned, a genuine pity stirring in his heart. The two of them were alone. Nobody stood with them, apart from the law enforcement officers. Stephen Abbott had driven himself and his wife here, and there appeared to be no one else waiting in the car. What kind of lives did these *Englischers* lead, what kind of friendships did they lack, that their people would allow them to face such a moment as this by themselves?

It didn't bear thinking about.

Joseph was gratefully conscious of the cluster of men who stood behind him. He could hear their breathing and the restless shift of their boots on the gravel. His bishop's hand rested warmly on his arm. The farm overflowed with people, come to show support however they could. The men would tend to the few animals the Hochstedlers had left. The women would clean the house, and deal with the laundry and other family needs, to spare Emma the trouble. Naomi would come and sit faithfully beside his fragile sister. Whatever help his busy neighbors could afford to offer would be quietly, generously given.

Joseph had lost a great deal today; that was true. And yet he remained far richer than these two in their fancy car. Joseph pulled free from the bishop's hand and strode down the drive until he met the couple and their entourage of khaki-clad county officers. The noise from the reporters died to a scuffling murmur, and Joseph knew the cameras were fixed on his face, waiting to see what he would do.

He held out his hand to Stephen Abbott, who awkwardly released his grip on his wife and accepted it. The *Englischer*'s hand was slick with sweat, and his eyes flickered nervously around the assembled Amish men.

"Thank you both very much for coming. It was kind of you," Joseph said quietly.

"We wanted—" Mr. Abbott faltered. He swallowed and went on doggedly, pitching his voice to be heard by the cameramen. "We wanted to express our deepest—our deepest condolences to you and your family on the loss of your parents—"

His wife's shoulders began to shake, and she pressed a crumpled tissue to her face. The reporters jostled excitedly, leaning around the deputies, trying to get a shot of Mrs. Abbott's face.

Joseph moved to stand beside Mr. Abbott, blocking the reporters' view. "Please bring your wife into the house. She can sit, and someone will make her a cup of tea."

The *Englischer* darted a glance toward the cameramen. Then he nodded.

"All right. Thank you. Thank you very much."

As the three of them walked toward the front porch, the Amish men silently parted to allow them to pass. Isaac fell in step beside Mrs. Abbott, keeping a respectful distance.

Just as they reached the steps, Joseph looked up, and his heart sank. Caleb stood framed in the doorway. His younger brother's jaw was set, his green eyes glittering like shards of mossy ice. Rhoda stood beside him, one pleading hand on his arm, her gaze fixed worriedly on her new husband's face.

Joseph stopped short, weariness falling heavily over him like a sodden blanket. He recognized that look on his brother's face, and he knew what it meant. This hard task Joseph was expected to do had just gotten a good deal harder.

CHAPTER FOUR

NAOMI CAME UP THE BASEMENT STAIRS INTO THE Hochstedler kitchen, cradling four full mason jars against her middle. The wooden steps were unevenly spaced, so she kept her eyes fixed on her feet until she arrived safely at the top.

"We're in luck," she announced as she stepped through the doorway. "I found more pickles, sweet and sour both. I don't think the family will mind if we open them. There are plenty more jars down cellar."

Nobody answered. The kitchen, which had held half a dozen busy women before she went downstairs, was empty.

Puzzled, she nudged aside a few crumpled balls of discarded tin foil to set the jars on the cluttered kitchen table. A hubbub of raised male voices came from the direction of the living room, and she tilted her head, listening. Likely that was where the women had gone, to see for themselves whatever new trouble was brewing. Should she go, too?

Nee, she decided. She shouldn't. Whatever was happening, it wasn't any of her business. From the look on Joseph's

face earlier, he'd had just about enough of nosy folks for
one day. She wouldn't add to his troubles, especially not
now that he'd asked her for her help.

Naomi felt a warm bloom of joy at the memory. It had
felt *gut* to be so matter-of-factly asked for help, as if she
were any other able-bodied woman in the community. Back
home, people still hesitated. Even her sisters-in-law shot
wary glances at her brothers whenever Naomi offered to
lend a hand.

Although Joseph had known about her restored health
for only a few days, he hadn't hesitated to turn to her when
he had a need she could fill. That made her all the more
determined to be a blessing to the Hochstedler family—and
to Joseph in particular. Unfortunately, it seemed she'd already caused him some trouble.

She hadn't meant to eavesdrop, but she couldn't help
hearing Melvin's disapproving remark about Joseph courting her. Maybe she'd been meant to overhear it. Joseph's
uncle seemed to be that sort of man. She could certainly
have avoided listening to Joseph's answer, though. She'd
halted, one foot on the first step leading up to the back door,
long enough to hear Joseph's denial.

Which, of course, was what she'd expected to hear, and
no reason at all to feel an odd twinge of disappointment.
She truly hadn't come to Johns Mill looking for a husband,
in spite of some of the teasing remarks her brothers' wives
had made.

Well, *ja*, she'd thought it might be . . . sweet . . . if *Gott*
blessed her with a family of her own, but she wasn't setting
her heart on it. She had plenty other blessings to be thankful for.

She was just grateful Melvin hadn't made his dig before
Joseph asked her to sit with Miriam, or perhaps he wouldn't
have considered Naomi at all. Since he had, the least she
could do was work hard and keep her nose in her own business. She'd start by replenishing the empty pickle platter.

She picked up one of the jars and tried to twist the silver ring holding the lid in place. It wouldn't budge. That sometimes happened when canned goods were stored with the rings left on. Naomi carried the jar to the sink and held the top under running water for a few seconds. As she waited for the ring to loosen, her gaze lingered on the word printed across the top of the lid.

Sweets

Naomi's heart constricted. Likely that would be Joseph's *mamm*'s handwriting, scribbled on a still-warm lid after a long day of canning. Levonia could never have guessed that this jar would be opened at her own funeral.

Naomi gently dried the jar with a red-checkered dishtowel. She set it on the butcher block counter and nibbled on her lower lip. Maybe she shouldn't open these, after all.

Then she glanced at the glass platter, empty but for a greenish-yellow puddle of pickle juice, firmed up her lips, and reached for a butter knife. Using its solid heel, she tapped a circle around the stuck ring and gave it another twist. This time it loosened easily, and Naomi used her fingernails to pop up the lid. The spicy scent of a housewife's last busy summer wafted into the kitchen.

Tears stung Naomi's eyes, but she blinked them away and began arranging the crisp slices in a pretty pattern on the platter. Her faith taught that death, even sudden, tragic death, was simply a part of life. Levonia had made these pickles to be eaten, and so they would be. Life would go on.

The men's tense voices grew louder, and the door leading into the living room flew open, banging against the wall. Naomi jolted around to face it, and a pickle slithered off her fork and plopped into the sink.

Caleb, Joseph's younger brother, strode through the kitchen, his face ruddy with anger. He didn't spare her a glance as he headed for the back door.

Joseph followed hard on his brother's heels. "Caleb, we need to talk."

Caleb turned, and Naomi drew a startled breath. She'd never seen such fury in the eyes of a man wearing Plain clothing.

"There's nothing to talk about. You wanted them in, Joseph. They're in. But I'll not pass pleasantries with the parents of that murderer in my father's house."

Naomi stood frozen as pickle juice dripped from her fork to the floor, not sure what to do. Neither man had glanced in her direction. They were too focused on each other.

"They came here alone, seeking our forgiveness." Joseph spoke evenly, only the muscle jumping in his cheek betraying him. "Our faith requires us to give it, even if they themselves were the ones who caused us harm."

Caleb laughed, a short, harsh sound. "Isaac couldn't have said it better. You're very trusting, Joseph, to follow him so blindly." He paused. "Or stupid, maybe."

Joseph's eyes flashed, but when he spoke, his voice was quiet. "We can't hold the Abbotts at fault for their son's actions. They've broken no laws."

"You think not?" Caleb shook his head without taking his eyes off his brother's face. "So you're stupid, then," he muttered.

"Mind your tongue, *bruder*."

Caleb tilted up his chin. "I speak the truth as I see it."

"Truth I could respect. This is nothing but temper," Joseph continued in a gentler voice. "Stop and think, Caleb. I know you're grieving, but *Daed* always said—"

"Don't." Caleb's voice cracked on the word. "Don't quote our father to me. You'll never begin to fill his shoes, so better you don't try."

Joseph flinched. "I know I am not such a man as our *daed*. But we're still brothers, you and I."

"Are we?" Caleb's eyes narrowed. "I'm not so sure. You go back and talk nicely to those *Englischers* if you can stomach it. I'm leaving." He reached for the doorknob. "Tell

Rhoda to pack our things and go home with her parents. Even living with a bishop looking over my shoulder will be better than staying here."

Joseph made an exasperated noise. "Go, then, if you're bound to it, but Rhoda is your wife, not mine. If you have something to tell her, you can do it yourself."

Caleb turned back around slowly. "And that's part of our trouble. I married the woman you wanted, and you've not been fit to live with since. Maybe you should think twice before you preach to me about forgiveness."

Naomi suddenly came to her senses, horrified. She shouldn't be listening to this. She had to excuse herself somehow. She had to—

"Stop it! Both of you! *Shemmt ehr!*"

A sharp female voice rang out behind her. Naomi looked over her shoulder to see Emma standing on the steps leading to the upstairs bedrooms.

Naomi was startled at the sight of her. From birth, Emma Hochstedler had been gifted—or cursed, maybe—with a breathtaking loveliness, but grief had taken a heavy toll. Today her oval face was washed of color, and her blond hair straggled from under her *kapp*. Caleb's twin looked exhausted and heartbroken—and angry. Her shadowed blue eyes spit sparks at her two brothers.

"For shame!" Emma repeated. "Having such an argument at all, much less here in our *mamm*'s kitchen, in front of Naomi! What would *Daed* have said to the pair of you?"

Her voice trembled at the mention of their parents, and both men went still and looked stricken. Caleb sent one shamed glance in Naomi's direction. Then he looked back at his brother, and his expression hardened. He slammed out of the back door without another word.

Joseph started after him, but Emma held up a hand. "*Nee*, let me speak with him. He may not listen to me, but he certain sure will not listen to you."

She lifted Caleb's winter hat from its peg on the wall. In

his fury, he'd gone outside bareheaded. Emma hesitated, looking down at the black hat in her hand. Then she slipped silently through the door, leaving Joseph and Naomi alone in the kitchen.

Naomi moistened her lips, her breaths coming unevenly. She didn't know what to say, how to apologize. It didn't help that her heart seemed to be doing some funny things. She felt dizzy.

"I'm so sorry for staying," she blurted out. "I didn't know what to do."

"I'm the one who should apologize." Joseph raked a hand through his hair. "Emma was right. It was rude to argue in front of you." His gaze sharpened as it skimmed her face. "You've gone pale. You should sit, maybe."

He pulled out one of the ladder-back chairs. Naomi started to argue that she was perfectly fine, then changed her mind and sat.

She *was* fine, of course, but her knees did feel wobbly and it was better to sit down than to fall down. Naomi felt an all-too-familiar flash of self-disgust. She was supposed to be helping this family, not requiring help herself.

Joseph pulled out a second chair and sat across the table, watching her.

"Are you sure you are all right?"

She nodded quickly. *"Ja."*

"Gut. Naomi . . ." He stopped as if he didn't know quite what to say next. Disappointment poked Naomi's fluttering heart.

No doubt he was rethinking the favor he'd asked of her, and who could blame him? She'd stood there like a dunderhead, listening to an obviously private conversation instead of discreetly leaving the room. A woman who'd do such a thing was nobody to have around when a family was suffering through such a difficult time.

He cleared his throat, and Naomi braced for the worst.

"If you want to reconsider sitting with Miriam, I'll understand."

"Joseph, I—" Naomi cut short a second apology and blinked. "What?"

"I couldn't blame you." Joseph glanced toward the back door. "The four of us are in a mess, and it's not fair to ask you to muck around in it with us."

"Oh, I don't mind. Truly I don't." When he shot her a skeptical look, she added, "Don't be discouraged, Joseph. What you've been through is enough to make any family strain at the seams, but in the end the stitching will hold. You'll see."

Joseph sighed. "If it does, it'll be *Gott*'s doing, and none of my own. I've no idea how to head up this family. Caleb's right enough about one thing. I'll never fill *Daed*'s shoes."

"You're doing all you can, Joseph. Caleb's just upset."

"He's gone mad as a bull, and he won't listen to reason. And Miriam won't come out of her room. She just lies balled up in her bed, crying. It's not only grief. There's more to it. All you have to do is suggest she come downstairs, and she trembles so hard, the bed shakes. I don't know how to help her, and that worries me. And Emma—" He broke off and shrugged miserably.

"Emma's suffering," Naomi finished for him. She hastened to add, "Of course, you all are, but—"

"*Nee*, you're right. We're all grieving, but Emma's got the worst of it. Worse even than Miriam, if you can believe that. Emma blames herself for what happened."

Naomi made a sympathetic noise of protest, and Joseph nodded.

"I know. It's not her fault, none of it. She knows how I've always felt about keeping separate from the *Englisch*, and she thinks I blame her for being friendly to the boy. I don't, of course. None of us do, but nothing I say makes any difference. Whenever I look into her eyes, I can see the hurt she's feeling. I just—" He stopped short. "I can't look in her eyes anymore," he finished finally.

The pain in his face made the tears start pricking at Naomi's eyes again. "It will get better, Joseph. If we give Him time, *Gott* can heal all our wounds. Even this grief, as deep as it is."

"I believe that, Naomi, but grief isn't the only thing we're coping with. We've got all that craziness out there by the road, too. The sheriff says it will take time for those folks to lose interest, and until then we're likely to have troubles with trespassers and the like. That's one reason I'm worried about leaving Miriam alone, but I'm having second thoughts about asking you to come here. We'll likely have a few run-ins over the next few days, and that's nothing you need to be dealing with."

"I'll come anyways, Joseph. I'm not afraid of the reporters."

"Naomi, that's kind of you, but—"

"I'm not being kind." She stuck her chin out as she spoke, holding his eyes with hers. "I'm being sensible, and you should be, as well. Like I told you before, I've had to stay in hospitals amongst the *Englisch* more times than I can count, and I got used to them. Oftentimes, they just don't understand. When they overstep their bounds, they just need somebody to speak plainly to them, make them see sense. I've had plenty of practice with that. Trust me, no Amish woman you'll find will be better suited to run a nosy *Englischer* off your porch!" She leaned earnestly across the table. "Joseph, perhaps this is *Gott*'s provision, for me to be here and to be able to stay with Miriam just at this time. If it is, don't you think we should accept it?"

She could see that he was thinking over what she'd said in his careful, serious way. That was another thing she liked about this man. He listened.

"It does seem providential," he admitted. "All right, Naomi. We'll see how it goes. You'll tell me, won't you, if you change your mind later? I don't want you troubled if this turns out to be unpleasant for you."

"I'm not going to change my mind, and I'll stay as long as you need me." She would, too, *Gott* willing. She couldn't quite tamp down the smile that tipped up the corners of her lips.

Joseph didn't smile back, but the tired creases at the corners of his eyes softened. "Then I thank you, Naomi. You're being very generous."

"If I am, then it's no more than you deserve. You've been so kind to me, and I'm thankful for the chance to help you until this storm blows by." Impulsively, she placed her hand lightly over his, willing him to believe what she was about to say. "That's what this is, Joseph, a storm, just an awful storm. Sooner or later it will pass, because that's what storms do. They come, and then they go."

He looked down at her hand lying over his, and Naomi flushed. She'd forgotten herself. She snatched it away and hid both hands safely in her lap.

"*Denki*, Naomi," he said quietly. "I hope you're right." He stood. "I reckon I'd best be getting back to the living room."

Naomi rose as well. "I'll get on with my work, then." She flashed him a quick smile before going back to the sink and the open jar of pickles.

"Naomi?"

"*Ja?*" She picked up the fork and readied the platter.

"I want you to know, what Caleb said about Rhoda . . . it's not true. Well," he added, "not entirely. I did have some notions about courting Rhoda, and I won't deny being disappointed when she chose Caleb. But I accept that she did, and I respect their marriage."

She paused, then shrugged and jabbed at a pickle. "Of course you do." It had to be painful, though, and now this fresh grief had piled on top of that earlier wound. Such a thing could bring any man to his knees. She glanced at him and smiled. "Don't worry yourself, Joseph. Likely, Caleb didn't mean half of what he said. Hard times make for harsh words, sometimes."

"My *daed* used to say that." Joseph's mouth softened as he looked at her. "You're a born encourager, Naomi." Just as her heart thrilled with the praise, his gaze slid to the half-filled platter, and he frowned. "Are those my *mamm*'s pickles?"

"Ja." Naomi frowned, trying to read Joseph's expression. "I hope it was all right to open them. There seemed to be plenty, and we were out."

"You can't serve those, Naomi."

"Oh!" She set the fork down, mortified. "I'm so sorry, Joseph. I should have asked. Of course you'd want to save these for your own family."

"It's not that." Something strange twinkled in Joseph's eye. "Try one."

Obediently she lifted a cucumber ring to her mouth and bit. A second later, her face contorted as she fumbled for a paper towel to spit the horrible thing into.

Joseph's mouth tilted into the first real smile she'd seen in days. "There's a reason there are so many of those jars down cellar, Naomi. *Mamm* was a *wunderbarr* cook, mostly, but she couldn't make a decent pickle to save her life. Never could." His eyes sparkled suspiciously, and he used the back of his hand to swipe at them.

"Oh, Joseph—"

He shook his head. *"Sell is awreit.* Not the first time *Mamm*'s pickles have brought tears to my eyes, trust me."

For a second, they stood there smiling at each other, tears glimmering in both their eyes. Before either of them could speak, the back door popped open and young Abby Mast poked her head in. The teenager's *kapp* was askew, and her round cheeks were bright with excitement.

"You'd best *kumm*, Joseph, and quick-like! One of the

Englischers sneaked into the yard and was bothering Emma, and Caleb took his camera away and broke it into pieces. The man shoved Caleb, and your *bruder* struck him! Right on the nose!" Abby's eyes were round as she added, "The sheriff's taking both of them to jail."

CHAPTER FIVE

❧

JOSEPH HAD NEVER BEEN INSIDE THE COUNTY JAIL before, but the sprawling brick facility didn't seem too different from other *Englisch* government offices he'd visited. They all had the same harsh, too-white lighting, the same tile floors with grime crusted in the corners, and the same unpleasant smells of disinfectant and over-boiled coffee.

A uniformed young woman sat at a desk inside a glass enclosure, her blond hair scraped away from her face into a businesslike bun. She slid open a small pane of glass when he approached and waited for him to speak, one eyebrow lifted.

"I'm Joseph Hochstedler. I've come to see about my brother Caleb."

"I've got this, Christy." Sheriff Townsend opened one of the double doors on the right side of the room. "Come along through here, Joseph. We need to talk."

The sheriff led the way down a narrow hallway, his shiny black shoes and heavily laden belt squeaking with each step. "I didn't lock Caleb up, Joseph, though he's lucky I didn't. I just stuck him in an empty office to cool off."

Joseph cleared his throat. "That was kind of you."

"Well, I feel for ya'll. Your family's been through a lot these last few days, and the reporter fellow was trespassing. On the other hand, your brother broke the guy's nose. That's aggravated assault, and the camera he broke was worth a tidy two grand. That throws us into felony territory, and it ain't like nobody's watching us, you know what I mean? It's already splashed all over the television news. I had to haul him in."

"I understand. We'll pay for the damage." It would take a big chunk of the small amount in the family bank account, but it was the right thing to do. "Is there any way I can get my brother released?"

"Well, that's the good news. The boys and I talked the reporter into not pressing any charges, long as you're willing to fork over the money for the camera. It took some doing, but we pulled it off. I know those fellows are driving you crazy, Joseph, and I wish there was more I could do about it. It'll die down soon, I expect. Bound to."

"I hope you're right."

"But that ain't going to happen if your brother keeps throwing punches. I thought you folks didn't believe in violence, anyhow. Don't your church frown on it?"

"*Ja*, it does. My brother made a mistake."

"Well, there's a hothead in every family, I reckon. I got a grandson that's a doozy, let me tell you." The sheriff pushed open a wooden door. Caleb sat in a plastic chair inside a cramped office.

"Your brother's here to get you, son, and you're free to go. I'd just as soon not see you back here again. From now on, you leave those reporters to my deputies, you hear?"

Caleb raised his head. "Tell your deputies to keep them off our property and away from my sisters and my wife. If they do their jobs, you'll have no more trouble from me."

The sheriff gave Joseph a resigned look. "You got your work cut out for you with this one. Good luck, 'cause I'm warning you now. I won't be able to cut you so much slack if there's a next time. Exit's down thataway. Ya'll can see yourselves out."

Joseph held his breath until he and Caleb had stepped through the metal door into the brittle winter sunshine. Then he unclenched a little. Titus was still tethered to the bike rack along the side of the facility, and no reporters were in sight. The sheriff's deputies must have put the fear of God in them. Joseph hoped that held for a while. He could use a spell of peace.

Neither of them spoke as they went through the routine of untying Titus and climbing into the carriage. Joseph un-snapped the side curtains, thankful for the chill in the air. Nobody would look twice at a snugged-up buggy today.

As they clopped home down the two-lane highway, the odors of canvas and horse, and the familiar feel of the reins in his hands, steadied Joseph's nerves. This was the world that made sense to him.

Caleb stared silently ahead. Joseph cleared his throat.

"Caleb—"

"I'm not apologizing." Caleb interrupted. "So don't bother trying to talk me into it."

"You struck a man, Caleb."

"I did." His brother turned to look at him. Caleb's eyes were the exact shade of green that *Daed*'s had been, but never once had Joseph seen this kind of hot defiance in his father's eyes. "And I'd do it again. He came out from behind the barn, shoving his camera at Emma, calling her name. I told him to stop, and he paid me no attention. Emma covered her face and turned away, but he didn't care. 'Look at me, honey. Just look at me, okay? One shot.' That's what he kept saying, over and over again. He wasn't going to listen, that one, and he wasn't going to back off, not without a fight."

"He's *Englisch*. They don't understand." Joseph's heart wasn't in his words. The thought of Emma being pestered like that turned his stomach. "But you understand, Caleb, and you know you shouldn't have laid hands on him."

"Don't rub my nose in the *Ordnung*, Joseph. Rhoda's father will do enough of that. If," Caleb muttered darkly, "I give him the chance. You're wrong anyhow. The *Englischers* understand plenty. They know we can't do anything, that we're hobbled by our church. We're weak to them, so they just press in harder and take whatever it is they want. Maybe you can stand by and see your sister hounded to tears, but I'm not about to."

"You should have found another way to stop it. You're a baptized member of the church, Caleb. When you made that decision, you agreed to accept the church's leadership in these matters."

"I should never have been baptized, then."

Joseph's heart jolted. "Maybe you feel like that now, but—"

"It's not just now. I've felt like that all along."

"Then, why—"

"Why do you think? I wanted to marry Rhoda. I knew she'd never consider me otherwise."

There was a beat of silence, punctuated only by the rhythmic sound of Titus's hooves hitting the asphalt and the squeak of the buggy wheels. Joseph tried to wrap his brain around what Caleb had just told him.

"You joined the church . . . you made a decision like that . . . for a girl?"

"For *the* girl." Caleb made the correction swiftly. Defiantly. "I did, *ja*."

Grief had pushed jealousy to the back of Joseph's heart, but it reared back up at Caleb's words. He forced himself to focus on the issue at hand. "That wasn't wise, Caleb. They caution us against that kind of thing. The decision to be baptized is between you and *Gott*, and it's never to be taken lightly. It's irreversible."

"*Nee*. It's not."

The cold weight of his brother's statement hit Joseph like a fall of snow from an overloaded branch. "You'll be shunned, Caleb." When Caleb didn't answer, Joseph went on. "Think what that would mean for Rhoda. You can't be so selfish as to put her through such a thing."

Caleb shifted on the buggy seat to face Joseph fully, his eyebrows raised, and a cold look in his eyes. "Interesting that you think first what my shunning would mean for Rhoda, not what it would mean for me."

"You know well enough what it would mean for you and for the rest of us. Why would you even consider such a thing?"

"Our parents deserve justice."

"Justice is not for us to seek. We have to leave that in *Gott*'s hands."

"Maybe you do."

Joseph started to answer, then tightened his lips and remained silent. There was no point arguing with Caleb while he was in this mood. He reined up Titus in front of the Lambrights' small house, and Caleb frowned.

"Your *fraw* is waiting with her parents," Joseph told him. "She'll be worried. You'd best go in and see to her."

Caleb's face shifted into resignation. Rhoda's father would have plenty to say about what had happened at the Hochstedler farm. As bishop, he would be forced to address his son-in-law's transgression sternly, lest he be accused of favoritism. In spite of everything, Joseph felt a grudging sympathy.

Caleb wasn't in for a pleasant time. Until he made up his muleheaded mind to get on his knees before the church and ask forgiveness, he'd be at odds with his wife's family and the rest of the community.

"Isaac will understand, Caleb. You were under pressure and you lost control of your reason for a minute. It's nothing any man amongst us hasn't been tempted to do, and under less trying circumstances than these. You'll ask forgiveness, and—"

Caleb made an exasperated noise. "Don't preach me a sermon, *bruder*. I'll likely get more than enough of those from Isaac and Rhoda both." Caleb swung out of the buggy, landing lightly on the ground. "We'll sleep here tonight, but I'll be along home tomorrow to help."

Probably not a *gut* idea, having Caleb on the farm while reporters were still milling around, not given the mood he was sporting. "Don't worry about that. The chores aren't much to manage these days."

"I wasn't talking about the barn work. Looking after Emma and Miriam is my responsibility as much as yours."

"*Nee*, it isn't. You've begun a family of your own. You've responsibilities in there now, too." Joseph jerked his chin toward the tidy white house. "You'd best be tending to them." He clucked to Titus, and the buggy rolled forward, leaving Caleb standing in Ida Lambright's carefully tended yard.

When he topped the last hill, Joseph breathed a sigh of relief. The stretch of road in front of the house was littered with plastic water bottles and blowing scraps of paper, but there were no reporters to be seen. He wasn't sure how the deputies had convinced them to leave, but somehow they'd managed it.

All the buggies were gone, too. Folks had no doubt returned home to see to their own evening chores. As much as he appreciated the support of the community, Joseph was relieved to see the empty yard. He'd had enough of people, even well-meaning folks, for one day. He was ready for things to get back to normal.

As always, Titus picked up his pace as the barn door loomed in sight. As they briskly wheeled past the house, Joseph's eyes lingered on the trampled earth, where countless buggies and horses had scraped deep ruts in the damp ground. His *mamm* would have kicked up a ruckus over that. She'd always fret when their turn to host church fell on a rainy Sunday. It ruined the yard, she said. The grass took weeks to fill back in, and some folks never minded where they drove their buggies and parked over her flower beds.

Now she wasn't here to be troubled. The painful reminder hit him squarely in the center of his hollow chest. *Mamm* wasn't here to fuss, and *Daed* wasn't here to tease her back into a good humor.

Things would never be normal again.

As they reached the barn, Titus shied sideways. Naomi came out, carrying the steel milk pail. Given the way she was listing to the side as she walked, it must have been brimful.

As he brought the carriage to a halt, she set the bucket on the ground and straightened up. The pale oval of her face and the white of her apron glowed in the fading light.

"Joseph," she greeted him quietly.

There was something about the way she said his name that he liked. Calm, straightforward. He'd always felt strange around the girls back when he'd gone to the youth singings. They were always giving him sideways glances and kittenish smiles that he didn't understand.

Caleb had always known what to say. He'd never missed a step, and he'd never lacked for a willing girl to drive slowly home under the moonlight. On the few occasions Joseph had invited a girl to drive, he'd ended up tongue-tied and his stomach had bunched itself up in knots as if he'd just been given a dose of his *mamm*'s spring tonic. Even with Rhoda, maybe especially with Rhoda, it had been so, and he'd always felt secretly relieved when he'd driven his empty buggy into the familiar peace of the barn. If one of those girls had popped out like this back then, he'd have been flummoxed, for sure.

Somehow seeing Naomi didn't disturb him at all. Strange, that.

He climbed down and started unhitching Titus. "I figured everybody had gone already. Are Katie and Aaron still here?" He'd thought the yard was empty, but given the sheer number of buggies, people had been forced to park creatively. Maybe he'd missed one.

"*Nee*, they had to get back to get the *boppli* settled so they went on home."

Joseph turned his attention from the buckle he was unfastening to Naomi's face. "They left you?"

"Emma asked me to stay on for a bit." Naomi twisted her hands in front of her stomach. "She said she needed to talk to us both once you and Caleb got back." She didn't ask the question, but he could hear it in her voice, so he answered it.

"Caleb stopped off at Isaac's to see to Rhoda. He won't be back tonight." Joseph frowned. "Emma needs to talk to us?"

"That's what she said. She hurried everyone else off." Even in the dim light, he could see Naomi's mouth curve into a small smile. "Your sister's a wonder. Folks were . . ." Naomi hesitated as if searching for the best word. "Worried," she finished finally. "They wanted to wait for you, but Emma was having none of it. She hustled everybody out the door, quick as quick, but nice as you please."

That sounded like Emma, the old Emma. She had the kindest heart in the county, and she was fiercely protective of those she cared about. She hadn't wanted her twin arriving home to a houseful of curious stares.

"The men had already done all the evening chores but the milking. Emma told them she'd do it herself, but I stole the pail and scooted out before she could catch me."

"That was kind of you."

She denied his praise with a quick shake of her head. "Not so kind. Melvin was hanging about the kitchen, and he makes me feel *ferhoodled*. Oh!" She stopped short. "I'm sorry. I shouldn't speak ill of your uncle."

"Don't worry yourself. You're not the first person Melvin's sent running for the barn, trust me."

Naomi smiled. "The cow did make for a real pleasant change."

Joseph chuckled, then froze at the sound of his own laughter, his fingers clutching the last buckle. He'd not thought he'd smile again, maybe not ever, certainly not anytime soon. And yet here he was, laughing in the barn and poking fun at his grumpy old uncle, just as he'd done a hundred times before.

He drew in a breath and felt his tense shoulders relax slightly. *Nee*, life would never be normal here again, but he was thankful for the slivers of ordinary that came his way. And grateful for the person who made it possible.

"I'd best be getting this milk strained and chilling," Naomi said. "I'll see you in the kitchen, *ja?*"

"Hold up." For some reason, he was reluctant to let her out of his sight. "I'll see to the horse, and then I'll walk with you to the house and carry that pail." He hurried to finish unfastening the harness and led Titus into his stall.

"I can manage."

"It won't take a minute. Besides when it comes to Melvin, two are better than one. He picks off the stragglers."

She didn't laugh, but he saw his reward for the joke in her gentle smile. She clasped her hands in front of her apron and stayed put, waiting for him to finish.

He'd just started to get Titus settled in for the night when a question occurred to him. "How are you getting home, Naomi? Is Aaron driving back over?"

"He offered, but I told him I'd walk it."

Joseph set the brush down. Titus had one more job to do tonight. "I'll drive you."

"Oh, no! No need for that. It's an easy walk, barely a mile, and it's a nice, fair night. Aaron left me a flashlight, and I've a *gut*, thick shawl, so I'm all set. I've walked farther, lots of times, since my operation."

"That's not what I'm worried about."

Naomi waved the argument away with one slender hand.

"The reporters are gone for the night. Even if they weren't, like I told you, I'm not scared of them. It's no sin to the *Englisch* to take photos, and they don't always understand why we don't like it. That man was being rude, but he likely didn't mean any real harm."

"Best you let me drive you," Joseph said firmly. When she looked at him with surprise, he softened his statement by adding, "It would be a favor to me. I'll not rest easy otherwise, worrying over you getting safe home. I'll hitch Titus back up, and you go tell Emma to come out here if she's something to say."

"Pardon my *bruder*, Naomi. Joseph gets bossy when he's tired." Emma spoke wryly from the doorway. She cast a wary glance over her shoulder as she walked into the barn. "I saw you drive up, but I couldn't get away from the house until now."

"Is it Miriam?"

"*Nee*, I gave her one of the pills the hospital doctor prescribed, and she's been asleep for the past hour. I didn't want her bothered by all the fuss about Caleb. It's Melvin. He's packing up to go home tomorrow, and he's about to turn the house upside down with it. He's asked me to ready up *Daed*'s and *Mamm*'s clothes for him to take back to Ohio with him, for himself and Nella, and now he's down cellar picking through the preserves. Apparently, somebody told him that *Mamm*'s sweet pickles were very different from everybody else's, and he thought they meant it as a compliment. He's loading up a peach box with them," Emma shook her head. "I suppose I should tell him differently, but I think it serves him right. I hope I'm standing right beside him the first time he tastes one."

Joseph shot a suspicious glance at Naomi, who returned it innocently. "I wouldn't mind seeing the look on his face myself, but since he's taking them to Ohio, I reckon we'll have to hear about it in one of his letters."

When Emma didn't agree, he looked in her direction,

and the expression on her face made his heart sink. He knew what she was going to say before she spoke, knew he'd already failed to do the one thing his father would have most wanted.

"That's what I came to tell you. I'm going to Ohio with him."

CHAPTER SIX

"EMMA." JOSEPH SAID ONLY HIS SISTER'S NAME, BUT he sounded so defeated that Naomi's heart ached for him.

"It's the best thing, Joseph." Emma spoke firmly, but Naomi had spent too many years around hurting people not to recognize the misery behind the matter-of-fact tone. "After what happened today with Caleb—"

"That was Caleb's wrongdoing. It had nothing to do with you."

"That man would never have pushed in if he hadn't been trying to get my picture. It had everything to do with me."

"But to go to Melvin's?" Joseph made a disgusted noise. "He'll work you to death, Emma, and you'll never please him or have any kindness from him. For me, maybe, or even Caleb it wouldn't be so bad, but you'll be miserable. I can't let you do it."

"You can't stop me." Emma drew in a deep breath and continued in a gentler tone. "You're my brother, not my father, Joseph, and I'm plenty old enough to make my own decisions. Nella's getting up in years, and she needs help with Henry. That's something I can do, something good. In time the *Englisch* reporters will lose interest, and I can come home. Until then, my being here is just going to cause more problems."

Something I can do, something good. Naomi understood the longing in Emma's words, and she knew the joy that came when *Gott* fulfilled it. Her heart swelled with a sisterly sympathy.

"I think you're right, Emma," Naomi said. "Once you're away, this will likely die down. I watched a lot of television news in the hospital. One day all you'd hear about was one thing, a few days later, they'd be talking about something else. People lose interest fast when there's nothing new going on."

Joseph studied her. Even in the dimness of the barn, she could see that he wasn't happy with her agreement to Emma's plan.

This was a very personal conversation, Naomi realized, too personal for her to be butting in. Although, she reflected ruefully, she seemed to find herself in the middle of these a lot lately.

"Excuse me," she murmured. "This is a family matter, so I'll leave you to it. I'd best be getting on back to Katie's anyhow."

"Nee!" Joseph and Emma protested together. They glanced at each other, and Emma spoke first.

"Forgive us, Naomi, if we've made you uncomfortable, but there was a reason I asked you to be here when I talked with Joseph. I truly do think it's best for me to go away, but I'm worried about Miriam. She's not doing well, and I'm afraid my leaving will only make her worse."

"Couldn't she go with you?"

Emma and Joseph exchanged a long look. Emma shook her head. "I don't think living in Melvin's home would help Miriam's recovery very much."

"It's not likely to be any too good for you, either," Joseph muttered.

Emma went on as if he hadn't spoken. "Melvin would never agree to it anyway, not unless there were no other choices. He and Nella have their hands full with Henry, and they wouldn't be willing to take on another person needing care."

Naomi understood that all too well. Plain folks often feared disability more than death. To die was the eventual lot of every man and woman, but to feel you were unable to contribute to the good of your family and your community, to feel like a burden on those around you, that was a fate far worse in their eyes.

Naomi had felt like such a burden to her loved ones for too many years, but her illness had been a physical one. Mental breakdowns were shakier territory, and some hard-liners like Melvin tended to blame the sufferer. She understood Emma's reluctance to bring her fragile younger sister into a situation where her emotional troubles might be viewed with more frustration than compassion.

"So," Emma was saying, "that leaves you, Naomi. Joseph mentioned that he'd spoken to you about sitting with Miriam some, but once I'm gone, there'll be the cooking to see to as well. Cleaning and laundry, too, if you're willing."

Joseph cleared his throat uncomfortably, darting an apologetic glance at Naomi. "We've not the money for full-time help, Emma."

"That's no worry," Naomi said firmly. "I'm happy to help all day for nothing, for as long as I'm needed."

Joseph shook his head. "I can't allow that."

"Joseph, you're going to need help," Emma started, but he interrupted.

"It's not right, Emma. Naomi has no husband to provide for her, and she must look out for herself. If I can't pay her fairly, I've no business letting her work here."

"I've already told you I don't want to be paid at all." Naomi felt a surge of impatient indignation. "Maybe Caleb shouldn't be the only one on his knees at the next church meeting, Joseph Hochstedler," she continued, "because that's your pride talking and nothing but. You've helped plenty of other folks in times of need, myself included. It's wrong of you not to take your turn at receiving help when you truly need it."

The words came out sharper than Naomi had intended, but Joseph's remark about her unmarried status had stung. He'd made it sound so . . . *final*, as if she'd no hope of anything else.

That wasn't true. Not that she was looking, but now that her health was better, marriage was at least a possibility. A widower, maybe. They didn't tend to be so particular as the young men did, especially the ones with a brood of children needing a *mamm*. Just because Joseph didn't see her as a potential wife didn't mean some other fellow wouldn't.

She blinked and found both Emma and Joseph staring at her, their mouths slack with surprise.

Emma recovered first. "Naomi, having you here may be every bit as good for my brother as it is for Miriam." The other woman crossed the dirt floor of the barn and drew Naomi to herself in a quick, hard hug. "Take *gut* care of these people I love while I'm away," she whispered fiercely in Naomi's ear. "Please."

"I will do my best."

Emma drew back, searching Naomi's eyes. Then she nodded. "*Ja*. You will do your best, Naomi, and that, I think, will be a very fine thing." She turned to her brother. "Melvin has told his driver to come at four a.m. He figures the *Englischers* won't be up and about at that hour, and so we'll get away with no trouble."

Naomi smiled. "He's likely right about that."

"So I'd best finish my packing." Emma squared her narrow shoulders, picked up the pail of milk, and headed toward the open barn door. Halfway there she stopped and sent one last warning look in her brother's direction. "Naomi and I have settled this between us, Joseph. Don't you go messing it up, now." Then she disappeared into the darkness.

Joseph stared after her for a few seconds. Then he shook his head and glanced at Naomi. "I'll have Titus hitched back up in just a minute, and I'll drive you over to Aaron's."

"That's truly not necessary, Joseph. It's an easy walk, and—"

"I think it's necessary. I've already been sideswiped once tonight by you and my sister. Do you think maybe you could let me have my way on this?"

Naomi liked hearing that wry humor back in Joseph's voice. "I suppose maybe I could."

Joseph tried to be quick, but the process of hitching a reluctant horse back to the buggy took every bit as long as the walk itself would have done. Naomi decided not to point that out, and she waited quietly until he had everything ready. She climbed into the buggy, accepting his supporting hand, and settled on the far end of the bench seat. The carriage creaked and sagged as Joseph boosted himself into the driver's spot.

"Here." Joseph retrieved a folded blanket from the seat in the back and tossed its soft weight into Naomi's lap. "If you tuck this around yourself real snug, you'll be warm enough, I reckon. Get on, Titus."

Joseph clucked briskly and flicked the reins. Although the horse's laid-back ears made it clear that he wasn't any too happy about being hustled out of his warm stall again, they were soon rolling down the bumpy drive toward the highway.

As they pulled onto the road, Joseph switched on the battery-operated headlamps, and Naomi shivered. She'd never liked being on the road at night. The lamps shone brightly enough that the way ahead was clearly visible, and there was plenty of reflective tape on the back of the buggy, but still. No matter what precautions you took, accidents were just likelier in the dark.

She unfolded the thick blanket carefully, tucking it around her legs and feet, although she really wasn't all that cold. Then she clasped her fingers together tightly, sitting bolt upright and looking forward at the patch of road visible in the short lamplight, thankful that the ride would be brief.

If she'd ever been courted, she might have grown used to nighttime driving, but that sort of thing had never been part of her life. Come to think of it, before this minute, she'd never once been alone with an unmarried fellow in a buggy at night. She'd rarely been well enough to go to singings, and when she'd gone, no young man had ever offered her a ride home. Of course, she'd not expected it, given how poor her health had been back then.

She'd heard other girls whispering about such drives, though, and she'd learned a few things. If a fellow took the longest route home, that meant he liked you. Sometimes they halted the buggy in a safe spot a little ways from the house to steal a few more moments with a sweetheart. If you were willing, they might even kiss you, or so she'd heard.

Naomi had always wondered what that would be like, to have a man seek you out that way, to feel his lips touching yours. She'd shyly asked Katie about it once. Katie had smiled a particularly sweet smile and said she couldn't explain it, that it was something every girl had to find out for herself.

Naomi cast a quick sideways look at Joseph. He'd not spoken a word since handing her the blanket. He seemed intent on the road and lost in his thoughts. Of course, he had plenty of things to think about just now, what with the trouble Caleb had caused and Emma's decision to leave with their uncle. Probably he wouldn't talk much at all during this short ride.

This was about as far from courting as you could get,

she supposed, but at least she was getting a taste of how it felt to roll along in the privacy of a buggy with a fellow you liked. Because she did like Joseph. She always had, and sitting here, just the two of them, as the dark fields rolled slowly past . . . well.

It wasn't unpleasant.

She left the silence between them undisturbed, as Titus's hooves clopped on the pavement and the buggy squeaked. Slowly she found herself relaxing. She wasn't sure exactly why. The road was still just as dark, and occasionally a car came whooshing by in the opposite lane, or worse, tearing up from behind to pass in a rush of stinky air. She didn't much care for that. Still, there was something peaceful about riding like this, something reassuring about how Joseph seemed so unbothered by the speeding cars. His strong hands gripped the reins loosely, directing his horse in an absentminded way that spoke of long practice.

Naomi was sorry when she made out Katie's mailbox coming up on the left-hand side of the road, and she had to smile at herself. Just a bit ago, she'd been thankful the road between the houses was short, and now she was wishing the drive had taken longer. Well, she reminded herself sensibly, she'd be happy enough for the short distance when it came time to walk it twice a day.

She braced herself against the side of the buggy, preparing for the turn, but Joseph never slowed. He drove right by the Lapps' house, continuing on the road leading into Johns Mill.

"Joseph?" Naomi spoke up as the mailbox slipped behind the buggy.

He startled and looked in her direction. *"Ja?"*

"You've missed the turn."

Joseph craned his neck to look over his shoulder. "So I have. I'm sorry, Naomi. I wasn't paying attention. Just let me get to where the shoulder of the road is more level, and I'll get us turned around."

A little farther on, he stopped and in a series of back-and-forths, worked to turn the carriage around. At one point, the buggy was broadside in the dark road, and Naomi held her breath, praying that no *Englisch* car would come whipping over the hill. But Joseph was deft and quick, and soon they were safely in the correct lane, heading back to Katie's.

They bumped gently into the gravel driveway. Warm light glowed through Katie's kitchen windows as Joseph drew close to the back steps.

"*Denki* for the ride, Joseph," Naomi said politely.

In the golden light, she saw him smile. "Nice of you to thank me for something you didn't want in the first place. *Du bisht welcome*. I'm sorry I was so featherheaded and drove by the first time. I could tell it made you *naerfich* when we had to turn in the road."

"That's all right. You did a good job of it."

"You're very kind."

Naomi smiled and took hold of the side of the buggy, preparing to hop out, but before she could, Joseph spoke again. "I mean that. I've told a lot of people how kind they are just lately. People have been generous to us, and I'm thankful for it. I've needed it. But you . . . you've done more to bring me comfort today than anybody else."

Her hungry heart swelled and bobbed like a fresh-made dumpling dropped in warm broth. "I've not done so much really, Joseph, but I'm glad if I've helped you."

"You have." He spoke with such decision, she was forced to believe him. He looked away from the lighted windows to the dark stillness of the rolling pastures. "And it's not so much by what you've done. It's something about you, yourself." He shook his head shortly. "I can't find the words to explain it. You know I'm no good with that kind of thing. But you rest me, Naomi, and I've not felt rested in a long while. So I thank you."

Her throat had closed up, as if all the gratitude she felt at hearing this had turned into a big lump of pure happiness and stopped up her pipes. She forced out a whisper, *"Du bisht welcome."*

"Can Aaron drive you over tomorrow, or should I come fetch you?"

Naomi was tempted to accept the offer. Another ride with Joseph, this time in the sweet, fragile brightness of a winter morning? That sounded lovely.

This man had more than enough on his plate, though, and she shouldn't add to it. "Aaron will drive me if I ask, I'm sure."

"All right." Something flickered across Joseph's face. Naomi couldn't be sure, but for a second there, she thought maybe she wasn't the only one who'd have liked another drive together.

"Do you need help down?" Joseph made a move to set the brake, and Naomi blinked and came to herself. What was she doing sitting here like a silly lump? He'd need to get on home. With Emma and Melvin leaving so early, the poor man would have a short night and a hard and troubled morning.

"I can tend to myself, *denki*. You drive back careful, Joseph, and I'll see you in the morning."

"See you in the morning, Naomi."

He waited where he was until she was opening the kitchen door. Then he clucked to Titus, and the buggy squeaked as he turned for the road.

Naomi squinted against the soft light from the gas lamp burning in the kitchen. Katie was sitting at the table, baby Sarah asleep in her arms and a half-eaten piece of cherry pie in front of her. Katie smiled as Naomi closed the door quietly behind herself.

"I saved some pie for you, if you want it. It took some doing, too. I believe this one's your best yet. You've finally got the handle on the pastry. Aaron's as happy as I am that you're staying on to help out with Miriam, just for these pies alone. He and I both are going to be fat as fritters, though, if your baking gets any better. Was that Joseph driving you home?"

"*Ja*. I didn't want to trouble him, but he insisted."

"Of course he did. He's that sort of man." Katie settled her sleeping infant more snugly against her bosom and tilted her head. "So? What did you two talk about on the ride?"

"Nothing. He barely said a word the whole time."

"*Ach*, well. He's got a lot on his mind." Katie freed one hand to scoop up her last bite of pie. "He was never one to talk much anyway, Joseph, and whenever he tried, he usually made a hash of it. I've always wondered if that's why he never courted to speak of, because he's so clumsy with his words. He doesn't know how to say the sweet things a girl likes to hear." Katie closed her eyes, smiling dreamily as she savored the pie. "Aaron was wonderful *gut* at that when we were courting. He always knew just the right thing to say."

Naomi picked up the empty plate and moved to the sink without answering, her mind lingering on the simple words Joseph had spoken back in the shadowed carriage.

You rest me.

Her heart skipped at the memory, and she smiled as she began to wash the sticky dish.

Katie was wrong. Joseph Hochstedler wasn't so clumsy with his words, after all.

CHAPTER SEVEN

❧

THE NEXT MORNING, JUST AFTER SEVEN, NAOMI started down the road with her best walking shoes on. She had a still-warm apple-raisin pie in her hands—and a smudge of guilt on her conscience.

She wasn't doing anything wrong, she reassured herself. There was no reason why she shouldn't walk the short distance to the Hochstedlers'. The air was nippy, but she had a thick coat and good stockings. And, as she'd assured Katie a few minutes ago, Naomi planned to cut through the fields and bypass the gaggle of reporters altogether.

She'd been truthful when she'd spoken to Joseph last night. Katie's Aaron was a kindhearted man, and he'd have driven Naomi if she'd asked him. She'd started to at breakfast, but then Aaron had mentioned needing to make a run to the vet to pick up medicine for a sick cow. Naomi didn't feel right about delaying him. Now that she was blessedly healthy, Naomi made it a point never to trouble anybody for something she could manage by herself.

Besides, if she was to be going to and fro every day, she

couldn't very well keep pestering Aaron for rides, could she? She'd have to walk sooner or later, so she might as well start out as she planned to continue. Once Joseph saw her arriving safe and sound, he'd see the sense in it.

At least, she hoped so.

The loose gravel strewn beside the two-lane highway crunched and rolled under her sneakers, and she stepped carefully, trying to balance the pie and watch her footing at the same time. It was tough going, but she only had to walk along the roadside for a short bit. Just ahead, she'd slip through the gate and head across the frost-silvered pastures to Joseph's house. That would make for easier walking, plus she wasn't any too fond of the cars whizzing beside her, fluttering her coat and bonnet.

There was the gate. Naomi's relieved sigh caught in her throat when she saw a little yellow car pulling to the side of the road ahead. It was the style *Englischers* called a "beetle," all rounded on top. She'd met somebody once at the hospital whose brother had driven one. Naomi had thought them funny-looking, but Cassidy had assured her that they were very fuel-efficient.

Naomi walked purposefully toward the gate, hoping the driver, whoever he was, hadn't pulled over on her account. She faced the chained gate with a new dilemma. The chain fastening the closure was drawn tight and fitted into a metal slot. It wasn't locked, but it was going to take both her hands to wrestle it free. She cast around for a safe place to set the pie, not liking the idea of putting it on the ground. Apple-raisin, she'd heard, was Miriam's favorite, and Naomi was counting on this treat to help her connect with Joseph's troubled sister.

"Excuse me. Miss?" A male voice spoke behind her.

Naomi turned, prepared to firmly shoo whoever it was on their way. When she recognized the sandy-haired man standing on the roadside, her eyes widened. "Eric? Eric Chandler?"

"Naomi!" Cassidy's brother hurried toward her, his wide mouth spreading into an exuberant grin. "I thought that was you! This is some luck! I knew from that last letter you wrote Cassidy that you were coming to Johns Mill to stay with your cousin, and I've been keeping an eye out for you ever since I got here."

"Eric, it's so *gut* to see you! What are you doing in Tennessee? Is Cassidy with you? She never answered my last few letters."

She knew the instant the words left her lips. Eric shifted his gaze over to the rolling fields, his mouth working as he tried to formulate a response.

"Oh, Eric, I am so sorry." She juggled the pie for a second to free up a hand and then reached to clasp his arm.

"She got an infection after her last operation, and it was just too much for her. I should have let you know. I've been . . . reading your letters, meaning to write and tell you, but I just couldn't do it. It's been six months now, but still . . . I can't get past it. I miss her."

The grief in his voice came through clearly, and Naomi's throat ached with sympathy. "Of course you miss her. You always will." She gave Eric's arm a gentle squeeze before releasing it. "But in time, the pain will ease, and you'll remember all the good things. She was such a sweet girl, your sister. So kindhearted and so funny. I'm real thankful for the time we spent together."

Eric brought his eyes back to hers, and his expression relaxed a little. "She liked you, too, Naomi. She always said you were her favorite hospital roomie ever. So where are you headed? Maybe I can give you a lift. I've got a little time to kill." He glanced at his watch. "The rest of the crew won't be along for another few minutes."

Crew? Apprehension tickled up Naomi's spine. "What are you doing in Tennessee yourself, Eric? I thought you were living in Atlanta."

"I did. Do. I'm here on assignment for *Atlanta Today*,

covering the Hochstedler murders. You've heard about that, right?" He chuckled and shrugged. "What am I saying, of course you have. You're right here in the middle of it all." His eyes met hers, and his smile faded. "Oh, gosh, Naomi. I wasn't thinking. Were they friends of yours?"

Naomi hesitated. "I know the family, *ja*. Are you going to the Hochstedlers now?"

"Yeah. We're all camped out there, at least for a few more days." He ran a hand through his shaggy hair. "This story's pure gold, a double murder, a crazy-rich attorney's son, and this sweet, innocent Amish girl. Folks can't get enough of it. The fact that all the Hochstedlers are so closemouthed just makes it all the more fascinating. Everybody's trying to get some kind of insider angle to set their story apart."

"I see."

Naomi's expression must have betrayed her, because Eric hurried on, "That's not why I stopped to talk to you. Honest, it isn't. I'm not asking you to give me dirt on your friends."

"Well, I'm glad because I wouldn't do it anyhow. Whether you all mean to or not, you're causing a lot of trouble for that family."

"If you're talking about what happened yesterday, my crew had nothing to do with that. Carl Simms isn't one of ours, but I've run into him before. He never thinks the rules apply to him, but I bet he'll think twice before squaring off with an Amish ploughboy again."

"Caleb works in construction," Naomi corrected him absently. When she saw the interested gleam in Eric's eyes, she wished she'd kept quiet. Maybe Eric wasn't trying to get information from her, but that didn't mean he wouldn't snatch it up if she offered it.

A white news van roared past and blew the horn. Eric threw up a casual hand. "That's my crew. I'd better get going. They're already ill as hornets because we thought we were going home today. The network was talking about pulling us, but when Simms got slugged, the execs decided to leave us here a little longer." Eric shook his head. "The guy's a piece of work, but he got some great photos of Emma Hochstedler, and she's the holy grail of this story. Nobody had any decent shots of her until then, and man, when Carl's hit the Internet, the whole world went crazy. Not hard to see why. That girl's smoking hot, and—" Eric flushed and threw a shamefaced look in Naomi's direction. "Sorry. I forgot who I was talking to. My apologies."

"Accepted. But, Eric, the Hochstedlers aren't a story. They're ordinary, decent people, and they're grieving." Her mind flickered to Joseph's weary face, and she pressed gently on the spot she felt likeliest to give. "Think how you'd have felt if people had crowded in on you after Cassidy died."

"I know," Eric agreed immediately. "I'd have slugged Simms myself, no two ways about it."

"Then can't you back off a little bit? There's not going to be anything exciting happening today, truly there isn't. Can't you tell the rest of them so and give this family some peace?"

"Naomi, trust me, it wouldn't make any difference. Nobody's going to listen to me. I don't have that kind of clout, and this story is huge."

"You could try." She hesitated, then went on. "Tell them Emma's gone. She left town before dawn, so nobody's going to get any new pictures of her today anyhow. Would that help?"

That sharp gleam was instantly back in Eric's eye. "Emma left? Where'd she go, Naomi?"

"I don't know." That was true enough. She didn't know exactly where Melvin lived, only that it was someplace in Ohio. "She's not here, and that's all that matters." Impulsively, she pushed the pie into Eric's hands. "Give them this and tell them it was from an Amish friend. I can be your . . . what did you call it? Your insider angle. Maybe then they'll listen."

"Aw, Naomi. Like I said, I didn't stop just to—"

She waved away the apology. "*Nee*, I know. But I don't mind telling you something that might *help* the Hochstedlers."

Eric lifted the pie and sniffed. "Man, this smells good. We've been going to that Amish café downtown for every meal, hoping to hear some gossip. The minute we walk in, though, the whole place goes silent as a church. Makes me too nervous to eat." He studied her for a minute, then nodded. "Okay. I'm not sure it'll do any good, but I'll tell them what you said."

The sound of hooves on pavement came from behind them. Burly Samuel Christner was driving toward them in a two-seater buggy, no doubt heading to Joseph's to help with chores. When he caught sight of her, the big man flicked the reins and sped his horse into a trot.

He was upon them in a minute and pulled to a stop. "Naomi, *kumm.*" Samuel spoke in *Deutsch*, sparing only the briefest glance at Eric. "I will give you a ride. Best you not be walking today."

The waves of suspicion rolling off Samuel were so strong that Naomi's knees quivered. She wasn't the only one who noticed.

"Go ahead," Eric murmured under his breath. "I don't want to get you in any trouble. Here." He slipped a card into her hand. "My number's on here if you need it."

Naomi nodded, tucking the card into the pocket behind her apron. She headed for the carriage, hoisting herself into the seat. She was barely settled when Samuel snapped the reins against the horse's rump. The carriage rattled forward, past the yellow beetle-car and on down the road.

"Are you all right?" Samuel asked. "Did that *Englischer* frighten you?"

"*Nee*, he was only being kind, asking if I wanted a ride." Naomi relaxed, relieved that Samuel's suspicions weren't directed at her.

"He wasn't being kind. He's a reporter, that one. I've seen his car parked in front of the house along with all the other vultures. It's *gut* I came along when I did, Naomi, or you'd have had yourself some trouble, maybe. This is no time to be careless."

The reproach in the carpenter's voice made Naomi's spine straighten a little. As if she'd have taken a ride with someone she didn't know! She was not so *schtupid* as he seemed to think. "I wasn't going to get in his car, Samuel."

Samuel only grunted. He wheeled into the driveway, past a gaggle of reporters, who tumbled from their warm vehicles to see who was arriving.

Samuel ignored them, keeping his eyes fixed straight ahead, but Naomi sneaked quick sideways peeks. Not so many as yesterday, and maybe once Eric told them the news about Emma, more would give up and go away.

She could hope anyway.

Samuel drove to the back, stopping just as Joseph came up from the barn. Joseph approached the buggy, giving them a confused smile.

"Kind of you to come by, Samuel, but there's no need. Barn work's done."

"Sorry I wasn't along earlier to help. I had some folks to speak to before I left town. Can we talk for a minute? There's some business I'd like to go over with you."

Joseph raised his eyebrows. "*Ja*, sure."

"I'll leave you two alone, then." Naomi jumped down from her seat. "Have you had breakfast yet, Joseph, or should I fix some?"

"I had cereal before I went to the barn, but Miriam could do with some food, if you can find something she'll eat. She's pretty upset about Emma's leaving." Joseph threw a worried look at the row of second-story windows. "It's been a hard morning for her."

Naomi thought regretfully of the pie she'd given Eric. It would've come in real handy just now. "I'll see what I can do." As she reached the back steps, she heard Joseph's deep voice behind her.

"How is it that you're driving Naomi this morning, Samuel? I thought Aaron was bringing her."

Naomi froze, one hand on the cold metal doorknob, waiting breathlessly to hear Samuel's reply.

"I don't know anything about that. I happened across her about halfway here. She was on foot, and one of those reporters was pestering her."

"She was *walking*?"

Uh-oh. Naomi twisted the knob and hurried onto the back porch. When she turned to shut the door, her gaze tangled with Joseph's. The reproachful glint in his eye promised that he'd be asking her about this later. She offered him a shaky smile, and pushed the door firmly closed between them.

Hopefully whatever business Samuel needed to talk about would take a while. She'd like a chance to gather her wits before she had to face Joseph.

CHAPTER EIGHT

✣

JOSEPH PULLED HIS GAZE FROM THE KITCHEN DOOR and forced himself to focus on what Samuel was telling him.

"*Ja*, she was walking. That's not a good idea, Joseph, not if she'll be coming here regular. The reporter had her cornered against your north fence, there where the gate's at. Looked to me like she was trying to slip through it to get away from him but couldn't quite manage the chain. She put a brave face on it, claimed the man was only offering her a ride, but she seemed spooked to me."

Cornered. Spooked. Those weren't words Joseph wanted to hear about Naomi Schrock. "It wasn't my intention for her to walk. I thought Aaron was to bring her, or I'd have gone to fetch her myself."

"Just a misunderstanding, then. Likely something came up to prevent Aaron, and she decided to walk, thinking nothing of it. Normal times, it wouldn't have been a problem. None of us are used to this"—Samuel gestured toward the news vans lining the roadside—"foolishness," he finished finally. "I've told Naomi it wasn't a good idea and that she must be more careful of herself. She seems a sensible girl. She'll likely see reason."

"I hope so." If not, this idea of her sitting with Miriam would be over before it got started. "What business did you need to talk about, Samuel?"

"*Ach*, well." Samuel's face fell, and he shifted his weight from one oversized boot to the other. "Folks thought I'd be the best one to speak to you. Not sure I agree with them."

Joseph raised an eyebrow. He'd once seen Samuel Christner hoist two hundred pounds of sacked concrete mix without so much as a grunt. When a man like Sam acted uneasy, a smart fellow paid close attention.

"*Vass is letz*, Sam?"

"Nothing's wrong. It's about your *daed*'s store. A group of us talked it out amongst ourselves, and we'd like to take turns running it for you."

The store? Joseph blinked. He'd barely thought about the store over the past few days, and he certainly hadn't made any plans to reopen it.

"The way we figure it," the other man went on, "you need little help here, what with the cows being sold off. The store's another matter. We've worked out a schedule. Just us men," Samuel hastened to add. "We'll have no women working there, not for now. If it suits you, we'll start today. Some of the wives went over last night and—" The other man faltered, then continued in a firmer voice. "It took some doing, but they got the job done in the end. They cleaned the whole place up real *gut*."

They'd scrubbed his parents' blood away, Joseph realized. The idea brought on a wave of nausea—and guilt. He should have seen to that unpleasant job himself, not left it to his friends' wives. He cleared his throat. "I appreciate the kindness, Samuel, I surely do, but I've no mind to re-open the store." He hated the idea of being trapped behind *Daed*'s counter, fending off reporters and curious locals.

"*Ja*, we figured it might be so, but we wonder if you've thought it through. Now that the dairy's closed, that store is your family's livelihood, Joseph, and that's nothing to set aside lightly. Besides, even if you've no interest in setting yourself up as a storekeeper, you'll need to sell the things that are already in stock."

Joseph weighed his friend's words with a sinking heart. Samuel was right, but if there was one thing *Daed* had taught him, it was never to foist a job he couldn't stomach onto somebody else. So long as he was able-bodied, a man did what needed doing himself, no matter how he felt about it.

If that store needed to be reopened, then he should be the one to do it.

"You're going to say it's your place to look after this." Samuel spoke Joseph's thoughts aloud. "I told the men you'd see it so, but we all agreed you don't need to be at the store right now. Not you, nor anybody connected to your family. That would just stir things up, and nobody wants that."

Samuel had a point. Joseph rubbed his chin. "The last thing I want to do is make things worse. Enough of our family troubles have spilled over onto the rest of you already."

"Don't worry yourself. Our hearts are grieving right alongside yours, and it's our joy to find some way we can help. It's nothing you wouldn't have done for any one of us if the tables were turned. Besides, that store's a real help for Johns Mill, Joseph. Your father's got things in on consignment from at least a dozen or so families, and there's not a one of them that couldn't use the money, being that the farms are failing. And right now, with all that's going on—" Samuel stopped short, and his face flushed ruddy.

Now it was Joseph's turn to finish Samuel's unspoken thought. "Right now, a lot of people will come to the store."

"*Ja*," Samuel agreed uncomfortably. "They will. They've been peering in the windows and asking at the café and the bakery when it'll be reopened. There's droves of 'em hanging around town right now, but likely they won't be here long. Best we make our hay while the sun shines."

Joseph stood for a second or two, his eye skimming the crooked row of vehicles parked along the edge of the road. Reporters huddled in knots of two or three, many clutching morning coffees that steamed into the chilly air. Even from here he could make out the logo of Miller's Café stamped on the disposable cups.

Joseph sighed, but Samuel was only talking sense. The dairy was gone, and the store was the Hochstedlers' livelihood, at least for now. He needed to tend to it, best he could. Providing was the man's part of looking after his family, and with *Daed* gone, that duty had fallen to Joseph. The fact that other Plain families were also depending on sales from the store made it an even heavier responsibility.

"All right, Samuel. I accept the kindness, and I thank you all for it. There might as well be some good to come to Johns Mill out of all this trouble. Sell as much as you can as quick as you can but take no other goods in on consignment. I don't know that I'll be keeping the store open for the long haul."

Samuel looked relieved. "Fair enough. If there's nothing else you need here, I'll drive back to town and get the store opened up." He grinned. "I'm first on the roster."

Joseph didn't have to ask why. Folks generally thought twice about misbehaving in Samuel's presence. The builder's sheer bulk was enough to settle most troublemakers.

He watched Samuel drive away, making sure his friend got past the growing huddle of *Englischers* without trouble. Several angled their cameras in the big man's direction, but nobody attempted to get in his way, and the buggy was soon out of sight.

Joseph mounted the steps and walked into the kitchen. Naomi stood at the stove, pushing strips of sizzling bacon around in a skillet with a long-handled fork. His mother's favorite blue bowl sat close by, full of eggs already whisked and ready for scrambling, and a loaf of homemade bread sat on the cutting board, with a knife handy by. Naomi looked up as he came in.

"I'll have this ready in a minute, and I'm making enough for you if you're still hungry." She smiled. "If the smell of bacon can't tempt Miriam to eat, I don't know what will."

"Naomi, why didn't Aaron drive you over, like we'd talked about?"

Naomi darted a guilty glance at him. She began forking the sputtering strips of meat onto the plate she'd lined with a paper towel to absorb the grease. "I didn't ask him. He had to make a run to the vet this morning, and that's in the opposite direction. I didn't want to hold him up. It all worked out all right."

"Samuel said a reporter was bothering you."

"Not bothering. Just talking to me and offering me a ride, which I didn't accept."

"Sam said you seemed frightened, that you were trying to get in the gate to cut through the pasture to get away."

Naomi carefully laid another bubbling piece of bacon on the plate. "Samuel was mistaken. I wasn't the least bit frightened, and I'd planned all along to walk through the fields. I'm not scared of *Englischers*, but their cars make me nervous, flying by so close. Plus, they stink. The cars, I mean. Not the people." As she speared the last bit of bacon with her fork, it popped viciously, spewing a glop of scalding grease on her hand. "Ouch!" Naomi exclaimed. She dropped the bacon on the plate and moved the pan to a cold burner before hurrying to the sink to rinse her burn under cool water.

"Let me see." Joseph came close and took her small-boned hand in his, turning it to check the damage. A spot the size of a dime was reddening against Naomi's pale skin.

"It's nothing," she murmured.

"It'll hurt worse if you don't tend it." He handed her a clean towel. "Dry it off."

He retrieved a paring knife from the dish drainer and moved to the aloe plant his mother had growing on the windowsill. He sliced off one of the thick lower leaves and squeezed out the clear gel.

"Here." He gently dabbed the goo on the burn. "This'll heal it up right quick. Put a bandage over it, and likely you'll be good as new by morning."

He glanced up to find Naomi's gray-green eyes fastened on his. It had been a long time since he'd stood so close to any woman not related to him. He was near enough to notice the sprinkling of golden freckles across the bridge of her nose and to see how well her mouth was shaped, with a sweet dent just above its middle.

She seemed flustered by his scrutiny. She bit down on her lower lip as her eyes moved back and forth between his. "*Denki*, Joseph," she murmured. "It feels better already."

"Don't walk here anymore, Naomi." The words came without thought, gruff with feeling. "Not until things calm down. Please."

"I won't, if it worries you."

"It does."

"All right. I'll get Aaron to drive me for the next few days anyhow." Their eyes held together for a second or two longer, then she gently tugged her hand free. "I'd best get the eggs scrambling. Would you hand down that tray on top of the cupboard so it'll be all ready to go? I want to get this food upstairs to Miriam while it's nice and hot."

Joseph retrieved the tray, glad for the excuse to turn away. Standing there, holding that small, damp hand in his own . . . he hadn't felt so light-headed and strange around a girl since he'd first taken notice of Rhoda. His heart hammered as if he'd run half a mile, and his palms had gone so sweaty that the smooth wood of the tray nearly slipped out of his grasp.

Naomi was as different from Rhoda as night was to morning. Joseph had always thought that Rhoda, with her smooth mahogany hair and dark eyes, looked like a farmer's wife should, curvy and strong, rosy-cheeked and full of energy.

Naomi was smaller and daintier, with a quiet, unhurried way about her. She'd always had plenty of gumption, though, in spite of her shaky health—or maybe, because of it. Even as a *youngie*, Naomi'd had more pluck than a lot of grown men.

Even so, when Sam had talked about her being cornered by that reporter, Joseph had felt a sudden sympathy for his hot-tempered brother. Maybe Naomi could hold her own, but Joseph still didn't intend to see any man, *Englisch* or Plain, bothering her.

He watched as she set up Miriam's breakfast tray, finishing it off with a steaming cup of tea. "I'll carry that up the stairs," he offered.

"No need." She tucked a napkin beside the cup and smiled up at him. "I expect you'll want to eat some breakfast and then get back to your woodworking. You likely have a good many orders waiting, ain't so?"

He hadn't thought of that, but *ja*, he did. The unexpected prospect of retreating to his woodshop bloomed into a hungry desperation. He hadn't realized until this moment how much he craved the normalcy of it, the peace of doing something he was good at instead of blundering around this house like a moth banging against the globe of a lamp.

It would be a sweet relief.

Still. He cast a worried look at the stairs leading to the family bedrooms. Miriam hadn't taken Emma's departure well, and today would be a hard day for her.

"Don't worry about your sister," Naomi said gently. "I'll

see to her just fine. No point in keeping a cat and still chasing the mice yourself, Joseph." She arranged a portion of eggs, bacon, and sourdough bread onto a plate and slid it in his direction before pouring a mug of tea from the chubby white pot sitting on the table. "Eat. Then get on outside and tend to your work. I'll let you know when lunch is ready."

"*Denki*, Naomi."

She didn't answer, only gave him one of her sweet, slow-blooming smiles. Then she lifted the tray and started for the stairs.

Joseph hadn't been hungry before. He hadn't cared about food for days. But as Naomi's footsteps creaked on the steps, he sat down at the table, picked up his fork, and started to eat.

CHAPTER NINE

✿

NAOMI MADE IT TO THE LANDING BEFORE SHE HAD to stop. Setting the tray on the small painted table positioned under the window, she pressed one hand against her pounding heart. She stood there for a moment, measuring her breaths and willing herself not to worry about the wave of dizziness that had halted her.

The tray was heavy, and there'd been all the stress of her surprise meeting with Eric. That's what this was. Mostly.

Because when Joseph had looked down into her eyes, holding her injured hand so gently in his calloused one, Naomi had known for certain sure what she'd been suspecting ever since their buggy ride the other night.

She had some new heart trouble brewing. And that was a problem.

She couldn't let herself fall for Joseph Hochstedler. He was a kind, good-hearted man, and he'd won her loyal affection years ago, but that was as far as it went.

Joseph had known her for years, and he'd never looked twice in her direction, not that way. *Nee*, he'd fallen for pretty, energetic Rhoda Lambright instead. Now that Rhoda had chosen Caleb, Joseph would soon find another girl to love, and it was plain enough what sort he fancied. Definitely not skinny, pale, ordinary ones like Naomi. And if he'd any idea she was getting a case of the flutters every time he glanced at her, he'd be sure to put a quick end to this arrangement of theirs.

Setting her heart on Joseph would be like putting a dozen loose eggs on a buggy seat. No matter how carefully you drove, sooner or later you were going to end up with a great big mess. She couldn't allow herself to be so foolish, not now. There was too much at stake.

Lying in hospital beds during her illness, weary and bloated from her medications, she'd watched the nurses bustle here and there tending to their patients. How wonderful, she'd thought, to be so needed, to be capable of doing such great good for suffering folks. She'd prayed with all her heart that the Lord might one day allow her some way to be useful, too. Now *Gott* had graciously given her more than she'd dared hope for, and she wouldn't spoil it by selfishly fretting for more.

Naomi took another steadying breath and wiped her damp palms down the front of her apron. Picking up the tray, she tackled the last stretch of stairs. She'd taken no more than four steps when she saw the huddled form on the varnished hall floor.

Miriam sat beside her half-opened bedroom door, her knees drawn up to her chin, her head buried in her hands. Her body shook as she struggled to breathe.

Naomi plunked the tray down at the top of the steps and hurried over. Crouching, she laid a gentle hand on the girl's shoulder. "Miriam?"

Miriam raised her head. Green-flecked brown eyes very much like Joseph's looked at Naomi through a film of tears.

"Can't breathe," she managed. "Tried to go downstairs. To help. But can't."

"*Sell is awreit*," Naomi soothed, not sure quite what to do. She cast her mind back, trying to recall tricks she'd seen nurses use to calm panicked patients. A memory sparked. "Breathe, Miriam," she said. "Breathe in while I count."

"Can't," Miriam panted, her voice high with fear.

"*Ja*, you can. Breathe in through your nose, one, two, three four, five," Naomi instructed. "Now hold that breath while I count. One, two, three, four, five. Now breathe out through your mouth, one, two, three, four, five." Some of the terror ebbed out of Miriam's expression. "*Gut*. Now, we'll do it again." Naomi made her voice sound like the nurses she remembered, kind but firm.

She counted out the breaths again, one by one. She'd no idea if she was doing this right, but since it seemed to be working, she kept it up. After three repetitions, Miriam's panic seemed to have subsided, although she still trembled.

"I'm sorry." Miriam's face twisted as tears streaked down her cheeks. "I haven't been out of my room, since—I haven't been out of my room. But now Emma's gone away"— the younger girl's voice broke—"and Caleb's not thinking straight. Joseph shouldn't have to manage everything by himself."

"He doesn't have to," Naomi assured her sturdily. "That's why I'm here."

"Joseph and Emma told me you were coming, but Melvin came up yesterday and said that I should be ashamed of myself, lying in bed when there was nothing really wrong with me. He said it went against our faith to mourn so, that it was sinful and lazy to let my brothers and my sister handle everything when I was perfectly capable of—"

"Don't you pay any attention to your uncle," Naomi broke in. "He's twisting our faith all out of shape, saying such things. You're not lazy, and you're not selfish, either. You're just upset, as anybody would be. You're going to get better soon enough."

Miriam shook her head miserably. "I couldn't even

make it down the hallway, Naomi. I'm such a coward. Every time I think about leaving my room, I just get so scared. I can't breathe. I can't move. It's awful."

"But you got yourself up and dressed, didn't you? And you've made it outside your door." Naomi slipped a comforting arm around the younger girl's shaking shoulders. "That's *wunderbaar* progress. Now, let's try standing up."

Naomi rose, tugging Miriam up with her. Briskly, she straightened the other girl's *kapp*, tucking stray tendrils of her curly brown hair back into place. "Now, you can go back inside your room, if you like. I'll bring your breakfast in, and we'll have a nice talk while you eat. I can tell you all about Katie's sweet new *boppli*. Or," Naomi hesitated, then forged on, "we could both go down to the kitchen so I can heat up your tea. It's likely gone stone cold, and I could use another cup myself. You can keep me company in the kitchen while I tell you all about how precious little Sarah is. Which will it be?"

Miriam's face fell as she studied her half-opened bedroom door. "I would like to go downstairs, but what if I have another spell?"

"What if you do? It won't bother me any, and there's nobody else here to see. We'll just do some more of that special breathing, and you'll calm right down, same as before."

"*Ja*, that helped." An uncertain glint of hope appeared in Miriam's eyes. "Will you stay right with me, Naomi? The whole time?"

"That's what I'm here for, ain't so? Come on. You've already managed the hardest part."

"All right." Miriam wrapped an arm tightly around Naomi's waist. "If you'll help me, maybe I can do this."

"Of course you can," Naomi assured her as they turned toward the stairs. "Just take your time, and—" She broke off. Joseph stood at the end of the hall, holding his sister's breakfast tray.

His face had lost most of its color, but he smiled encouragingly. "You'd best hurry before I eat your share of breakfast, Mirry. Turns out, Naomi is a right *gut* cook."

"You'd better not!" Miriam stepped in his direction, clutching Naomi tightly. "I can smell that bacon from here."

Their voices were light as they teased each other, their words heartbreakingly ordinary. Only their shadowed eyes and Miriam's shuffling steps hinted at their recent troubles. Joseph watched his sister's approach intently. The tray tilted dangerously in his hands, but his smile stayed firmly in place.

Naomi's heart swelled with a fierce joy. That *schtinker* of an uncle would do better to hold his tongue. These Hochstedlers were the bravest folks she'd ever met.

"Why don't you take the food on down, Joseph?" Naomi suggested. "We'll follow behind."

"Wait," Miriam protested breathlessly. Joseph froze in mid-turn, his brow creasing with concern.

Miriam released Naomi's arm and snitched a strip of bacon from the plate. She bit into it, flashing a determined smile at her brother. "You're right, Joseph. Naomi has done *gut*."

"*Ja*," Joseph agreed huskily. His gaze met Naomi's in a way that had her pulse stuttering out of rhythm again. "She has done wonderful *gut*."

He walked down the steps before them, his wide shoulders blocking most of the view. Naomi followed with Miriam, careful not to rush her. Naomi understood how wearying it was to stand and walk after even a few days of being bedridden.

Besides, Naomi's knees were feeling a little wobbly, too.

Once downstairs, Joseph strode ahead to place Miriam's breakfast on the table, but Miriam faltered on the last step, looking around the kitchen.

Naomi's heart constricted with sympathy. After she'd lost her own mother, it had been especially painful to set

n

o-
d

le.

is

he
at

ss-
r."
ng.
e
m
ph
re
ni
e any

er
for
wed.
air.
le
and
ould

ou

mi."
ent
ok

foot in the kitchen, a room where *Mamm* had spent so much time.

As Naomi fumbled for something comforting to say, Joseph turned and caught sight of his sister's face. He crossed the room and took Miriam's arm.

"Come," he murmured, leading her toward the table. "Sit." He pulled out a chair with his free hand.

Miriam looked up at him, her face stricken. "This is *Mamm*'s place," she whispered.

"It was, *ja*. Now it will be yours. The faces around the table change . . ." He trailed off, looking expectantly at Miriam.

"But *die familye* goes on," she finished softly. "*Grossdaddi* said that when *Grossmammi* passed. I remember." She sat, and Naomi released the breath she'd been holding.

Joseph took the plate of food and the teacup from the tray and arranged them in front of his sister. When Miriam dipped her head for her silent mealtime prayer, Joseph stayed beside her, resting his hand on her shoulder. There was something so tender about the gesture that Naomi found herself blinking back tears. She couldn't imagine of her brothers dealing with her half so patiently.

When Miriam had finished praying, she picked up her fork, and took a small, deliberate bite of eggs. "*Denki* cooking breakfast, Naomi," she said when she'd swallowed.

"*Ja*," Joseph echoed as he pulled out his own chair. "*Denki*." The look he sent her over his sister's head made it clear that he was thanking her for more than the food, and Naomi's joy expanded inside her breast until she could barely breathe.

"*Du bisht welcome*," she murmured. "Joseph, would you like another cup of tea? There's plenty in the pot."

"*Ja*, and you can sit down and have some with us, Naomi."

"Please," Miriam added insistently, so when Naomi went to retrieve the teapot from its spot on the counter, she took out another cup as well. She paused at the table to pour the still-warm tea into Joseph's cup. Her arm brushed his sleeve as she did, and her heart did another one of its crazy leaps.

"Sit here, Naomi." Miriam patted the seat next to her own. When Naomi had sat down, Miriam smiled, tears shimmering in her eyes. "That is Emma's place. I am glad for you to sit in my sister's spot while she's gone."

"I imagine Emma will be wishing soon enough that she was back in that chair," Joseph muttered.

"Maybe she'll come home all the more quickly, then." Miriam's voice already sounded stronger. She scooped a second fluffy bite of egg onto her fork, and Naomi smiled. Another thing she'd learned in the hospital—a good appetite was often the first real sign of improvement.

Someone knocked on the kitchen door, and Miriam jumped, spilling egg on the table. For a second, Naomi feared Miriam was going to bolt, but then Rhoda pushed open the door and stuck her dark head inside.

"It's only me," she said. "Well, me and *Daed*. He's tending the horse. Star started limping on the way over, and *Daed* is checking his hoof. I've come to spend the day. Miriam, how good to see you in the kitchen!" Rhoda leaned to give her sister-in-law a gentle hug. As she did, she set a crumb-sprinkled pie plate on the table. "How are you feeling?"

Naomi didn't hear Miriam's reply. She stared at the dish uneasily. That was Katie's plate, the old one with the dent in the rim that Naomi had borrowed. Last time Naomi had seen it, it was full to the brim with a warm apple-raisin pie. How in the world had Rhoda ended up with that?

"I'll see if Isaac needs help with the horse." Joseph took one long drink of his tea then rose.

"He wants to talk to you anyway." Rhoda sighed as she sank into the chair Joseph had left empty.

"Are you all right, Rhoda?" Joseph asked.

Her conscience pricked her. She hadn't explained that she knew Eric, but surely that wasn't really important.

She looked up from her tea to find Rhoda studying her. "Well," Rhoda said, "I suppose it's a blessing the fellow had enough sense to return the pie tin, especially since you borrowed it from Katie." Rhoda seemed to suspect there was something Naomi wasn't telling, but she was either too polite or too burdened by her own troubles to ask about it.

"*Ja.* You're right," Naomi agreed. "I guess I wasn't thinking clearly."

"Of course you weren't," Miriam said staunchly. "I would've been scared witless if an *Englischer* came up to me like that. It's hard to think straight when you're frightened."

"That's true." Rhoda's expression softened as she looked at her new sister-in-law. "So we must try hard to trust *Gott* and fight back our fears, ain't so? Just like you are doing right now, Miriam. You must help me follow your good example."

Her voice wobbled as she spoke. Miriam reached out and clasped Rhoda's and Naomi's hands in her own and gave a gentle squeeze.

"We will all help each other," she whispered. "Every day until the sun comes back out. That's what sisters do, ain't so?"

"*Ja,*" Rhoda said shakily.

"*Ja,*" Naomi agreed with a smile. She stretched across the table and took Rhoda's free hand in her own, closing the circle.

Likely most folks in Johns Mill were thankful they hadn't been called by *Gott* to suffer the trials of the Hochstedlers. However, if Naomi could have wished herself anyplace in the wide world, she would still have chosen to be sitting at this kitchen table, holding the hands of these two sad-eyed women, who considered her a sister.

And that's who she was to the Hochstedlers—all of them.

An honorary sister. She'd best try to remember that the next time she started feeling silly around Joseph. After all, being loved in this way truly was a precious thing and a great deal better than nothing.

Even if it didn't always feel that way.

Chapter Ten

"There we go." Joseph flicked out the offending bit of gravel with the hoof pick he'd retrieved from the barn. He straightened and rubbed his back. "Good as new."

"*Denki.*" Isaac released the horse's bridle and gave the leg a firm pat. "I hope it wasn't there long enough to cause any real damage. Star's a hardworking horse, and I wouldn't want him to go lame."

"I'm more cowman than horseman, but I don't think he will. Do you have time to come in for a cup of tea, Isaac?"

The older man shook his head. "*Nee*. I'll need to get back to the bakery to help Ida. We've a big delivery coming today. Ever since they showed up"—he nodded toward the reporters grouped along the roadside—"we've had more business than we can handle."

"They're good for business, *ja*, but I'm glad enough to see fewer of them out there today." A sheriff's cruiser drove slowly by, and some of the men stepped back off the edge of the yard, carefully staying on the right-of-way next to the road. "Seems like Sheriff Townsend has settled them down some, at least. They are staying off the property, even without the deputies here full-time now."

"I don't know whether it was the sheriff or your *bruder* we should credit for that," the bishop observed dryly. "That's something I need to speak with you about, Joseph."

Joseph shifted so that his back was toward the road. The heaviness in Isaac's tone told him that he was about to hear something unpleasant, and he didn't want any camera capturing his reaction to it.

"Caleb?"

Isaac nodded. "I've been talking to him. Or trying to. I'm afraid I've not seen much return for my efforts."

"*Ach*, well. Don't blame yourself. Caleb has always been *schtubbich*."

"I fear this is more than stubbornness, Joseph. Even my *dochder* cannot reason with him. They argued last night, and he left in a temper. He's not been back, and she's very upset."

Joseph inhaled the sharp winter air through his nose. "*Ja*, it would be so. He behaves like a wounded animal, my *bruder*. His pain and anger blind him, and he tramples whoever's standing closest to him."

"Hurt and grief are dangerous companions when they have not been surrendered to *Gott*. I've told Caleb this. I've tried to counsel him as a father would do, but he seems unwilling to listen."

Frustration rumbled in Isaac's voice, and Joseph felt a pang of understanding sympathy. This bishop and his *fraw* had been blessed with only the one daughter. While Rhoda had her share of spirit, she was basically a sweet, obedient girl. Nothing had prepared the bishop for a son-in-law like Caleb.

"I don't wish to cause you alarm. Your family has suffered pain enough already. But, Joseph, I feel I must be honest with you. I am very worried over Caleb—and Rhoda, too.

If he doesn't turn away from this path of revenge and anger, I fear we could lose them both."

"Lose them?" Joseph's heart dropped. Apparently, Caleb was in an even darker place than Joseph had thought. "You think Caleb's going to jump the fence?"

"He's only hinted as much so far, but *ja*. That is my concern. I think this root runs deep, Joseph, that the outburst with the reporter is only the edge of a much bigger problem. Caleb's heart is not at rest here among us; perhaps it never has been. I suspect that your brother professed a faith he did not truly believe, and now his lie has come back to trouble him, as such lies tend to do."

The truth of the bishop's words struck painfully home. Caleb had even admitted as much—that he had joined the church only because he wanted to marry Rhoda.

Joseph didn't know what to say, and after a moment, Isaac cleared his throat. "I wanted to let you know of my concerns so that you can also seek opportunities to speak to your *bruder*'s heart, to remind him of the blessings and ties he yet has here among us. A fresh appreciation for these things may turn him from this path, if anything can."

If anything can. Joseph wondered if anything could. If Rhoda, the very reason Caleb had entered into a false covenant with the church in the first place, hadn't been able to sway him, Joseph didn't have high hopes for much else doing the job. "I will talk to him, of course. But he's less likely to listen to me than to you, Isaac."

"Well, we will do our best, we will ask *Gott* for help, and we will not give in to discouragement. We must be patient with your *bruder*. This will not be fixed overnight, for sure. Remember, the prodigal did not turn from his ways easily."

Neither would Caleb. Joseph remembered how their father had been so concerned about Caleb, and how joyful he'd been about the marriage he believed would help bind his son's heart to the church. *Daed* would have been so grieved by this. This was what he'd always feared for Caleb, that his younger son's temper would pull him from his faith and his family.

Joseph couldn't let that happen, couldn't let his father's deepest fear become reality. He'd find some way to turn Caleb's heart. He had to.

"Tell Rhoda not to fret, Isaac. I will make Caleb see reason," he promised grimly.

"Tread carefully, Joseph. Those who stray are not won home with harshness. When the prodigal came back, he was received with kindness, *ja?*"

A muscle jumped in Joseph's cheek as he gritted his teeth. "I will show him kindness."

"*Gut.*" Isaac clapped him on the back approvingly. "Although," he added, "that reminds me of something else I meant to speak to you about. There may be times when our kindness could be misinterpreted."

"What do you mean?"

"Only this. If you truly want to be rid of those *Englischers* down at the road, you might tell Naomi to stop feeding them pie."

"*Vass maynsht?*" Joseph asked, confused. Isaac was talking in riddles.

"Today one of them presented me with an empty dish and his thanks to Naomi for his breakfast. It is well enough to be friendly, but if a man doesn't want crows in his cornfield, he'd best not feed them in his yard, ain't so?"

"*Ja,*" Joseph agreed, but he still didn't understand. "Naomi gave one of the *Englischers* a pie?"

"So it seems." Isaac chuckled. "If they want pie, tell them to come to my bakery and pay for it. We've plenty. Speaking of that, I must get back. Rhoda is staying here for the day to help however she can. Best for her to keep busy just now. I will come fetch her in the evening." The older man climbed into the carriage, and Joseph stepped back to allow him space to turn his horse.

As the bishop drove away, Joseph looked at the kitchen windows. He heard the low murmur of female voices, a reminder to focus on the blessing of this day. Miriam had finally come downstairs.

He'd barely been able to believe it when he'd seen Naomi leading his sister toward the steps. None of them had been able to coax Miriam out of her room, not even Emma, though she'd tried her best. Somehow, though, Naomi had managed it.

Maybe it was her eyes. When Naomi looked at him a certain way, he wanted to do whatever she asked of him, too.

He'd best question her about this pie business. Isaac's story was a puzzle—and a fresh worry. Joseph should probably go back inside now and get to the bottom of it.

Then again, maybe not. The bishop's concerns about Caleb weighed heavily on Joseph's heart, and the thought of unraveling yet another tricky problem made his head ache. Besides, Rhoda was in there, and Joseph didn't relish the idea of looking into his sister-in-law's eyes and seeing the pain his *bruder* had caused.

Nee, he decided. He'd follow his first plan and go out to his woodshop. Whatever had happened this morning, Naomi was safe enough now. He'd best spend a few hours with his hands busy and his mind occupied with something other than trouble while he still had the chance.

Because more trouble was coming; that was for certain sure. Sooner or later his brother would show back up, and trouble followed Caleb like a doting hound.

CHAPTER ELEVEN

❧

TWO MORNINGS LATER, NAOMI COUNTED BLUE AND
yellow triangles out of the basket Miriam had brought
down from her room. She arranged them on the freshly
scrubbed kitchen table, trying to copy the pattern of the
quilt square in front of her.

This was harder than it looked. She had all the pieces in
the right spots, but still the corners stuck out unevenly.

She glanced at Miriam, whose head was bent over her
own square, her fingers flying as she stitched in tiny, effi-
cient movements.

"I don't think I've got this right," Naomi worried aloud.

Miriam craned her neck to peer over the basket. "You
have the triangles turned the wrong way. Here." The younger woman set her own work beside her second cup of tea
and rearranged Naomi's square. The disjointed bits trans-
formed into a yellow star on a blue background. "There,
now. Ready to stitch."

"Denki." Naomi picked up two triangles and began
slowly sewing the narrow seam that would bind them to-

gether. "You'll have yours finished before I get mine started, Miriam. I've never seen anybody sew as fast as you."

"I like quilting. It's fun, not like making clothes. I enjoy picking out the colors and the patterns and matching them together. *Mamm* says—" Miriam caught herself, and her fingers stilled. For a second, the kitchen was heavy with silence, then she drew a breath and continued, "*Mamm* used to say there was a lot of satisfaction in bringing order and beauty out of a bunch of scraps. I agree with her."

Pretending to focus on her own square, Naomi watched Miriam blot a tear from her eye, then resume her sewing with trembling fingers. Naomi started to speak but thought better of it. Instead, she drew a soft, slow breath and returned her attention to moving the needle in and out of the fabric pressed between her thumb and forefinger.

Even when a person had her faith to cling to, grief was hard going. There were no words Naomi could say to make it easier. Best simply to pray silently that *Gott* would comfort Miriam's heart as only He could do.

Miriam glanced toward the battery-operated clock ticking on the kitchen wall. "Rhoda has been gone a long time to gather the eggs, ain't so? Do you think she's all right?"

"Likely she's found something else that needed doing while she was outside. You know how that goes."

Miriam's stitching slowed to a stop. "I should have gone myself. Tending the chickens is my job. But," she faltered, "going outside . . . I just couldn't. I know there's not near so many folks down by the road now, but still . . ."

"That's all right, Miriam." Naomi looked the other girl in the eye. "You've been getting dressed and coming downstairs every day, and you're sure doing a better job of quilting than I am. The rest will come in *Gott*'s good time. Rhoda did not mind going for the eggs today, and soon enough you'll be collecting them yourself. Like you said, there are hardly any reporters hanging round anymore. Before long, they'll all be gone."

"But there are still a few. What if one of them bothers her? I know that *Englischer* scared you the other day. I saw it in your face when Rhoda brought in the pie pan."

Naomi flinched. Nobody had mentioned the pie again, and she'd hoped it had been forgotten.

"I wasn't frightened," she assured Miriam quickly. "He just surprised me, that's all. He was very polite. Nobody's going to pester Rhoda, so don't fret yourself. Anyhow, Joseph's out there, and he'll let no harm come to her."

"*Ja*, that's true." Miriam relaxed against the back of her chair. "He's always been fond of her. For a while Emma and I thought . . . but then Rhoda chose Caleb. And now Joseph loves Rhoda as a sister, and he wouldn't let anybody bother her, not if he could help it."

Naomi recalled the look on Joseph's face that awful day when Rhoda had driven up to Katie's home, disheveled and beside herself. Naomi's heart thumped painfully, and she bent her head, forcing herself to focus on her quilt square.

She didn't share Miriam's love of quilting—or her skill. No matter how hard she tried, she couldn't make her stitches like her companion's tiny and uniform little dashes. Muffling a sigh, Naomi reached for another triangle to add to her growing star.

She wouldn't argue with Miriam, of course, but personally Naomi would rather make a dress or a shirt any day. When you made clothes, it didn't matter so much if your sewing wasn't perfect. The stitches were just supposed to do their duty and hold the fabric together. Nobody cared if they were pretty or not, and that made the work peaceful.

She came to the end of her thread, tied a knot, and clipped it off. As she reached for the spool, she noticed Miriam staring at the clock again, her sewing limp in her hands. Miriam caught Naomi's eye and looked embarrassed.

"I always got back in from the chicken coop in about ten minutes," she explained sheepishly. "Rhoda has been gone for twice that already."

Likely Rhoda was only stealing a few moments of privacy. Nobody knew exactly where Caleb had gone after he'd left the Lambrights' home, and no one had heard from him since. Rhoda was doing her best to be calm and cheerful in front of Miriam, but of course she must be worried. "I'm sure Rhoda is all right, but if you want, I will go check on her."

Miriam bit her lip, plainly uncertain about being left alone in the house. Finally, her concern for Rhoda overrode her fear. "*Ja*, go. But please be careful, and come back quick, all right?" She plucked Naomi's unfinished quilt square from her fingers. "I'll finish this for you while you're gone." She tilted the basket to check the remaining scraps. "We'll need more fabric soon if we're going to make enough squares for a full-size spread. Between the three of us, we've nearly got these pieced already."

Naomi laughed. "That's mostly your and Rhoda's doing. I'm afraid I'm little help."

"That's not true! You help more than you know. It's wonderful kind of you to sit and quilt with me, Naomi, especially since I can tell you don't enjoy it."

"I enjoy being with you, and that's what counts. Pleasant company makes everything better." Naomi winked. "Even quilting." She rose and collected her shawl from the peg by the door. "I'll hurry back."

Miriam nodded and bent over the bright bits of fabric as Naomi slipped out into the chilly yard.

There was a damp promise in the air, more like rain than snow. Maybe she'd make soup tonight, Naomi thought, as she hurried across the brown grass toward the coop. There were plenty of canned vegetables down cellar. She'd seen them when she went for the pickles on the day of the funeral. Soup would be warming on a day like this, served bubbling hot with a cast iron skillet of crisp cornbread. It would scent the air while it simmered, too, and that was such a comforting thing on a wintry day.

She was mentally ticking through the ingredients for her *mamm*'s favorite vegetable soup recipe by the time she got to the coop. She reached for the door latch, then halted as she heard Rhoda's tearful voice inside, mingled with the satisfied clucks of well-fed chickens.

"Caleb, you don't mean what you're saying! You can't see past your anger. *Daed* says if you will only put your trust in *Gott*, in time this grief will ease, and—"

"I don't want to hear what your father thinks, Rhoda. I've had more than enough of that already. I don't care how much Isaac preaches at me, I won't stand by and see the man who murdered my parents go free. I'll track Trevor Abbott down myself if I have to."

There was a short silence, punctuated by Rhoda's soft, sobbing gasps.

When Caleb spoke again, there was a frustrated edge to his voice. "You still haven't answered my question. Are you coming with me or not?"

"Caleb." Rhoda's voice broke on her husband's name. "Please, don't ask me this. I can't—I can't choose between you and my faith."

"You're going to have to because I'm leaving either way. With you or without you."

Horrified, Naomi backed away from the coop. She had to get Joseph.

When she burst through the door of the woodworking shop, Joseph glanced up from the rocking chair he was piecing together.

"What's wrong, Naomi? Is it Miriam?"

She shook her head breathlessly. Somewhere in the back of her mind, it registered that she shouldn't be struggling so hard to breathe after such a short sprint. "Caleb's in the chicken coop with Rhoda. He's jumping the fence, Joseph, and he wants her to go with him."

Joseph set the curved bit of wood down on a nearby shelf and started for the door. As he passed her, his face grim with frustration, he muttered, "So Isaac was right. No surprise there. My *bruder* spreads trouble like a head cold."

As they left the shop, they saw Rhoda running toward the house, her hands pressed to her face. Joseph watched her for a minute, then, shaking his head, he strode toward the coop.

Naomi followed Rhoda, her heart still chittering oddly in her chest. Naomi sent up a fervent prayer that Joseph would be able to talk sense into his brother. If he couldn't, if Caleb renounced his baptism now, he would pile sorrow upon sorrow for his family and his community.

When Naomi hurried through the back porch, she found Miriam standing frozen, clutching the back of a chair so tightly that her knuckles were white. Beside her on the table, the quilting basket was tipped on its side, bright squares spilling out recklessly.

"Naomi? Rhoda—she just ran through crying." Miriam's voice shook. "Those *Englischers*—"

"*Nee*," Naomi broke in quickly. She placed a reassuring hand on her friend's arm. "It was nothing like that, truly. It was only Caleb. He came by, and they argued, that's all."

"They argued?" Miriam asked with difficulty. Her breath was coming far too fast, and she looked to be on the brink of one of her attacks. "About what?"

"You're upsetting yourself, Miriam. You should sit down."

"Caleb's leaving us, ain't so? That's why Rhoda's crying." Miriam's whole body trembled as she waited for Naomi's answer.

Naomi gently stroked Miriam's sleeve. "Caleb's upset, but Joseph is talking to him."

"It won't do any good," Miriam whispered. "*Daed* was the only one Caleb ever listened to, and *Daed*'s not here."

Naomi's heart sank at her friend's bleak expression. All the *wunderbaar* progress they'd made was slipping away like water down a drain.

"Miriam, let's not worry ourselves. Things may come

right yet. Why don't we finish off these quilt squares before supper? If you help me, maybe I can even get mine sewn right-side-up the first time."

"I can't." Miriam was gasping quick and hard like a frightened sparrow. "Not right now. I have to . . . I have to go upstairs."

"Maybe we should try our special breathing. Come on, I'll count. One—"

"Ich kann naett!" Miriam's voice was sharp with desperation. She shook off Naomi's hand and stumbled toward the steps.

"I'll come with you."

"Nee! I need to be alone. Please, just . . . leave me be, Naomi." Miriam ran up the steps, and a few seconds later, her door slammed shut.

Naomi struggled with a sinking disappointment as she gathered the teacups for washing. It was too bad. Things had been going so well.

As Naomi set the cups and saucers beside the sink, her eye caught on a bit of brightness on the floor. A finished quilt square lay crumpled beside Miriam's chair.

Naomi picked it up and turned it over in her hands. Sure enough, there were her childish stitches, looking all the more crooked next to Miriam's perfect ones. In all the confusion, someone had stepped on it, pressing dirt into the dainty colors.

Oh, what a shame, Naomi thought sadly. What a terrible, terrible shame.

CHAPTER TWELVE

❧

EVEN BEFORE JOSEPH DUCKED INTO THE CHICKEN coop, he was frustrated. There was plenty he'd like to say to his brother right now, but none of it was particularly kind. He had no idea how to approach this in the way Isaac had suggested, but he had to try.

Caleb stood in the corner of the small building, *Mamm*'s plump black-and-white hens milling around his feet. His gaze was fixed on the half-filled egg basket his wife had left behind on the earthen floor, and he didn't look up when Joseph entered. "If you've come to lecture me, *bruder*, you can save your breath."

"Fine. You do the talking, then. You can start by telling me why your *fraw* just ran across the yard, crying."

"Rhoda doesn't understand." Caleb moved restlessly, startling the hens closest to his boots. They squawked and flapped their wings before settling back to their pecking and scratching. "None of you do."

"Maybe you should explain."

"All right." Caleb looked up and met his gaze squarely.

"I will. The Abbotts are hiding Trevor, Joseph. They're using their money and their friends to squirrel him away someplace while they wait for things to calm down."

Joseph frowned. "Do you know this for fact, or do you only suspect it?"

"Everybody knows it. A wealthy family like that? They're not about to just turn their son over to the police."

Joseph paused, choosing his tone carefully. "Things everybody knows usually come from gossip, Caleb. If there's any truth in such talk at all, it's likely not much."

"I knew you wouldn't listen."

"I am listening. I just think . . ." Joseph trailed off, fumbling for the right words, words Caleb might actually hear. "I think pain and anger keep a person from seeing clear sometimes, that's all."

His brother made an impatient noise. "You sound like my wife."

"And you sound like you're the one who's not willing to listen." The sharp words came too quickly for Joseph to stop them. His brother's expression darkened.

"I'm telling you, the Abbotts are lying to all of us." Caleb dug into the pocket of his pants. "Look at this, and maybe you'll see what I mean."

"What are you doing with a cell phone?" Joseph watched his brother swipe a finger across the tiny screen, making the device light up. How many other rules had Caleb skirted since his baptism? Plenty, Joseph figured. Frustration and impatience knotted heavily together in the pit of his stomach.

When Caleb held the phone out in his direction, Joseph made no move to accept it. "Whatever it is, I don't need to see it."

"You can't hide from this, Joseph. Not for much longer anyhow. There are stories all over the Internet, crazy stories about Emma, about *Daed* and *Mamm*. They're saying there was more to it, that Emma and Trevor were in love and that *Daed* had forbidden it. That he was beating Emma because of it. Beating her, Joseph, our *daed*! That Trevor was only protecting her, doing what he did."

Joseph felt a metallic sickness rising in the back of his throat. He swallowed hard. "So? Let them tell their lies. It makes no difference to us."

"*Ja*, it does. I think the Abbotts are behind these new stories. They want to make *Mamm* and *Daed* out to be in the wrong, so people will have more sympathy for Trevor. At the start of this, the public stood with us, but now, as these lies are sneaking out, opinion is starting to turn. They're making Trevor into some kind of hero."

"That would take more than a few silly stories, surely. People cannot be so *dumm* as that."

"You think not? Do you know why you haven't seen any sheriff's deputies driving by this morning?"

"There aren't so many reporters here today. They aren't needed."

"They're needed elsewhere. Somebody spray-painted hateful words on half the store windows in Johns Mill last night—the ones belonging to the Plain folks. The police are in town taking pictures and trying to figure out who did it."

Stunned, Joseph weighed his brother's words. Isaac hadn't mentioned any such thing when he'd dropped Rhoda off earlier this morning, and the bishop surely would have known about it. Then again, maybe Isaac had kept this disturbing news to himself, feeling the Hochstedlers had enough trouble on their plates already.

"I am sorry to hear of it, but we can't control how others feel about us nor what they do, Caleb. We can only control how we answer, and *Gott* calls us to answer with—"

"Forgiveness, *ja*," his brother interrupted impatiently. "I've sat through the same sermons you have, Joseph. Maybe that worked in the past, but the world has changed. Plain folk can't keep sticking their heads in the sand and refusing to stand up for themselves, not if they want their families to survive."

They. Their. Joseph's heart twisted at his brother's choice of words. Caleb had already separated himself from the rest of them. "It isn't our way to return evil for evil."

"Justice isn't evil. Stop spouting church doctrine and just listen to me for a minute. We've never questioned that *Gott* uses us to bless our neighbors. You'd be the first to help a man put out a fire in his barn, or help a widow bring in a crop her husband's death left standing in their field. We don't think of those things as stepping on the fingers of *Gott*, do we? Why should helping Him bring about justice be any different?"

Joseph wasn't sure how to answer that question, so he sidestepped it. "You knew the positions of the church before you were baptized, Caleb. That was the season for questions and doubts. Now's the time to set such things aside and trust the guidelines of our faith."

"Right now, I see little there worth trusting."

Joseph's breath was coming hard and quick. Dealing with his brother's stubbornness was like trying to cut a rock with a butter knife. "So what are you figuring to do, Caleb? Turn your back on your church? On your family?" When he got no answer, Joseph pressed on, "What about Rhoda? Will you turn your back on her, too?"

Caleb's eyes cut to him sharply. "That's my business, *bruder*, not yours."

"Maybe not my business, but certainly Rhoda's. These consequences you're courting will fall on her head as well as your own."

"*Ja*, there will be plenty of consequences for us but none for Trevor Abbott. I know you've no particular fondness for *Englischers*, *bruder*. In that one way you were always more like Melvin than *Daed*. How can this seem right to you?"

"Caleb—"

"He shot our father, Joseph. *Daed*, who was so tender-hearted that he hated to put down a suffering animal. He shot *Daed* first, they say, which means *Mamm* saw it. Then that boy turned his gun on our mother and shot her. Twice."

"*Schtopp.*" Joseph squeezed his eyes shut, but the images Caleb's words brought into his mind remained. A wave of pain and grief swelled and staggered him.

"And Miriam," Caleb continued relentlessly. "She may never get over what happened, as sensitive as she is, but she's lucky even to be alive."

"*Nee.*" Joseph set his jaw and clamped hard onto the fraying lifeline of his faith. "It wasn't luck, Caleb. It was *Gott*'s provision that Miriam was spared. We must focus on that and be thankful."

He opened his eyes to find his brother studying him. The skin above Caleb's new-married beard was pale, and his eyes glistened icily. "His gun jammed, Joseph. You can read *Gott* into it all you like, but that's what the police say happened. Trevor would have killed our little sister, too, but his father's pistol jammed on him, and he couldn't do it. You forgive him, *bruder*, if you can. Me, I'm going to find him, if I have to go to the ends of the earth to do it."

A horn blared from the direction of the road. "That's my driver." Caleb moved toward the door, and wordlessly, Joseph stepped aside to let him pass.

There was nothing more he could say. Caleb still wore the Plain shirt and trousers *Mamm* had made for him, but there was nothing Plain about the look in his eyes or the tilt of his chin. Their common ground, what little there'd been left of it, had crumbled away, leaving a gaping pit between them. Joseph saw no way to bridge it.

His brother paused with his hand on the door latch and spoke without turning his head. "I'll come back in a week or two, once Rhoda's had time to calm down. While I'm gone, she should give careful thought to what she wants to do. Will you tell her this?"

"I will tell her."

There was a short, hard silence. Caleb still didn't turn, but his shoulders flexed, as if he were fighting some inner battle.

"Look after her." The words came out stiffly. "You and I . . . we don't see eye to eye, maybe, and I haven't forgotten you had your own feelings for Rhoda. Even so, I'm asking you this as my brother." He hesitated then added roughly, "Please."

Joseph had to clear his own throat before he could answer. "I will look after your *fraw*, best I can, as if she was Miriam or Emma."

Caleb nodded shortly. Then he pushed through the wooden door, leaving it swinging on its hinges.

Joseph stood alone in the musty coop, the impact of Caleb's decision settling heavily in his gut. He didn't bother to look out the small window to watch his brother leave. In the most important way, Caleb had been gone before he'd even showed up this morning.

If *Daed* had been here, he'd have found some way to make his younger son see reason, but Joseph had failed yet again. That didn't bode well, because now, with Caleb and Emma gone, even more responsibilities had fallen upon Joseph's shoulders. Miriam, the store, this farm, and now, to some measure at least, Rhoda were all left to his care.

His mind went back over the memory of Rhoda stumbling toward the house, blind in her grief over her husband's decision. And small wonder—Joseph flinched at the choice Rhoda was facing. If she followed Caleb away from the church, she'd be shunned by her own family. If she chose to remain, Rhoda's future would be bleak. Although still bound to her husband, she wouldn't be allowed to accept any support from him. She'd have to rely on her parents and the charity of others until she figured some way to earn a living for herself.

Joseph sighed as he leaned over to retrieve the egg basket she'd forgotten. He'd carry it into the house before he went back to the workshop to finish the rocking chair.

When he entered the kitchen, Naomi was at the sink, rinsing a soiled fabric square under a stream of water. A basket of quilt pieces was tumbled sideways on the table, and the chairs were askew, as if people had risen from their places in a hurry. Miriam and Rhoda were nowhere in sight.

More trouble. Joseph felt a wave of weariness as he set down the basket. He had a sudden desire to throw a couple eggs just to see them smash.

"What happened here?" he asked, dreading the answer.

Naomi glanced over her shoulder. Tiny worry lines creased the corners of her eyes, but the smile she offered was sweet. "A little setback, that's all. Nothing to worry over. Only, someone stepped on this quilt square Miriam made and smudged it. I'm just washing it out."

Joseph went to stand beside Naomi, watching as her nimble fingers massaged the dirt out of the pretty fabric. Miriam had always loved quilting. Surely the fact that she'd taken her needle up again was a good sign. A tiny spark of hope sputtered in the darkness of his heart as he studied the dainty square. "Will it be all right, do you think?"

"*Ja*, sure. With some work and a bit of patience." Naomi's gray-green eyes met his with a quiet certainty that steadied him. "Everything will be all right, Joseph."

He knew she wasn't only speaking of the quilt square. As he looked into her face, her gentle smile grew, warming him.

Joseph couldn't seem to pull his gaze away from hers. He was oddly reminded of the time he'd ventured out to the county fair with a bunch of other *youngies* and had been enticed onto some sort of twirly ride. He'd never experienced anything like that before, and he'd felt awful *grank*. Just in the nick of time, he'd discovered if he fixed his eyes on the metal pole in front of his face, the crazy spinning didn't bother him near so much.

Looking down into Naomi's eyes, he felt the same grateful relief as he had back then. The ugliness whirling around him blurred, and he was almost able to believe that what she'd just told him was true.

That somehow, someday, his life would come right again.

CHAPTER THIRTEEN

❧

HOLDING HER BREATH, NAOMI FLICKED THE REINS on Titus's back. The gelding walked forward obediently, and the buggy bumped out of the drive and onto the two-lane road. Not a car was in sight, and she sent a fervent prayer heavenward thanking *Gott* for that mercy.

She was an uncertain driver on the best of days, and she didn't need traffic to deal with. She'd finally convinced Miriam to venture into town, so she had more than enough on her plate as it was.

"Isn't it a perfect day?" she asked brightly. "Hard to believe it's the end of December. Such sunshine, and the air's just cold enough to nip your nose but not cold enough to make your toes ache."

There was no answer from the other two occupants of the buggy. Rhoda was hunched beside her on the buggy's bench seat, staring blankly at the lovely morning. Two weeks had passed since Caleb had left Johns Mill. Rhoda had continued coming faithfully to the farmhouse to help out, but lately Naomi found herself dreading the other woman's arrival. With every passing day, Rhoda grew more silent and withdrawn, and Naomi had caught the worried glances Miriam was giving her sister-in-law.

Having Rhoda to fret over wasn't helping Miriam's situation. On the other hand, Rhoda was hurting just as much as Miriam was, and she needed just as much sympathy and understanding. Naomi understood that, but the two of them were a lot for one person to handle.

Today, though, was all about Miriam. This trip was a milestone for her, and it had been slow in coming. Miriam hadn't set foot off the Hochstedler farm since she'd been brought home from the hospital. Over the past couple of weeks, Naomi had coaxed her into staying in the kitchen longer and longer, mostly by sewing quilt squares with her. Tedious as that was, she would have cheerfully hand-sewn miles of seams to keep Miriam from hiding in her bedroom.

At least Naomi's stitching had improved with all the practice, so that was something, too.

A few days before their quiet Christmas, she'd talked Miriam into venturing outside to the woodshop to see what Joseph was working on and to bring him some ginger cookies they'd baked. The expression on Joseph's face when he'd looked up from his lathe to see his sister had given Naomi a touch of spring right in the middle of the sodden winter morning.

The gratitude in his eyes had made her bounce on her toes with joy. She'd walked back to the house arm-in-arm with Miriam, aglow with thanksgiving. *Gott* had answered her prayers. She was truly making a difference.

Since then, she and Miriam had taken a treat to Joseph in the middle of each morning, and Miriam had grown more relaxed each time. She'd even stopped glancing at the road, since there were no reporters there to see anymore.

Now she was making this trip to town, to visit Mary Yoder's fabric shop. It was a big step for Miriam, and Naomi intended it as a surprise for Joseph. He'd gone with Aaron to an auction, and he wouldn't be back until late afternoon. He'd given Naomi permission to take the buggy into town, and she knew he'd be delighted to hear that his sister had gone along.

"This sunshine is nice, ain't so, Rhoda? Such a welcome change after all the rain we've had." When Rhoda didn't answer, Naomi glanced over her shoulder. "You're in the shade back there, Miriam. Are you keeping warm enough? I put an extra blanket in if you need it."

"I'm fine."

The two words were barely audible, but at least they proved that Miriam was still capable of speech. Her eyes were wide as a frightened colt's, but she was breathing okay.

So far, so good.

Still, Naomi swallowed a sigh of relief when she turned the horse into Katie Lapp's drive. Talkative Katie and sweet baby Sarah would fill the silence in the buggy and cheer everybody up.

She set the brake on the buggy, and half turned on the seat so she could face both women. "Wait here, *ja?* I'll run in and help Katie bring Sarah out." When Rhoda made a move to climb into the back, Naomi put a gentle hand on her arm. "I think Katie would best sit beside Miriam, don't you think? That way Miriam can help with the baby. I can't do that while I'm driving."

Rhoda nodded dully and settled back on her seat, but Miriam, Naomi noticed, perked right up.

"I'll move everything so there's plenty of room," the younger woman said. She picked up the blanket and the neatly folded cloth shopping bags and stowed them on the buggy floor.

"Gut!" Naomi turned aside to hide her smile. Miriam was really looking forward to seeing the baby, and hopefully Sarah would keep her pleasantly distracted for the rest of the trip.

When Naomi hurried into the kitchen, she was relieved
to see Katie standing there pulling on her gloves, her black
bonnet and shawl already in place.

"I heard you driving up," her cousin said cheerfully.
"We're both all ready to go."

"That's a blessing! I don't dare leave Rhoda and Miriam
alone too long." Sarah, bundled to the tip of her nose,
squirmed happily in her pink cloth sling seat on the table.
Naomi leaned down and kissed the little girl's forehead
before unfastening her and lifting the infant into her arms.
"Come on, sweetie-pie. You're just the tonic Miriam needs.
And for goodness' sakes, Katie, once you get in that buggy,
talk."

Katie laughed, the sound delightfully normal after the
strained drive. "Nobody ever has to tell me to talk, Naomi.
To hush, maybe, but not to talk."

Naomi smiled, but she couldn't quite find the breath to
answer. Sarah suddenly seemed very heavy. "Here." She
handed the baby to Katie. "Maybe you'd best carry her."

Katie's eyes sharpened as Naomi pressed one hand on
the table to steady herself. "Are you all right? I haven't
liked to say anything, but you've seemed exhausted lately,
and you're going to bed mighty early these days. I'm getting worried. Is helping at the Hochstedlers' turning out to
be too difficult for you?"

"*Nee*," Naomi answered quickly. "I'm fine. I just don't
like to drive on the road. I've never had much practice with
it, and it always makes me shaky."

That was true enough, but Katie's questions worried
Naomi a bit. She'd been feeling more tired than usual, but
she'd told herself it was simply because she was coping
with so much just now . . . running a household, struggling
to help Miriam past her fears, and trying to comfort Rhoda
as she pined for her stubborn husband.

Then there was Joseph. The weary sorrow in his eyes
when he looked at his sister and at Rhoda made Naomi long

to comfort him, too. She tried her best to make his life easier, but there seemed so little she could do.

Still, when he thanked her quietly for her help or for a particularly good meal, or for bringing a cup of hot *kaffe* out to his woodshop on a chilly, rainy afternoon, she felt as if she'd at least done something.

Her heartbeat was slowing back down, and her breath came easier. Likely what she'd told Katie was the truth. Managing the buggy on the road and dealing with the two unhappy women had just stretched her nerves a little. She was fine.

Katie laughed again as she tucked Sarah's blanket around her. "You've always been such a nervous Nelly about driving. Me, I love it! Aaron fusses at me sometimes for going too fast. Do you want me to drive today?"

Naomi shook her head. In her private opinion, Aaron was right about Katie's daredevil driving. Naomi didn't think her nerves were up to that this morning, and she didn't want Rhoda and Miriam unsettled, either.

"I'll manage, *denki*. I need the practice, and the traffic's light now that all those reporters are gone."

Katie frowned. "They aren't all gone. Aaron took his turn minding the Hochstedlers' store yesterday, and he said a few were still hanging around, taking photos. I know that won't bother you, nor me, either if we bump into one of them, and I doubt Rhoda would even notice, poor girl. But what about Miriam?"

A feather of worry tickled across Naomi's shoulders, but she shivered the feeling away. "I think it'll be fine. We won't go anywhere near the store, so nobody's likely to bother us. Even if a reporter does try to speak to us, you and I will straighten him out quickly enough. Anyway, it's important for Miriam to do this. Her fears about town are starting to settle in, Katie. Once they do, she'll find it much harder to break free of them."

"Maybe you're right. My *grossdaddi* always said the

best thing to do was get back on the horse that threw you as soon as you were able, or you'd be fearful of him from then on."

Just as Naomi had hoped, once Katie and Sarah were settled in the buggy, things improved. Katie chattered merrily, telling tales about new motherhood that had everybody laughing. Out of the corner of her eye, Naomi even caught Rhoda smiling a time or two. More important, Miriam held baby Sarah on her lap for the rest of the drive into town. She was so absorbed in cooing at the infant that she didn't glance up when Naomi turned the buggy off Main Street in order to avoid coming within sight of Hochstedler's General Store.

Sooner or later, Miriam would have to face that place, too, Naomi suspected, if her recovery was to be complete. But not today.

Naomi secured Titus carefully in the parking area beside the brick building that housed the local fabric shop. The other three women clambered out of the buggy, passing the baby off one to another as they did. As they headed toward the sidewalk, Naomi positioned herself behind Miriam, scanning the street for anyone who looked remotely like a reporter.

She didn't see anybody except ordinary folks, mostly Plain, going about their morning business, and she breathed a grateful sigh. If they managed to complete this errand in peace, it would be another big step forward for Miriam.

When Naomi stepped into the cozy store, she was instantly overwhelmed by all the colorful bolts of material arranged by shade on the walls. Naomi's lack of quilting skills extended to shopping for fabric. She didn't see how anybody made decisions with so many pretty things to choose from.

Clothing was more straightforward. If you needed a new dress, you looked at the few solid colors approved in your district. You compared prices and chose a bolt of decent quality in a shade that you hadn't recently had and that, hopefully, looked reasonably nice on you. And that was that. Simple.

This process was anything but simple, but Naomi could see right away that this trip was exactly the right thing to do for Miriam. The younger woman's eyes lit up, and she hurried to the bolts of pink and green fabric arranged on the right-hand wall.

"Here, Katie," Naomi offered. "Let me hold the baby while you go help Miriam choose the fabric for the border of the quilt. You know a lot more about all this than I do."

Katie smiled. "You won't have to offer twice. I love shopping for quilting fabric. Isn't it lovely in here with all these beautiful colors? It's like we left winter outside and walked into a flower garden!" She transferred Sarah into Naomi's arms then joined Miriam. Soon the two were gathering samples from the swatches offered beside each bolt and comparing them, heads tilted together.

Rhoda sank onto one of the wooden chairs in the corner, a spot usually occupied by elderly shoppers who needed to rest their aching feet. She stared down at her clenched fingers, her narrow shoulders slumped, oblivious to Miriam and Katie's enthusiastic chatter.

Naomi shifted Sarah's soft, warm weight in her arms. Given that little spell she'd had in Katie's kitchen earlier, it was probably wisest for her to sit down herself. She settled in the chair next to Rhoda.

"You don't want to look at any fabric?" she asked, nestling Sarah more comfortably on her lap. Now that Miriam was safely occupied, maybe she could manage to spark some interest in Rhoda's lifeless eyes as well.

Rhoda shook her head. "Not today."

The unseasonable December sunlight beat through the large window behind them, toasting Naomi's back pleasantly. It was so nice and warm in here. She began freeing Sarah from some of her outer clothing. "My goodness, Katie has this poor *boppli* wrapped up as if we were in the middle of a blizzard. No wonder her cheeks are pink! I'm not much of a quilter, but I might look at some new dress fabric while we're here. The sign over there says they're having a sale. What do you think? Should we take a look?"

"I've no need of a new dress, and I must watch my budget carefully just now," Rhoda said quietly.

Naomi's hands faltered, with only one of Sarah's plump arms out of her little coat. How could she have been so thoughtless? Of course Rhoda would be watching her spending. Caleb had said he'd be back in a week or two, but that time frame was already past. With her husband gone, so was Rhoda's means of support. She'd have to rely on her parents financially until Caleb returned and made his full repentance before the church.

If he ever did.

"I'm sorry," Naomi whispered. "I wasn't thinking."

Rhoda attempted a smile. "It's all right, Naomi. I'm sorry, too. I know I've not been very good company for you and Miriam. I've even thought perhaps I should stop coming over every day. Miriam and Joseph have enough troubles of their own to deal with. But selfishly, I just couldn't." A sparkle of tears glittered in the shop's bright lights. "I felt I'd lose my mind if I stayed home, and I just couldn't face working in the bakery with *Mamm* and *Daed*."

Naomi shifted Sarah into the crook of her right arm and used her left to give Rhoda a warm hug. "Don't be silly. We want you with us, Miriam and I." She started to mention Joseph, too, but then held back. Perhaps that wouldn't be wise, given the circumstances. "This is a hard time, *ja?* But it will end, and in the meantime you have friends and family to love you and pray for you. *Gott* has not left you, Rhoda, and neither will we."

Rhoda drew a shaky breath and nodded. "I know. *Daed* says the same. That's the best comfort I have, at least for now." Her glance strayed to Sarah, happily snuggled in the circle of Naomi's arm. The baby was fascinated with her tiny fist, clenching it and unclenching it in front of her own wide blue eyes. The ghost of a smile flickered across Rhoda's lips. When she spoke again, her voice was stronger. "Why don't you let me mind Sarah while you look at the dress fabric?"

Naomi started to protest, but the yearning in Rhoda's eyes stopped her. Babies were wonderful *gut* company for hurting folks. During her illness, when her older brothers would bring her little nieces and nephews to see her, she'd always felt uplifted, no matter how dark the day had seemed beforehand.

So instead of arguing, she nodded. "That would be real helpful. I'm not used to juggling a *boppli* while shopping, and she does get a bit heavy sometimes."

When Naomi transferred the infant into the other woman's arms, Rhoda's faint smile bloomed into a real one. "That's because she's getting so big already. Aren't you, sweet girl?" When Rhoda glanced at Naomi, the smile she'd beamed at Sarah stayed in place. "Shoo, now. Go look at your fabric. We'll be fine. And Naomi?" Rhoda added as Naomi rose to her feet. "*Denki* for being so kind to me."

"*Du bisht welcome.*" Naomi gave the other woman's shoulder a gentle pat.

As she walked across the tiny store to the bolts of dress fabric angled on the back wall, Naomi's feet barely touched the polished oaken floorboards. This outing idea had been risky, but it had turned into a rousing success, for Rhoda and Miriam both. She could hardly wait to see Joseph's face when he found out.

When she reached the selection of fabric, she forced herself to focus and studied the bolts thoughtfully. In spite of her protests, Joseph had insisted on paying her a small wage, and she could easily afford the material for a new dress.

She trailed a gentle hand along the smooth fabric, moving past the girlish lavender and plum shades to the more somber, matronly colors.

She generally preferred lighter shades, but maybe this time she should choose something a bit darker. Miriam and Rhoda were wearing black, of course. They were in mourning for Elijah and Levonia and would be wearing no other color for at least a year.

The black dresses Naomi had worn after her own mother's death were back in Kentucky. Lately, though, she'd felt uncomfortable tripping around the house in her light-colored dresses. She didn't want her friends to think she was unfeeling.

Maybe this brown would be a good compromise. She fingered the fabric. It seemed to be a nice, sturdy cloth, too, and it would last for years.

Normally that would be a positive, but she had to admit, the thought of wearing such a muddy color for so long didn't exactly thrill her heart. Still, showing sympathy for the Hochstedlers' feelings was more important than indulging her own tastes.

"Don't buy that." Katie halted beside her. She was on her way to the counter, several swatches of material in her fingers. "This one would suit you much better." She indicated a deep plum shade. "It'll put some color back into your cheeks."

That light tickle of fear touched the back of Naomi's neck again. When she'd first come to Johns Mill, Katie had exclaimed delightedly over how wonderful Naomi's color had become since her operation. Today not only was Katie calling her pale again, but there had been that odd sinking spell in the kitchen earlier.

Surely there couldn't be some sort of problem with her heart? At her last appointment, her doctors had assured her everything looked fine, and she wasn't scheduled for another checkup with her cardiologist for months.

Katie bent closer, lowering her voice, "I wasn't sure to start with, but you were right. This trip to town was a wonderful idea. Miriam's perked right up, and she's had a lovely time choosing her fabric."

Naomi glanced at Miriam, who was telling Mary Yoder, the store owner, how much fabric she wanted of the various swatches she'd brought to the counter. Naomi pushed her private worries firmly to the back of her mind. "That's an answer to prayer, for sure."

"Since she's doing so well, what do you think about popping into Miller's and having a piece of pie before going home? It's only a couple of doors down from here."

Naomi shook her head. "I don't know, Katie. Miriam's doing real well, *ja*, but maybe it's best not to try too much on this first trip."

"Oh." Katie's face fell. "I'm sorry. I've already mentioned the idea to Miriam. At first she looked a little *naerfich*, but then she said a piece of apple-raisin pie sounded real *gut*."

"Well." Naomi looked at Miriam, still smiling and chatting with the plump store owner. Miriam did seem to be doing fine, and if she wanted to go to Miller's, maybe it wasn't such a bad idea. "All right. We'll head that way as soon as we finish settling up with Mary." Naomi hesitated, glancing between the brown and plum dress goods. Impulsively, she lifted the bolt of deep plum cloth off its brackets and headed for the checkout counter.

"That's a smart choice." Her cousin approved. "Good for a *maidel* or a married woman, either one, ain't so?" Katie asked the loaded question with a teasingly lifted eyebrow, and Naomi laughed.

"I've no reason to worry about that." She didn't, and there was absolutely no reason for her mind to jump in Joseph's direction at the suggestion, either. "I just don't want to be wearing bright clothes around folks who are grieving."

"I see." Katie nodded easily, but Naomi thought she saw

a flicker of doubt in her cousin's eyes. "Well, this'll do just as well for that, and it'll rosy those cheeks of yours back up, too."

She hoped Katie was right, and a change of dress colors was all that was needed to bring some pink back into her cheeks. In any case, she wouldn't allow herself to worry about her health until it was time to follow up with her cardiologist. Right now, she was living the life she'd always dreamed about, and she wasn't going to let silly fears—or even sillier hopes—spoil it.

CHAPTER FOURTEEN

❧

AFTER LEAVING THE STORE, THE WOMEN PAUSED TO stow their fabric in the box secured on the back of the Hochstedler buggy. Then Katie and Miriam led the way toward Miller's Café, walking arm-in-arm.

Katie chattered about the new quilt she was planning. Miriam was quieter, and her eyes darted nervously toward the road, but as near as Naomi could tell, she seemed to be doing all right.

Rhoda walked beside Naomi, Sarah cuddled against her left shoulder. Naomi had hoped the *boppli* would be a distraction for Miriam, but now it was Rhoda who seemed oblivious to everything but the baby. Her face had lost its tense, worried expression as she murmured softly into Sarah's tiny, shell pink ear. Naomi smiled to herself as they walked along the sidewalk.

Joseph was going to be so pleased when he heard about all this. She could hardly wait to tell him.

Sporting simple cream curtains and a hand-painted sign, Miller's Café was as Plain and wholesome as its young owners, Ellen and Micah Miller. The tiny restaurant offered a limited menu: sandwiches, soups, and desserts, ordered at the counter, deli-style. The food wasn't fancy, but it was all made from scratch and delicious. The café was a popular spot for Plain folk and local *Englischers* as well.

As the women entered, the comforting aromas of freshly baked bread and roasting meat wafted over them. Although it was barely eleven o'clock, the lunch rush had already started, and a line of customers snaked halfway down the store. Miriam shrank back at the sight of all the people, and Naomi bit her lip.

There was no way she could ask Joseph's sister to wait in this lengthy line, brushing elbows with so many strangers. Maybe this hadn't been such a good idea, after all.

"The line is a bit long, ain't so?" Naomi remarked. "Rhoda, why don't you and Miriam take Sarah and go sit at that booth in the corner? Katie and I will get pie for all of us and meet you there in a few minutes. All right?"

"No pie for me, *denki*, but I would like a glass of milk, if you'd be kind enough to get it for me." Rhoda juggled Sarah, trying to reach the little cloth bag she had looped over her elbow, but Naomi waved her off.

"Don't worry about paying now. You and I can settle up later. Go get that table before somebody else does, and we'll be there soon."

Naomi waited until Rhoda, Miriam, and Sarah were safely seated in the secluded booth. Then she and Katie joined the fast-moving line of customers headed to place their orders at the counter.

"Poor Rhoda." Katie sent a sympathetic glance toward the corner where their friends were seated. "She's having such a hard time with all this, and who can blame her? I can only imagine how I'd have felt if Aaron had left me so soon after our marriage."

"*Ja*, it's been very difficult for her." Naomi checked the prices posted on the chalkboard above the counter and busied herself pulling bills out of her bag. She felt certain that Rhoda's refusal of pie had more to do with her budget than her appetite, so she counted out enough to purchase a slice for Rhoda as well.

"Everybody wonders what's going to happen," Katie was saying. "Folks are split right down the middle over it. Half of them say that Caleb is sure to come back when his grief settles down a little. The rest think this was bound to happen sooner or later because Caleb's always been so *schtubbich*. They say he only joined the church because Rhoda made him, and that he never meant to stay. What do you think?"

"I don't know. What kind of pie are you going to get?" Naomi asked desperately. She'd noticed a couple of nearby *Englischers* giving them curious glances and whispering. Katie was as sweet as a ripe strawberry and she had a big, kind heart, but she truly did love to talk—sometimes a little too much. Naomi didn't want to gossip about the Hochstedler problems at all, but particularly not in this crowded café, where anybody might overhear.

"I always get sweet potato pie. It's my favorite. What does Joseph say? Does he think Caleb will come home?"

"He hasn't said." Clearly her cousin wasn't going to let go of this subject easily, so Naomi added, "Let's not talk about this, all right, Katie? Rhoda wasn't sure about coming along today because she knows everybody's gossiping about Caleb. She's suffering enough without her friends picking over her troubles behind her back, ain't so?"

"Oh!" Katie's cheeks flushed a mottled red. "*Ja.* Of course you're right. I'm sorry, Naomi, my tongue runs away with me sometimes." They were almost at the counter now, and Katie glanced at the bills in Naomi's hand. "Are you buying Rhoda some pie?"

"I was planning to." Unwilling to share Rhoda's confession about her money troubles, Naomi added, "I always think I don't want pie until I see everybody else eating theirs. I thought I'd get her a piece just in case. If she really doesn't want it, I can always wrap it up and take it along home to Joseph."

"Let me buy it." Katie flashed a knowing look at Naomi, and Naomi realized her excuse hadn't been necessary. Of course Katie understood Rhoda's financial situation perfectly. Everybody in their district did. "I will tell her it's a thank-you for looking after the baby for me today. I love Sarah to pieces, and I love being her *mamm*, but now and then it's so nice to be able to think about something else for just a little while, you know?"

Naomi nodded, but of course, she didn't know, not really. She could imagine, though, what a sweet blessing it must be to have such a darling baby. Not to mention a handsome husband who looked at you with his heart in his eyes, like Aaron did whenever his Katie bounced into a room.

"Naomi?"

Naomi blinked as Katie jostled her elbow. They were at the front of the line and Ellen Miller was waiting, pen in hand.

"Oh, I'm sorry! I was woolgathering."

She and Katie quickly placed their orders, paid, and collected their laden trays. As they neared the corner booth, Naomi's smile faded, and her heartbeat quickened. Rhoda sat at the table jogging Sarah on her lap, but Miriam was nowhere in sight.

Naomi picked up her pace, hurrying toward the table so quickly that Rhoda's milk sloshed out of the glass onto the paper lining the plastic tray. "Where's Miriam?"

"She went to the washroom," Rhoda replied without looking up from Sarah's face. "I offered to go with her, but she said she was fine to go by herself, so I let her. That's all right, isn't it?"

Relief washed over Naomi. "*Ja*, that's fine. That's very good." She glanced in the direction of the wooden door leading to the restroom area, willing her hammering heart to slow back down. Miriam was fine.

She and Katie busied themselves setting out the various pieces of pie and drinks, then Katie settled down with Sarah on her lap. As Katie and Rhoda argued good-naturedly about Katie's gift of pie in exchange for Rhoda's baby-sitting, Naomi's eyes kept drifting back to the closed door. Miriam hadn't yet reappeared.

"Oh!" Rhoda jumped up from the booth, bumping the table and making all the plates and forks rattle. Sarah made a startled wail of protest, but for once, Katie ignored her baby, staring over Naomi's head, her eyes wide.

Naomi stiffened. She turned her head, already suspecting who she'd see behind her. Sure enough, Caleb stood there, looking grim and uneasy.

"Can we talk, Rhoda?" he asked quietly.

Rhoda didn't seem able to speak. She nodded.

"Not here." For the first time, Caleb spared a brief glance for Naomi and Katie. "Let's go outside, *ja?*"

Rhoda swallowed, her gaze fastened hungrily on her husband's face. She gave another stiff nod and started for the door, Caleb following close behind.

As soon as the café door shut behind them, Katie turned to Naomi, vibrating with excitement. "*Is sell naett ebbes!*" she exclaimed over Sarah's escalating wails. "Caleb has come back! This is wonderful *gut* news!"

"*Ja,*" Naomi agreed, "wonderful *gut.*" But her mind skipped back to the look on Caleb's face, to that muscle she'd seen twitching in his set jaw.

She hoped Caleb's return meant good news for Rhoda; she truly did. But somehow, she wondered.

She glanced apprehensively at Katie's eager expression. Plainly, her *kossin* was gearing up to talk this whole thing to death. Naomi snatched her napkin from her lap and placed it beside her untasted pie.

"I'll run to the washroom and check on Miriam while you settle Sarah," she said as she rose to her feet. "I'll be back in a minute."

Without waiting for Katie's answer, Naomi hurried across the café. Just as she opened the door to the restroom area, a booming female voice echoed down the narrow hallway.

"What do you think you're doing, young man? Leave that poor girl alone! I mean it, now—*get!*"

Suddenly an *Englisch* man pushed roughly through the doorway, making Naomi stagger backward. He strode through the café, head down, stuffing a cell phone into his shirt pocket.

Naomi rushed into the tiled corridor leading to the restrooms. "Miriam?"

"She's back here, honey—and you'd better come quick!"

Naomi rounded the corner where the door to the ladies' room was located. Miriam was huddled in a terrified knot on the floor, her face buried in her hands, her black bonnet sliding off the back of her head. The middle-aged *Englisch* woman kneeling beside her looked up as Naomi ran toward them.

"I'm not sure what happened," she said, pitching her voice to be heard over Miriam's frantic gasps. "When I came out of the bathroom, that man had her cornered, taking pictures of her. He had her by the arm, the poor little thing, so she couldn't get away. No wonder she got scared. Made me so mad! I whapped him good with my pocketbook so he'd turn her loose."

Naomi dropped to the floor, putting her arms around Miriam, who was struggling to pull air into her panicked body. Indignation burned hot in Naomi's stomach, and she understood Caleb Hochstedler a good deal better than she had before.

"It's all right, Miriam. He's gone, and I'm here. You're safe."

"You got some more friends out there that can help you, honey? I'll go get 'em if you want." The plump *Englisch* woman hoisted herself to her feet with some difficulty. "Just tell me where they are."

"Yes, please. My friend's in the corner booth to the right. She has a baby with her. Thank you, Miss—"

"Mona. I'm Mona Carter. Here." She opened her bulky purse and rummaged, finally offering a lavender business card. "I sell real estate, so that's got all my contact information on it. If you need me to tell the police what happened, you just let me know. In fact, I'll call them myself right now, if you want me to!"

"*Nee,*" Miriam choked out. "No police! I can't—please. I just want to go home. Please, Naomi."

"Bless her heart," Mona murmured. "I'll run get your friend." Her footsteps echoed heavily down the hallway.

Naomi pulled Miriam closer. "We'll rest here for a minute, just until you catch your breath, and then we'll go home. Everything will be all right, you'll see."

She put as much conviction in her voice as she could, but she had no idea if Miriam believed her. To tell the truth, crouched here on this floor, with all her bright hopes wilting like flowers after a freeze, she wasn't sure she believed herself.

CHAPTER FIFTEEN

❧

THE HEAVILY ADVERTISED FARM AUCTION HAD BEEN a disappointment, and Aaron and Joseph were back in Johns Mill before lunchtime. As they rolled through town, Aaron nodded toward the parking lot outside of Yoder's Fabrics.

"Ain't that your buggy, Joseph?"

Joseph looked over in time to catch a glimpse of Titus, tethered to a hitching rack.

"Looks to be. Naomi must have come into town to visit Yoder's. She's got Miriam sewing again, and I heard them saying they were near about out of some things they needed to finish the quilt they're working on."

He scanned the area as Aaron's buggy rumbled past the parking lot, but Naomi was nowhere to be seen. She must already be inside the store.

"She's a good helper, is Naomi." Aaron flipped up a lazy hand to wave at a friend driving in the opposite direction. "I wasn't too sure when Katie asked her to come stay after the baby came. I remembered Naomi the way she used to be, always frail and lagging behind the rest of us *youngies*. I worried Katie was asking her out of pity and making more work for herself in the bargain. It didn't turn out like that at all. She carries her load as well as anybody now, Naomi does."

"*Ja*, she does." Joseph struggled with himself for a moment longer before adding, "Stop here, Aaron, will you? I'll walk back and drive Naomi home."

Aaron veered to the left and slowed the carriage to a stop. "Sure nice of you to take such trouble for Katie's *kossin*."

As he jumped down from the buggy, Joseph shot his friend a suspicious look. Aaron's mouth was straight and serious above his short beard, but his blue eyes twinkled mischievously.

"Naomi's not had much experience driving," Joseph explained sheepishly. "She's said more than once that managing a horse on a road with cars makes her *naerfich*. I don't want her getting frightened into an accident. That's all."

"That's what I said. It's kind of you to take such care of her. 'Course, best I remember, it was always so, *ja?* Naomi wasn't the only one lagging behind the rest of us. Wherever she was, there you were as well, more times than not. Funny, ain't it, how the past repeats itself? *Mach's gut*, Joseph." Aaron gave his friend one last, knowing smirk, then clucked to his horse, making the carriage lurch forward.

As Aaron rolled toward home, Joseph began walking back toward the parking lot where he'd seen Titus.

The twinkle in Aaron's eye was nothing new. Ever since he'd reached marriageable age, Joseph had gotten sly looks anytime he'd so much as mentioned a single girl's name. Courtships in their community played out quietly, and folks liked guessing which *youngie* was pairing off with whom. When wedding plans finally filtered out, people were always interested to see if they'd guessed correctly.

Joseph wasn't so young anymore, and it had been a while since anybody had hinted that he might be courting. Now it seemed folks thought he might be settling on Naomi Schrock.

Maybe he was.

A notion that had been lurking in the back of his thinking for some days now came front and center. Joseph slowed his pace as he faced it fully for the first time.

Aaron was right about Naomi. She was a kind girl, and a smart, steady worker. The way she'd rolled up her sleeves and helped him out with Miriam was proof of that. Lately she'd also been helping with Rhoda, who was in nearly as bad a shape as his sister, thanks to his rock-headed brother.

Between the two troubled women, Naomi's days couldn't be easy. Yet every evening when Joseph came in from his woodworking shop, she had a smile on her face and a hot supper readied on the stove.

It was more than that, though.

Ja, Naomi was a *gut*, cheerful helper, but Joseph could have said the same of many other *maidels* he knew, and he'd never given them a second look. There was something special about Naomi.

She drew him, Naomi did. It was like when his *mamm* had baked her homemade bread. She'd always joke that the men knew just when to turn up in the kitchen for a hot slice fresh from the oven. It was true. No matter where he was on the farm on baking day, he'd catch a whiff of yeasty bread and sense it was time to make a detour by the kitchen.

Naomi was like that. That sweet gentleness she carried with her seeped through the whole farm, calling to him. He'd be in the middle of working at his lathe and suddenly he'd cock his head and think, *I wonder what Naomi is doing?*

He didn't always go see, of course, but oftentimes he'd wander into the house on one excuse or another. As soon as he saw Naomi sewing at his kitchen table, the white curve of her neck peeping out below the golden hair coiled under her *kapp*, he always felt a strange rush of fierce, peaceful joy.

Joseph's stomach rumbled, reminding him it was near midday, and he hadn't eaten since an early breakfast. Maybe he could convince Naomi to have a quick lunch in town before they headed back to the farm. Miller's Café was handy by. They could stop in there and get a sandwich before they started home.

The more he thought about the idea, the better he liked it. Now that Rhoda was at the house all day and Miriam was spending more time out of her room, he'd barely had a word with Naomi in private. It would be sensible to seize this chance to talk to her alone. He could ask some questions about his sister's progress that he wouldn't like to ask in front of her.

Very sensible, *ja*. But the truth was, when he thought of Naomi sitting across a table from him, just the two of them alone, something far less than sensible happened to his insides.

He'd like that, he realized. He'd like that a lot, having Naomi all to himself for a little while. He'd best hurry, though, or she might finish her shopping and head home without him. Joseph stepped up his pace.

He rounded the corner of the Johns Mill post office and stopped short as his shoes hit the gravel of the parking area. The buggy was still there, he noticed with relief, but he seemed to have arrived just in time.

A woman stood on the far side of the carriage. He could see the hem of a Plain dress and small black shoes through the spokes of the wheel. She wasn't alone, though. He could see trouser legs, too. Joseph frowned. Whoever was talking with Naomi had taken the precaution of standing on the far side of the buggy, allowing some privacy from the road.

Joseph didn't like that much.

"*Nee*, I can't!"

The woman's voice sounded broken, and Joseph strode faster along the side wall of the post office. He wasn't sure what was happening behind that buggy, but whatever it was, he was going to put a quick stop to it.

When he finally had a clear view, he stumbled to a clumsy halt, unsure what to do next. Rhoda stood beside the buggy, looking up at Caleb with a stricken expression. Both of them were too absorbed in each other to take any notice of Joseph.

"You mean you won't." Caleb's reply was low and bitter.

"Caleb—"

"I need to do this, Rhoda. It's the only way I'll have any peace."

"You'll find no peace in taking revenge, Caleb."

"I'm not planning to kill Trevor Abbott. I'm only going to do my best to make sure he answers for what he did."

"I think maybe you want him to suffer as you are suffering. Caleb, I understand how you must feel, but *Daed* says you must forgive and leave Trevor's punishment in the hands of *Gott*."

"I wish you'd stop quoting Isaac to me." Caleb's voice was hard. "You're my wife now, Rhoda. Your loyalty should lie with me, not with your father."

"It does." Rhoda's voice broke on the assurance. "But I was baptized into the church before I became your wife. I must answer to *Gott* even before I answer to you."

There was a heavy beat of silence. Joseph's pulse pounded in his ears. He knew he should back away out of earshot, but his boots seemed rooted to the ground. So much that mattered hinged on what Caleb said next.

"So if I leave to search out Trevor, you'll shun me, then, Rhoda? Like the rest of them?" Caleb spoke roughly, but Joseph heard the pain under the words. Even as a small *kind*, Caleb had always blustered like a March wind whenever he was hurting.

"If the church says to, and you know they will. Otherwise, I would be in sin myself. Until you're truly repentant and turn away from this way of thinking, I won't have a choice."

"*Ja*. You will have a choice, Rhoda."

Caleb stared into his wife's eyes, and though she was trembling hard, she faced him down. Joseph's heart sank when his brother's expression shifted. Holding his wife's gaze, Caleb pulled off his black hat and dropped it in the gravel at her feet. "So be it, then."

As he turned away, leaving Rhoda behind him, Caleb saw Joseph standing at the edge of the lot. When their eyes met, Joseph felt the punch of Caleb's anger as solidly as if it had been delivered by a fist.

Caleb halted, looking as if he were about to speak. Then he set his jaw and disappeared around the corner of the post office.

Joseph didn't waste time wondering if he should follow. Caleb had the bit in his teeth now. If Rhoda hadn't been able to turn him, Joseph certainly couldn't. Caleb would leave the church in search of what he was calling justice, and he'd be shunned for it, even by his new wife.

Rhoda had picked up her husband's hat. She turned hopefully when Joseph approached, but her face fell when she saw he wasn't Caleb.

Joseph had no idea what to say, except, "I am sorry."

"He wanted me to go with him."

"I heard. I shouldn't have been listening, but—"

"I wanted to go," Rhoda confessed wretchedly. "*Daed* warned me I might feel that way. We've been married so short a time, Caleb and I. It's natural, *Daed* said. But he said that I am the best chance Caleb has. If I stand firm, if I am true to my own faith, and Caleb has to bear the brunt of his decision, then he will come back."

Maybe, but Joseph doubted it. Some cows herded easy. Some cows would run you down or break their own legs jumping a fence rather than be forced through a gate they didn't like the look of. Joseph knew better than most which of those groups Caleb fell into.

He couldn't think of anything to say that would be helpful, so he stayed silent. Rhoda glanced up from the hat in her hands. The sadness in her eyes told him she understood what he wasn't saying out loud.

"I don't think *Daed* knows Caleb as well as we do," she whispered.

"Maybe not." Joseph drew a deep breath, trying to dislodge the brick that was sitting so heavily on top of his stomach. "Isaac is right about one thing, though. If anything can make Caleb turn back, it'll be you, Rhoda. It'll be the way he feels about you."

Rhoda's lips trembled. "I believed that once, too. But now I don't think it's enough, Joseph, not for Caleb. A woman's love could never be strong enough to hold a man like him to a faith he doesn't share, not for long. My father warned me of that when I told him I was going to marry Caleb, but I didn't listen. I should have. I was wrong to choose him, Joseph. I should have waited for—" She broke off abruptly, then whispered, "Someone else."

His heart thumped once, hard, as he looked down into her tear-soaked eyes. Before he could think how to answer, someone spoke behind him.

"Joseph?"

Aaron's Katie stood at the edge of the buggy, clutching her baby against her. He could tell from her expression and the way her eyes darted from Rhoda to him and back again that she'd heard at least some of what Rhoda had said. His heart plummeted.

Katie was a kindhearted woman, but everybody knew if you told her a secret, it'd be all over Johns Mill in half a day's time. No telling what she'd do with this. And, of course, the first person she'd tell would be Naomi.

Joseph felt sick. Well, he supposed it served them all right for having such personal conversations in the middle of town.

"*Ja*, Katie. It's me. Aaron's already headed for home. He dropped me off when we saw the buggy here. Do you need a ride back?"

Katie shivered, like a dog coming in out of a storm. "I'm sorry. I was just—Naomi sent me out to bring round the buggy. Miriam's having one of her spells—a bad one."

"Miriam's here? In town?"

"Yes, Naomi's inside with her," Katie said. "You'd best go in, too, Joseph and help. We'll drive the buggy to the front of the café. Get in, Rhoda. You can hold Sarah while I drive." When Joseph didn't move, she urged, "Hurry, Joseph! Miriam's in a real state."

Joseph sprinted around the corner and into Miller's Café. The scene inside made his stomach lurch with angry disgust. His sister was huddled, glassy-eyed at a table near the door, surrounded by gawking *Englischers*. Thankfully, a few Plain women had come to stand near Naomi, turning their backs to the crowd and doing their best to shield Miriam from view. One young *Englisch* boy had his phone out, lifted above the black bonnets of the women, aiming it toward Miriam. When he caught Joseph's glare, the teenager blanched and slipped the device into his pocket.

Joseph muttered under his breath as he shouldered gently through the protective circle of women, dropping down in the chair next to his sister.

"Miriam?"

His sister was too lost in her terror to answer him. Her eyes were fixed straight ahead and her bonnet was askew, her face smudged and mottled, mucus running from her nose.

Joseph's heart spasmed with pity and anger at the sight. He cast a reproachful look at Naomi, who was white as skimmed milk and more flustered than he'd ever seen her. She met his eyes, and for a second he thought she was going to burst into tears.

"A man," she whispered. "He caught her over near the restrooms, started taking photos. He wouldn't stop, and he frightened her."

Anger bubbled up inside him, bringing along a spate of frustrated questions. Why had Naomi brought Miriam to town in the first place? Maybe Naomi wasn't frightened of pushy *Englischers*, but Miriam was, and for good reason.

He started to speak then caught himself. This wasn't the time.

"Come, Mirry." He slid his arms under his sister's knees and behind the small of her back. He lifted her easily and turned toward the door just as Katie reined Titus to a stop in the road outside. "It's all right. I'm here now, and I'm taking you home."

Chapter Sixteen

❧

LATE THAT AFTERNOON IN THE HOCHSTEDLER kitchen, Naomi bent to open the gas oven. A hot breath of air, smelling richly of roast beef, puffed into her face. She carefully lifted the heavy lid and poked at a potato with a fork. It was done to a floury perfection, so she snugged the lid back down and lowered the heat.

She was thankful roast beef was *gut* left over because it was unlikely anybody in this house had an appetite tonight. Rhoda had left with her father an hour ago, still clutching her husband's discarded hat, her face frozen into miserable disbelief. She hadn't said much about what had happened in town, but Naomi had pieced it together. Caleb had asked his wife to leave Johns Mill with him, and she'd refused. She'd held on to her faith and lost her husband.

Rhoda's problems made Naomi's heart ache, but they were the least of her worries. Even after they'd arrived safely back at the farm, Miriam had trembled and cried uncontrollably. Naomi had finally given her one of the pills the hospital doctor had prescribed.

The younger woman was upstairs sleeping now, and she'd likely sleep through until the morning. Naomi felt in her bones that the pushy photographer had wiped out all the promising progress Miriam had made. It would be twice as hard to recover that lost ground after such a setback.

The trip to town that Naomi had planned so pridefully had been a terrible mistake. She'd known her feelings for Joseph would lead her into trouble if she wasn't careful, and so they had. She'd been overcome by a foolish desire to be noticed by him, and now she felt sick at the mess she'd created.

Naomi tied her black bonnet over her prayer *kapp* with shaky fingers. Then she pulled her shawl off the peg by the kitchen door and wrapped it around her shoulders before picking up the thermos of coffee she'd brewed. She paused with her hand on the doorknob and whispered a prayer for *Gott*'s help.

It was almost time for Aaron to come for her, so she couldn't put this off any longer. She had to face Joseph and ask his forgiveness. He'd barely spoken to her since they'd returned home, and he'd gone out to his woodshop as soon as Miriam had fallen asleep.

After the sheltered warmth of the kitchen, the evening air felt bitterly cold. A sneaky wind found the vulnerable spot between the top of her shawl and the bottom of her bonnet, making her shiver. She walked in the fading light toward the glowing window of Joseph's woodshop, and summoning up all her courage, she rapped on the doorframe. She could hear the sound of the lathe inside, so she wasn't surprised when Joseph didn't answer.

She edged the weathered door open. Joseph had his back to her, bent over his lathe, peddling with his foot as he carefully chiseled the curve of a table leg. Fragrant curls of wood fell away as he worked. They scented the room with a fresh, promising aroma, mingled with the sharp tang of varnish.

Clutching the warm thermos in her hands, Naomi stood silently, unwilling to startle him and risk him spoiling the piece. As she waited, she studied the space Joseph had claimed for his own, back in the day when this farm had been a busy dairy with plenty of uses for every sheltered spot.

She'd been surprised the first time she'd seen this room. She'd expected something more professional looking, more like other woodworking shops she'd visited. Joseph's shop was nothing like those. Long and narrow, with an earthen floor and no source of heat, it had been built as a lean-to attached to the barn. It had probably housed the family pig at one time or another or been used for grain or equipment storage. It wasn't much, but Joseph had turned it into a functioning woodworking shop.

It was neat and efficiently organized. Tools hung on the rough wall shared with the barn, and there was a scrap box in the corner where Joseph collected the odds and ends of wood rather than allowing them to stay where they dropped. The three worktables were clear of clutter, and a couple of finished pieces were set close to the door, old sheets tucked around them to protect them from dust.

Naomi recalled the crib Joseph had brought to Katie's house. How amazing that such a lovely thing could be created in such a humble place. Her gaze lingered on Joseph's hands as they guided the chisel in its groove. That's the secret, she thought, the *Gott*-given skill in those sure, strong fingers. That's where the beauty comes from.

But as she watched, Joseph made an exclamation of frustration. He lifted his foot off the pedal, slowing the spinning lathe. He thumped the chisel down on the table and ran a finger along the spindle leg.

"Ruined," he muttered.

Naomi cleared her throat. "Joseph?"

He didn't jump, but his broad shoulders stiffened. When he turned to face her, he offered her a tired smile.

"Naomi. I didn't hear you come in. Is it suppertime already?"

"*Ja*, almost. The food's keeping warm in the oven. I came out a little early because I wanted to talk to you. I . . . brought you some coffee." She stepped forward and handed him the thermos.

He accepted the peace offering and set it down beside the lathe. "*Denki*," he murmured. "It's cold in here, so *kaffe* will be welcome. How is Miriam?"

"Still sleeping."

"Sleep is the best thing for her, I expect."

Naomi nodded. Her heart was pounding so hard that she felt dizzy, but she needed to get this done. She leaned a hip against one of the tables to steady herself.

"I want to say how sorry I am, Joseph, about today. It seemed a good idea, going to Yoder's. Miriam was so excited about the idea of choosing the new fabric." Naomi's fingers nervously pleated and unpleated the material of her apron as she spoke. "I figured the trip was a good way to get her to go into town. It was very unwise of me. I should have asked you about it first, but I wanted to surprise you. I hoped . . . It doesn't matter what I hoped. I made a mistake, Joseph, and I'm very sorry for the trouble it caused."

"You are forgiven." Joseph spoke quietly, simply. His eyes met hers, and she saw no condemnation there. All she saw was a sad weariness that hurt her laboring heart even more. "I was angry at first, but I have had time to think it over. Your idea did not turn out so well, but I know your only thought was to help my sister. It is not your fault that the man behaved as he did. But next time, it would be wiser to tell me your plans. It might be better that I should go with you on such a trip, *ja?*"

"Yes, of course." Those words he'd just said . . . *next time* . . . brought up another thing she needed to ask him. "Do you still trust me to come stay with Miriam? If you don't, I will understand."

He'd started unscrewing the top of the coffee thermos, but at her words his chin came up swiftly. "Do you want to stop coming?"

"*Nee*! It's just that . . . I've made such a mess of things." Naomi shrugged miserably. "I wasn't sure you'd want me to."

"I said you were forgiven, Naomi. I meant it. We will forget about this and move on."

"All right, then." Naomi's insides unclenched. That had gone a good bit better than she'd expected. Joseph Hochstedler, she reflected, not for the first time, was a very kind man. "What are you making today?"

"A mess." His frustration was clear in his tone. "I'm trying to finish a sewing table for Mahlon's Rosie. I'd like to get it done because I've kept her waiting too long already, but I keep bumbling. This is the sixth leg I've ruined this afternoon."

"I know that feeling," Naomi said earnestly. "I don't know much about woodworking, but maybe you shouldn't try to do that particular thing today. Some things take a delicate hand to get right, and they're hard to do well when you've had an upsetting day."

He was watching her with his head tilted, and his face was more relaxed than it had been when he'd first turned around. "Is that so?"

"It is. That's why I never try to make piecrust when I'm upset. It always turns out leathery as the bottom of a boot if I do. If I've had a bad day, I make bread. Bread dough you can punch to your heart's content, and that only makes it rise better."

"I see." A smile flickered across Joseph's face. "And have you been punching any bread today?"

Naomi could feel her own lips tipping up in response. "Four loaves are waiting inside on the counter, but you're having molasses cookies for your dessert. So maybe you should put that table leg off until tomorrow?"

"I think I will have to, but I'm not sure tomorrow will be

any better." Joseph rubbed the back of his neck wearily. "I guess you heard that Caleb's leaving."

"I figured as much. I'm sorry, Joseph."

"Caleb's always fought harness. It's just the way he's made, I guess. *Daed* could manage him, but I'm no good at it. Still, what comes to Caleb will come from his own hand. I'm more worried about Miriam." He sighed. "And Emma."

"You don't think Emma's all right in Ohio?"

"Nobody who lives with Melvin for long can be anything other than miserable. Emma sent me a letter, and she doesn't say a word about how awful it is, but I can read what she's not writing. It's got to be hard, first losing *Mamm* and *Daed*, and now being worked half to death . . . it makes me sick to think of it."

"Maybe she won't have to stay there much longer."

"I don't know about that. I'd hoped to bring her home soon, but after what happened with Miriam today, I reckon Emma had best stay where she is for a while yet. The Oak Point community is more conservative than ours, and they don't cater to the tourist trade. Nobody's likely to trouble her there." Joseph gave a humorless laugh. "Except for Melvin."

Naomi tried to think of something comforting to say, but she couldn't come up with anything that didn't sound stupid, so she held her tongue.

Sometimes when *Gott* was walking a person through a valley, there was simply nothing you could say. The truth was the truth, and there was no dodging it. Emma would have to stay where she was and make the best of things for a while longer. And Joseph would have to deal with his own helplessness where his sister's happiness was concerned. In time, the Lord would lead them out again into the sunshine, but until then the best friends stayed close and kept silent.

Joseph wrenched the table leg off the lathe and slung it into the scrap box. Naomi jumped, and an equally startled mouse skittered out from under the box and wiggled into a hole in the sawdust-covered earthen floor. "I should be doing better with this," he said angrily.

"You're a good woodworker, Joseph. Anybody can have a bad day. You must not take it to heart."

"I'm not talking about the table. I'm talking about the family. It's in my charge now, and it's falling apart. I should have found a way to keep us together. That's what *Daed* would have expected, what he would have wanted. I try to do well, as he'd have done, but no matter what I do, I can't seem to shift things back as they should be."

Naomi took a step forward, then halted herself just before she reached out to touch Joseph's arm. She clenched her hands together instead. "Your father never had to deal with what you are dealing with, Joseph. I think even he might have struggled with this, ain't so? You must not judge yourself by the outcome, as long as you have done your best. The rest we must leave in *Gott*'s hands."

He was listening closely, his brown eyes intent on hers. How dark his lashes were, she thought, and as long as a girl's. His mouth was shaped well, too, and he had a nice, strong chin. Some men with chins like that were trouble, but not Joseph. He held the reins to his own determination with a steady hand. It was unlikely to take him anyplace he didn't wish to go, as long as he didn't lose his faith.

"In the darkness," Naomi added softly, "we cling to what *Gott* showed us in the daytime, *ja?* It is like picking your way through your bedroom at night. We remember and we choose our path correctly, even though we cannot see."

"My father said something like that, just before—" Joseph stopped. "*Daed* believed that, too."

"Your *daed* was a wise man," Naomi said. She heard the jingle of a harness and the creak of a buggy and glanced out the window. The light from Aaron's buggy lamp beamed into the yard. "I have to go, but I will see you tomorrow, *ja?*" She turned toward the door, hesitated, then looked back over her shoulder.

Joseph was still watching her, and when he caught her gaze, his eyes crinkled in the corner, just like always. After the chill she'd felt from him on the ride back from town, seeing that familiar, gentle friendliness made her want to weep in relief.

She drew in a shaky breath. "*Denki*, Joseph, for your forgiveness and for allowing me to keep helping out here. I will try to do better."

There was a short beat of silence before he answered her. "I think you're doing well enough, Naomi."

Naomi shut the splintery door quietly behind herself, smiling as she did. He hadn't said much just then, but the firm certainty in his voice had reached past her guilt and set the last of her fears to rest.

Like his shop, Joseph's words might not seem like much on the surface, but there was a good bit of beauty in them, if you knew where to look.

Chapter Seventeen

✿

THE NEXT MORNING, JOSEPH LOOKED THROUGH the barn door and saw the bishop's buggy slowing on the road, getting ready to turn into the drive. Joseph forked one last bit of hay into Titus's stall, his sigh of relief clouding white in the wintry air.

So Rhoda had come today, after all.

Working in his woodshop yesterday, he'd mulled over what had passed between them next to the buggy, especially the regretful words Rhoda had choked back at the last minute. He'd understood what she'd nearly said, and he also understood why she would never say it.

What he hadn't understood, at least not right away, had been his own reaction. There'd been a time, only a few weeks ago, when hearing that Rhoda regretted marrying Caleb—that she wished she'd chosen Joseph instead—would have knocked him to his knees. The idea that she'd never even considered him as a husband had been a cold comfort, but at least it had been something.

Then yesterday he'd heard from her own lips—or nearly

anyway—that she wished she'd chosen him instead. He'd waited for the firestorm of feelings to hit—the grief, the regret, knowing that what had been done could not be undone, that he'd missed what he'd wanted most by a whisper.

Instead he'd felt only pity for this sweet, strong girl who was in the middle of a trouble not of her own making—and who'd need every ounce of her faith to walk through the barren life that stretched ahead.

If he could lift any trouble off her shoulders, he'd gladly do it, but he wasn't in love with Rhoda any longer. Now his heart hoped for something—or someone—else.

Naomi.

He smiled as he set the pitchfork back in its place. Just the thought of her made a shy warmth bloom in his chest. The feeling was a sweet relief after the past months—like waking up one morning and discovering that an ache that had been plaguing you for weeks had eased overnight.

When the Lambright buggy rolled to a stop, Rhoda climbed out with none of her former energy. She shot a furtive glance in Joseph's direction on her way to the back steps. He gave a friendly nod, but she turned so that the side of her black bonnet shielded her face.

Well, at least she hadn't let the brief, almost-admission from yesterday shame her into staying away. That was best forgotten by everyone—including Katie Lapp. Joseph had been praying that for once in her life, Katie would find the strength to hold her tongue, and apparently, his prayer had been answered. Naomi had given no sign this morning that Katie had gossiped.

He was thankful for that. After the tumult of yesterday, they all needed an ordinary day, some kind of reassurance that things could get back to normal.

Or at least what passed for normal these days.

He'd expected the bishop to turn the buggy back toward town, but instead Isaac set the brake and clambered down.

"Joseph, may I have a word with you?"

"*Ja*, sure. It's a sharp morning, Isaac. Come into the house where it's warmer, and we will sit down with *kaffe*."

The bishop threw a look in the direction of the farm-house and shook his head. "Best we talk here, I think." The older man's voice sounded tired, and his shoulders were slumped. Whatever the bishop wanted to talk about, it was bad news.

"All right." Joseph straightened, bracing himself for the blow.

It took Isaac a moment. He stared off over the fields for a moment before his eyes cut back toward Joseph. The bishop cleared his throat. "We met last night, and the decision was made. We will move forward to place Caleb under the ban."

Joseph had known this was coming, that it had to come, but there was something hard about hearing it spoken aloud. "I understand."

"We could find no way around it." They'd tried. The pain and grief roughening Isaac's voice told Joseph that much. But in the end, of course, they'd had no choice.

Joseph sighed. Caleb was sowing trouble with a gener-ous hand. Having a shunned son-in-law was a shameful thing for a man in Isaac's position—and watching his daughter's suffering would cut deeply. If Caleb didn't re-turn, there would be no hope of *kinder* to brighten Rhoda's life and Isaac and Ida's old age. The Lambright family would wither into nothing.

And it could easily have been far worse. If Caleb had convinced Rhoda to leave the church with him, this kind-hearted man would have been forced to shun his only child.

"There is nothing else you could have done." Because Joseph understood what Isaac was waiting for, he added, "I will abide by the church's decision."

"We must both do that, *ja*, however much it grieves us.

But we must not give up hope, Joseph. We will pray, and we will wait. Many people return to the faith once they are made to feel the full consequences of their decisions. Caleb has his faults as all of us do, but I believe—I have to believe—that his heart will lead him back to us in *Gott*'s time."

Joseph nodded. Privately, he'd caught himself doubting that even prayer could turn a heart as stony as his younger brother's, and he was shamed by his lack of faith.

Nothing was impossible for *Gott*. Joseph believed that. Lately, though, with trouble piling on trouble, he'd wondered how bad the Lord planned to let things get before He stepped in.

Isaac glanced toward the house. "My *dochder* is grieving especially hard. She has come along this morning to say goodbye to Naomi and your sister. After what happened yesterday at Miller's, Ida and I arranged for Rhoda to stay with some relatives in Pennsylvania for a while. We hope the change of scene and company may be helpful for her. When Caleb comes home and makes his repentance, Rhoda will rejoin him as his wife. We all pray that will happen soon."

"My brother has caused your family a peck of trouble, Isaac. I am sorry."

Isaac shook his head and held up a hand to wave off the apology. "That trouble is not your fault. My family, like yours, must bear whatever trials *Gott* in His wisdom allows."

There didn't seem to be much more to say, but still the bishop remained where he was, looking uncomfortable. Joseph waited, but when Isaac said nothing, he asked, "Is there something else?"

"I'm afraid there is, *ja*. The sheriff came to see me yesterday. He'd been at the chamber of commerce meeting, and there was some news." The older man sighed and raked a hand through his salt-and-pepper beard. "Some representatives from an *Englischer* movie studio down in Georgia were there."

"Why would such people be in Johns Mill?" Joseph hoped the answer wasn't what he suspected. It couldn't be, surely.

But, of course, it was.

"They want to make a movie about what happened to your parents, and they would like to film it here. The sheriff came to speak with me because he knew it would impact our community."

Ja, it would. Joseph shook his head in disbelief as Isaac went on.

"The commissioners were all very excited about it, the sheriff said. Lots of money coming into the town, and maybe more movies coming behind this one, if the studio likes it here. Other towns have done well with such arrangements, they said. To the *Englischers*, this seems a good thing. Me, I am not so sure, and the sheriff agrees. We believe this will only cause more trouble."

Joseph believed that, too. He rubbed his forehead and tried to think, but his brain seemed to have shut down operations. "For my family especially."

"*Ja*, with your sister in her delicate state, this is of even greater concern for you." The bishop's lips tightened. "Sheriff Townsend showed me some unpleasant photos on his phone. Apparently, the man from the café has sold them to the people who buy such pictures, and the sheriff reckons he made a tidy sum from it. We fear that sort of thing will only get worse after this film is announced. Especially since—" Isaac paused. "We haven't wanted to trouble you, but other things have happened, too."

"I heard of it, the spray-painting."

Isaac looked relieved that he wouldn't have to explain. "The sheriff is concerned that he won't have the manpower required to prevent such things from happening once news of this film gets out. He and I will do what we can to discourage the commissioners from allowing the production company to work here, but we doubt we will succeed. Even if we do, there seems to be no way to stop the making of the movie itself, whether it is filmed in Johns Mill or elsewhere. Sheriff Townsend says we must prepare for . . . intrusions, either way."

Intrusions. Joseph's muscles tensed. Miriam couldn't go through what had happened at Miller's again. "When will all this start?"

"Soon. That's what they said at the meeting, the men from the studio. It will take them some time to get organized, but they are moving as quickly as they can, making preparations. They plan to announce the movie in only a matter of weeks. All this attention that confuses and troubles us, it excites them. They see money in it, and they want to move forward before the interest dies back down." The bishop shook his head, looking out over the back fields. "Two innocent people were murdered by a troubled boy who'd probably seen one too many of the movies they make. So what do they do? They try to profit from it by making another one, before this situation is even put to rest. Such thinking I will never understand."

"*Nee*, it is not something easily understood."

"Joseph, perhaps it would be better to send Miriam to stay with Emma, at least for a while. Your uncle's community is more sheltered, and likely Miriam could stay there unbothered."

Joseph was silent, not knowing how to explain that his sour uncle would be none too enthusiastic about taking another refugee niece into his home. Melvin would agree to it if Joseph pressed him, because it was expected that he would support his family in a time of difficulty, but he would do so with ill grace.

Joseph didn't want to put sensitive Miriam into such a situation. He was already none too happy about Emma living in that household. He realized with a pang that this movie business meant that Emma wouldn't be coming home anytime soon, either.

And that wasn't the worst of it, he realized suddenly. His heart fell hard and deep, like a rock into a well.

Isaac was still waiting for some reply, so Joseph murmured, "I will think on it."

The bishop nodded, satisfied. "*Ja.* Think and seek *Gott*'s guidance. That is always the wisest thing to do."

The back door opened, and Rhoda came down the steps, holding carefully to the handrail as if she were three times her age. When she reached the bottom, she looked up, and her gaze caught with Joseph's. She froze, her face pale and blank.

"Come along, Rhoda," her father commanded gently. "We'd best be getting back home. You've packing to do yet." He nodded to Joseph and went to climb into the buggy.

Rhoda walked around the side of the buggy, and Joseph offered her his hand to help her up. It was an automatic courtesy, one he'd offered to his mother and sisters countless times, but Rhoda hesitated one telling second before placing her hand in his.

"I'm sorry, Joseph," she whispered in the scant second their heads were close together. "Please forgive me."

He wasn't sure exactly what Rhoda meant. Was she asking his forgiveness for her slip of the tongue yesterday or for not being able to keep Caleb among them?

It didn't matter. Either way his answer was the same.

"There is no need." He held her hand steady as she climbed slowly into the seat. "May *Gott* go with you, *schwesdre.*"

Sister. Rhoda looked down at him, and he saw a glimmer of relief in her sad eyes. When she answered, her voice was stronger. "I know He will. You take *gut* care, Joseph."

After Isaac's carriage had rattled away, Joseph remained standing where he was. A painful heaviness settled over him, feeling unpleasantly familiar.

He'd felt the same when he'd learned Rhoda had promised to marry Caleb—as if a bright doorway had slammed shut just in front of his nose, leaving him alone in a smothering darkness.

He'd had to accept the truth then, just as he had to now. Caleb had been officially set outside of the Plain community. Unless he reversed himself, something Joseph had never known his brother to do, he would remain separated from his family for life. It felt like another death, that, and as frustrated as Joseph had been with Caleb, the fresh loss cut deep.

Now, with this movie, *Englischers* were brewing more trouble for his family. He'd be mired in the muck of it for years, from what Isaac had told him. That was bad enough, but it went further.

He couldn't ask anyone to face such a future with him. The quiet hope that he'd been nursing since Naomi had crept into his heart would have to be set aside. No sensible woman would consider marrying a man who was dragging such a load of manure behind him anyhow. And by the time this was finally over, if it ever was, it would almost certainly be too late, just as it had been with Rhoda.

The spicy smell of frying sausage drifted out from the kitchen. Naomi would be nearly done cooking breakfast, and she'd be expecting him. She'd sit down at the table with him, likely, as she'd done every morning for weeks now. She always sipped a cup of tea while he ate, a gentle smile rounding her cheeks whenever his eyes met hers.

Suddenly the thought of eating made a choking bile rise up in the back of his throat. Instead of going inside, he turned and made his way blindly down the sloping yard toward the old dairy.

Chapter Eighteen

❧

NAOMI SIGHED AS SHE NAVIGATED THE LAST OF THE steps, balancing the heavy tray in her hands. Miriam had eaten next to nothing, and the kitchen was as empty as it had been when she'd gone upstairs. The place she'd set at the table was still undisturbed, meaning Joseph hadn't come in for his breakfast. He was running very late this morning.

She set the tray beside the sink and tiptoed to scan the yard. Joseph was nowhere in sight.

She'd peeked out of the upstairs window earlier and seen the bishop's buggy pulling up. What a relief that had been— until Rhoda had come in and said her goodbyes. Miriam had wept, and Naomi's joy had deflated into concern.

Rhoda hadn't explained much, only that she would be going away for a while. Likely, she was trying not to upset Miriam any more than she had to, but Naomi knew there must be more to it. Katie had hinted as much last night, something she'd seen or heard pass between Joseph and Rhoda when she'd gone for the buggy. Naomi had felt far too tired to listen to Katie's gossip, and she'd cut her cousin off in mid-sentence. Now, she wished she'd been more patient.

Naomi scraped Miriam's uneaten sausage, eggs, and toast into a bowl to take out to the chickens, feeling uneasy. The fact that Joseph hadn't come in for breakfast was worrisome. Born and bred to the rigid rhythms of milking schedules, the man followed his routine as faithfully as the sun.

Naomi reached for her bonnet and shawl. She'd run these leftovers out to the chickens a little earlier than she'd planned. If she happened to bump into Joseph while she was out in the yard, well, that would just be a happy accident.

The delighted hens clucked greedily over the scraps, even though Joseph had already filled their hanging metal feeder with scratch and layer pellets. He'd finished the chores then. So where was he?

Naomi collected the warm brown eggs from the nesting boxes, even though there were only half so many as there would be a few hours later in the morning. She nestled them in the empty bowl and carried them back to the house.

Pausing by the steps, she glanced in the direction of the woodworking shop. She could check there before she went inside to finish the dishes. Normally Joseph didn't go out to the shop until after breakfast, but maybe today he'd changed his mind. She set the eggs carefully on the top step and started across the yard.

But when she eased open the creaky door, the little lean-to was empty and still as neat as when Joseph had tidied it the previous night. He'd not been in here yet this morning.

Naomi lingered inside the door for a moment, inhaling the sharp odor of freshly sawn wood. Such a *gut* smell, she thought, bringing to mind both old things and new. It was the scent she most associated with Joseph.

She liked it very much.

Naomi stepped back into the yard, closing the door carefully behind herself. Hands on her hips, she surveyed the farm. Well, wherever Joseph had vanished to, Naomi couldn't trouble herself about it any longer. She ought not leave Miriam alone in the house for very long, even though the only thing the other girl seemed to want to do right now was huddle in her bed.

Naomi was halfway to the house when a flicker of movement caught her eye. She peered in the direction of the old dairy. Somebody was definitely moving around in there. It must be Joseph, although what he was doing inside that unused building was anybody's guess.

Naomi paused for only a second before turning down the path leading to the rectangular stone building. She wasn't being nosy, not really. She needed to check with Joseph about breakfast, didn't she? She couldn't keep it warm on the stove forever.

The door leading into the building was huge, but it swung on its hinges with only a little push. It creaked loudly, but Joseph, standing with his back to her, surveying the long line of empty milking stanchions, didn't turn his head at the noise. He stood still as a fencepost, and something about the set of his shoulders made a cold dread settle in Naomi's breast.

"Joseph? Is everything all right? Your breakfast's waiting."

"This is a *gut* place." Joseph spoke without turning his head. "Strong built, made to last. It served our family well for a hundred years, and it would do another hundred, with a little scrubbing."

"A lot of scrubbing." Naomi wrinkled her nose, eyeing the cobwebs hanging in the corners and the mouse droppings on the floor. "But, *ja*. It could be made right easily enough. Are you thinking of reopening the dairy, then?"

"I'd figured to." Joseph drew in a deep, slow breath and released it. "Once things got straightened out, I was going to study up on it and see if I could meet the *Englischers*' milk regulations somehow without going broke. But not now. I'm going to have to let it go. It's a shame." He touched the wall with one hand. "It's a *gut* place. It should be in use."

The sadness in his voice cut at Naomi's heart, but she thought she understood. Lots of Plain folks were getting out of farming-related businesses, and looking for other ways to make a living, just as Joseph's *daed* had been forced to do.

An idea occurred to her. "You could turn this into a woodworking shop, maybe. It would be a real good space for that."

Joseph didn't seem to have heard her. Naomi edged closer until she was standing behind him. She reached out to touch his arm, then stopped herself at the last minute.

"What is it, Joseph? What's truly troubling you?"

He drew in a slow breath and glanced at her over his shoulder. "Did Rhoda tell you that Caleb's being placed under the ban?"

Ah. So it was that. "*Nee*," she answered quietly. "She didn't. Miriam was already so upset about Rhoda going away . . . I suppose she didn't want to add to it."

Joseph's throat flexed as he swallowed hard. "*Ja*, of course Miriam will be upset. This will set her back even more." He shook his head sadly.

"Maybe for a little while, but Miriam will regain the ground she's lost, you'll see. You mustn't give up hope, Joseph. We will all pray that *Gott* will turn Caleb's heart quickly."

Joseph made an irritated noise. "*Gott* will have to do that if it gets done, and even then, I doubt it will be quick. Caleb listens to no one but himself, and his anger holds its heat longer than most. The Lord will have His work cut out for Him with my *bruder*, for sure, but I must leave it with Him. I've got more than enough trouble to manage—and from what Isaac told me, there's more coming."

"What do you mean? What did Isaac say?"

"The *Englischers* are making a movie about what happened, and they want to film it here. So things aren't going to get any better, Naomi, not for a while, at least."

She listened as he recounted what Isaac had told him. Her heart sank lower with each word until she could barely breathe.

"Oh, Joseph." Nothing she could think of to say seemed near strong enough. "I am so sorry to hear this."

He turned his head then and looked at her over his shoulder, his eyes meeting her own. "I am sorry, too, Naomi. I had finally begun to hope for . . ." He broke off, his gaze tracing her face, lingering oddly—and sweetly—on her lips. "Better things," he finished finally.

Joseph's voice was matter-of-fact, and the words were simple, but that hungry sorrow in his eyes made her insides tremble strangely. What exactly, Naomi wondered with a sudden, desperate fierceness, was it that Joseph had been hoping for?

He turned his head away. "This is not what I wanted, but hard times make for hard choices. I'm leasing out the farm and moving up to Ohio with Miriam."

"Oh!" That one word was all she could manage. Joseph was leaving Johns Mill, Miriam, too. All this—all this work and purpose and goodness was ending, and she would have to go back to Kentucky, to her brothers and their kind, impatient wives.

The realization hit her like a rush of icy air, as if someone had snatched off the warm blanket she'd been snuggled under, leaving her vulnerable. She shivered, crossing her arms over her chest and digging her fingers into the flesh of her arms.

"I can work at Melvin's dairy," Joseph was saying. "I'll get a small house someplace nearby. Emma can tend to Miriam during the day. That'll get her out of Melvin's house, and hopefully the rent of this place will give us enough to live on. Melvin's pay won't be much, and he'll expect me to work for less anyhow because I'm family. I can do some woodworking on the side to make ends meet. We'll get by, I expect."

"Do you think Miriam will do all right there? Isn't Oak Point a little"—Naomi struggled for a kinder way to say *dreary*, or *miserable*—"more strict than what you all are used to?"

"It is. It's not such a pretty place as Johns Mill, nor so friendly. But that's the kind of place we need because it doesn't attract so many tourists. As long as Emma and I are both with her, I think Miriam will do all right. We should have a quiet time there." He sighed. "If you can manage on your own today, I'll drive into town and speak with a real estate agent. I've no love for the idea of involving *Englischers* in this, but I don't want to lease the farm to a Plain family, not with everything going on. It wouldn't be right to pass our troubles on to others."

Naomi heard the weary disgust in Joseph's voice, knew how much he'd hate the prospect of turning his beloved farm over to people he couldn't bring himself to trust. And yet because it was the right thing to do for his family and the community, he'd force himself to set his own feelings aside. She nodded miserably.

"I'll manage all right. Oh!" A memory stirred. "That woman who helped Miriam at the café, she was a real estate agent. She gave me her card, and I put it in my bag. She was a real *freindlich* person, Joseph. Maybe you should go see her."

"That one who thumped the fellow with her pocketbook?" A smile flickered across Joseph's lips. "*Ja*, I will talk to her. If I must deal with an *Englischer*, I'd rather deal with her. Go fetch her card, please, and I'll hitch up. I'd best get this moving quickly."

"Mona seemed like she'd be a real good manager. Explain things to her, and I'm sure she'll figure something out." Naomi straightened her shoulders. "There will be a lot of work to do, getting the house ready. You must tell me what you want done, and I'll get started on it."

"*Nee.* Such heavy work will be too much for you, especially as fast as I'll need it finished. I'll ask help of the church. Many hands will make the work lighter."

"It wouldn't be too much for me." She hated the idea of the well-meaning church members descending on this home, as they doubtlessly would once Joseph made his request, sleeves rolled up and ready to work. They'd be here from early to late, until the house was emptied and ready for its new occupants.

She'd have no more quiet times with only Joseph and Miriam, no more opportunities to pretend, for this last, little while, that these precious folks were her own to look after.

"I don't want you overdoing," Joseph stated flatly. "I know you are stronger since your operation, but all the work you've been doing for us has tired you. I can see it. Your face is paler than it was when I first saw you again, and I've noticed you stopping to lean on the furniture when you think I'm not watching. I won't have you stretching yourself any thinner. Besides, this way we can wait until just before we leave to start packing up, which will keep things normal for Miriam as long as possible. This will be very upsetting to her, and I'd rather you stay close beside her while all the work is going on. She's comforted by you. Will you do that for me?"

I would do anything for you. The admission almost slipped past her lips; she had to bite down hard to keep the words in. "Of course."

"*Denki.*" He cleared his throat roughly. "You have been a comfort to me, too, Naomi. I am thankful for your help, and I will not forget it."

She would not forget, either. Not ever, what joy it had been to be here, to help this kind man. "*Du bisht welcome.*"

"I'll let you know when we're leaving as soon as I know

myself. I reckon you'll need to make arrangements to go back to Kentucky, won't you?"

"Ja." Naomi forced a smile. "I suppose so."

Joseph didn't smile back. "I will miss you, Naomi."

Naomi's breath caught in her throat. Once again, the words were simple enough, but there was something in Joseph's expression that made her arms prickle with hopeful goose bumps.

"I will miss you, too," she whispered.

He looked down into her eyes, and for one, long, breath-stealing second, she thought he was going to say something else, something not so simple. Something that . . . mattered.

Instead he only blinked and looked away. "I'd appreciate it if you'd get that card for me, Naomi. I'd best get on into town."

"Sure." Feeling strangely embarrassed, Naomi turned abruptly toward the door, bumping into the supporting post just behind her. "Ooh!"

"You all right?"

"Ja. I'm fine. It's just so dim—it's hard to see where I'm going," she murmured as she slipped through the door.

That wasn't entirely true, she realized sadly. She could see where she was going well enough—or more important, where she wasn't going.

And it was breaking her poor, foolish heart.

Chapter Nineteen

❧

"DO WE REALLY HAVE TO GO LIVE AT OAK POINT? I . . . don't like the idea of leaving home." Miriam fisted her hands restlessly in the rumpled covers of her bed.

Joseph forced himself to meet his sister's eyes squarely. "I know, and I'm sorry, Miriam. But I do think it's the best thing; otherwise I'd never ask it of you."

He'd hated to break this news to his sister today. Things had been going a bit better just lately. Miriam still wouldn't set foot out of the house. She wouldn't even cross the yard to feed the chickens.

She'd finally come downstairs again yesterday, though, and she'd sat at the table with Naomi, making a half-hearted attempt to do some sewing. It wasn't much, but it was the most she'd done in the past five days, and it had given him hope that maybe Miriam would start improving, as she'd done before.

He didn't want this news to be a setback for her, but given what the real estate agent had told him yesterday, he hadn't seen a way around it.

"I've explained to you about the movie, Miriam. Don't you think it's wise we should be someplace else while all that is going on here?"

"*Ja*, I guess so." Miriam leaned her head against the simple oak headboard and squeezed her eyes shut as if she were in pain. "I just don't understand. Why would people want to make movies about such terrible things?"

That was a question Joseph couldn't answer, so he didn't try. "I know this feels hard, Mirry, but things have fallen into place so quickly. It seems like *Gott*'s provision. The real estate agent, Mona, who helped you back at the café, has already found somebody to rent the house, and for a higher price than I'd hoped for. The fellow jumped on it as soon as she told him about the farm, without even coming out to see the place for himself."

He counted that last bit as an extra blessing. Joseph wasn't sure how he'd have managed an *Englisch* stranger poking through the house, not with Miriam in this condition. Mona had explained that the renter was a writer researching the Plain lifestyle. Apparently, he was so delighted to have the opportunity to live on an actual Amish farm that he'd signed a three-year lease agreement on the spot.

"I'm supposed to go to the office today to sign the contract." He hoped that there was something in the paperwork to discourage the renter from breaking the lease agreement early. From what he'd seen, most folks who hadn't been born to the Plain life couldn't stomach it for very long. "According to Mona, we'd need to move in about a month." The anguish he saw in his sister's red-rimmed eyes made him hasten to add, "Won't you think about it, Miriam? Ohio may not be so terrible once we get there. We'll be with Emma again, and I know how you've missed her."

"*Ja*, I would love to see Emma. Traveling so far is what frightens me most. We'll have to go in a car, too." Miriam shook her head. "I don't think I can do it. To go outside, to ride in a car with an *Englisch* driver? I'm sorry, Joseph. I truly am, but I just don't think I can." Miriam's breath had begun coming sharp and hard, as if she was spiraling into one of her attacks.

Joseph felt a rush of guilty concern. This was why he'd chosen to talk to Miriam here, in her bedroom, the place where she seemed to feel the safest. He'd done his best to make this as easy for her as he could, but in the end, there was nothing for it. Once news of this movie got out, he wouldn't be able to protect Miriam in Johns Mill. Neither of them had a choice, not really, and he didn't know what he'd do if he couldn't convince Miriam to attempt the trip.

"I'll be right there with you the whole time, and I'll help you all I can. What if we ask the doctor if he can give you a pill, to make you sleep on the ride? That would be easier, ain't so?"

"*Nee*, that would be even worse." Miriam shook her head more furiously, tears spilling down her cheeks. "To be . . . helpless like that, outside. *Nee*, I can't stand the thought of it, Joseph. I'm sorry to be such a coward, but I can't help it."

Miriam's voice held such shame and desperation that Joseph's heart cracked open. He cast a despairing look at Naomi. She'd been standing by the door, offering her silent support and sympathy as he'd broken this news to his sister.

She crossed the room to sit next to Miriam on the bed. "Maybe not a pill to sleep, then, *ja?* Just a pill to relax you a little and make the trip easier on your nerves. And I'll pack plenty of food so that you won't have to stop at restaurants on the way. You can take your quilting squares and work on them in the back seat, maybe. That'll make the miles fly by, I reckon. Once you're there, it'll be wonderful *gut*. You'll see. Quiet, I bet, and nobody but Plain folks everywhere you look. You'll like that part of it, ain't so?" Naomi patted Miriam's hand.

Miriam swiped the tears off her cheeks and sighed. "If all the people up there are like Melvin, I don't know that I'll like it so much as you say. He's not such a pleasant man, our *onkel*."

She didn't sound any happier about the prospect of the trip, but still, Joseph marveled at the change in her voice. She'd been crying buckets a second ago, and now she was grousing about Melvin in a way that sounded nearly normal. Naomi had an amazing touch with his sister; that was for sure.

"*Ja*," Naomi answered with a chuckle. "You're not telling me anything I don't know already. I've met him. Sour as an unripe persimmon, that one." She pursed up her mouth comically, and amazingly Miriam's quivering lips tipped up into an almost-smile.

She grasped Naomi's hands with both of her own. "Will you come with us to Ohio, Naomi? If you and Emma and Joseph were all there, I think maybe I could manage all right. Do you think you could?"

Naomi cast a helpless look at Joseph, but he had no help to give her. He'd not been prepared for this, and he wasn't sure what to say—especially since a part of him wanted to hear Naomi's answer as badly as Miriam did.

"*Nee*," Naomi said gently. "I can't go with you. I'll be going back to Kentucky."

"You don't want to do that," Miriam argued, her voice gaining strength. "You've told me so, time and again. You like working and being useful and busy, and your brothers and their wives don't need you like we do. You've been happy with us, haven't you?"

Joseph held his breath as he waited for Naomi to speak. Naomi seemed to be having a little trouble with it, but when she finally answered, she sounded sincere.

"I have been very happy here with you, Miriam. I'm sorry, too, that our time together has come to an end, but there's nothing for it. I couldn't come along with you to Ohio. I'm not really family, you know, and it wouldn't . . ." Naomi seemed to be searching for the right words. "Give the right appearance," she finished at last.

"Joseph." Miriam turned her pleading eyes to his. "Naomi will be unhappy in Kentucky. Couldn't you find some way that it would be all right for her to come with us?"

Joseph didn't answer. His mind was turning over what Miriam had just said—that Naomi wasn't looking forward to returning to Kentucky. It had never occurred to him that she wouldn't be glad to go home to her family. That she might truly be happier staying with Miriam . . . and with him . . . in spite of all their troubles. Was that true? He'd felt grimly sick ever since he'd set his hopes about Naomi on the shelf, but he'd thought it was the best thing to do, for her sake. The possibility he'd been wrong set his heart to pounding.

Naomi had risen from the bed and was smiling down at Miriam. "It will be all right, Miriam. *Gott* has a way of working these things out for the best. Now I'm going downstairs. I feel like baking today. When you smell something delicious, that's your cue to come to the kitchen, all right? We'll have some tea and a treat and start cutting our new material so you'll have plenty of pieces in your basket to work on during your drive."

Naomi flashed a sympathetic look at Joseph as she passed him. When she walked out the door, the whitewashed bedroom seemed dimmer, as if the sun had ducked behind a cloud. Funny, that, how Naomi brought such brightness into any room, just by being in it.

From the way Miriam's expression crumpled as soon as Naomi was out of sight, it was clear his sister felt the same way. She shot him a guilty look. "I'm sorry. I'm being selfish."

"*Nee*, Miriam. I'm asking a lot of you, I know."

"And I know you wouldn't ask me this at all if you saw any other choice." She stopped and swallowed hard. "I am willing to try the trip, if you really feel it's for the best."

Joseph sent a thankful prayer heavenward. "I do think so, Mirry. I truly do."

"I shouldn't have asked about Naomi coming with us. I could see it embarrassed you. You have such a hard job now that *Mamm* and *Daed* are gone, and instead of helping you, I only cause you more trouble."

"You are no trouble to me, Miriam, and I understand how you feel about Naomi. She's been a great help to you during a terrible time, and of course, you will hate to lose her company."

"She *has* helped me, more than anybody else could. When she is with me, that is the only time I feel peaceful." A fresh tear rolled down Miriam's face, but she swiped it away quickly.

"*Ja.* I know what you mean." Joseph's mind drifted back to the way he felt walking up from the barn each morning and evening. Through the windows, he would see Naomi moving about the family kitchen. Then when he walked through the door, she would glance up from her work and smile a welcome at him. She never said anything special, but something about those smiles warmed his belly as much as the steaming food she set on the table.

More, even.

He realized that Miriam was watching him closely, her eyes clearer and sharper than they'd been for a long time. He cleared his throat uncomfortably, feeling as if he'd been caught sticking a grubby hand in the cookie bin before supper. "Naomi has a restful way about her, certain sure."

"You'll miss her, too, then?" The question was innocent enough, but Joseph suddenly felt as if he were balancing on a very thin board.

Even so, there was only one way he could answer that

question honestly. "I will miss her. Like I said, she has been a great help, and she's a hard worker."

Miriam kept her eyes fastened on his as she smoothed out the quilt over her knees. "Is that the only reason you will miss her, Joseph? Because she has been such a hard worker?"

"Of course not! She's not a plough horse. She is good company, Naomi is."

"*Ja*, she is. I don't know what it is about her. She's very quiet, mostly. When we sew together, I end up doing most of the talking."

That was actually one of the things Joseph liked best . . . Naomi's gentle stillness. "She speaks when she has something to say. She's very kind, and she can be funny, too. Like she almost made you laugh just then about Melvin. She manages to make things nicer somehow, even in a house like this, with so much sorrow and trouble. I don't know how to explain it, but—" He glanced up to find Miriam studying him and broke off in midsentence.

"I think you are explaining it very well," his sister said dryly. "And do you know what else I think?"

"What?"

"I think Naomi would make some man a wonderful good *fraw*. She'd be such a blessing for him and all his family, with her sweetness and her big heart. And I think, if the right fellow came along, Naomi would be very happy to have a home of her very own, instead of moving from one brother's house to another all the time. That's what I think. What do you think, Joseph?"

He didn't answer her question. Not aloud anyway. But his long-suffering heart produced its own answer with a fire-hot certainty.

The answer was *yes*. Yes, he thought Naomi would make a wonderful *gut* wife. The best wife any man could wish for, in fact.

He couldn't say such a thing to his sister—or to anybody

else for that matter. And something about the way his sister was eyeing him, with the beginnings of hope in her eyes, was making him *naerfich*.

"I should get out to the woodshop. I've work to finish if I'm to get all my outstanding orders completed before we leave."

Miriam nodded slowly, still not taking her eyes from his face. "All right. Me, I think I will rest up here, at least until Naomi's baking is done. So if there is anything you might like to speak to her about before you go out, you won't be disturbed."

Joseph stopped with one hand on the dented brass doorknob and looked hard at his sister.

"I can think of nothing I need to speak to Naomi about that I would not wish for you to hear, *schwesdre*."

He spoke firmly, but to his astonishment, Miriam, for the first time since their world had fallen to pieces, laughed. It was soft, and it was brief, but it was definitely a real laugh.

"Maybe you need to think a little harder then, *bruder*."

Joseph went out the door, shutting it firmly behind him. His head spun as he walked down the stairs into the kitchen.

Naomi was unscrewing the metal top off a canister of flour. She glanced up at him and smiled, but she didn't speak. She'd gotten out his mother's old pie board, and she sprinkled a generous handful of flour over it. Then she measured a cupful into a crockery bowl, frowning seriously as she did.

She looked sweet, standing there. The dress she was wearing was a new one. He'd noticed her sewing on it up in Miriam's room, but today was the first day she'd worn it. It was a deep, rosy shade, and it lent its color to her face, making her neatly coiled blond hair seem even lighter. It was still stiff and new, and its thick sleeves made her slim arms, busy in their work, look even daintier somehow as they poked out beneath the folded-up fabric.

That dress looked more like a woman's than a girl's. She

really did look like a man's wife, busy at her morning work. It was his kitchen, so she could easily have been his own young *fraw*, baking for their family.

The thought shuddered him, the way a loud clap of summer thunder could shake the walls of even the sturdiest house. His face stung hotly, and his mouth went suddenly dry.

"Did you need something from me before you go to town, Joseph?" She cut a quick glance at him and gave him a half smile before returning her attention to the dough she was forming in the striped bowl. "I can leave this for a bit if you do. It's only a piecrust." She looked up again, and her easy smile dimmed as she studied his face. "Is something wrong? You're all flushed. Are you feeling well?"

Would you ever consider me as a husband, Naomi?

The question burned in his mind, begging to be asked, but instead he said, "I'm well enough, *denki*. You're making a pie?"

"*Ja*. Apple-raisin. Or at least I hope so." She darted another look at him. His heart did a somersault. "We'll see how it turns out."

"I thought you never made pies on difficult days. This sure feels like a difficult day to me."

Naomi sighed and dusted a snowfall of flour off her hands into the bowl. "*Ja*, I know it must feel so, for both of you. Hard for Miriam to hear about the move, and even harder, I think, for you to tell her about it. But you did it kindly, Joseph."

Her praise warmed him. "She's agreed to go, but the trip won't be easy for her."

"*Nee*, it won't, but with your help she'll get through it all right. In the meantime, I'll do my best to get her in a good frame of mind before you leave. This pie is Miriam's favorite, ain't so? I'm hoping that the smell of it will be enough to lure her into the kitchen." She tilted her head and gave him a mischievous smile. "That's why I decided to take a chance on the pastry. You'd best say a prayer that it will work out well."

Why was his heart beating so hard? He stood as if he'd grown roots into the kitchen floor, watching her as she spooned snowy lard into the mound of flour. She worked the mixture briskly with a wire pastry cutter for a second or two, then she arched an eyebrow at him.

"Is there something else you need from me, Joseph?"

Ja, there is. That deep, certain part of his heart sounded off again.

"Was it true what Miriam said? Are you not looking forward to going back to Kentucky?"

Naomi's hands slowed. "I hope you don't think ill of me. I love my family, Joseph, I do. But I'm the youngest, you know, and the only girl. I was sick for so long, and such a trouble to everybody, that it's no wonder they still see me as someone they must look after."

"Your brothers must miss you, though."

"I suppose they do." Naomi spoke cheerfully, but something in her voice told Joseph that she didn't really believe what she was saying.

He frowned. "Aren't they kind to you?" He remembered the way the Schrock boys had jogged off and left their frail sister struggling behind. Maybe that hadn't changed as much as one would hope.

"They're kind. It's just they're all so busy with their own families, they've little time to fret over me. They've been real pleased that I've been so happy in Johns Mill." She offered him a rueful smile. "It got me out from under everybody's feet for a while."

Joseph's opinion of Naomi's brothers dipped another several notches. "I see." No wonder she didn't want to go home. "And have you been happy here? Truly happy?"

"Ja." This time her answer came quick and sure. "Happier than I've ever been in my life. It's been so *gut* to be

here, helping first with Katie and her sweet *boppli*, and now you and Miriam."

Happier than I've ever been. Did she mean that? Joseph probed gently to find out. "I can't think being here with us during this time could be very pleasant."

"It has been for me. Not," she added quickly, "that I'm happy for your troubles. Of course it's not that. It's just . . . I've never been like you, Joseph. You've always been strong. But me, I've felt useless for so much of my life. You can't understand how much it's meant to me to be allowed to help you all. It's given me a real feeling of purpose, and that's been the biggest blessing I've ever had. I thank *Gott*—and you—for giving me the chance."

"It was you who took a chance, coming here with reporters at the door and the whole family in a mess."

"Ah, well. I didn't mind that."

She sounded as if she meant it. His heart was pounding so hard now, he could barely think. All his common sense was slipping away from him, like reins sliding through slack fingers. Something strong deep inside him was taking control, like a horse took his head when the comfort of his barn came into view after a long ride home.

"Do you like to take chances, then, Naomi?"

She laughed, and the gentle sound tickled up the back of his neck like playful fingers. "Oh, *ja*, I do. I spent so long not taking any at all, you know. *Mamm* wouldn't let me do anything the least bit risky while I was so frail. So I guess now I take them whenever I can to make up for lost time!"

He'd forgotten how to breathe, and he was feeling pretty light-headed, but it didn't matter. He forged ahead. "I can think of another chance you could take, then, since you like them so much."

She looked up at him, the metal cutter motionless in her hand. "And what would that be, Joseph?"

"You could marry me." He could hear his pulse banging

away behind his eardrums. "You could marry me and come to Ohio with us. As my wife," he added stupidly, as if a *schmaert* girl like Naomi needed him to spell everything out.

Both her gray-green eyes and her mouth opened wide, and the cutter fell against the side of the crockery bowl with a clatter. "Oh!"

"It seems sensible," he rushed on desperately. "You're none too eager to go home to Kentucky, and Miriam's sure to do better if you came along to Ohio with us. And I—" he stopped. He couldn't say . . . what he wanted to say. Not now, not with her looking at him with that flat astonishment in her eyes. "It's past time I married. *Daed* said so just before . . . he thought so, too. Unless," he added, "there's some other fellow you like the look of."

She worked her lips twice before she seemed able to answer him. "*N-nee.* There's no other fellow. But—"

He didn't want her to finish that sentence, not yet, not while she had that shocked look on her face. "Don't answer me now. I've sprung this on you sudden, and you'll need to think on it. I'm going out to the woodshop for a while, and then I need to drive to town to sign the paperwork at the real estate office. Likely I'll not be back until suppertime." He hesitated another awkward second, then he forced his legs to work and got out of the kitchen as fast as he could.

He didn't take another breath until he was inside his shop. He sank down on the cold earthen floor, his back pressed against the door, his heart hammering.

He never did anything like that, quick-like, without thinking it through. And proposing to a girl, well, his father had stressed to him time and time again growing up, that such a choice was one of the two most important ones he'd ever make. And the way he'd done it, just blurting it out like that. He'd bumbled it badly, just like he always did when it came to saying the right words.

Ja, he'd likely made a mess of things, all right, talking about marriage to Naomi like that, out of the blue. He waited for reality to sink in, to feel a sense of embarrassment or regret or something similar that he'd made such a *zwickel* of himself.

But when he remembered what he'd seen in Naomi's eyes the split second before her surprise kicked in, what he felt wasn't regret at all. *Nee*, it was something lighter, and stronger and far more promising.

He couldn't be sure because he hadn't felt this way in a long, long time. But as near as he could remember, this felt an awful lot like hope.

Chapter Twenty

❧

THAT EVENING AS NAOMI WASHED THE DISHES she'd used to make the chicken casserole now steaming on the table, her gaze kept drifting out the window at the rapidly darkening yard.

Joseph had returned from his appointment in town a couple hours ago. She'd seen him driving up, and a thrill had run through her, starting at her toes and ending at the top of her head. She'd barely been able to breathe, waiting for him to come inside.

But he hadn't.

She'd seen him unhitching Titus and leading the horse into the barn. He'd paused on his way out, casting one long look at the house, but then he'd disappeared into his woodshop, shutting the door behind him.

Now he was late for supper, and Naomi's nerves had stretched to their breaking point. They'd been thrumming crazily all day, ever since he'd dropped that abrupt proposal in her lap and scooted out the back door like a scalded dog.

Her heart had been so out of rhythm that she'd had to make the casserole sitting down.

Naomi had wondered, like any *maidel*, about what a proposal might be like. Such things weren't talked about much back in Kentucky, so she'd had to use her imagination. Most of the time, they seemed to happen on buggy rides, late at night, clopping home from a Sunday night singing. She knew at least one of her brothers had proposed that way.

David hadn't told her anything about it, of course, but her sister-in-law had. Driving her home that evening, David had taken a long detour around a pond, and he'd paused in a pretty spot. She'd known then, Lena said, that something was afoot. And right there, sitting in the buggy, he'd asked her to be his wife, offering her a pretty whistle he'd whittled to mark the occasion.

Her future sister-in-law hadn't known what to think of David's choice of gifts. Mostly if a present was given, it was some nice, practical thing that the girl could use in her new home. But Lena had laughed when David had explained that she only had to whistle, and he'd come running for the rest of his life.

Naomi had liked that way of doing things; it seemed both sweet and funny. She'd hoped that—if she ever did have a boy propose to her, which seemed increasingly unlikely—that he might do something like that.

One thing was for certain sure. She'd never imagined she'd be proposed to standing elbow deep in piecrust— because marriage seemed sensible and because the fellow's sister didn't want to lose Naomi's company.

All in all, she'd rather have had the whistle.

She hadn't been worth much for the rest of the afternoon, and making a decent pastry was out of the question. The pie had turned out terribly, but she'd baked it anyhow. Miriam had come down and politely picked at the tough-crusted mess before settling in at the table to do some quilting.

After scraping the remains of Miriam's pie into the scrap bowl, Naomi had tried to join her, but sewing was another skill that was beyond her abilities today. After she'd poked her finger with the needle and bled on the cheery yellow cloth, she'd given up and decided to do a bit of cleaning in the kitchen instead.

At the sight of the blood welling out of Naomi's finger, Miriam had gone pale. She'd risen unsteadily from her chair, claiming to have a headache, and disappeared upstairs as quickly as she could. Naomi had felt bad, but perhaps it was for the best if Miriam stayed safely upstairs for the rest of the afternoon.

Naomi and Joseph needed to talk.

She'd gone over and over their earlier conversation in her head, looking at it from every angle, trying to make some sort of sense of the crazy twist her day had taken. She hadn't been successful.

She felt the same way as she had the day her doctor had explained the operation that could fix her heart. That day, she'd sat in the medical office, hands clenched so hard, her fingernails had printed angry little half-moons in her skin.

She'd felt terrified and hopeful all at once, just as she felt right now. It had been overwhelming, and she'd asked the cardiologist question after question, repeating many of them as she struggled to convince herself that what he was promising her—the possibility of a healthy, useful life—could truly happen.

She had a few questions for Joseph, too. Naomi cast an agonized look at the relentless clock ticking on the wall. If he didn't hurry up, Aaron would be here to take her back to Katie's for the night.

She couldn't wait until tomorrow. She just couldn't.

She dropped the pot she'd been absentmindedly rewashing into the dishwater and dried her hands on a towel. Enough was enough. If Joseph wouldn't come to her, she'd go out to Joseph.

She made it all the way to the barn door before realizing that she'd hurried outside without her shawl or her bonnet. She tucked her hair carefully under her *kapp* and smoothed down the front of her dress, listening to the unmistakable sounds of milk hitting a stainless steel pail.

Joseph was running late with the chores. That must be why he hadn't come in for supper on time. It made sense, given that he'd had to spend part of the day in town, seeing to the rental agreement about the house.

She hesitated. Maybe she should have waited instead of rushing out here.

Nee, she told herself firmly. Joseph had started this. All she was trying to do was to finish it, and he'd already made her wait the whole, long afternoon. She pulled open the barn door and stepped inside.

The temperature in the snug barn was several degrees warmer than the yard. Daisy, the milk cow, was nose-deep in her grain, and the calm old Jersey flicked a disinterested gaze in Naomi's direction.

Joseph was bent over, milking quickly, the strong, white jets streaming forcefully into the pail. He stopped and straightened up on the stool when he saw her.

"Naomi. Is Miriam all right?"

"She went up to her room a bit early, but that's not why I came out here. I just . . . I thought we should talk before it was time for me to go home."

He looked at her, his cheeks mottling red. "I suppose we should, *ja*."

Impatient with the delay in her evening routine, Daisy turned a grain-encrusted nose in Joseph's direction and mooed irritably.

"I need to finish up here," Joseph said. Naomi detected a whiff of relief in his voice. "I'll be up to the kitchen in a few minutes. Best you wait for me inside where it's warm."

"All right." Disappointed, Naomi turned and started toward the door. When she reached it, though, she halted, one hand flat against the cold, rough wood. Then she squared her shoulders and turned. "*Nee.* Aaron's likely to be along to pick me up soon, and I'd rather not put this off until tomorrow. I won't sleep a wink if I do. You're a dairyman, ain't so? You can talk while you milk well enough, I reckon."

The tempo of Joseph's milking slowed for a pace or two, then sped back up. "I reckon I can, *ja.*"

She edged closer, watching his muscles flex as he methodically stripped the cow's bulging bag of its milk. Naomi swallowed and gathered her courage.

"Before—" Her voice cracked on the word. She cleared her throat and tried again, "Before, back in the kitchen. You asked me to think on the idea of marrying you."

He shot a glance out of the corner of his eye at her and nodded, once. Then he turned his eyes back to Daisy's deflating udder. "And have you? Thought on it?"

What a question. "I've not been able to think of much else, all the day long. That's not something a fellow usually flings at a girl with no warning."

He glanced at her again and nodded sheepishly. "Suppose not."

She waited for him to explain, but he kept working silently, the steady pulses of his milking marking the passage of time. Naomi inhaled air that smelled of warm milk and the rich, dark molasses mixed with the sweet feed Daisy was crunching, and she prayed for patience.

"Before I give you an answer, I've a couple questions of my own, if you don't mind."

Joseph stripped the last of the milk from Daisy's back teats and slid the lid onto the pail. He stood, scooting the three-legged wooden milking stool over out of the way.

"Ask me whatever you like, Naomi. I'll answer you, best I can."

"All right." Now that the time had finally come to ask the question that had been burning in her breast all afternoon long, she was reluctant to ask it. But she had to know, so she did. "Did you mean it?"

Daisy's rhythmic chewing, the sound of a hen cackling in the chicken coop, the rattle of a loose shingle in the wind on the roof. Those were the only sounds she heard over the ragged thump of her own heart.

Joseph studied her, his brows drawn together. Was he going to answer her or not? She shivered nervously, and he frowned.

"You're cold." He set down the pail and jerked a heavy chore jacket off a hook on one of the barn's supporting wooden posts. As he came close, her gaze fastened on his face. The closer he came, the harder she found it to think—and to breathe.

Finally, he was standing only a step away. Reaching around her, he settled the musty jacket on her shoulders. Her breath came in quick, shallow puffs as their eyes met.

She'd rarely stood so close to a man not related to her, never had a man do something so intimate as this. His eyes were gentle, and a little sad, as he smoothed the rough fabric over her arms. Then he put his hands back down at his sides, but his gaze stayed connected with hers.

"*Ja*, Naomi," he said quietly. "I meant it. I'd not have joked with you, not about something like that."

"All right." She nodded jerkily. "I . . . wasn't sure."

The corners of his lips twitched upward slightly. "I must've made a real hash of it, if you couldn't tell."

"I've never had anybody ask me before. So I didn't know."

Something flickered in his eyes, but it was gone before she could figure out what it was. "We've that in common, then. I've never asked anybody before, so I reckon we'll have to figure the rest of this out together. If, I mean, you do decide to . . ." He trailed off, looking uncomfortable. "I don't mean to rush you for an answer, Naomi. I know it's a big decision, and I'm bringing little enough to the table. It's only sensible for you to think it through."

Sensible. Naomi's mind flitted suddenly to a schoolmate back in Kentucky. Like Naomi, Lyddie had never been too pretty or sought after by the boys, but she'd had her share of romantic dreams, just like all the other girls. Then a year ago, she'd up and married an overwhelmed widower with a brood of nine children.

"I know Amos Byler ain't so much," Lyddie had admitted to Naomi with a practical shrug. "He's skinny as a beanpole and gray as a cat, and he's no more in love with me than I am with him. He mainly wants a *mamm* to look after his young ones. But I'm sensible enough to know I'm not likely to get any other offers, and I've always wanted a family of my own. Amos is a kind man and a *gut* father, and he makes a decent living with his chicken houses. That's enough for me."

Naomi had stood up with Lyddie at her wedding, and she'd secretly felt a bit sorry for the bride. Still, that match had worked out all right, hadn't it? Lyddie had a sweet baby son of her own now, and she seemed content with her choice. If she'd held out for romance, likely she'd still be alone.

Naomi blinked and refocused on Joseph. "You'll be leaving pretty soon, ain't so? That doesn't leave much time for thinking, seems to me."

"I reckon you're right about that. Isaac will understand how things are, and I think he'd work with us to make a quick marriage, if that's what we want. But you should take enough time to be real sure, Naomi."

"Are *you* real sure, then, Joseph?"

The question came out before she could stop it. She was torn between wishing she could call it back and wanting to hear the answer so badly, she could barely bring herself to breathe.

Maybe he would say . . . something. Just a little something that would sweep away the silly disappointment she'd felt and make all this seem less . . . Amos-like.

He looked at her and the silence stretched out between them for what seemed like just a hair too long. Then he nodded.

"*Ja*, Naomi. I'm sure. I'd never have asked, otherwise."

She pressed her lips together to keep them from wobbling. Amos Byler couldn't have said it any plainer.

So there would be no come-a-running whistle, not for her. But there would be this kind man, and a *gut* life, a better one than she'd ever expected to have, if only, like Lyddie, she had enough sense to be grateful for the blessings *Gott* was offering her instead of pining for the ones He was not.

"Then I don't need any more time to think about it. I will marry you, Joseph. Just as soon as you like."

CHAPTER TWENTY-ONE

❧

JOSEPH HESITATED ON THE SIDEWALK, STUDYING the buzzing throng of people inside Isaac's bakery. It was crowded today. Not good, since he needed a private word with the bishop if he wanted to start the wheels turning for his wedding to Naomi.

A hopeful warmth spread through his chest, just as it had done every time Naomi's acceptance of his bumbling proposal came to mind. He still couldn't quite believe it was true. It would take some time to sink in—maybe more for him than for most. Changes had always come hard for him.

This change, though, was one well worth making. Joseph agreed with his church's encouraging position on marriage, believing it provided a sturdy structure both to a person's life and to the community at large. He'd have married before now, if things had gone differently with the dairy—and with Rhoda. Still, even when that disappointment had been fresh, he'd never given up on the idea of finding a wife. He'd even said as much to Naomi once, sitting at Katie's kitchen table.

Funny now, to think how angry and hopeless he'd felt that last morning of the old days, before his world had broken apart and shifted into something new. He remembered the jumbled heat of his feelings for Rhoda with a strange lack of connection, as if they'd belonged to someone else.

He guessed, they had, in a way.

What he felt for Naomi was different. It was simpler. Cleaner. Stronger even. As usual, he couldn't put the right words to his feelings, not even in his own head. But he sensed a deep rightness to this, and that sense of purpose had propelled him into town bright and early this morning.

He hadn't expected the bakery to be so busy already. He could leave the discussion for another time, he supposed, but he'd prefer to get this seen to. He hoped Isaac would understand the need to move the wedding along quickly, but you could never be certain about such things, especially not when you were asking a church leader to depart from the tried-and-true way of doing things.

An *Englisch* man jostled against him on his way to the door.

"'Scuse me," the stranger muttered automatically. Then he paused, darting a curious look into Joseph's face.

Joseph nodded politely, but he quickly turned his head, pretending to study the handwritten list of specials taped to the inside of the bakery's window. The man hesitated a second or two, but finally he went on through the door.

Joseph relaxed his clenched fingers and sighed. The last thing he needed today was to have somebody recognize him as one of the Hochstedlers. He'd best get off this sidewalk or that was going to happen for sure. He pulled open the glass door and walked into Isaac Lambright's bustling business, simply named The Bakery.

The warm air smelled richly of coffee, baking pastries,

and vanilla, and there was a low hubbub of voices. Joseph edged through the crowd toward the front of the store, careful not to make eye contact with anybody.

Unless he missed his guess, a good many of these folks were reporters. They had the look of it. The ones in line were talking on cell phones and juggling wide-strapped shoulder bags as they waited in the rope of people winding up to the glass-fronted counter. The ones who were already seated were tapping on paper-thin computers, their faces pinched in concentration. Most had cups of coffee positioned next to the phones lying flat on the table, their glances darting from screen to screen.

It didn't bode well, so many *Englischers* back in town. Johns Mill had been calming down, but it looked like this movie business had already stirred things up again.

Behind the counter, Isaac's wife, Ida, was busy taking orders. Her matronly sister Betta stood beside her in Rhoda's old spot, filling them quickly. Joseph slipped past the line and flipped up the wooden partition leading to the employee area.

Before he could duck through, Isaac popped out of a doorway, like a hound ready to bark at an intruder. Looked like Joseph wasn't the only one made uneasy by the throngs of *Englischers*. Isaac relaxed when his eyes met Joseph's.

"*Guder mariye*," he said, beckoning Joseph into his combination office and storeroom. "I'm glad to see you. I was planning to make a run to your place this afternoon, so you've saved me a trip. Wait just a minute."

Isaac went behind the desk. As the bishop rummaged in the center drawer, Joseph's eye lit on a large plastic tote sitting in the middle of the floor. It was stuffed with plastic greenery studded with pinecones and red berries. Isaac was storing away the bakery's Christmas decorations.

Joseph fingered one of the garlands trailing out of the storage bin. They'd never put up decorations at home, of course, and privately Joseph had been taken aback when he'd seen them in The Bakery. More proof of the compromises that were being made in order to keep the tourists happy, he supposed.

Still, *Mamm* had always made a fuss over Christmas, especially second Christmas, the day when family visited and shared good food and games together. This year, the holiday had passed by quiet-like, barely marked at all.

He felt a quiet sadness as he tucked the rest of the greenery into the tote. He looked up to find Isaac studying him, the older man's eyes gentle. He held out a large, brown envelope in Joseph's direction.

"Here. This has all the records for the store, the deposits we've made, the payment for the pieces your *daed* had in on consignment. We've settled it up for you. There are only a few things left over now, since we haven't been restocking. Folks bought you out, or nearly so, with their Christmas shopping. So we men think it's time to close down the store. Unless you've decided to restock, that is. Have you?"

Joseph weighed the envelope in his hand. The money would be useful, but there was only one answer to Isaac's question. "*Nee*. I'm no storekeeper, Isaac. I thank you for seeing to this. It has been a blessing."

"*Ach*, well. I did not do so alone. Many helped."

"I am grateful," Joseph replied simply.

The bishop nodded, accepting the gratitude as easily as he would extend it, when it came his turn to be on the receiving end of such a gesture. "What brings you to town today, then, Joseph?"

"I've come to discuss a personal matter with you. I'm sorry to trouble you at your work, but—"

"That is all right." Isaac's eyes sharpened. He went to the door and closed it halfway, leaving a careful gap so that he could hear what was going on in the busy bakery. It was a simple gesture, but a new one, and Joseph recognized it for what it was. Isaac was keeping a protective eye on his own wife and family, as best he could. Joseph wasn't sure if Isaac was worried about Trevor, the reporters, or Caleb, but clearly things had changed in Johns Mill for more folks than the Hochstedlers.

"So," Isaac said, "what is it you want to talk about?"

"Two things. I want to let you know that Miriam and I are going to be moving to Ohio for a while, at least until this movie business is over and done with."

Isaac blew out a long, slow sigh. "Not happy news for your friends here, but like I said earlier, that may be the best thing. And you realize, Joseph, that it's not just the filming of the movie that's going to stir up trouble. Later, when it's showing in the theaters, things will likely get even worse, Sheriff Townsend says."

Joseph nodded. He'd thought of that already. "We're renting out the farm for three years at least. After that, we'll see what happens."

"*Ja*, you never know. Maybe you'll like it up in Ohio. We'll miss you, of course, but you've family there. Everybody understands."

Joseph made a noncommittal noise. Maybe folks didn't understand things so well as they thought, not if they were assuming that living closer to Melvin counted as a positive.

Isaac's eyes twinkled. "Who knows? You might start a family of your own even."

Joseph cleared his throat. "That was another reason I've come to see you, Isaac. I need to ask you about the possibility of marriage under some . . . special circumstances."

"Oh?" The teasing twinkle faded from Isaac's eye, replaced by a wary interest. He sank into the chair behind the desk. "Ask then, and we'll see if I have an answer for you."

Joseph swallowed and offered the speech he'd rehearsed on the ride into town. "I have asked Naomi Schrock to be my wife. She's accepted, but in order for her to move with us to Ohio, we'll need to get married soon." When Isaac lifted an eyebrow, Joseph hurried to explain. "It would be much simpler for us to travel together, and it would make the trip easier for Miriam as well. I was hoping the church would see fit to help us move through the process right quick."

"Naomi." There was no mistaking the surprise on the bishop's face. The old chair squeaked as he shifted. "You've decided to marry Naomi?"

Joseph nodded. "*Ja*. Soon, if that's possible," he added, in case Isaac had missed the sticking point.

Isaac took a couple of long moments to think before giving his answer. "Well, you're both church members in good standing, and your age is no concern. You are both old enough to make such a decision with wisdom. I'll need a letter from her bishop in Kentucky just to verify her standing in the church, but I see no trouble with allowing such a thing to move forward quickly, given the circumstances. You can be published this coming Sunday, if that will suit."

Relief washed over Joseph like a splash of warm water. That had been easy enough. "It will suit."

"I will speak to the ministers, then, and we will begin the process."

"*Denki*." He turned to go, but Isaac's voice stopped him.

"I think this is a wise decision, Joseph. Naomi seems to be a levelheaded girl. I have found no foolishness in her. Her long illness has taught her patience and wisdom, I think, and she has a sincere gratitude to *Gott* for being spared to work and serve others."

"Naomi has shown our family great kindness, for sure."

"Some have built marriages on much less firm a foundation, and they've paid a steep price for it. Love grows after a marriage just as well as before it, maybe better. Naomi may not be the first girl your heart would have chosen, but she will be a *gut* help and a comfort to you and to your family, and that is what counts most."

Everything Isaac was saying was true. Somehow, though,

his words fell wrongly on Joseph's ears. It sounded as if Naomi were a mare Joseph was buying, and not a particularly choice one.

He started to argue then caught himself. Isaac had agreed to the speedy timetable. Joseph had gotten what he'd come for. A wise man chose his words carefully in such a situation.

"*Denki.* I'll let Naomi know that you have approved it, and we will begin to make our plans."

Back out on the street, Joseph started toward the parking area, then paused. He weighed the envelope Isaac had given him, feeling the bumpy outline of the keys through the thin paper, thinking hard. He turned and strode down the street toward Hochstedler's General Store.

He managed to turn the key in the balky lock and slipped in without being noticed. The old oilcloth shades were pulled down behind the windows, leaving the big store dim, but Joseph didn't need light to know where he was. All he had to do was close his eyes and breathe.

The scent of the place yanked him backward in time. If somebody had asked him yesterday what this store smelled like, he wouldn't have been able to say. But now he knew. It smelled of wood and lemon oil and a whiff of mustiness that had probably been trapped in the cracks of this old building since time began.

Even though the Hochstedlers had run the store only a short time, the scent reminded him sharply of his *daed.* Joseph half expected to see his father walk out of the storeroom, his tan shopkeeper apron tied around his middle, smiling.

Involuntarily, Joseph glanced toward the counter, then quickly away. He shook his head, trying to clear it. He'd not come here to remember or to dwell on what had happened inside these walls. He had other business to attend to.

He headed toward the storeroom, scanning the store as he went. As Isaac had said, the place was near emptied out, with only a few leftover items here and there. That ugly quilt of Rowena Miller's that *Mamm* had taken out of pity, knowing she'd never sell it. A few blank-faced dolls and wooden spinning tops. A cardboard box filled with half-pint jars of blackberry jam. Most of the shelves were empty.

Good, then. It would be that much easier to close it up. He should talk to Mona and see whether it would be wisest to rent the place out to another business or to sell it outright.

He flicked on the light in the storeroom, and it sprang into an artificial brightness. The church allowed businesses to run electricity and to have telephones. Computers even, in some places, although *Daed* hadn't gone that far. He'd decided to keep his ledgers by hand, just as he'd done with the dairy for years. Those handwritten ledgers were neatly stored on a shelf down in the basement, and Joseph made a mental note to pack them up for the move.

Joseph reached for the phone and pressed a button. The dial tone buzzed in his ear. Quickly, he punched in the number he'd memorized and waited for the answering machine to pick up. When it did, he cleared his throat.

"This message is for Emma Hochstedler, staying with Melvin Hochstedler, from her brother Joseph in Tennessee. Please let her know—"

There was a click as the receiver on the other end was lifted.

"Joseph?"

Joseph stopped, astonished. "Emma? Is that you?"

"*Ja!* It is me! Oh, it is so *gut* to hear your voice!"

"Yours, too. What were you doing in the phone shack?"

"Hiding," Emma admitted guiltily. "I needed a few minutes to myself."

"What a blessing for you to be there when I happened to call."

"Well, that's not quite so unlikely as you might think. I walk down here most every day, saying I need to check for messages for home. They think it's foolish, because there never is a message, but they don't argue too much. I linger as long as I can. It's cold, but it's peaceful enough. Folks here don't use the phone any more than they have to."

Joseph shifted guiltily, making the old floor beneath his boots creak a protest. "I should have called you before now, I reckon."

"That's all right. I've appreciated your letters, although I could do with less descriptions of how fine everybody's cows are looking. I see more than enough cows here, although they're such sad-looking beasts, nobody's likely to brag on them. Melvin doesn't keep his Jerseys near so sleek as you and Daed always did."

Joseph wasn't surprised. "That costs money, especially in winter. You won't catch Melvin spending on anything he can make do without."

"*Ja*, things are pretty lean here. I don't think Melvin's doing much better with his dairy than *Daed* was those last few years, and of course, he's got no family able to help him. Henry can't even feed himself without help, and Nella's legs bother her a good deal. She spends a lot of time in her rocker."

No wonder Emma sounded so tired, Joseph thought. He could guess who was carrying most of the burdens in Melvin's home. "That must mean a lot of work for you."

"I am thankful to do it. I am blessed to have family that is willing to take me in, after—everything that happened. I try not to forget that."

Joseph's heart constricted. He doubted very much that Emma would be allowed to forget that, not while she was sitting down at Melvin and Nella's table. "I'm sorry. I wish—"

"There's nothing for you to apologize for," Emma cut in quickly. "I'll have to get back soon, so let's not waste our time. I'm starving for news from home. Have you heard anything from Caleb since the church placed him under the ban? Is Miriam any better?"

"There's no news of Caleb, not yet. Miriam was doing much better, but she's had a setback." He described the incident at the café while Emma made worried noises. "She won't leave the house now, but at least Naomi's got her coming downstairs and sewing again. I'm thankful for that."

"I am, too. *Gott* sent Naomi to us for sure. She has been such a blessing."

"Ja." Joseph smiled. "She has been."

"I wish I could be there to help out, too." His sister sighed. "I was hoping maybe I would at least be able to come back for a visit, but if Miriam can't even go to Miller's without being bothered, I suppose I'd best not. It's too bad, though. I miss you all so much."

"You won't be missing us much longer. We're coming to Ohio, Emma."

His sister's gasp of joy came clearly through the receiver. "For true, Joseph?"

For true? As long as he could remember, that childish expression had been Emma's response to any happy surprise.

"For true."

"Oh, Joseph! Goodness, I'm crying, I'm so happy! When will you be here? How long will you be able to stay?"

"In a month or so, if all goes as expected, and we'll be staying for a long while. That's why I was calling, so you could tell Melvin to keep a lookout for a house for rent. A small one," he added quickly. "We won't have much to live on, but I've rented out the farm, so we'll have that income. If Melvin will hire me on at the dairy, we'll scrape by well enough, I reckon."

"Joseph, I don't understand. You want to rent a house? *Here?*"

"Unless you think we would be better off staying with Melvin and Nella."

"You'd be better off in the barn with those poor skinny

cows," Emma said wholeheartedly. "But Joseph, for you to think of coming here . . . things at home must be worse than I'd thought. What's going on? Tell me."

He sketched out what sparse details he knew about the *Englisch* movie. Emma listened without interrupting, but the heaviness of her silence came across the connection.

"It will be a while, then, before we can all come home," she said when he'd finished.

"A while, *ja*. But even if we can never come back to Johns Mill, we will be all right, Emma, as long as we hold on to our faith and to each other."

"Listen to you, *bruder*." Emma chuckled softly. She'd always been a great girl for laughter, and Joseph was glad to hear a hint of it in her voice again. "You sound so much like *Daed*. Well, it will be a real blessing for me to have you and Miriam close enough to visit, that's for sure."

"To visit? You'll be living with us, Emma."

"*Nee*," Emma said quietly. "*Ich kann naett*. Henry needs a good deal of care in the night, and Nella isn't able to tend him by herself anymore. I must stay on here, but if you work at the dairy, at least I will be able to see you every day. Miriam, too. You will have to bring her when you come to work. It is not an easy house, this one, but she cannot be left alone, so we will have to make the best of it."

Joseph cleared his throat. "She will not be left alone. Naomi is coming, too. I've just come from speaking with Isaac. We are to be married, Naomi and I, as soon as we can make the arrangements."

"*Vass hosht ksaw?*"

Now it was Joseph's turn to chuckle. "I said that Naomi is coming to Ohio, too. As my *fraw*."

"Oh, Joseph! That is *wunderbarr* news! I am happy for you both. Naomi is one of the sweetest girls I know, and I will be glad to have her as my sister. When is the wedding to be?"

"Soon. A few weeks, likely. Isaac has agreed to let it move forward quickly."

"Isaac? But why are you talking to him? The wedding will be in Kentucky, won't it?"

"Ah." Joseph fumbled for an answer. Of course Emma would expect Naomi to be married from her home. That's the way things were always done. Somehow, though, he hadn't even thought of it, and Naomi hadn't said a word when he'd mentioned speaking to Isaac instead of taking it before her bishop in Kentucky. "There's no time for a big wedding. I want to keep this simple . . . given how things are. Naomi understands that."

"Ja." The syllable came softly through the phone line. "I am sure Naomi would be willing to do whatever you ask, but . . ." Joseph sensed that his normally outspoken sister was choosing her words carefully. "I wish *Mamm* were here. She could talk to you better than I can about such things."

"Just say what you need to say, Emma," Joseph suggested shortly. He couldn't believe he'd not so much as thought to ask Naomi about the wedding location, and it made him irritable.

"All right, *bruder.*" A spark of Emma's former spunk strengthened her voice. "I will. Naomi's life has been plenty hard enough already. Don't make it harder by being thick-headed. Of course she'll agree to whatever you suggest, but that's all the more reason why you shouldn't let her."

Joseph frowned at the phone in his hand. "You're talking in riddles, Emma."

"Naomi"—his sister paused as if struggling for words—"has always thought a lot of you," she finished finally.

Joseph raised his eyebrows as he realized what Emma was getting at.

She was saying Naomi had always cared for him.

"We have always been *gut* friends, Naomi and I," he admitted carefully, testing the waters.

"It was more than that for her. I've seen it for years, ever since we were all *youngies*, and I wasn't the only one, either. It was plain enough to anybody who had eyes. Your kindnesses to her back then meant little to you, but they meant a great deal to her. Of course, you never took any real notice of her, and with her health problems and all, nobody expected it could go anywhere. But now that it has . . . well. Be gentle with her. It's a great responsibility to be trusted with someone's heart, Joseph. If that person cares for us more than we care for them, we can hurt them very deeply without meaning to."

He was still trying to wrap his mind around what his sister was suggesting, but the regret in Emma's voice was so clear that he couldn't let it pass unchallenged. "What Trevor did wasn't your fault, Emma. You must stop blaming yourself."

"*Ja*," his sister whispered sadly. "It was my fault." Through the line he heard a loud knocking, and Emma called out, "Just a minute, please! I'm sorry, but I have to hang up, Joseph. Someone else has come to use the phone. I will talk to Melvin about your news. Call again as soon as you can."

"I will. *Mach's gut*, Emma."

He hung up the receiver, and the silence of the near-empty store resettled around him. His eye lit on one of his father's tan aprons, still crisp in its newness, hanging on a peg by the door leading into the storefront. Originally, there had been two aprons hanging there. The other peg was empty now.

Joseph drew in a deep breath, then picked up the key he'd laid on the table. There was no time today for dwelling on the past. He had to get back to the farm as quick as he could. If what Emma said was true, if even a little of it was true, he had some fences to mend with Naomi.

CHAPTER TWENTY-TWO

❧

SHE PROBABLY SHOULDN'T BE DOING THIS.

Naomi hesitated, one hand flat against the rough wooden door leading into Joseph's woodshop. Then she ignored the twinges coming from her conscience and pushed it open.

The workroom lay still in the January afternoon. Wintry sunlight streamed through the windows, illuminating the dust motes floating in the air. Naomi breathed in the cold, piney scent, and her heart fluttered with a special mix of joy and nerves that had come to mean Joseph to her.

He had been gone a long time. She'd been on pins and needles all afternoon wondering about his talk with Isaac. She'd tried to stay calm for Miriam's sake, but her ears had perked up at every sound coming from the road. She'd risen from their quilting to go to the kitchen sink more times than she could count, just so she could peek out the window.

Twice she'd seen *Englischers* stopped on the side of the road snapping photographs of the house. The rest of the time, it had mostly been trucks rumbling by, interspersed with a few buggies.

It had never been Joseph. His errand had taken much longer than expected. She wondered why.

As soon as Miriam had gone upstairs to take a nap, Naomi had snatched her shawl and headed for the chicken coop. She couldn't stay in the house another minute. On the way back to the kitchen with the basket of eggs, her gaze had snagged on the woodshop door, and temptation had won out.

Naomi shut the door softly behind herself. She felt closer to Joseph here than anyplace else on the farm. It was so like him to take a place nobody else had wanted and turn it into something useful. She saw his quiet, dogged responsibility in the way the tools were set so neatly in their places, and of course, in the lovely pieces that were waiting for delivery, she saw his skill.

She tugged an old sheet off a finished rocking chair and ran a finger down the gleaming wood. Joseph had been working on this piece for days, a gift Matthew Troyer had ordered for his new *fraw*. The chair was simple, but beautiful in its very plainness. Like everything Joseph made, this rocker was the best of its kind, strong and fine and useful.

She lowered herself into the chair. Someday soon Matthew's Ellen would rock their *boppli* in this, no doubt, and whenever she did, she would feel the loving thoughtfulness of her young husband surrounding her like an embrace.

How sweet that would be for her.

Naomi pressed her lips together and tightened her fingers on the glossy arms of the rocker. It was a sin to be greedy. She knew that. She'd cut her teeth on such teachings, sitting beside *Mamm* in church meetings. It was wrong to be ungrateful for *Gott*'s blessings or to envy others because He had seen fit to give them gifts that He'd chosen in His wisdom to withhold from you.

She'd had plenty of opportunities to learn this during her illness, when it had been so tempting to feel jealous of others whose hearts were strong and healthy. She'd thought she'd learned this particular lesson well, but right now she seemed to be having some trouble remembering it.

Assuming all had gone well with the bishop today, Joseph would soon be her husband. That alone was gift enough from *Gott*. She'd never expected to have any husband at all, much less one such as Joseph. She should be nothing but grateful.

Instead, as the day had dragged on, she'd fretted, dwelling on the idea that Joseph had likely hoped once that Isaac would be his father-in-law. Wondering, when he'd gone to speak to the bishop today, if he'd wished he could be there asking to publish his intentions to marry Rhoda instead of Naomi.

Now she was sitting here in a chair he'd made for another man's wife, wishing that when Joseph had offered her marriage, he'd looked at her just a little like Matthew Troyer looked at his Ellen. Or even as he'd looked at Rhoda that awful morning she'd come barreling up Katie's driveway in the pony cart.

She was being childish. Once, when Naomi was about five, she'd gone to the county fair with her family so *Daed* could look at the livestock. There had been a man selling funnel cakes there, hot, twisted masses of sweet, fried batter covered with a heavy dusting of powdered sugar. They had smelled heavenly. Her brothers had gotten several to share, but her *mamm* had led Naomi away to look at piglets without letting her have so much as a bite. Fried dough, especially bought in a place like the fair where there might be bad germs, was not on Naomi's special heart-friendly diet.

She'd cried over it, and *Mamm* had gently scolded her in *Deutsch* by the pigpen. One must learn to accept what one could not have, even little girls. It was shameful to fuss, and besides, it did no good.

Naomi leaned back in the chair, the gentle curves of the piece fitting her body as if it had been made for her, instead of Ellen Troyer. She closed her eyes and used one foot to rock the chair gently on the hard, earthen floor. Her nerves had kept her anxious all day, and it felt *gut* to rest here for a minute.

Perhaps once she was married to Joseph, she should write to Lyddie. There might be some comfort in exchanging letters with another woman who'd married a man who didn't love her, but who'd made it work so well.

Ja, that's what she would do, Naomi thought, yawning. She would write to Lyddie.

Her thoughts slowed, growing heavy and dull with sleep. Naomi's chin dipped down, and her body relaxed.

"Naomi?"

She jolted awake, and for a second didn't remember where she was. She pressed one hand against her startled heart and looked up to see Joseph standing in the doorway of the woodshop, looking puzzled.

"What are you doing out here?" he asked.

"Oh! *Ich binn sorry*," she whispered, standing up. She had to push a little on the arms of the chair to do so. Her legs felt oddly stiff and weak. "Miriam was resting, and I was tired of staying in the house. I shouldn't have come in here, I know, but—"

"You are welcome to come in whenever you like, Naomi. I was just surprised to see you sleeping out here, that's all."

Naomi twisted her fingers together, feeling foolish. "I sat down to try out the chair, and it was so comfortable, I guess I nodded off."

Joseph smiled. "That's a fine compliment, seeing how cold it is in here. You should get yourself back into the house and get warmed up. I'll come inside in a minute, and we'll talk."

Naomi started to ask him how his meeting with Isaac had gone, but she felt oddly reluctant to do so. Joseph would tell her sooner or later, she supposed.

"You must have gotten cold yourself, driving home. I'll

make some *kaffe* for you to have when you come inside." She turned to tuck the sheet carefully over the rocker. "This chair is beautiful, Joseph. Matthew's Ellen will be well pleased with her gift, I'm sure."

"Naomi?"

She halted on her way to the door and turned to find Joseph watching her, looking uncomfortable.

"Ja?"

"If you would like a rocker for yourself, you've only to ask. I'll make you one as a wedding gift, if that's what you want."

A wedding gift. Naomi's mouth went dry, and she had to fight to swallow. "So Isaac has approved our plans, then?"

"He has. He was kind about it. Afterward I stopped in at the store and called up to Ohio so Melvin could start looking out for a nice house for us."

A house for us. Her brain kept replaying phrases Joseph spoke, wondering over them. "Oh, Joseph! A house of our own." A smile spread over her face like butter on warm bread. "That's so exciting!"

Joseph smiled back, but he shook his head. "Don't get too excited. Melvin's idea of nice and yours may be different. We won't be able to afford much, in any case, so whatever house we get will likely be small and need some fixing."

She didn't care. It would be her home, hers and Joseph's. Naomi lifted her chin. "I will not complain," she promised him.

"Nee." Joseph stubbed the toe of his boot into the sawdust on the floor. "You never do complain, Naomi, but once we're married, I hope you'll tell me, straight out, anytime you want something. I can be"—he hesitated a second before continuing—"thickheaded when it comes to guessing such things, but I've no wish to see you unhappy."

Once we're married. Naomi's heart caught mid-beat at his words, and her smile widened. "You're not so thickheaded, Joseph."

"Emma says different. I happened to catch her in the phone shack when I called, and she nearly tore a strip off my hide when I told her I'd been to see Isaac about marrying us here in Johns Mill. I never even asked you about that, Naomi, and it was selfish of me. Would you rather get married in Kentucky? I'm not sure if your bishop will understand our situation as Isaac does, but if it is important to you, we can wait if we have to. I'll move on up to Ohio with Miriam, and we can be married afterward, just as well."

Naomi thought quickly. Her bishop was a very kind and devout man, but he was also old and set in his ways. He was not prone to bending rules, no matter how logical the argument was. He was one of the reasons that her own surgery had been delayed for so long, against the worried urging of her pediatric cardiologist. Bishop Charlie Atlee hadn't felt comfortable approving a confusing heart surgery that he couldn't square with his beliefs. He'd finally relented, but it had been a very near thing.

Charlie would never agree to shortcut a marriage process, and she privately feared that if she delayed very long, the wedding might not happen at all.

She shook her head firmly. "*Denki*, but I think we should be married here. My brothers and their families will come if they can, but I'd really like to keep it simple. I'm as close to Katie as I am to anybody in my family in Kentucky. Maybe she will let me be married from her home. I can ask her."

Joseph's brow furrowed in concern as he studied her. "Are you sure, then, Naomi? Weddings are special times for girls. I don't want you regretting anything later."

"I won't. I am . . ." She halted, searching for the right word. It came to her quickly. "Content," she finished firmly. "I am content, Joseph, with what you have planned. Truly."

One corner of his mouth tipped up. "All right, then. We'll go ahead with things as they are. And you can tell me just what you'd like me to make for you, and I'll get right on it."

Naomi smiled back, but she shook her head. "Please, don't trouble yourself. You haven't the time to make me anything, not if you're going to finish all your other orders."

"I'll make the time. I'm not offering you much as your husband, Naomi. I know that. You might as well take what little I do have to give."

The best furniture he could make for her. His unfailing kindness. A home of her very own. Those were the things Joseph was offering her. Joseph wasn't giving himself near enough credit. Those were fine things, far better than any whistles or romantic looks.

"I'll like anything you make, Joseph," she murmured, feeling strangely shy. She'd not expected this, and she didn't want to put Joseph to any extra trouble. "But don't you think maybe you should wait until we're in Ohio? If you make me something now, it would just be another thing for us to move, ain't so?"

He looked a little taken aback, but he nodded readily enough. "I suppose you're right. Anyhow, if you want a rocking chair, there'll likely be time for me to make you one after we are settled, before any babies start coming along."

Babies. Naomi could feel her cheeks flushing hot as the wonder of that word dawned fully upon her. Of course. She and Joseph would have children, likely. Strong-shouldered sons with Joseph's unruly cowlick and his gift of working with wood, or sweet girls, maybe, with his green-flecked eyes and a hint of his smile.

She felt a desperate need to get off somewhere by herself. She wanted to turn this idea over and over in her mind, considering it from every promising angle, like a toddler scurrying off to a corner to examine a stolen treasure. "I'd . . . better get back. I will see you in the house, Joseph."

She got through the door and snatched up the egg basket

she'd left beside the barn. But she made it only halfway across the yard before she had to stop and catch her breath, pressing her hand hard against her hammering heart.

Joy shifted hard into fear, as she faced what she'd been pushing aside for weeks. These spells of hers were getting worse.

Something wasn't right.

She'd been assuring herself that she was only nervous and overexcited, but she'd just fallen asleep sitting in a freezing-cold barn simply because she'd sat down for a moment. She couldn't remember the last time she'd been able to go up the stairs without having to stop on the landing to catch her breath.

She'd tried not to think about it. She hadn't wanted to think about it, to consider what this might mean. There was far too much at stake for her to have something wrong with her health right now.

But now Joseph was talking about babies. That idea made her feel as warm and gooey as a fresh brownie and took every bit of the starch out of her knees, but it also meant that she couldn't brush aside these strange symptoms anymore.

She needed to make an appointment to see a doctor, and soon. At least she knew where to go. When Naomi had announced her plans to come to Tennessee, her doctor back home had insisted on giving her the name of a good cardiologist in Knoxville.

The question was how she'd get there without making a big—and hopefully unnecessary—fuss. A trip so far out of town would require an *Englisch* driver. That cost money, and it would probably take all the cash she had just to pay for the doctor's visit. Besides, the reliable drivers around here were shared by all the families, and word of her errand would certainly leak out. She'd rather keep this quiet.

Naomi's mind lit on the card Eric had given her, tucked carefully away in a keepsake box back at Katie's. She'd been on pins and needles after the pie incident, but Joseph had never mentioned it, and she'd not had to explain. If the other reporters were back in town, likely Eric was here, too. If he was, he would drive her to her appointment if she asked him. She was sure of that.

She resumed her walk across the yard with a purposeful step. Tomorrow she would take Eric's card and the cardiologist's number down to the phone shack on the other side of Katie's house and make the necessary calls.

Likely, she was worrying over nothing, but before the wedding plans went any further, she'd best find out for certain.

CHAPTER TWENTY-THREE

❧

JOSEPH IMPATIENTLY BRUSHED ASIDE THE CURTAIN on the kitchen window and peered at the still-dark road. No sign of Naomi, not yet. She and Aaron were running late this morning.

He glanced at the clock on the wall. It was well past time for milking, but Daisy would have to wait a little longer. He wasn't going out to the barn until he'd talked with Naomi.

Thanks to his interfering *onkel*, Joseph had some apologizing to do. Barely a week had passed by since he'd let Emma know of his plans to marry Naomi, and already Melvin was causing trouble.

Joseph glanced at the crumpled paper in his hand, and the anger he'd been battling since last night rose like bile in the back of his throat. The letter had been in the mailbox yesterday morning, but Joseph hadn't gotten around to opening it until after Naomi had gone home. By the time he'd reached the final sentence, he'd been mad at both Melvin and at himself.

He should have seen this coming. He would've if he'd been thinking straight.

Truth was, he'd been featherheaded for days, ever since Naomi's pretty eyes had lit up when he'd talked about finding them a house in Ohio. Then, when he'd made that offhand remark about the *kinder* he hoped *Gott* would bless them with, she'd blushed just the color of those pink roses that tumbled over the back pasture fence at the beginning of every June.

Ja, that blush had pretty much finished him off. He hadn't been able to think straight since. And now, Melvin had ruined everything.

He smoothed the letter and read it for the dozenth time. Phrases written in his uncle's spidery hand leapt out at him, each one worse than the last.

Emma has told me of your plans to marry the sickly maidel.

Poor choice for a fraw.

Disgraceful hurry.

The look of wrongdoing.

Only one reason couples marry in such haste.

Shame. Foolishness.

And finally, the sentence that had struck a chill right down to the marrow of his bones:

I have written to this girl as well, in your father's place.

He recrumpled the paper and prayed for the hundredth time that Naomi's letter had been delayed, so that he could warn her of this ahead of time.

He lifted his head and looked sharply toward the window, listening. *Ja*, that was the clop of hooves and the jingle of harness. Aaron's buggy was coming to a stop in the yard.

He moved to stand just inside the door, waiting impatiently. He heard Naomi's soft voice, and the deep rumble of Aaron's reply. No doubt she was thanking him for the ride, even though it was a daily routine for them now. Naomi was always careful to thank a fellow for anything he did for her, no matter how small it might be or how often he did it.

Just as he heard Aaron's sharp urge to his horse, the doorknob turned, and Naomi pushed open the door. She gasped, her clear, gray-green eyes widening as she saw him standing so close.

"My, you startled me, Joseph! I never expected to see you in the house. I'd thought you'd be in the barn by now." She began to untie her black bonnet, her pale brows drawn together in concern. "Is something wrong?"

That's exactly what he wanted her to tell him. He searched her face before he answered, looking for trouble. He saw none. Naomi only looked flummoxed by being pounced on. Other than that, she seemed perfectly normal.

His muscles relaxed in a rush of sweet relief. *Gott* had answered his prayers. She'd not received Melvin's letter yet. Now, if he could convince her to hand it over to him unread, he'd burn the awful thing to ashes.

Naomi's frown deepened, and she glanced past him toward the stairs. "Is Miriam all right?"

"*Ja*, she is still sleeping, I think. There is nothing wrong. Except—" He broke off. How exactly was he going to explain this?

"Except what?"

He drew in a deep breath. "I must ask you to do me a kindness, Naomi. And I will not be able to explain very well why I am asking you for it."

She was watching him closely. A tiny smile tickled over

her lips, but she nodded seriously. "I will do any kindness you ask of me, Joseph, if I can. What is it?"

"Soon you'll be receiving a letter from my uncle in Ohio. I would ask you to give it to me without reading it. Will you do that?"

Naomi had turned to hang her shawl and bonnet on the pegs beside the door. He saw her hands falter. "You don't wish for me to read this letter? Why not?"

He couldn't explain, not in any way that wouldn't make things worse. "All I can tell you is that I think it's necessary that you give it to me unopened." She still had her back to him. She was fussing over hanging her shawl just right, so he couldn't judge her expression. "I ask you to trust me in this, Naomi," he added desperately. "Please."

She finally got the shawl draped properly and turned to face him. "I do trust you, Joseph," she said quietly, "but I'm afraid I cannot do what you are asking. Melvin's letter arrived yesterday, and I have already read it."

His heart crashed to his boots, and for the first time in his life, he nearly said one of those words Caleb used to mutter whenever one of the cows slashed him in the face with a mucky tail.

"*Ach*, Naomi. I'm sorry. I truly am. I can guess what it said because I've had a letter from him myself. Melvin's troubles have made him a sour, suspicious old man. You mustn't pay any heed to what he wrote."

"Perhaps your uncle could have been kinder, but he's right, Joseph. I mean"—a little flush crept up her neck to stain her cheeks—"not about everything, of course. He's not wrong, though, that some people might think and say things if we marry so quick."

And that was another thing he hadn't even thought of, until Melvin had pointed it out. "Does that bother you? That people may talk?"

"*Nee*, not really. That's the kind of truth that cannot be

hidden for long, ain't so? People will know soon enough. If they want to make themselves look foolish gossiping about us beforehand, it's of no concern to me."

He couldn't keep his lips from curving up into a grin. "*Gut.* And I hope you will forgive my uncle. I'm going to speak to him about this. It won't happen again." It wouldn't. Joseph would see to it.

"Maybe Melvin could have chosen his words better, but in his way, I think he was trying to look out for you as a father would." Naomi tilted her head, considering him like a worried sparrow. "And he's right about another thing, too, you know. You could find yourself a better wife than I, Joseph, easily enough. A prettier, smarter girl that you"—she paused delicately—"could have more feelings for than just friendship. Me, I don't have so many choices, so this decision is easier for me. But you . . . well. This hard season will not last forever, though it may seem so just now. Marriage is for life. I wouldn't want you to have regrets."

Melvin's letter must have been worse than he'd thought. Joseph was not a violent man, but at that moment, he could have cheerfully wrung his uncle's stringy neck. "I'm not going to have any regrets about marrying you, Naomi. You're the most—" Footsteps sounded on the staircase, and he glanced over his shoulder to see Miriam coming slowly down. She smiled shyly at the two of them.

"I'm sorry. I hope I am not interrupting anything."

Joseph fell awkwardly silent, and his sister shot him a teasing glance. He was torn between being grateful to see that familiar expression on her face and feeling acutely embarrassed.

He wasn't sure what he'd been going to tell Naomi after what she'd said about him finding a "smarter, prettier girl" but he knew it wasn't something he'd have wanted his sister to overhear.

"Not at all," Naomi reassured Miriam. "I was just about to tell your *bruder* that I need to leave at lunchtime tomorrow. I have some business to attend to in Knoxville in the afternoon."

She reached above the stove to pull a skillet out of the cupboard. "I can have scrambled eggs ready right quick if you'd rather eat before going out to the barn, Joseph."

Joseph frowned, distracted from his concerns about his uncle's letter. There was something odd about the way Naomi had skipped so lightly over that thing about going into town. "What kind of personal business? Is Katie going with you?"

"Joseph!" Miriam scolded as she went to the small gas refrigerator to retrieve the eggs. "You mustn't ask too many questions. Maybe Naomi has things she must see to before the wedding." His sister smiled at Naomi as she handed her the bowl of brown eggs. "I wish I could go with you, Naomi. But I . . ." Miriam shivered and shook her head sadly.

"That is all right." Naomi smiled warmly at Miriam. "Get the butter for me, too, would you, please?"

When Miriam turned away, Naomi glanced at Joseph. When their eyes met, her expression became serious. "It's just something I need to tend to, Joseph, that's all." A smile quivered over her lips, and she dropped her voice to add, "I ask you to trust me in this."

He still would have liked to know what errand was taking her all the way to Knoxville and how she planned to get there. However, there was little a man could do when he'd just had his own words thrown back in his face.

He nodded reluctantly. "All right, then. Do as it suits you." He shot a cautious look in Miriam's direction. "That letter we were speaking of? I'd like to read it, if you wouldn't mind." No matter what Naomi said about Melvin's intentions, Joseph planned to take his uncle to task, and he wanted to be sure he had his facts straight when he did.

Naomi lifted her eyebrows as she dropped a thick pat of homemade butter into the heating skillet, but she nodded. "I'll bring it with me tomorrow morning."

Miriam halted beside the table, three plates stacked in her hands. Her eyes darted between Joseph and Naomi. "What letter?"

"Who just scolded me for asking questions about private things?" Joseph lifted an eyebrow.

His sister's shoulders relaxed. She wrinkled her nose at him as she'd done back when she was a little girl, and she began setting the breakfast table.

"Best take up my plate, Miriam. I've got to get out to the barn. Daisy will be tired of waiting on me to do the milking, for certain."

Naomi nodded. "I'll put your breakfast in the oven to keep warm, and I'll have the *kaffe* hot when you come back with the milk. There's a chill today."

"*Denki*," he said quietly. "We'll talk soon again, Naomi." She glanced up from the eggs she was cracking and gave him another little smile.

Once outside, he trudged across the frost-crisped yard toward the barn. Naomi was right. It was sharp today. Or maybe he was just missing the gentle warmth of the kitchen.

He halted, the steel milk pail swinging from his gloved hand and turned to look at the house behind him. Naomi was framed in the glowing kitchen window, frowning slightly, intent on the eggs she was scrambling. Joseph's sore heart turned over ponderously, like an old dog stretching aching bones in the heat of the sun.

She used to frown at him like that when they were *youngies* and he'd drop behind to walk with her after her brothers had leapt ahead. She'd urge him to go ahead, not to miss his fun because of her. She'd told him over and over that she didn't mind walking alone.

Maybe she hadn't minded, but he had minded for her. She was a nice girl, and he'd always thought she'd deserved better treatment. Now he knew for certain sure she did. There was no "sweeter, prettier, smarter girl," not for Joseph, but he could hardly blame Naomi for thinking that way, given how he'd behaved.

Naomi Schrock deserved the best any fellow could give her, especially one hoping to be her husband. But what had Joseph offered? A blurted-out proposal, with no soft words, no little sweetnesses.

He'd no excuse for that. He had two sisters, and he knew well enough what such things meant to girls. He was no better than Naomi's thoughtless brothers, no better than Melvin himself, to ask so much while treating her so carelessly in return.

She was a wonderful girl, Naomi was. The best kind of girl. She should have had it all, the moonlit drives, the quiet, shy talks, the little sweets or gifts a fellow offered when he was trying to woo a sweetheart.

He'd given her none of that, just a bald-faced offer of marriage and a quick, embarrassing wedding.

Joseph watched for another second or two, until Naomi took the skillet off the heat and moved out of the window's frame.

Then he blinked. He was cold to the bone, and his heart was pounding hard in a combination of shame and determination.

He'd made a muddle of this, but maybe he could still set things right. He'd think it through while he finished the chores. He'd always found it easier to think out in the barn.

Hopefully he'd come up with some ideas. If he planned to court Naomi Schrock before she became his wife, he was running out of time.

CHAPTER TWENTY-FOUR

❧

THE NEXT AFTERNOON, NAOMI BUCKLED HERSELF into the passenger seat of Eric's tiny car, hoping the forecasted snow held off until she was safely back home again. She was trying not to be nervous, but this felt very different from the minivans and trucks she'd ridden in before. The seats in those vehicles were higher up, much like riding in a buggy. This car was so low-slung, she might as well be sitting on the road itself.

Still, beggars shouldn't be choosers. "Thank you very much for driving me."

"You're welcome. So we've got about forty-five minutes to kill, according to my GPS," Eric said as he pulled onto the highway. "Why don't you tell me what this is all about?"

"I told you already. I have a doctor's appointment."

"That's all you told me." He gave her a quick, sideways glance. "I'm not trying to be nosy. It's just . . . I'm a little worried. Is something wrong, Naomi?"

She sure hoped not. She offered him a smile. "That's what people go to doctors' offices to find out, ain't so?"

"Are you having symptoms? You must be, or you wouldn't have made the appointment in the first place." Eric drummed his fingers on the steering wheel as he waited for a buggy to take its turn at the four-way stop. "I'm sorry, Naomi. Cassidy and I were so happy that you got better, you know? That you had a chance for a normal life like you always wanted."

The past tenses Eric was using made her stomach clench, reminding her that his sister hadn't been blessed with the same chance. Maybe she should have chosen somebody else to drive her for this errand, but Eric had seemed the simplest choice. She'd never considered the painful memories her situation might bring up in him. She'd been focused only on herself.

"This appointment is just a precaution," she reassured him gently. "I'm not having any of the symptoms I had before." She wasn't. That much was true. She was having new ones, but Eric didn't need to know that.

He gave her a suspicious look as they turned on to the four-lane highway heading out of Johns Mill toward Knoxville. "I don't understand, then. What's going on, Naomi? I'd like to help if I can."

"You are already helping by driving me to the appointment. And you must let me pay for your fuel." She'd brought all the cash she had, and she prayed that it would be enough to cover both Eric's gas and the cost of the doctor's visit. Before she'd left Kentucky, her doctor had said this particular cardiologist was accustomed to seeing Amish patients. Hopefully he would have some sort of reduced-fee schedule for folks without insurance.

"You're not paying me a cent. I'm happy you asked me." He gave her a rueful grin. "I kinda miss having a kid sister to look after, you know? But I still don't think you're being straight with me. This feels like a rush appointment, and you've told me at least six times not to mention it to anybody. What's with that?"

Naomi glanced at the dashboard clock. They'd been in the car a grand total of eight minutes. She'd best go ahead and give Eric a piece of the truth. Maybe then he'd quit probing.

She tightened her interlaced fingers and forced herself to speak brightly. "Well, the truth is, I'm getting married."

"What?" Eric braked so hard, they both jolted against their seat belts. Muttering under his breath, he flipped on the blinker and moved the car onto the shoulder of the highway. Horns blared as other vehicles whizzed by, but he ignored them. He shoved the car in park and twisted to face Naomi. "You're getting married?"

"That's right." She craned her neck to look behind them. "Are you supposed to be stopped here, Eric? The other drivers seem upset."

"Never mind them. You're serious?"

"Yes."

"Wow." Eric leaned against his seat and shook his head, still staring at Naomi. "Wouldn't Cassidy have loved this! Our Amish little sister is getting married. I don't know whether I should shake this guy's hand or punch him in the nose. So who's the lucky man?"

Naomi hesitated, unsure what to say. Eric was a friend, but she couldn't afford to forget that he was also a reporter.

"We are alike in so many ways, but we are different in this, Eric. Among the Plain, engagements are considered very private things. Even friends are often not told until the wedding is planned and everything is in order. They may guess, but they do not know for sure."

"Oh." He looked taken aback. "I'm sorry. I didn't know that."

"That's all right. Of course you didn't know."

"Well, congratulations. Or best wishes, or whatever is the right thing to say."

"Thank you." She turned her eyes expectantly to the front, waiting for him to merge back into the speeding traffic.

Instead Eric cleared his throat.

"I'm probably trampling all over a whole bunch of Amish taboos right now, Naomi, but this fiancé of yours. He isn't the guy you've been working for, is he?" Eric's eyes searched hers. "Oh, wow. He is."

"Joseph Hochstedler is a *gut* man, Eric," she said quietly.

"Well, he's better than that hotheaded brother of his from all I've heard. But man, Naomi . . ." He trailed off, looking uncomfortable. "There are all kinds of stories going around about that family. Most of them probably aren't true, but that doesn't mean trouble can't come from them, especially since you folks never want to get in front of the cameras to tell your side of things. And I don't know if you've heard, but there's likely to be more publicity coming. I just hate to see you getting tangled up in all this."

"Eric—"

"Nope," Eric cut in quickly. "For Pete's sake, don't tell me anything else, Naomi. Do you have any idea what this kind of information is worth? Don't tell me, and don't tell anybody else, either, especially not about the wedding." The urgency in his voice made her draw back. "You have no idea what kind of media storm that little tidbit could unleash."

"I'm not about to go around blabbing, Eric. I'm not so *dumm* as that. Anyhow, I wasn't involved in what happened, and except for the sorrow of losing his parents, Joseph had no part in it, either. We're small potatoes. Nobody's likely to care if we get married or not."

"Trust me, they'll care plenty. This story is smoldering under the surface, but it could flame up again at any moment. People are fascinated by all this, so it's had a longer shelf life than stories usually do. And your Joseph isn't as small a potato as you may think. That shot of him shaking Stephen Abbott's hand the day of the funerals? You wouldn't believe how much money that brought. Only one guy had the best angle, and let me tell you, he cleaned up. Adding more romance to this story right now would be like throwing gasoline on a bonfire." Eric ran one hand through his shaggy hair. "My producer would totally lose his stuff if he found out there was a Hochstedler wedding planned. I wish you hadn't told me."

"I only told you I was getting married. You guessed the rest."

"It wasn't hard. Never try to play poker, sis. Any card player worth his salt would read that face of yours like a book." He checked the traffic over his left shoulder before pulling back out onto the highway. "If it's okay with you, I'm going to turn on the radio. Otherwise, I'm going to want to ask you questions, and we're both better off if I don't do that. Okay?"

"Okay."

Eric pressed buttons on his dashboard until he found a Christian station. Since he had to do a lot of fiddling to find it, Naomi doubted it was a station he usually listened to, and she appreciated his kindness in trying to find something he thought wouldn't offend her. She didn't recognize any of the songs, but it was nice of him to make the effort.

They rode in silence until they reached Knoxville. Eric pressed more buttons on the cell phone in the holder attached to his dash, and an electronic female voice guided them to a large brick building across the street from a sprawling medical center.

Naomi glanced at the hospital's crowded parking lot and suppressed a shudder. No telling what all those folks were dealing with. No doubt some of them were experiencing one of the hardest days of their lives. Others would be experiencing the very last day of their lives, or of the life of someone they loved.

But, she reminded herself, kind nurses and doctors were there working, and no doubt babies were being born today, too. Joy bloomed right in the middle of sorrow, often as not. A person just had to decide which she was going to focus on.

"I don't know how long my appointment will take," she explained apologetically to Eric. "Feel free to go wherever you like. I can wait here if I am finished before you get back."

"There's nowhere I need to go. But hold up a second." He levered up on one hip and pried a wallet out of his back pocket. He flipped it open and thumbed through its pockets. "Here. Take this in with you, just in case." He handed her a silver card.

She accepted it automatically turning it to read the writing. Then she tried to return it. "This is your credit card."

"I saw you going through your purse a few times on the way over, counting your bills. I know you don't have insurance, and you're obviously worried about having enough cash. If it turns out that you don't, just put it on my card."

"Oh, Eric, that's very nice of you, but I couldn't do such a thing."

"Sure you can. If you don't need it, fine, but if you do, you'll have it. Please, Naomi. We could both use one less thing to worry about, I think."

Naomi hesitated then nodded. She could take it in with her, if that made Eric happy. She didn't have to use it. "*Denki*. You are very kind."

"You're welcome." He smiled, his eyes gentle and sad. "I'd offer to come in, but honestly, doctors' offices make me break out in a cold sweat ever since . . . these days. But I really hope you get good news, Naomi."

She smiled back as she opened the car door. "So do I."

Eric wasn't the only one who got *naerfich* in doctors' offices. Naomi's whole body tensed the minute she walked into the beige and ice blue waiting room. She'd never been in this particular office before, but it felt far too familiar.

As usual, she was by far the youngest person there. Most of the other folks were gray-haired, and several had oxygen

tanks parked by their chairs. Naomi went to the half-moon
reception desk and picked up the pen to sign herself in.

The plump, middle-aged receptionist gave her a brief
professional smile. Curiosity glinted in the woman's dark
eyes as she scanned Naomi's clothes. She flipped the chart
around to look at the name. "Naomi Schrock?"

"Yes."

The woman tapped keys on her computer and frowned at
the monitor. "We have the records from your cardiologist in
Kentucky, so we'll just need you to fill out a couple of forms
for our office." She clamped papers to a clipboard and
handed them to Naomi along with a ballpoint pen. "Dr. Lawson has been called away, so a nurse will be doing your
initial evaluation. I assume that's all right?"

Naomi bit her lip. Her cardiologist back home had told
her this doctor was accustomed to seeing Amish patients,
that he understood their ways and their boundaries. Well,
she'd just have to hope that understanding extended to his
staff.

"That's fine."

She settled in a nearby chair, nestling her small tote bag
between her feet so she could balance the clipboard on her
knees. She'd barely finished the forms when a nurse with
iron gray hair and a no-nonsense expression beckoned to her.

"I'm Deborah," the nurse said over her shoulder as she
walked Naomi through a maze of examination rooms. "I'll
be doing your examination today. Dr. Lawson was called to
emergency surgery." She led the way into a small room and
bumped the door shut with one substantial hip, studying a
little tablet she held in her hand. "Hop up on the table,
there, please. You're having some symptoms?"

"*Ja.* I mean, yes."

"I understood you, don't worry about that. We get a lot
of Amish folks in here. So what's going on?"

"Mostly I'm just getting tired too easily," Naomi explained. "I've been working more, so hopefully it's nothing, but I thought I'd best check."

Deborah nodded as she checked Naomi's blood pressure. "Always good to be sure, hon." The nurse pulled the stethoscope from around her neck. She plugged the ends in her ears before sliding the metal piece under Naomi's cape to the fabric just above her heart.

The nurse's expression shifted, and Naomi knew.

She knew before Deborah told her that she needed to do an EKG and a sonogram in the office, even though the nurse's face never registered anything after that first unguarded moment. She knew, even though Deborah told her that the results would have to be gone over by Dr. Lawson himself, so there would be no answers that day.

Something was wrong. The cage that she'd escaped was closing, and once again she was on the wrong side of the door.

Before leaving, she was given a time to call in to speak with the cardiologist in a few days, proof that the practice really was accustomed to dealing with Amish patients. Naomi counted out the bills from her purse with surprisingly steady fingers, grateful for the substantial discount she received as an uninsured patient, paying with cash. She had enough money, and that was a blessing.

Somehow that little success made her feel better. She mustn't let herself get upset. She must trust *Gott*, just as she'd had to do when she'd been sick before. Whatever happened from here on, she'd accept His will with all the grace and courage she could muster. She'd witnessed Miriam and Joseph Hochstedler doing that very thing, as they walked through their troubles, so she had good examples to follow.

What, she wondered, should she tell them about all this? She tucked her deflated wallet back into her bag as she thought it over. She'd wait, she decided. She'd hold off until after she'd talked to the doctor before discussing this with

Joseph. She hadn't said anything before because she'd hoped that today she'd get a quick reassurance that nothing was really wrong.

That hadn't happened, but she still didn't know anything for certain. The concerned expression on the nurse's face might have meant nothing at all. Naomi wouldn't know for sure until the phone call with the cardiologist—if then. Probably they would want to run further tests. Doctors almost always did.

She'd wait until after the phone appointment, but then she'd have to talk this over with Joseph. Her stomach dipped as she realized what that talk would likely lead to . . . but then she pushed the thought out of her mind.

She wouldn't cross that bridge until she had to. She'd gotten through the roughest parts of her long illness that way, by living one day at a time, and enjoying whatever blessings she was given to the fullest.

Outside Eric was waiting in his tiny car. He glanced up as she opened the door.

"How'd it go?"

She managed a smile. "They ran some tests, but I'll not know anything for a few days." She didn't want him to ask any more questions, so she quickly changed the subject. "Is there anything else you need to do in Knoxville while we are here?"

Eric's smile dimmed. He understood, she realized, without her having to say a word. "There's nothing I need to do, but I'll take you anyplace you want to go, Naomi. Anyplace at all."

"Just home." She settled against the seat and sighed. "Thank you, but I just want to go home."

They drove back in a companionable silence. By the time they'd hit Johns Mill, the light was beginning to dim, and the promised snow had begun to fall. Great, fat flakes drifted down like wet bits of lace.

As Eric pulled into the Lapps' driveway, Naomi leaned

forward against the seat belt. A horse and buggy waited near the front porch. She frowned, peering through the dim light.

Sure enough, that was Titus standing in the falling snow. What was Joseph doing here? Miriam could never have ridden over to the Lapps'. She couldn't even force herself to venture outside the house. What was going on?

Well, there was only one way to find out.

She turned to Eric. "Thank you for the ride."

"I was glad to do it, Naomi. If you need another ride for follow-ups or anything, please don't hesitate to ask."

"I will let you know. *Denki-shay*, Eric."

Joseph walked out of the shadows on the front porch, and Naomi was thankful for the screening snow. He wouldn't be able to see who was driving; not that he would have recognized Eric anyway. Even so she hoped Joseph wouldn't ask any questions. She had a feeling he'd not approve of her having a reporter drive her anyplace, no matter how well she knew him.

She got out of the car and hurried toward the porch. "Joseph! It is a surprise to see you here! Is something wrong with Miriam?"

"Nee." He was frowning slightly, watching Eric turn his car around. "Miriam is all right. Katie and Aaron have gone over with the *boppli* to visit for a few hours, so I came here. I don't recognize that driver. Who is it?"

"Oh, that's *gut!*" Naomi skipped over the question. "Miriam will enjoy playing with Sarah. But you should have stayed there, Joseph, to enjoy the visit, too."

The distraction seemed to work. As Eric's beetle-car scooted safely off down the road, Joseph dropped his gaze to his feet. *"Ja*, well. I had other plans." He kicked one boot against the post of the porch, as if suddenly interested in the soundness of the wood. "The truth is, I asked them to come over. I needed them to keep Miriam company so I could be here to meet you when you got back."

"Oh?" In spite of her new worries, sweet warmth expanded in her breast. What a very Joseph-like thing to do. "That was real kind of you, but I'm sorry you put yourself to such trouble on my account."

"It was no trouble." He kicked the post again. "If you're not too worn out from your trip, I was wondering if you would like to go for a ride."

Naomi crinkled her brow, puzzled. "A ride? Now? Wherever to?"

The glow from the battery-operated lantern in the living room window revealed a tide of red rising into Joseph's cheeks. "Nowhere in particular. It'll be right pretty, maybe, with the snow falling. We'll stay off the main roads, so you'd have no need to feel *naerfich*. So? What do you think? Would you like to go for a drive with me, Naomi?"

Naomi didn't understand what was happening for a couple more seconds, and when the truth finally dawned, she was too astonished to answer right away. She'd seen the bravest boys asking the prettiest girls similar questions at the singings she'd attended, all with the same hopeful, shamefaced expressions. *Can I drive you home, then?*

But nobody had ever asked Naomi such a question, not until this minute.

The prickly worries of the day slipped away, replaced with a grateful, glowing joy. Maybe she didn't know what her future held, but right now, in this moment, she was happier than she'd thought she'd ever be.

Joseph Hochstedler had come courting, and she meant to enjoy every second of it.

"*Ja*," she answered shyly. "I think a drive in the snow with you would be wonderful fun, Joseph."

His slow, answering smile warmed her all the way to her chilly fingertips. "That's what I hoped you'd say."

Chapter Twenty-Five

❧

JOSEPH OFFERED NAOMI HIS HAND AS SHE CLIMBED into the waiting buggy. Her slender fingers pressed gently down on his as she boosted herself up. Feeling as skittish as a teenager, he hurried around to climb in himself.

"It's a sharp night," he said, reaching to pull a thick blanket from the back seat. "Best tuck this around you real snug."

"Denki." She shook the heavy fabric open and layered it over her dress. He waited until she was well settled, then snapped the reins on Titus's back and clucked to the horse.

"Don't worry," he reassured her as he pulled onto the road. "We'll only be on the highway for a minute."

"I am not worried, Joseph."

There was a strangely determined note in her voice, and he shot her a curious look. It was no use; he couldn't read her expression in the dim glow from the battery-operated lights Caleb had installed on the buggy dash a few years back.

"Courting lights," his *daed* had called them with an

understanding chuckle. Newer buggies came with such lights, but until Caleb got to tinkering, the Hochstedlers had made do with a kerosene lantern hung on the side of the buggy. These lights were stronger and made night driving far easier.

His father had tweaked their position so that they cast some light into the depths of the buggy as well as the road ahead. When Caleb protested, *Daed* had given him a knowing look and a shake of the head. "*Gott* sees well even in the dark, son. But your *mamm* and I will sleep better if other folks can see you, too."

Joseph cast around in his mind for something to make small talk about. He was rusty at this. He'd never courted much. Once he'd set his heart on Rhoda, he'd not so much as looked at another girl.

Until Naomi.

He turned off the highway onto a narrow lane, glancing warily at Naomi as he did. This little road wasn't often traveled by *Englischers*, but it was a favorite among the Plain *youngies* in the area. It wound its way through conveniently secluded pastures, and there was a bridge over a tumbling creek that was a well-known smooching spot. The road's real name was Cobbler Creek Road, but it had a descriptive nickname that he hoped Naomi hadn't heard.

She shifted in the seat and lifted an eyebrow. "We're taking Kissing Creek Road?"

So she had heard the name. He felt his cheeks burning in spite of the chilly air. "I'm not—I didn't think . . ." He was stammering like a fool. "I was only looking for a quiet place to drive. I know you don't like being on a road with cars, especially in the dark."

"It is a *gut* choice, Joseph. There'll likely be no traffic on this little road tonight, and it'll be real pretty with the snow falling down, ain't so?"

Naomi sounded so placid that Joseph's own nervousness

melted, like the snowflakes falling on Titus's broad back. "I reckon we'll see."

Naomi was easy for a fellow to be with. She always seemed content, so peaceful and calm. Spending time with her felt like slipping into the comfort of the house after working long hours outside in the cold. It warmed him all the way to his bones.

They clopped along the quiet road in silence for a few seconds. Then he cleared his throat.

"I've mailed off a letter to Melvin, Naomi. I did my best to make things clear to him. If he says anything else unkind to you, you must tell me, and I will deal with him." With Melvin, it was more like *when* than *if*, and he wanted to be sure Naomi was prepared.

Naomi turned from the snow swirling outside the buggy and looked at him. "You are planning to work for Melvin at his dairy when you go to Ohio, ain't so?"

"When *we* go to Ohio," he corrected quietly.

Naomi lowered her head so that her bonnet shadowed her face. "When *we* go," she repeated, and he heard the hint of a smile in her voice.

That made him happy.

"*Ja*. I will be working for him. He can speak to me however he likes, but I'll not have him speaking to you rudely. Nor Miriam, nor Emma, not in my presence anyhow."

"Is that really what you want to do, Joseph? Work for your *onkel*?"

"It'll suit. Dairying is all I know, and Melvin needs the help, so it makes *gut* sense."

"That is not what I asked, and dairying is not all you know. You know woodworking, too."

True enough, and he was less keen on spending his days working cows if it also meant working with Melvin. He knew his cantankerous uncle too well to feel any different, but he'd already thought this through.

"Melvin's community isn't as friendly with the *Englisch*, and there's not so much trade. It's smaller, too, so not many customers among the Plain folks, either. I don't think my woodworking will be much help to us. Oh, I'll take my tools up and try to add some money to the household, but I don't expect it'll amount to anything. Don't worry yourself. With the dairy work and the lease money from the farm, I should be able to provide for you all right, so long as we're careful."

"I know you will provide for me, Joseph, but I also would like to see you happy."

They'd just driven onto the small bridge, and the horse's hooves hit the wooden timbers with muffled beats. Naomi was looking out over Titus's back, her profile hidden by the sides of her bonnet. When Joseph slowed the buggy to a stop, she glanced at him, the pale curves of her face barely visible in the dim light coming from the dash.

"I would like to see you happy, too, Naomi." He searched his mind for the *gut* words to say, the right words that always seemed to slip past him somehow. "As your husband, I will do my best to make you so."

"*Denki*, Joseph." She answered him seriously, but her lips curved into a gentle smile. "As your wife, I will do the same for you."

As your wife. In just a few weeks, he and Naomi would be bound together before *Gott* for the rest of their lives. Maybe he should have felt some caution about that, some uncertainty, especially given the circumstances. Instead he felt only a sense of deep relief. He still couldn't quite believe this sweet-hearted girl had agreed to marry him, Joseph Hochstedler, with his stumbling tongue and all his trials and troubles. His heart swelled with gratitude . . . and with something else, too, something deeper and surer.

Naomi Schrock was the woman *Gott* had set aside for him, and he loved her with everything that was in him. He always would. He recognized that truth with the same joyful thump of sureness as when he chose just the right piece of wood for a project.

This one right here. Only this one will suit.

Swamped by a crazy swell of rising joy, Joseph stopped thinking altogether. He leaned forward, cupping Naomi's chin gently with one hand, and he kissed her.

Her lips were soft and warm under his, and when he drew back, her eyes were round with surprise.

"Oh!" The word rushed out on a quick, unsteady breath. Her eyes searched his, and Joseph knew that the next thing he said mattered more than anything he'd ever said before. He felt a twinge of panic.

"I'm no *gut* at this," he murmured, holding her gaze desperately with his. "The talking, I mean. I'll likely make a muddle of it, same as always, but I want you to understand before we take this any further. You are a fine person, Naomi, and the sweetest woman I've ever met. I can't offer you much, but you deserve the best of me, and you'll have that, such as it is. With *Gott*'s help, I'll give you the happiest life I can."

In the flickering light from the dash lamp, he watched her expression soften. She reached out a tentative hand, laying it lightly against his cheek. No other woman had ever touched him so, and he raised his own hand to press her chilled fingers more closely against the warmth of his skin.

For a second, they simply sat there looking at each other, as snowflakes fluttered gently into the buggy, falling to melt on the blanket and her shawl. Then Titus snorted impatiently and shook his head, jingling the metal of his harness.

Joseph was suddenly aware of the chill and the fact that Naomi's hand was trembling under his touch. How *schtupid* of him. "You're shaking with cold, and the snow's picking up. We'd best get back." He released her hand and shifted to reach for the reins.

"Wait," she whispered. "Please. Wait just a minute."

When he turned to look at her, she leaned quickly forward, and her mouth met his for the second time.

Her lips had chilled, but they instantly warmed again, melting sweetly against his own. For a few heart-catching seconds, the snow-muffled world around them disappeared.

When she drew back, the icy air hit his face like a dash of cold water. She straightened her bonnet, darting a self-conscious look at him as if waiting for him to speak.

His heart was beating so hard, he was sure she could hear it. He didn't know what to say. He desperately wanted to say the right words, the sweet words, the sort of words that fell from Caleb's lips as easily as rain from the edges of the roof.

Unfortunately, he wasn't Caleb. He didn't have any notion of what to say to a girl who'd just surprised him with such a kiss, and his befuddled brain seemed to have shut down operations.

All he could think about at the moment was how badly he wanted to kiss her again.

"Tuck up warm," he said gruffly. "Wind's getting up, and I can't have you getting sick before the wedding."

Judging from her reaction, that wasn't the right thing to say. Naomi drew back, her face falling into shadow, but she said nothing. Meticulously she readjusted the thick blanket over her lap and faced stiffly forward.

He hesitated for an awkward minute, wishing, as he'd done a thousand times, that he could call the wrong words back and try again. He never could, though, so finally he snapped the reins on Titus's back and started the buggy rolling.

"I'm taking you to my house," he told her. "It's closer, and you can warm up well before driving home with Aaron and Katie."

"If that's what you want, Joseph."

Her voice sounded so sad and unsteady that he yanked Titus to a sudden stop.

She twisted on the seat to look at him, her brow creased with alarm. "Is something wrong?"

"Taking you home is not what I want. What I want, Naomi, what I really want, is to stay out here, alone with you, so I can kiss you again. The truth is, I want that so much that maybe it's best if we're not alone again in the dark until after we're married."

"Oh!" Once again, the little word rode on a quick, broken breath of surprise, but when Naomi continued, a hidden smile added warmth to her voice. "Maybe we'd better get on back then, *ja?*"

He flicked the reins on Titus's back. As the horse started forward, Joseph felt an unaccustomed glow of satisfaction.

Most likely he hadn't used the best words. He never did. But for once, somehow, it seemed he'd managed to say the right thing.

CHAPTER TWENTY-SIX

NAOMI SNEAKED A GLANCE AT THE KITCHEN CLOCK as she and Miriam cleared away the lunch dishes. It was nearly one o'clock, and she was supposed to call the cardiologist at two. Soon she'd have to excuse herself and start the walk over to the phone shack.

She'd kept pretty calm over the last few days, but this last bit of waiting was stretching her nerves to their limits. Her heart thumped as she scooped leftover beef casserole into a plastic storage container. When Miriam dropped a metal pot lid on the stove top, Naomi jerked, her elbow knocking over a half-empty glass of water.

"Oh, I'm sorry." Miriam hurried to dab the spill with a dishtowel. "I startled you."

"It's not your fault," Naomi protested with a shaky laugh. "I'm just jumpy today."

"You've been jumpy a lot lately," Miriam pointed out with a smile. "'Specially around my brother, I notice."

"Oh!" Naomi's cheeks burned as she fumbled for an answer.

"Stop teasing Naomi, Miriam," Joseph said mildly as he came down the steps. As he passed his sister, he gave her prayer *kapp* a tug, making it slip sideways on her head.

"*Shtobb sell*, Joseph!" Miriam exclaimed in irritated dismay. She straightened the skewed *kapp* and tucked curling strands of hair back into place.

"See? You don't like being teased so well yourself." Grinning, Joseph sidestepped Miriam's swat.

"I don't like you mussing up my hair, that's what I don't like! It's hard enough to keep this crazy stuff where it's supposed to be without you jerking it sideways." Miriam sighed deeply. "I wish I had hair like yours, Naomi, so nice and smooth. It always looks *gut*."

Naomi laughed, the upcoming call temporarily forgotten. It made her heart sing to hear these two squabbling good-naturedly back and forth like any ordinary brother and sister. "Well, I like the color of your hair best, Miriam. Such a warm brown, like the caramel inside a good chocolate candy. We must be satisfied with what *Gott* sees fit to give us, I reckon."

"I suppose." Miriam shot a sisterly smirk in her brother's direction. "Are *you* satisfied, Joseph? With what *Gott* has seen fit to give you?"

Joseph studied Naomi with a gentle warmth in his eyes that made her curl her toes tightly in her small black shoes. "*Ja*. I am very well satisfied."

Her heartbeat sped up so suddenly that she had to grip the back of a nearby chair to steady herself. Fortunately, the two Hochstedlers were too busy needling each other to pay any attention.

"Stop looking at Naomi all calf-eyed. I was talking about your hair, *bruder*."

"Maybe you were," Joseph replied calmly, "but I wasn't." His mouth turned up in a smile so swift and bright that Naomi's breath caught painfully someplace between her lungs and her lips. "Naomi, could I talk to you for a minute? Someplace away from my nosy little sister?"

Naomi went hot and cold all at the same time. Ever since those kisses shared in the snowy buggy, she'd felt this way around Joseph—jittery and excited. More than anything in the world, she wanted to relax into the promise of a future together with this wonderful man, but the upcoming call to the cardiologist's office had hung over her head like a sullen thundercloud at a picnic.

Well, in just a little while, that part would be over. The storm would begin, or the sun would come back out. Either way, at least she'd know what she was facing.

Miriam laughed as she carried the last plates over to the sink. "Go on with him, Naomi, and I'll start on these dishes. That'll save us both time. You might as well know from the start that Hochstedler men are all as stubborn as goats." She threw her brother another narrow-eyed glance. "Not so much nicer to look at, either."

In response, Joseph gave the strings dangling over his sister's shoulders another quick tug. As Miriam squealed and grabbed at her crooked *kapp*, Joseph headed for the back door. He opened it and gestured for Naomi to follow him onto the unheated back porch.

The painted gray floorboards creaked under her weight as she walked out and stood by the humming water pump. Joseph closed the kitchen door carefully behind them, and Naomi's heartbeat quickened.

Was Joseph finally going to kiss her again? After what he'd said in the buggy, Naomi had confidently expected he would, but so far, nothing. In fact, he seemed to be spending even more time in his woodshop these past few days.

That had been . . . disappointing, and he made no attempt to close the small gap between them now, either. Instead he lowered his voice and said quietly, "I want to thank you, Naomi, for helping Miriam. Just then, back in the kitchen, it felt like old times."

Naomi nodded, trying not to feel let down. "She is doing

much better." She hesitated, then added, "So long as she doesn't go outside."

The smile on Joseph's face dimmed. "*Ja*, that is still a problem. She can't set a foot in the yard without fear. I'm praying she'll start making improvements there soon. If she can't even walk to the chicken coop, I'm not sure how we'll manage the move to Ohio."

"We will have to trust *Gott* and do our best to help her," Naomi said. "Miriam will have to do her best, too. It won't be easy, but one way or another, we'll get there, I reckon."

"You're right." Joseph agreed. "We will. Having you along will be a big help to her, I know. She's so happy about the wedding. In fact, I'm hoping maybe she'll want bad enough to come to Katie's to see us married that she'll find the courage to go outside. That could happen, don't you think?"

"It could, maybe." Naomi managed a bright smile in spite of the niggling frustration she was feeling.

She might not know much about engagements, but she suspected most fellows would rather kiss their girls than stand around talking about their sisters. If Joseph had been engaged to Rhoda, maybe he'd be doing less talking right now.

The bubble of secret joy that had been buoying Naomi up since their buggy ride deflated a bit. Maybe that sweet, breath-stealing time together hadn't meant quite so much as she'd thought.

If you can't have what you want, Naomi, make the best of what you do have, her mother's oft-repeated advice whispered in her memory.

She was being foolish and ungrateful. Joseph was kind, and he was good, and it was blessing enough to be his second choice.

"Didn't you need to walk to the phone shack?" Joseph was saying. "Will you check the messages while you're

there? I'm hoping Emma will have called with news about
a house for us."

"I'll check, *ja*."

"I'd like to walk with you, but I'd best get back out to the
woodshop. I've some orders to fill yet, and time's getting
by. Still"—Joseph pulled a simple watch out of his pants
pocket and studied its scratched face—"if you'd rather I
come along, I can probably—"

"I'll be fine to go on my own," Naomi interrupted quickly.
"Miriam doesn't mind staying in the house by herself, but
she wouldn't like being all alone on the farm. Anyhow, I've
only one call to make. I won't be gone long."

"All right. When you get back, will you come out to the
shop for a minute?" Joseph paused at the back door to smile
at her, and her silly heart hammered its usual frantic response. "I've something to show you. Besides, maybe you'll
have *gut* news to share."

Oh, she hoped so. "*Ja*, I will come to the shop."

Naomi watched him walk across the yard, her eyes lingering on the broad set of his shoulders beneath the old
black chore coat he wore. When he'd disappeared into the
barn, the breath she hadn't known she was holding whooshed
from her lungs.

"*Gott*, please," she murmured desperately, "let there be
good news." Then she ducked back into the warmth of the
kitchen to retrieve her bonnet and her own coat and shawl.

The phone shack was only a mile away, but the shortest
walk to it lay across bumpy, winter-hard fields. It was rough
going, and Naomi had to stop twice to catch her breath
before she got there.

She was relieved to see that the tiny wooden building
was empty. She'd dealt with cardiologists often enough to
know that if she wanted to speak to the busy doctor, she'd
best call at the exact moment she'd been assigned. Anybody
using the phone would certainly have gotten off it for a

medical call to be made, but the news would've been all over Johns Mill before the sun had set. She didn't want that to happen.

She wasn't the only person who needed to make calls at a specific time. Such calls were common enough that an inexpensive battery-operated clock ticked beside the phone. She had five minutes to spare, so she decided to go ahead and check the messages.

There was no new message from Emma, but sandwiched between various messages for the neighboring families, there was one for the Hochstedlers. Mona, the real estate agent, needed Joseph to come in to discuss the lease arrangement for the farm.

Naomi jotted the message on the notepad kept on the rough wooden shelf and folded the paper so it would fit in the pocket behind her apron. Then she pulled out the card from the cardiologist's office, lifted the receiver, and carefully punched in the number.

She was promptly put on hold by the receptionist, and seconds ticked by slowly. She prayed silently as she waited, but even so, by the time the doctor picked up, the phone receiver was slick with sweat from her hand.

"Is this Naomi?"

"Yes." His immediate use of her first name was reassuring. Doctors unfamiliar with the Amish tended to call her Miss Schrock.

"This is Dr. Lawson. I've reviewed the results of your tests, and I'm afraid we do have some areas of concern. It's a good thing you came in when you did."

"Oh." Naomi found it difficult to breathe. "It's serious, then?"

"Fairly serious, yes." The doctor hesitated, and she heard him sigh. "Normally I'd ask you to come in so we could discuss this in person, but my grandparents are Plain, and I understand how difficult it might be for you to get to the office. I'll tell you as much as I can over the phone, so long as you agree that you'll come in for another appointment as soon as we can arrange one. All right?"

"All right." Naomi swallowed. "Is it the Wolff-Parkinson-White again?"

"No, I believe you have a damaged heart valve. I can't be sure, of course, but I'd guess it was damaged during the ablation procedure. Nicked just the tiniest bit, maybe. It happens."

"But that was two years ago. I only started having these symptoms within the past few months."

"That could make sense. It's like a tiny tear in a piece of fabric. At first, it's not so bad, but over time, the tear widens and it becomes more of a problem. Especially if you're giving your heart a workout. The nurse said that you had been more active lately than you've been in the past, right?"

"*Ja*. That's so." She took a deep breath. "What does this mean?"

"You'll have to have another operation. But," he hurried on, "that's the bad news. The positive news is that, if we replace the valve, there's a good chance that you can go on to live a normal life."

"A good chance."

"Yes."

"But it might go poorly, this operation? I might not recover fully?" *Or at all?*

The doctor paused before he answered. "There's always that possibility, but I'm optimistic."

Optimistic. The pediatric cardiologist had been optimistic about the first procedure, too, so optimistic that he'd swayed her bishop to agree to it. In fact, he'd presented Naomi's recovery to health as a sure thing.

Obviously, it hadn't been, and she hated the idea of asking her family or her community to fund another operation. Communities worked together to shoulder such hospital bills, and Naomi's had been substantial—and only recently paid off.

Which brought up another question. "This valve replacement surgery—is it more complicated than the first procedure I had?"

"Yes. Much."

Naomi's heart sank. *Complicated* in medical jargon was another word for *expensive*.

"And if I don't have this operation? What will happen then?"

"You'll die," Dr. Lawson told her bluntly. "Not right away, but soon enough. Sooner if you keep on working like you've been doing. The symptoms you're experiencing will get worse until the valve quits working altogether."

"I see."

"I'm sorry, Naomi. I know this is hard to hear but try to focus on the positive. It's likely that we can fix this. I understand there will be some financial difficulties to overcome, but I'll work with you. I'm sure the hospital will, too."

"Denki." Her doctor and hospital in Kentucky had done that as well, but even so, the amount owed had been huge.

"Do you have any more questions for me right now?"

"Nee." He had answered them all, just not in the way she'd been hoping.

"I'm going to transfer you to the receptionist now so she can make you a follow-up appointment. You agreed to that, remember? We'll talk more then and get this surgery on the books. Okay?"

Smart of him to get her to agree up front, and to remind her of that now. He really was familiar with Plain folks. There was nothing to say but, *"Ja,* I will come to the appointment."

The earliest one she could get was two weeks out. The receptionist apologized, but Naomi wasn't upset about the wait. She had plenty of things to sort out in the meantime, like how she was going to tell Joseph about all this. She sank onto the wobbly wooden stool, looking out the shack's window at the quiet road as she tried to think things through.

She didn't waste time wondering what Joseph would say. She knew him well enough to know. His face would go white and tense, the way it had been those first weeks after his parents' deaths, but he would tell her it was fine. He'd say they would be married as they'd planned and figure the rest out as they went. He'd take this new trouble onto his shoulders just as he'd taken the ones that had come before, quietly, doggedly.

Faithfully.

Hot tears prickled, and she dabbed at them with her sleeve as resolve built inside of her. She'd been a real help and a comfort to Joseph. He'd said so himself. She hated the idea of becoming a burden to him now, of seeing his eyes change when he looked at her . . . not full of hope and sweet affection anymore but filled with duty and resignation.

She'd seen that on the faces of her brothers every time they opened the bills for their monthly installment payments on her hospital debt. They'd never once complained, at least not in front of her. They weren't bad folks, and they'd look after Naomi for the rest of her life if it came to that.

Still, she'd hated causing such trouble for the people she loved best. She'd tried to help all she could, and she'd been so relieved when that account had finally been paid off. Even afterward, though, her brothers tended to look at her with a certain grim, kindly patience that reminded her silently of the sacrifices they'd made on her behalf.

She couldn't tell Joseph the truth about this. She couldn't stand the prospect of Joseph thinking of her the same way her family did. Maybe that was selfishness, but since she knew how he'd react to this news, there was another side to consider. She couldn't in good conscience bring more troubles into Joseph's life right now, not if she could help it.

And of course, she could help it. They weren't married yet.

She clenched her hands together and bowed her head. She'd spend some time praying here, seeking *Gott*'s guidance and resigning her will to His. Then she'd go back to the Hochstedlers and try to find some truthful, but vague way to explain to Joseph that she couldn't marry him, at least not right away.

And unless *Gott* surprised her with a miracle, quite possibly not at all.

CHAPTER TWENTY-SEVEN

❧

JOSEPH BLEW TINY CURLS OF WOOD AWAY FROM THE project he was working on and frowned. The oak leaf he'd been carving had come out lopsided. It was going to take a lot of thought and some careful, tedious work to get it fixed so that it would match the others twining up the sides of the headboard.

He sighed and set the small chisel on the workbench. A local *Englisch* couple had ordered the piece three months back, and he'd hoped to get the carving finished today. As frustrating as it would be to set this piece aside, he'd best not work on it anymore this afternoon. He'd been trying to keep himself busy while he waited for Naomi to return, but he'd gone featherheaded, his normally nimble fingers stiff and clumsy.

That was all right. He'd spent his time cleaning up the woodshop. Likely it wouldn't be long until Naomi was back.

Funny how that thought perked him right up. He whistled tunelessly under his breath as he brushed shavings onto the floor and put tools back in their appointed spots. As he reached for the old broom slanted in one corner, he paused.

The broom had been discarded from *Mamm*'s kitchen, the red paint on its wooden handle worn off where she'd gripped it. A memory of his mother sweeping out her kitchen in that ferocious, energetic way she'd had washed over him. The sharp pain he'd begun to anticipate whenever his parents came to mind jabbed hard, but then it subsided quickly.

He halted, broom in hand, and poked at his grief as he'd poke at a sore tooth, gingerly, carefully. He missed his parents. He would miss them always, but the raw edges of that sudden wound had scabbed over. His brutal grief had softened into a gentler sadness. It could be he had simply gotten used to his sorrow, but he thought maybe there was more to it.

His gaze drifted to the sheet-covered surprise against the wall, waiting on Naomi, and a bubble of joy freed itself from his sore heart and tickled upward.

Naomi had made the difference. She—and the future he was planning with her—had shifted his heart forward into hope. No man could keep grieving for lost days when the days to come beckoned him with such sweet promise. *Gott* had been merciful for sure, and Joseph was deeply thankful.

The door creaked, and he turned, instantly alert. Naomi peeked in.

"Joseph? I'm back. I am sorry it took me so long."

His welcoming smile faded as his eyes skimmed her face. She looked pale, and there were fine lines across her brow and around the corners of her eyes. Something was troubling her.

He started to ask about it, then stopped, unsure if he should. Lately Naomi had seemed shy about answering questions. She'd even been cagey about the reason for today's trip to the phone shack, and Joseph had dropped the subject. He wasn't sure what sort of personal wedding preparations women made, and he didn't want to pry.

He didn't want to step wrong, and whenever he opened his mouth, that was likely to happen. The hopes building in his heart felt fragile and teetery, as if he were balancing eggs, one on top of the other. He needed to be careful.

"There was one message on the machine for you," Naomi was saying. She slipped a hand beneath her apron and came out with a folded scrap of paper. "It wasn't from Emma, though."

A message. His heart went oddly cold and hot at the same time. A message, but not from Emma? He could guess who'd called—and that explained the strained look on Naomi's face. "Whatever Melvin said, don't pay it any attention. I'd not have asked you to check the messages if I'd thought he'd call. He usually mails his nonsense."

"The message wasn't from Melvin." She wiggled the scrap until he took it from her. "It's from the real estate agent. She needs you to meet with her."

Then what's wrong? Why are you sad? He wanted to ask her, but he couldn't think of quite how. The questions felt as clumsy in his mind as the chisel had felt in his hand a moment ago.

He glanced only briefly at the paper before pocketing it. Whatever Mona wanted, he'd deal with it later. His eyes refastened on Naomi's face as he tried to guess what was troubling her.

She was looking around the workshop. "Did you say there was something you wanted to show me?"

"Ja." He'd been waiting for this all afternoon, but now that the moment had come, he was reluctant. Something felt off.

He didn't like it.

A tiny smile curved the corners of Naomi's lips as she watched him. "So then?" she prodded. "What is it?" Her eyes lit on the headboard. "Is it the bed for the Johnsons? That's coming along real well, ain't so?"

She brushed past, leaving a fresh scent of clean laundry and starch behind. She walked to the piece and traced the carving, her finger lingering on the awkward leaf.

"I know," he assured her quickly. "That one hasn't come right for me yet, but don't worry. I'm going to fix it."

"I wasn't worried, and nor should you be," Naomi retorted right away. "Maybe you shouldn't fix it at all. My *grossmammi* always left one little mistake in every quilt she made, on purpose. She told me it was a reminder to both herself and the people who bought her quilts that perfection belongs only to *Gott*."

"Your grandmother sounds like a very wise woman."

"She was." Naomi tilted her head, studying the deformed leaf. "Besides, this one crooked one makes the others look even more beautiful." She glanced over her shoulder at him. In that angle, in that moment, there was something so graceful about her, so sweet, that his heart stalled in his chest. "I knew you were a skilled woodcarver already. But do you know, Joseph, it is not until now, when I see your best work next to this little bumble, that I understand how fine your carving really is."

His eyes connected with her gray-green ones, and his stilled heart jolted back to life with a painful thump. Suddenly, more than anything in the world, he wanted to take this woman in his arms and kiss her.

Lately he'd been feeling that way pretty much every time Naomi was within arms' length. Earlier on the back porch, he'd babbled on about Miriam just so he could keep from gathering Naomi close and tasting her sweet mouth again. It was a good thing—a very good thing—that Isaac had given them permission to be married soon. How did young folks wait for months to be married?

He'd have gone crazy if he'd had to wait that long.

He cleared his throat. "*Denki-shay*, Naomi, but that headboard's not what I wanted to show you." He edged around a worktable and picked up the covered piece, plunking it in the middle of the sawdust-littered floor. "This is."

As Naomi came near, he yanked off the old sheet. The stinging scent of fresh varnish clouded the air as the glossy cradle he'd finished just last night came into view.

"Oh, Joseph!" She bent to inspect the intricately carved wood. "*Du hosht gut gedu!* What beautiful workmanship! I've never seen finer!"

"I am glad you like it. It's yours."

Her head snapped up, her eyes wide. "Mine?"

"This is my wedding gift to you." He smiled at her confused expression. "I know we talked about a rocker, maybe, but . . . The husband is supposed to give his *fraw* something useful, *ja?* I pray this will be useful to our family. Soon, if *Gott* wills it, and often."

Her cheeks pinked up, and she looked down at the cradle, caressing the wood with a gentle hand. "You must have worked very hard to finish it so quickly, and when you have so much else to do."

Naomi's voice was choked with emotion. It didn't sound much like happiness, though, and he didn't like the way she wasn't meeting his eyes. Joseph frowned.

"*Vass is letz*, Naomi? Something's troubling you. Tell me and let me help."

"*Ich kann naett.*" The whispered refusal was so unexpected that it hit Joseph like a slap. What did she mean, *she couldn't*?

"Of course you can. And you should. Your problems are my problems now."

"*Nee.*" She spoke sharply. It was strange, hearing that tone in Naomi's soft voice. She was breathing fast, her small bosom rising and falling rapidly. "We are not married yet, Joseph."

Joseph's heart constricted. Him and his stupid, clumsy ideas.

"Naomi, if I've stepped wrong somehow with this cradle . . ." He floundered to a stop. As usual, he had no idea how to put what he wanted to say into words. "*Ich binn sorry.* I'm just happy to be thinking about the future again. To be expecting good things ahead instead of being sad about the past. But I sure didn't mean to make you uncomfortable."

She looked up at him then, one quick shy glance that had his heart pounding. "You didn't make me uncomfortable, Joseph. The cradle is a beautiful gift." She looked back down and murmured, "Even sweeter than a whistle."

Her words were reassuring, but she still looked like she was about to cry, and he had no idea what she meant about a whistle. He started to ask, then decided he'd better not wander off on any rabbit trails, not until he had this settled. "Then what's the trouble?"

She took a halting, raggedy breath. "I think . . . I think we need to slow things down a bit, Joseph."

His frown deepened as he worked to decipher the expression on her face. "Slow things down? What things? You mean the marriage?"

"*Ja.*" She was avoiding his eyes again and twisting her hands together nervously.

"I thought speeding up the wedding was all right with you, that we were agreed." He paused to gather his courage before adding, "Are we not agreed, Naomi? Do you want me to tell Isaac we've changed our minds?"

She didn't answer. She only stood there, looking at her feet. Tension and hurt stole what was left of his patience. "Speak up, Naomi, and tell me what you want to do." He gestured roughly at the cradle between them. "I've been honest enough with you about what I want, I think. Now you need to be honest with me about what you want . . . or don't want."

"I don't want us to make a mistake, Joseph, by rushing into something too quickly." She still wasn't looking at him. He wished she would. He couldn't find his feet in this conversation, and he needed to see her eyes.

"Do you need more time? I can tell Isaac to wait until the next church meeting to publish us. We can be married at the meeting after that just as well."

"But—"

"Naomi." He couldn't stand much more of this. He needed to know. "If you don't want to marry me, you can tell me so." He gave a short, hard laugh. "It's not like I haven't had this happen before, after all. At least you're not marrying my brother, so I reckon that's something to be thankful for."

"It's not that." She looked into his face then, and he saw tears shimmering in her eyes. "I do want to marry you, Joseph. Only you."

She sounded sincere enough. His annoyance and fear fell by the wayside, and suddenly he'd had enough of the distance between them. Maybe he didn't know how to draw her close with words, but there were other ways.

Better ones.

He closed the gap between them in two strides and gathered her into his arms. At first she held herself stiffly, but then she relaxed against his chest, although he could feel her shaking. He rested his cheek on the top of her bonnet and spoke quietly, as he would to a spooked calf.

"I don't know what's wrong, Naomi, so I'm not sure how to fix it. But I'm here, as long as you want me to be."

"I'm sorry, Joseph." Her voice was muffled against his chest. "Truly I am. But—"

He couldn't let her finish that sentence. "I don't want you upset, Naomi. If you need more time, I'll give it to you. I've got to go into town anyhow to speak to the real estate agent. I'll speak to Isaac, too, and put things on hold, just for now. All right?"

Her hands were against his shirt, and he felt her fingers stirring restlessly against the fabric. She sighed, and he held his breath, praying she wasn't going to press him to cancel their wedding altogether.

"All right. For now, we'll postpone. Thank you, Joseph, for understanding."

He didn't understand any of this, but he nodded anyway, relieved. "Of course."

Naomi drew a shaky breath and moved to step out of his arms. Before she was beyond his reach, he bent down to touch her lips lightly with his own.

He'd kissed her to reassure himself as much as anything, but it didn't turn out that way. This kiss felt different from the sweet ones in the buggy. And afterward, when he looked into her eyes, he saw a sadness that made his insides ache.

"I'd best get back to the house now, Joseph," Naomi murmured. She gave him one fleeting smile, then ducked her head. Clutching her shawl around herself, she slipped out the door.

He looked after her for several painful heartbeats, then he squared his shoulders. He might as well hitch Titus up for the drive into Johns Mill. He'd go by to see Mona and Isaac both while he was in town, and he'd use the driving time to see if he could puzzle out what was going on with Naomi.

Before he left the workshop, he picked up the discarded sheet and threw it back over the cradle. Picking up the shrouded form, he tucked it gently in an out-of-the-way corner.

For the time being, at least, it wasn't something he particularly wanted to look at.

Chapter Twenty-Eight

❧

EVER SINCE HE'D BEEN OLD ENOUGH TO TAKE THE buggy into Johns Mill on his own, Joseph had appreciated the quiet drive, and today was the best sort of day to make the eight-mile trip. The winter sun shone with an unseasonable warmth, there wasn't much traffic, and Titus was in a cooperative mood.

He was too unsettled to enjoy it. He kept replaying the conversation with Naomi, and every time he did, he worried a little more.

He wondered who she'd talked to on the phone. He wished now he hadn't listened to Miriam's advice about minding his own business where Naomi's errands were concerned. He didn't like guessing. His mind picked at the uncertainty, like a ravel in a sweater.

If Melvin hadn't upset her, then who had? Somebody from back in Kentucky maybe? Could be one of her brothers had spoken against the marriage.

Joseph turned that idea over slowly, considering it from various angles, the way he did a piece of furniture when it wasn't coming right. It made sense. He'd likely caution Miriam or Emma the same way if one of them was thinking about marrying a man with so many troubles.

That realization didn't make him feel much better. Joseph shifted uneasily on the bench seat of the buggy. Had Naomi been so unsure about marrying him that it had taken only one conversation to convince her to put off the wedding? She didn't seem that sort of woman. She was sweethearted, but she seemed to know her own mind well enough.

Unless, maybe, she'd felt so sorry for him and his family that she'd agreed to marry him out of pity. That sounded like something Naomi might do. She was always so happy to be helpful, and she never minded being put to trouble for somebody else.

Marrying a fellow out of sympathy and a desire to be useful was taking that a little far, but if any woman would do such a thing, Naomi would. But now, perhaps she was thinking better of it.

Irritably, Joseph snapped the reins on Titus's back. The horse flicked an annoyed ear backward and grudgingly picked up his pace.

Only one thing was for certain sure right now. Since that phone call, everything had shifted sideways, and he needed to know why. A man couldn't fix what he didn't understand. Whoever Naomi had spoken to had made her uncertain enough about their marriage that it was having to be delayed a couple of long, extra weeks.

The way Joseph figured it, that made it his business, no matter what Miriam said. He wasn't about to push Naomi into anything. Still, maybe he shouldn't have been so quick to back off without pressing her for some explanation. After all, thanks to Rhoda and Caleb, Joseph had already learned one hard lesson in this area. Waiting silently on the sidelines didn't work out so well for him.

The thought that his future with Naomi might slip away altogether hit him hard, and as he passed the Johns Mill

City Limits sign, he reached a decision. As soon as he got back to the house, he'd ask Naomi about that phone call, straight out. He'd feel a lot more comfortable once he knew all the facts.

At least, he hoped he would.

He rolled the buggy into the parking lot behind the small realty office and pulled the hitching rope out of the back seat. He tied Titus off to the small wooden rail in a corner of the lot and headed inside.

Mona's office was small and, thanks to a flickering jar candle on top of a filing cabinet, smelled strongly of gardenias. The unoccupied secretary's desk in the cramped reception area was littered with papers, and three **FOR SALE** signs with big, smiling photos of Mona and mud-caked metal legs leaned against the right-hand wall. Nobody was in sight, but a machine was whirring somewhere in the depths of the building. Joseph cleared his throat loudly.

"Be right there," a female voice called. A few seconds later, Mona bustled up the narrow hallway. She was studying the sheaf of papers in her hands, a pair of bright purple reading glasses perched on the end of her nose. "Sorry, honey, it's crazy here today. My secretary's baby got up with a fever, so she's out, and—" Mona glanced up, and her welcoming smile drooped. "Oh! Joseph!"

"I got a message that you needed to speak to me about the lease. Is now a good time?"

Mona sighed. "As good a time as any, I guess." She didn't seem happy to see him, and that was a puzzle. The last time he'd been in this office, Mona's plump, well-powdered face had been wreathed in smiles. "Come on back to my office, Joseph. We need to have a little talk."

In the tiny office, Mona gestured Joseph into a floral armchair and settled herself behind the desk. Taking off her reading glasses, she folded them with a click and set them beside a candy jar filled with wrapped peppermints.

She clasped her chubby hands together on the scribbled-on calendar covering her desktop, and then finally, she spoke.

"Joseph, honey, I don't know but one way to tell you this. I goofed up."

"I don't understand. What happened?"

"Ian McMillan called me yesterday, and that's when I figured it out."

"Ian McMillan." Joseph recognized the name. "He's the man who is leasing the farm. The *Englisch* writer studying the Amish lifestyle."

"Right. He phoned to make sure we knew he wanted to lease the home fully furnished."

Joseph nodded. "You told me that already. It's not a problem. Apart from our livestock, we'll be leaving most everything. We're hoping to come back in a couple of years, so we've no interest in moving all our belongings." Joseph had made arrangements to store a few special items over in the Lapps' barn, but he'd resigned himself to leaving the rest of it for the renter's use. He wasn't thrilled with the idea of an *Englischer* pawing through his family's belongings, but it had seemed the most sensible thing to do.

"Right, I know. I'd told him that, but he kept going on and on about how he wanted everything left exactly as it is now, all the furniture in place just like you have it. He was being so persnickety, I got suspicious. I asked some questions, and I guess since the lease was already signed, he didn't mind answering them. Joseph, I don't know quite how to tell you this." Mona plucked a folder from the teetering stack at her elbow and centered it on the calendar, her brightly lipsticked mouth trembling. "This McMillan isn't just any old writer. Turns out he's the screenwriter for the movie they're making, the one about your parents."

"What?" Joseph could only manage the single word. He felt as if the carpeted floor had dropped out from beneath him.

"I'm so sorry, Joseph. I honestly had no idea! Nobody had even heard about the movie when he contacted me about leasing an Amish farm in this area. Thinking back, I should've guessed something. I mean, he did ask for a farm specifically on your side of the county, and when I mentioned your place coming on the market, he snapped it up so fast, it nearly made my head spin. I ought to have smelled a rat right then. Usually you can't rent out an Amish farm in this town for love or money, not to anybody but another Amish family." She made a helpless face. "They're real picturesque and all, but that whole no electricity thing . . . it's a real sticking point for regular folks. This fellow didn't so much as blink, just said he was willing to bring his own generator and make do as best he could. That's why I moved so quick to get him to sign the papers. I knew you didn't want to lease it out to another Amish family, and I didn't figure you'd get any other nibbles. I only meant to help you, but I've made everything worse." She massaged her temples. "Given myself a migraine to boot. This whole situation just makes me sick!"

It wasn't doing him any favors, either. Joseph rubbed his chin as he tried to think this through. He hadn't much liked the idea of leasing his home out to any *Englischer*, but to lease it to such a man as this . . . *nee*. There was no way Joseph could stomach it. He'd have to find some other way. "Cancel the lease."

Mona shook her head. "I wish I could. I tried to feel him out about that, but the minute he got the idea that's where I was headed, he shut me down quick. The lease is legally binding, so if you want to get out of it, you'll have to go see an attorney. And even then . . ." The older woman plucked a tissue out of a cardboard box perched on the corner of her desk and dabbed at her eyes. "I can't tell you how sorry I am about this, Joseph."

"I do not blame you, Mona, and you mustn't blame yourself." Joseph meant that, but it didn't fix the mess he was in. First the new uncertainty with Naomi, and now this.

"That's kind of you, honey. Here." Mona handed him the file folder. "These are copies of the papers you and McMillan both signed. I think you should talk with an attorney and see if there's some way to get out of the lease." She hesitated. "I'm not sure if I should even suggest this, since I've already made such a mess of everything, but maybe you should go see Stephen Abbott. I've worked with him on closings plenty of times, and I've got to say, normally I don't much care for the man. Stephen's slicker than spit, but trust me, if anybody can find you a loophole, he can. Plus, he's probably not too keen on this whole movie idea, either, so he might be inclined to help you out."

Joseph opened the folder, skimming the papers. Much as he hated the idea of consulting an *Englisch* lawyer, Mona was right. The lease was written in such legal jargon that he couldn't make sense of it. He'd need an expert's help to get out of this agreement. Stephen Abbott had as much at stake as Joseph had, maybe even more. Surely the lawyer would at least offer some advice, given the circumstances.

He wasn't looking forward to getting in deeper with these *Englischers*, though. It never paid off. Like Mona— maybe she'd meant well but look how it had turned out. Whenever these folks got involved, troubles multiplied like flies in a barnyard.

Joseph flipped to the last page in the folder and froze for a horrified second. Then he stood up so fast that the overstuffed armchair scooted several inches backward on the carpet.

"Joseph! My goodness, you startled me. What is it?"

"Mona, this McMillan, does he have a copy of these papers?"

The real estate agent's blue eyes were wide as she stared up at him. "Well, yes, he does. Both parties get copies. Why?"

Joseph looked back at the paper. There, neatly typed, was the forwarding address he'd provided for Mona when they'd filled everything out.

Melvin's farm in Ohio.

"I'm sorry, Mona. I need to go."

"Joseph, wait—" Mona struggled to her feet, but Joseph was out the door before she could finish her protest.

He strode down the street, headed for the store building and its telephone. He had to let Emma know that the movie-making people had Melvin's address. Thanks to Joseph, the troubles his sister had left behind in Johns Mill were about to catch up with her.

If they hadn't already.

CHAPTER TWENTY-NINE

❧

NAOMI PICKED UP ANOTHER APPLE FROM THE TABLE and cut it into quarters before tossing it into the big stockpot. Levonia Hochstedler had stored a crate of fall apples down in the cool of the cellar, and they'd begun to get soft and wrinkly. It was past time to deal with them, and Naomi had decided to make a small batch of apple butter.

It was late in the day to start such a project, so she'd need to do it in stages. Apple butter took forever to cook down, and she had to keep an eye on it so that it didn't scorch as it thickened. There wouldn't be time enough for that today. She'd cook the apples and grind them this afternoon, then she'd store the unflavored applesauce in the refrigerator overnight. First thing in the morning, she'd set a heavy-bottomed pot on the stove and simmer the apple puree with some spices over a low heat. She'd have the butter canned before she left tomorrow afternoon.

Since Miriam wasn't having a good day today, she was unable to help, but Naomi didn't mind working alone. The apples kept her hands busy while her restless mind picked over her troubles, trying to flip them around so that what she desperately wanted could somehow also be what she felt was right to do.

She hadn't managed it. On the one hand, she wanted to marry Joseph Hochstedler, worse than she'd ever wanted anything in her life. Standing out in the shed earlier, looking at the crib he'd fashioned for the babies he hoped they'd have together, she'd longed for the future he was offering her. And when he'd taken her in his arms and rested his cheek against the top of her head . . . well, the sweetness of that had almost been more than she could bear.

She loved Joseph with the whole of her flawed heart. Unfortunately, that was exactly why she shouldn't marry him.

Love, real love, Naomi had always been taught, was not so much a feeling as a decision of the will. Love was a determination to strive after the good of others, even when it conflicted with your personal desires.

Especially when it conflicted with your own desires.

She didn't know what the future held for her health. Only *Gott* knew that. She did know that either she'd have to undergo an expensive operation, or she'd lose her strength and die young. The doctor had made that plain enough—and if he hadn't, her difficulties going up and down the cellar steps with an apron full of apples today would have done so.

Perhaps if the circumstances were different, she could have snatched a bit of happiness. Joseph wasn't the sort of man to step aside from difficulties. He'd offered her marriage, and he'd keep his word, if she wished it, no matter what her health troubles meant for him financially or personally. For a little space of time, at least, Naomi could have everything she'd dreamed of.

More, even.

But that would be selfish. Naomi chucked an apple quarter into the pot so hard that water and vinegar splashed onto the table.

She blotted the spill with the dishtowel she had tossed over one shoulder and sighed. The idea of marrying Joseph—of having his strong shoulder to lean on in the teeth of the unexpected storm whirling around her was awfully appealing, but that wouldn't be love, would it? She couldn't saddle this *gut* man who was already bearing up under a mountain of troubles with the additional burden of a sickly wife. At best, Naomi would bring along a dowry of medical expenses he could ill afford; at worst, she'd be yet another source of grief to a family already reeling under it.

All afternoon she'd been hoping she could find some way around it, but no matter how many times she turned the matter over in her mind, she came up with the same conclusion. She had to find some gentle way to break off their engagement.

She dabbed her eyes with the rough material of her sleeve. She wouldn't cry over this. Not yet, not here. Later, maybe, when she was safely alone in Katie's spare room, but not now. If she started now, she wasn't sure she'd be able to stop, and Joseph was likely to be back from town any minute.

Please, Gott, help me. Help me to accept Your will in this. Give me Your peace, and the strength to do what I should do.

Thirty minutes later, the apples had softened. She was pressing the fruit through the hand-cranked mill into a waiting bowl when she heard the soft rumble of the buggy rolling up the drive.

It seemed a lifetime before Joseph came into the warm kitchen, accompanied by a blast of chilly air. He shut the door, taking his hat off, as he always did, but instead of hanging it on the peg, he stood looking at her, holding it in front of him. Naomi glanced at him, her eyes catching on that little cowlick of hair that always stood up on his forehead, and her knees went weak.

He would have been such a fine husband, this man.

"Naomi." Joseph's voice sounded strained. "I have some news." He looked around the room before returning his gaze to hers. "Where is Miriam?"

"Upstairs. Asleep, I think. She's had a hard morning, and she had to take one of her pills."

The sadness in Joseph's eyes deepened, but he nodded. "We can talk well enough here, then."

Naomi's busy hands went idle as she searched his face for clues. Whatever news he'd brought home with him, it wasn't good. "*Is alles awreit*, Joseph? What did Mona need to talk to you about? Is there a problem with the lease on the farm?"

"*Ja*. There is, a big problem."

Naomi listened horrified as Joseph explained that the writer leasing the farm, the Ian McMillan they'd all been thanking *Gott* for, was actually the person writing the script for the movie about his parents' murders.

"Oh, no." She sank into a chair, clasping her sticky hands together. "That is . . . upsetting."

"*Ja*, well. I'm afraid we've even more trouble than that." His throat flexed as he swallowed. "Turns out we can't move to Ohio after all."

"Why not?"

"It was my doing. I needed a forwarding address on the paperwork, and I foolishly put down Melvin's. And of course, that was on Ian McMillan's copy of the lease."

Naomi sucked in a sharp breath. "Oh, Joseph!"

Joseph circled his hat restlessly through his fingers. "I went to the store to call Emma, but there was a message from her waiting on the machine. Some reporters have already come around the farm, pestering, taking pictures. She can barely set foot outside. They've trespassed all over the dairy and upset my *kossin* Henry. They've got the whole community unsettled. It's a quiet town, no tourism to speak of, and they aren't used to such things. It's been very upsetting to everyone, and they've little idea how to handle it. If we move there, it's likely to get worse, so their bishop told Melvin that he thought it best if we stayed put, at least for the time being."

"I'm so sorry, Joseph! I'm the one who suggested you go to Mona about leasing out the farm. I feel this is partly my fault."

"It isn't." Joseph's denial came quick. "You did nothing wrong, and you weren't mistaken about Mona. She meant well, and putting that address on the paper was my mistake." He squared his shoulders. "This change in plans is just something we must accept. *Gott* opens and shuts doors as He sees fit, and it seems that Ohio is not His will for us."

"What are you going to do?"

"*Ich vays naett*," Joseph admitted quietly. "I don't know. I'm not sure it's wise to stay here in Johns Mill, but I don't know where to go, if not to my uncle's. I must pray and think about it before I decide. One thing, though, is certain. Even if we do move, it will not be so soon as I'd hoped, so it's no longer necessary for us to rush into a marriage." He paused, then added, "That is what you wanted, ain't so?"

Naomi clenched her fingers together under the veiling tablecloth before she answered him. "*Ja*," she agreed in a voice that sounded surprisingly normal. "That is what I wanted."

He crossed to the table and sat, placing his hat on the cloth next to the stockpot of gently steaming apples. He looked at Naomi directly, and she forced herself to meet his gaze.

"Naomi, it seems there's another wave of trouble coming in my family's direction. It may be God's will that I stand here to face it, although I'm not certain I can stay on the farm. I'm going to try to get out of the lease, but there's no telling if that'll be possible."

"Mona should never have allowed that man to lease your farm in the first place. Isn't there anything she can do?"

"It seems not. I'm not blaming her. *Daed* always said, when you do business, inside the faith or out of it, treat others as fair as you can, but make sure you look to your own good, too. I didn't check the details as close as I should have, and the trouble I've ended up with is more my fault than anyone else's." Joseph cleared his throat. "With that in mind, there's something I'd like to say to you."

"All right."

"Given the situation I'm in, I've not much good to offer you as your husband, and it may be a while before that changes." He paused. "I've no place for sure to live, no work that could support a family, and most likely more trouble coming from this movie situation. You made it clear enough earlier that you were having some doubts, and I think maybe I sweet-talked you into just postponing the wedding instead of calling it off altogether. Selfishly, I still want to marry you, Naomi, but the truth is, right now I can't see my way clear to take care of a wife. And I'd guess any doubts you had about marrying me before are multiplying like spring rabbits." He lifted his chin. "If you'd rather we break off our engagement altogether, I will understand."

A silence fell, punctuated by the drips of applesauce falling from the idle mill into the pot it was perched on. She knew Joseph was waiting for her answer, but she remained silent, tussling hard with her conscience.

She knew from the look on his face the answer he was hoping for, and more than anything, she wanted to give it. But she sat silently as wave after wave of guilty thoughts, sharp as splinters of glass, washed over her.

This kindhearted man wasn't so selfish as to ask her to stand by him during this fresh set of troubles, even though he wanted to. Couldn't she do at least as much for him?

Naomi had struggled with many faults in her life, but

she'd never thought of herself as a selfish woman. Yet right now, with her heart laid plain alongside Joseph's, she clearly was more self-centered than she'd ever imagined.

She tightened her hands until her short nails bit into her skin. "I'm not having doubts about you, Joseph. You'd make any woman a fine husband. But—" She stopped. This was very hard. "This does seem a real poor season to be thinking of marriage." She had to pause and swallow, but then she ploughed ahead. "It might be wisest to go back to the way things used to be, don't you think? I will continue to come over and help with Miriam and the housekeeping, and you and I will be *gut* friends, just like we always were."

Joseph's face tightened, but when he spoke his voice was gentle—and sad. "Is that what you want, Naomi? For you and I to be only . . . *gut* friends?"

Naomi struggled to find a way to answer him honestly. In the end, she sidestepped the question. "It seems the sensible thing. It's settled then. Things between us will go back to the way they were, *ja?*"

She stood, even though her knees were quaking, and reached for the big, slotted cooking spoon resting against the side of the stockpot. She ladled another load of soft apple chunks into her mill and turned the handle.

She could feel Joseph's eyes on her, but she didn't dare look at him. If she saw even a hint of pleading in his brown eyes, even the whisper of a wish that she would still agree to be his wife, she'd never be able to hold to this course.

Joseph cleared his throat raggedly. Even so, when he spoke, his voice was raspy. "*Denki*, Naomi. It comforts Miriam very much to have you here, so long as it suits you to keep coming." He got to his feet. "I'll speak to Isaac and let him know that . . ." He trailed off. "I'll let him know," he finished finally.

"Working here suits me well enough for now." She gave

him a determined smile. "I won't be staying in Johns Mill much longer, likely, but until I head back to Kentucky, I'll be along every morning, same as always."

Looking up was a mistake. Their eyes caught, and just as she'd feared, what she saw glimmering in his eyes hit her hard in the pit of her stomach. Hurt and sorrow, and a tired resignation that made her queasy.

She looked back at the apple mush she was pushing through the mill. "Supper will be simple tonight. Just leftover roast sandwiches and some soup. These apples are going to take most of my kitchen time today. I will call you in from your workshop when it's time to eat."

There was another short silence, except for the grinder squeaking its protest with every turn.

"*Denki*, Naomi," Joseph repeated quietly. Then he clapped his hat back on his head and was out the door in another blast of wintry air.

Naomi paused to watch him striding hunch-shouldered across the barren lawn toward the cold sanctuary of his woodshop. He walked like a man two decades older than he was, and in that she recognized something she'd been too shy, too unsure of herself, to fully believe until now, when it was too late.

Joseph had truly cared for her.

The truth of it crashed over her, and she dropped into her chair, breathing half-breaths, her heart pounding crazily. This *gut*, gentle man had cared for her, and she'd just broken his heart.

Naomi had known plenty of pain. She'd suffered with her illness, she'd buried her parents, and one terrible summer morning she'd stood beside the grave of a five-year-old nephew who'd fallen to his death from her brother's barn loft.

She had known pain, *ja*. But she had never known, not in her whole life, any pain worse than this—worse than hurting this man she loved—and who, as hard as it was for her to believe, loved her back.

More than anything, she longed to follow him, to hurry into his arms and tell him she'd changed her mind. But the situation she faced was still just as unyielding as it had been before. This pain was awful, but it changed nothing.

If she didn't hurt Joseph now, she would only hurt him worse later. Herself, too, because she would have to watch him pit the remains of his strength against the financial and physical hardships that mounted ahead of her, like a moth senselessly beating itself to death against the globe of a burning lamp. She didn't think he could win, but she would have to watch him lose everything he had left trying, knowing she was the cause of it all.

And that . . . that was the only thing she could imagine that would be worse than this.

CHAPTER THIRTY

✿

"YOU MUST NOT BE DISCOURAGED, JOSEPH." ISAAC pitched his voice low as they walked down the busy sidewalk toward the bakery's parking area. "We drive ourselves into confusing places when we take the reins of our lives into our own hands. It is *Gott*'s job to guide us in whatever direction He deems best. Ours is to follow willingly, even when the path doesn't lie along a road we ourselves would choose."

Joseph smothered a sigh. He'd hoped to keep this uncomfortable meeting brief, but after he'd explained that the wedding was off, the bishop had insisted on walking him back to the buggy. Isaac meant well, but Joseph wasn't in the mood to listen to a sermon.

"*Ja*," he agreed shortly. "It seems marriage isn't in *Gott*'s plans for me."

They rounded the corner revealing Titus standing patiently in front of the Hochstedler buggy. The bishop stopped at the edge of the sidewalk. Joseph halted, too, out of politeness, relieved that this painful discussion was nearly over.

Isaac held up a finger, as he often did when preaching.

"*Nee*, Joseph. You should not let this disappointment put you off marriage altogether. A *fraw* and *kinder*, these are blessings that every man should hope for. In time, you will find the one *Gott* has set aside for you."

Joseph nodded, but he wasn't so sure Isaac was right. He couldn't imagine ever loving another woman, not the way he loved Naomi. Could be *Gott* meant for some men to stay single.

"I'd best get on," he murmured politely. "I have another appointment here in town to keep yet."

"Of course. *Mach's gut*, Joseph. I will be praying for you."

"*Denki*," Joseph answered. As the bishop walked back to the bakery, Joseph unhitched Titus and hoisted himself into the buggy.

Well, the wedding was officially off, and at least he should feel relieved the unpleasant meeting with Isaac wasn't still hanging over his head. He didn't, though. He couldn't seem to feel anything but miserable. Ever since his conversation with Naomi, his heart felt as if it had been dragged over gravel.

Yesterday, when Naomi had looked at him across the kitchen table and had so quickly agreed that their marriage be canceled, it had knocked him to his knees. In spite of the unsettling news he'd brought home, he'd half expected her to reassure him in that quiet, steadfast way she had. He'd wanted her to say that whatever challenges he faced, she would face alongside him. He'd no right to ask her for such a thing, but he'd secretly hoped she'd offer it.

It was what he would have done, had the tables been turned, and he'd truly believed that Naomi cared for him as he cared for her. Or that she was beginning to.

Instead she'd shrugged off their marriage plans like an unwanted shawl. It stung, that. In the end, he'd been wrong about Naomi, just as he had been about Rhoda. *Ja*, he was a pretty poor scholar when it came to understanding women.

Joseph shifted restlessly on the buggy seat. He needed to push this out of his mind for the time being. He had the rest of his life to learn to live with his misery. Today he was meeting with Stephen Abbott, and any Amish fellow meeting with an *Englisch* lawyer had best keep his wits about him.

Abbott's law office was located in an elegant old home on the outskirts of town. Joseph was temporarily flummoxed as he pulled to a stop in the yard. Unlike most businesses in Johns Mill, there was no hitching rail here. Not surprising, since Plain folks rarely dealt with attorneys, but it posed a problem.

After considering his options, Joseph tied Titus to the lowest limb on the stately oak tree in the middle of the front lawn. He winced as the horse began to crop at the short grass, strangely green for the middle of winter. He'd just have to hope this meeting was over before Titus did too much damage.

He retrieved the folder Mona had given him from the buggy seat. As he turned toward the white-columned house, a sheriff's car slowed on the road and turned into the drive, stopping beside him.

Sheriff Townsend hoisted himself out of the tan cruiser. He mumbled into the radio clipped to his shoulder, then crossed in front of the idling car to where Joseph waited.

"Joseph." The older man threw a thoughtful glance at the building behind them. "I'd appreciate a word with you if you've got a minute."

"A minute only, I'm afraid. I have an appointment with Stephen Abbott."

"Do you, now." The officer's gaze sharpened, and he reared up on the toes of his boots to peer into the empty buggy. "You here by yourself?"

"I am alone, *ja*. Is there some problem, Sheriff?"

"Well, I don't know if there is or not." Townsend scratched

at his chin. "You ain't heard nothing from that brother of yours lately, have you?"

"I have not. Why?"

"I thought maybe that's why you were here. I had a complaint about him from Mr. Abbott just the other day. Seems your brother's been doing some jackleg investigating. Caleb's contacted some of the Abbotts' friends, trying to get a bead on where Trevor might be holed up."

"I see." Joseph wasn't surprised. Caleb didn't change course easily once he'd set his mind on something. "Is he breaking the law by doing this?"

"Not technically, but he's skirting it. If he does get in touch with you, now, you be sure and tell him he'd best leave the detective work to the authorities. All right? He's stirring up an anthill that would be better left alone. So far Stephen Abbott's cooperating with law enforcement, but he's not willing to stand by and see his son clobbered from behind in some dark alley."

Joseph recalled what Caleb had said about the Abbotts using their money to keep Trevor out of sight. How much cooperation was really going on, he wondered? Then he shut the thought down. If he allowed that question to take root in his mind, especially after what had just happened with Naomi, he'd soon find himself traveling down the same road Caleb had taken.

"My brother's looking only for justice. Trevor is in no danger from Caleb. That isn't our way."

The sheriff lifted an eyebrow. "That photographer he punched might see things a little differently. Caleb's gone rogue, Joseph. How can you know for sure what he will or won't do?"

An uneasy chill snaked its way up Joseph's backbone. Townsend had a point. Caleb had stepped well beyond the restraints of their faith. There was no telling what he might do in the heat of his temper and his grief.

"Like I said," Townsend continued, "if you do talk to Caleb, do your best to make him see reason." The sheriff nodded toward the stately old house. "And watch yourself in there, all right? Just between us, Stephen Abbott's got deep pockets, powerful friends, and a real flexible conscience. He's also got a wife who's on the verge of a nervous breakdown, and his son's accused of murder. You annoy him right now, it'd be like poking a rabid raccoon with a short stick." The officer let his advice sink in before adding, "I'll let you get on to your meeting. Won't help you any to keep Abbott waiting. You be sure to let me know if you hear from Caleb, now."

Townsend waited for Joseph's nod before lumbering back to his car. Joseph watched the sheriff drive away, then he headed up the curving walkway to Abbott's law office.

The dark green front door opened into an echoing, high-ceiling space, smelling strongly of lemon furniture polish. A severe-looking secretary was tapping on a computer. She glanced up, one eyebrow arched, but Joseph didn't have time to offer his name before Stephen Abbott appeared in a doorway on the right side of the hall.

Joseph hadn't seen Abbott since the day of *Mamm* and *Daed*'s funeral. The man in front of him bore only a passing resemblance to the shaken *Englischer* who had stumbled up his driveway, one arm around his trembling wife. He had some color in his face now, and he stood a good deal straighter. Abbott smiled and held out his hand.

"Joseph! Good to see you. Come on into my office. Eileen, hold my calls, please."

Joseph shook the attorney's hand, which felt oddly greasy, as if it had recently been oiled. He fought the urge to wipe his palm on his pants as Abbott led the way into a spacious office. Motioning Joseph into a red wing chair, the lawyer settled on the opposite side of an immense desk.

"Can I get you anything? Coffee? Hot tea?"

"No, please. I don't need anything." With difficulty, Joseph dragged his eyes away from the elaborate carvings trailing up the sides of the desk. Impressive work, but too showy for his tastes. "I thank you for meeting with me, Mr. Abbott. How is your wife?"

"A little better." A shadow crossed the other man's ruddy face. "Thanks for asking. She's under the care of an excellent doctor, and he's got her on some medication that seems to be helping. Of course, until all this business with Trevor is settled . . ." He trailed off and cleared his throat. "You said on the phone that there was something I could help you with?"

"*Ja*, I hope so." Joseph handed him the folder containing the copy of the lease.

Abbott put on a pair of silver-rimmed reading glasses and glanced over the papers as Joseph explained the situation.

When he'd finished, Abbott looked sharply over the top of his glasses. "I understand that you're not pleased about who this McMillan works for, but are you sure you want out of the lease? This is a good bit of money, more than you're likely to get from anybody else, and it was my understanding that you and your sister were relocating to Ohio."

Joseph wondered how, exactly, Abbott had known about that. "I was, *ja*, but those plans have changed."

"I see." Abbott steepled his fingers on top of his desk. "Do you think it's wise, though, to stay here in town? I mean, the movie's going to be made whether this particular fellow rents your house or not. There'll be plenty of publicity, the studio will see to that, and all the fuss that goes with it. It won't be easy, especially with your sister in such a delicate state of health. I really"—he leaned forward, holding Joseph's eyes with his own—"*really* think you should go ahead and make that move out of state."

The lawyer's tone was friendly enough, but there was no

mistaking the message in those unflinching eyes. *Watch your step.* Sheriff Townsend's warning echoed in Joseph's memory.

"That won't be possible," Joseph replied evenly, "but I thank you for your concern."

"Oh, I am concerned. Very concerned." Abbott removed his glasses and set them to the side. "I think you're making a big mistake. This round of publicity won't be like the last one. I've heard some things, things maybe you're not aware of."

There was something in the other man's expression that Joseph couldn't quite decipher. "What things?"

The lawyer leaned against the high back of his leather chair. "Let's just say this movie isn't going to take quite the same slant as the previous news articles did. This publicity may prove to be far more . . . painful for your family."

More painful than what they'd already dealt with? That seemed unlikely. "I'm not sure I understand what you mean."

"I've read the outline that the studio's approved for this film. It's not for public view, of course, but my family has always supported the arts, and the producer happens to be an acquaintance of mine. He did me the favor of giving me a preview. I'm afraid your family—at least in the draft I read—doesn't come off too well. Your parents particularly."

Joseph's heartbeat sped up. He found himself measuring his breaths, the way his father had taught him to do when his temper was rising. "I don't see how that could be possible. My parents did nothing wrong, Mr. Abbott."

The attorney shrugged gently. "I'm not saying they did. But movies have more license to explore the nuances of a situation. More creative freedom, as it were. This film isn't a documentary, you see. It's based on a true story, but it doesn't pretend to be one. It's just entertainment."

Entertainment. Joseph shook his head. "This makes no sense to me."

"I'm sure it doesn't." Abbott's sympathy felt as oily as his hand. "But then so many things in this world don't make sense. Not much we can do about that, I'm afraid. This, though"—he thumped the lease with one finger—"this we can certainly do something about. I'll make a phone call or two. You won't have to lease your farm to this fellow if you don't choose to. But like I said, Joseph, I'd think seriously about going ahead with your plans to move away, at least for the time being. You sure you don't want to think this over a little longer?"

Joseph stood. This conversation had his skin prickling the way it did during the height of a summer thunderstorm, just before lightning struck. He needed to get away by himself to someplace quiet and try to think all this through. "I would like to get out of the lease if you can manage that. Can you give me an idea of what your time will cost?"

Abbott took his time rising from his own chair. "Don't worry about the money, Joseph. I'm happy to make a few calls on your behalf, as a gesture of my goodwill. This terrible tragedy happened to both our families, just like you said that day at your home. Remember?"

"*Ja*. I remember."

"It's one of the finest tenets of your faith, that way of thinking. Who knows?" Abbott's smile didn't reach into his eyes. "If you'll stick to that, the publicity may be kinder to you. Of course, given the relationship you have with the press right now." The lawyer shrugged. "I certainly wouldn't count on them cutting you much slack. But we'll hope for the best."

He extended his hand, and Joseph saw no way short of rudeness to avoid accepting it. The other man's fingers clamped around his own, and Abbott leaned forward as if he were about to share a secret. "Since I'm doing you this favor, you might consider talking to that hotheaded brother of yours for me. Rein him in, get him to settle down and start behaving himself. That would make things a lot . . . easier . . . for everyone concerned."

Joseph withdrew his hand without answering. Abbott held his gaze for a second longer, then clapped him on the back before throwing open the office door. "Good to see you, Joseph. Give your family my best, won't you?"

The lawyer's voice was pleasant, and he'd agreed to sort out the lease trouble for free, something Joseph was fairly certain wasn't a courtesy often extended in this office. He'd gotten what he'd come for, but talking with Stephen Abbott was a lot like sticking a hand into murky water. Unpleasant feeling, and you could never be sure about what lurked underneath the surface.

He could add understanding lawyers to the growing list of things he wasn't good at. Still, he'd understood enough that he wasn't overly sorry to see that Titus had pulled up an uneven circle of the Abbotts' grass and dropped a pile of steaming manure in the middle of his expansive lawn.

On the drive home, Joseph barely noticed the occasional trucks and cars rumbling by as he methodically sorted through what Abbott had told him. His sense of unease grew as he fit the puzzle together. There were pieces missing yet, but he could see enough to distrust the picture that was forming.

He should've listened more closely to Caleb. Maybe his brother was too rebellious to mold easily into the Amish faith, but he'd never been stupid. Now, after talking with Stephen Abbott, Joseph suspected that Caleb had been right all along. Abbott would do whatever it took to protect his son from the consequences of his actions—including investing in a movie that spun the story in Trevor's favor at the expense of the truth.

Joseph had no idea how he was supposed to steer his family through this. He'd have to talk to Isaac and see what the bishop suggested. No matter what Joseph did, though, one thing was for sure. More tough times were coming for him and those he loved.

He registered that truth dully. A better man would be thankful that *Gott* had protected Naomi, grateful that the woman he cared for wouldn't have to walk through this mess alongside him.

Maybe Joseph should be thankful, but right now he couldn't muster up much gratitude. His heart, having suffered blow after blow, felt strangely dead. It was like that instant of blankness when a fellow sliced his finger open with a chisel. The blood welled up right off, but just at the first there was no pain.

That came later.

A small car whizzed past, honking its horn and causing Titus to sidle sideways. Joseph tightened his slack grip on the reins and spoke soothingly to the startled animal. When he glanced up, the vehicle had pulled over to the side of the road ahead, taillights and blinkers flashing. A young man got out and walked toward the approaching buggy.

Joseph felt a fresh surge of irritation. He didn't want to deal with some pushy *Englisch* stranger, not now, not today. He wanted to get home and close himself off in his workshop, get his hands busy and try to find a scrap or two of peace.

The man advanced with his hands extended and a determined look on his face. Joseph started to swerve around him, but then he narrowed his eyes. That was Naomi's driver, wasn't it? The one who'd driven her to Knoxville.

All right. Maybe he'd stop after all. Joseph had a few questions for that fellow, and right now he was in just the right mood to ask them. He slowed the buggy, drawing it as far off the sloping shoulder of the road as he dared. The man Naomi had called Eric came to the side of the buggy, his expression grim.

"I want to talk to you."

"Do you." Joseph made the words a statement rather than a question, since there didn't seem to be much question about it. Any fellow who'd flag you down in the middle of a road obviously wanted something. "I want to talk to you also."

"I'm going first." The younger man fixed Joseph with a steely stare. "Just so you know, I really hate doing this. Just because I'm a reporter doesn't mean I enjoy sticking my nose in other people's business. But the more I thought about it, the madder I got."

Joseph frowned. This fellow was a reporter? Naomi sure hadn't mentioned that.

"Just say your piece," Joseph ground out, feeling both hurt and annoyed.

"All right, I will. Naomi's one of the sweetest girls I know, and you're a poor excuse for a man if you don't take a lot better care of her than you've been doing. I don't know much about how you folks handle things," the other man went on, "and I don't mean to be disrespectful of your religion or anything like that. But I don't care what church you go to, a man doesn't send any woman he cares about to an appointment like that alone. She was scared to death, did you know that? She acted brave, but I could tell. Seeing her sitting there, counting her cash over and over again, worrying over whether she'd have enough . . . it just killed me. She didn't use my credit card but I wish she had. At least then somebody would've done something for her."

What was this crazy *Englischer* talking about? "I don't understand. You gave her a credit card? Why?"

The *Englischer* sputtered. "You really have to ask? Why do you think? Because I wasn't going to let her go into that cardiologist's office worried about money on top of everything else!"

Cardiologist. Suddenly all the confusing bits of information whirling in Joseph's brain clicked together into a terrible certainty.

"*Hah*, Titus!" Joseph snapped the reins sharply on the horse's back and the buggy lurched forward, causing the *Englischer* to stumble to the side of the road.

Joseph didn't spare him a backward glance. The reporter would have to look after himself.

He had to get home.

CHAPTER THIRTY-ONE

❧

NAOMI SWITCHED OFF THE GAS STOVE BURNER AND used a pot holder to pluck the hot lid off the water-bath canner. A cloud of steam wafted upward, heating her face as she set the lid to the side and reached for the rubber-tipped tongs.

"Spread out the towel, Miriam. This batch is ready."

Miriam quickly doubled the bath towel on the table to protect its wooden surface from the heated jars, then stepped back as Naomi began transferring the dripping half-pints of apple butter.

"Look at those cute jars." Miriam laughed softly. "We've never canned in such small amounts before. *Mamm* always used pints. Quarts sometimes, even, if it was something everybody liked."

"*Ja*, they are little!" Naomi smiled, dabbing at her damp forehead with one sleeve. It was wonderful *gut* to hear Miriam laugh. "Since this was only a small batch of apple butter, there wasn't much to work with."

She didn't add that with only Joseph and Miriam living at home now, there was no point canning big jars of anything. It would take the two of them long enough to get through these small ones.

Maybe Miriam figured that out for herself, because as she stood looking at the growing line of tiny jars, her smile dimmed. The younger woman picked up a dishtowel and began blotting the jars dry. She was silent for a moment, then she said, "Well, they are the sweetest jars, and they will look real pretty on the breakfast table, ain't so? You must tell Katie thank you for sharing them with us."

"I will," Naomi promised with a smile.

It was slow going, but Miriam was getting better. She'd not been farther than the doorstep since that last disastrous trip to town, but at least she wasn't hiding in her room these days. She got up every morning, dressed, and helped around the house. If a person didn't know Miriam's troubles, they'd never guess there was anything wrong with her—unless they asked her to go out of doors.

Given what the future held, this improvement was *Gott's* providence. Hopefully now, once Naomi was gone, Miriam could manage the housework on her own.

Unless the canceled wedding caused another setback.

Naomi had braced herself to see Miriam upset over that news today, but apparently Joseph hadn't yet told his sister what had happened. Naomi wasn't sure what to do, so she had simply let things be. She didn't think her heart could handle Miriam's disappointment, not when her own was so fresh.

In a strange way, it had been comforting, going about the kitchen today as if nothing had changed, as if the future she'd been so joyful about was still possible. At first she'd felt less than truthful, but then she'd decided it was all right to enjoy this final bit of happiness, like savoring the last sunshiny afternoon before winter started in earnest.

As she set the last jar on the table, Naomi heard the buggy rattling into the yard, and her heartbeat fluttered. "Joseph must be back from town."

"*Gut.* Likely he'll want to try a bit of this apple butter on some fresh bread for a snack. It was always one of his favorites. He—" Miriam cocked her head, listening. Her face changed, the fear that was never far away sparking back into her eyes. "Something's wrong."

Naomi set down the tongs. "Don't go jumping at shadows, Miriam. He's not even come into the house yet. There's no reason for you to think such a thing."

"He's stopped in the yard instead of driving the buggy to the barn. He never does that." A high note of panic had crept into Miriam's voice.

Come to think of it, Joseph did always drive Titus straight to the barn. "I'm sure it's nothing," Naomi soothed. "He probably has something to unload."

However, the minute Joseph came through the door, Naomi knew that Miriam was right. Something was wrong, for sure and certain. His eyes found hers and locked on.

"Miriam, would you leave Naomi and me for a minute?"

Miriam's fingers worried the damp dishtowel. "What's happened?"

Joseph's face gentled as he glanced at his sister. "It's all right. I promise you. I just need to speak with Naomi. Alone. Please."

Miriam hesitated for another moment then nodded. She folded the dishtowel neatly over the lip of the sink and went toward the stairs.

As Miriam's soft footsteps padded up the steps, Naomi struggled to read Joseph's expression. What had happened in town to give him such a hard look?

He waited until he heard the soft thud of Miriam's bedroom door closing before turning to Naomi.

"Why didn't you tell me you were sick again?"

Naomi's stomach gave a nauseating roll. He knew. Somehow, she couldn't imagine how, but somehow, he'd found out. "Oh, Joseph."

He stepped forward, searching her face. "You haven't been well for weeks." Suddenly Joseph snatched off his hat and flung it at the table. It landed half over the little row of cooling jars and settled crookedly. "I should have seen it myself. I did see it, some of it, but there were so many other things going on . . . It was wrong of you, Naomi, to keep such a thing from me. Especially when—" He stopped short. "It was wrong of you," he finished roughly.

She'd never seen Joseph this angry before. It was a sight to behold, for sure, the way his brown eyes flashed like autumn leaves catching flame in a bonfire. Who knew this quiet man had so much fire in him?

"How did you find out?"

"That *Englisch* driver of yours. Eric. The reporter. The one you've been giving pies to, ain't so? There seem to be plenty of things you forget to tell me. *Ja*, your reporter friend flagged me down, worried over you, and he told me. I'd sooner have heard this news straight from you, Naomi."

She didn't know what to say. The whole world was crashing down around her. "I'm sorry, Joseph."

"Are you? Then you'll tell me now. Everything, Naomi. All of it."

So she did. Quietly she told him what the doctor had said, watching the lines etched into his face deepen as she did.

When she'd finished, she added, "I am sorry for not telling you before. But I wasn't sure I really was sick, not to start with. The trouble came on slow. Even when I knew there was something amiss, I didn't want to believe it. I kept hoping—kept praying—it would just . . . go away."

Joseph's face had gone white, but his expression didn't soften. "You've known for a while, though. Long enough to go to the doctor. Yet I had to hear from some *Englischer* how I was hurting his friend, making you sicker, as if he cared more for you than I did. Than I *do*. Naomi"—he stepped closer and took her wrists in his hands—"you should have told me this. It was my right to know and to help you, if I could."

It wasn't really anger in Joseph's voice, Naomi realized. It was hurt. Somehow that was too much for her, that she'd hurt this man when all she'd wanted was to find a way to protect him, to keep him safe from the shadow looming over her life. Tears welled up into her eyes, but she couldn't dab them away, not with Joseph holding fast to her hands, so she finally lifted her chin and just let them streak down her cheeks.

"It was *my* right not to tell you." She choked the words out.

"But why, Naomi?"

"Because it couldn't do any good!"

"What craziness are you talking? No good it could do? Have I not always helped you? Always? How could you not trust me with such news?"

"Because I didn't want your *help*, Joseph. I wanted—" *Your love.* The words almost slipped past her lips.

"Well, you'll have my help now, want it or not," Joseph answered back fast—and stubbornly. "I'm going to the next appointment with you, and we'll make the arrangements for you to have this operation."

She shook her head. "It's expensive, Joseph, and who knows if it will even work?"

"The doctor said it would, likely."

"*Ja*, and they said the same about my last operation, but look how that turned out. A surgery like this will cost thousands and thousands of dollars. I've already put that load on my church at home once, and I can't ask them to—"

"We won't put the whole of the burden on them. I'll take out a loan on the farm. I'll sell it if I have to."

"*What?*" She froze, staring at him.

"It's good land and worth plenty. It should pay enough." He meant it. She could see it in his eyes.

"*Nee!*" Naomi hadn't stomped her foot in years, but she

rapped her heel hard against the scrubbed kitchen floor. "You will not do such a thing, Joseph Hochstedler!"

"A man does what he must for his wife."

"I'm not your wife!"

"You will be. *Nee*, don't shake your head at me, Naomi. This is why you were so quick to cancel our plans, ain't so? Not because of my troubles, but because of your own. Well, I'll not have it so. I won't leave you to go through this on your own."

This conversation was exactly the one she'd been trying to avoid. Joseph wasn't talking about love anymore. He was talking about duty. Just as she'd feared, she and her troublesome health had become a burden this man would wreck himself trying to bear.

She wouldn't allow that. But she couldn't stay here and break her heart arguing with him, either. She wrenched her hands free of his and moved past him toward the back door.

"Naomi—"

She halted at the door, but she didn't look back at him. "I know you only mean to be kind, and I thank you for that. But I don't need your pity, Joseph. I've had enough of that for a lifetime already. Please. Leave me be."

"Joseph?" Miriam called from upstairs, her voice trembling. "Is everything all right?"

"See to your sister," Naomi said over her shoulder as she slipped outside. "She's frightened, and she needs you."

She stumbled down the steps and into the yard. Her heart was already pounding, and she wouldn't be able to get far before she had to stop. She looked around desperately for some quiet place where she could gather herself together in peace, someplace Joseph wouldn't think to look for her right away.

Not the barn. Titus was still standing in the drive, the buggy hitched behind him. As soon as Joseph had finished comforting Miriam, he'd have to see to his horse, so the barn offered no sanctuary.

Her eyes lit on the empty dairy building. She could hide out in there until she'd gathered herself together. She hurried down the hard-packed path as quickly as she could, cracked open the wooden door, and slipped inside.

The long, low building was dim and silent. Shafts of thin winter sunlight slanted through the smudged panes, full of swirling motes of dust. She'd comforted Joseph here, on that hard day when Rhoda had left town and Caleb had been placed under the ban. This empty building was as good a place as any to cry over might-have-beens.

Naomi edged into the shadows and leaned against the pitted brick wall, burying her face in her shaking hands.

She heard the creak of the door and Joseph's voice at the same time. "Naomi?"

Her stomach clenched, and she answered without taking her hands off her face. "Joseph, please. *Ich vill noch bisli zeit.*"

"*Ja*, I know you want time, Naomi." Even though she had her eyes squinched shut, she knew when he came closer, felt each step he made in her direction. "But I'll not leave you out here to cry by yourself. We don't have to talk yet if you're not ready. But at least I can stand here with you, and that I'll do. Here." She heard a rustling noise, and the warmth of Joseph's coat slipped over her shoulders. "You keep forgetting your shawl."

The heavy fabric smelled of him, was warm from his body, and it jarred loose painful memories. He'd sheltered her with his coat before, that day in the barn when she'd said she would marry him. Something broke apart inside of her, and she struggled against it.

"Miriam will be upset," she whispered. "She'll need you. You should go back inside."

"You're the one who needs me right now, Naomi, although you're mighty stubborn about admitting it. I want to help, and I don't understand why you're not willing to let me."

He sounded annoyed. Anger flushed through her, and

she lifted her face from her hands. "You're right, Joseph. You don't understand! You don't understand what it's like to be a burden to the folks you love, all your life. You don't know what it's like to see how frustrated they are when yet another bill comes in the mail or when the tests don't come back good, even though you've tried so hard to do everything the doctor said to do."

He studied her, his face incredulous. "You've never been a burden, Naomi. People care for you. Of course they will want to help you."

"Well, I don't want to be helped! People have helped me all my life—even after my operation, nobody would let me do much of anything. I didn't know *how* to do much, but back home they wouldn't let me even try. When Katie asked me to come help her with the baby, I was so happy. Do you have any idea what that was like? How wonderful it felt to finally be the one scrubbing floors and washing dishes for somebody else? I could do those things as well as anybody, and Katie even let me do some cooking. She didn't care how many times my dishes went out to the pigs. She just let me keep trying until I got it right. She even thanked me. Then after your parents died, I'd learned enough to really help you and Miriam—I felt like *Gott* had finally answered my prayers. And when you asked me to—" She stopped and swallowed hard. "But now it's all over."

"Nothing has to be over, Naomi. You and I, we can still get married. We can—"

"*Nee.*" She shook her head. "You deserve better than to have some sickly *fraw* on your hands, running up bills, not even able to bear you children, likely—" She realized what she'd said and flushed. "I'm sorry, I'm . . . upset. But—"

"*Sei shtill*, Naomi." Joseph gently spoke the simple words Plain children often heard from an adult when they were speaking out of turn, when their tongues outran their *gut* sense. *Be still. Be quiet.* "Here." He pulled a handkerchief out of his pocket and offered it. When she hesitated, he added, "You'd best take it. Your nose is running."

Horrified, she snatched the scrap of cloth out of his fingers and pressed it to her face. She darted an embarrassed glance at Joseph, but he was looking around the empty building, his expression sad.

"When *Daed* told me he was going to close the dairy, he explained to me all his reasons why this was best for the family. They were *gut* reasons, sensible ones. He told me that he had prayed over this decision long and hard, and that he felt *Gott*'s leading, and I knew my father well enough to know that he was a smart and careful man. I knew him well enough to trust him. And yet I resisted him over it, and even up until the day he died, there was a little rift between us. I regret that."

The thoughtful pain in Joseph's words jolted Naomi out of her own hurt. She wiped her nose carefully and said, "You loved the dairy, Joseph, and why not? It had been in your family for so many years. Your father must have understood your feelings. You have nothing to regret."

He looked down at her, and his eyes crinkled in a warm and tender way that had her stomach tickling. "*Ach*, Naomi. Being married to you, I'm afraid it may be bad for my soul. You see no wrong in me, even where there's plenty. *Nee*, I was thinking only of myself back then, just as you are now."

Naomi frowned. "I don't believe I'm being selfish, Joseph."

"*Ja*," he argued mildly. "You are. It's selfish and prideful to be willing only to give help and not accept it when you truly have need. You've said as much to me yourself, when you wanted me to let you come here to help Miriam. You were right. Helping others is a blessing, and like all blessings, sometimes it is ours to have, and sometimes others must get their turn. You've blessed me beyond measure, Naomi, coming here in our hardest hours, bringing your light with you. Now that you've got your own troubles, you're asking me to leave you alone in the darkness?" He shook his head. "That I will not do, and it's wrong of you to ask it of me." He crooked a finger under her chin, nudging her face upward.

She looked up to meet his eyes, ready to argue, but her protest died unspoken. He was so close, gazing down at her, that even in the dim light she could see what was in his eyes.

It wasn't pity, after all. What resistance she'd mustered wilted into nothing.

"I love you, Naomi. At first, I thought the timing was poor, to fall in love when my life's in such a shambles. I was wrong. It's been *Gott*'s best gift to me, this love, growing during the hardest time of my life, like a thistle pushing up through rocky dirt."

She smiled in spite of everything. Joseph and his choice of words. "So our love is like a thistle, then? Not a rose or a violet? But a pesky weed? With prickles?"

He smiled back, and the tenderness in his face made her catch her breath. "*Ja*, a thistle. Roses are fussy and take lots of care, and they die if you look at them sideways. Thistles grow best in the hardest places. Maybe they've prickles aplenty, but they're strong, Naomi. You can't hardly kill a thistle once it takes good root, and they bloom real pretty in their time. And when that time is past, their seeds will have scattered as far as the wind blows. Young thistles will spring up, sturdy and strong, far as the eye can see." His thumb stroked her chin gently. "Wouldn't that be something?" His lips quirked.

She understood what he was suggesting, and fresh pain poked at her heart. "Joseph, like I told you, I don't know if—"

"We don't have to know. All we have to do is trust *Gott*'s will and go faithfully through whatever doors He opens." Joseph looked around the vacant building again. "And stop

waiting outside the doors He chooses to close." He searched
her eyes so intently that the world around them faded into
unimportance. "So what will it be, Naomi? Like I said the
other day, I've little enough to offer you just now, but what
I do have is still yours if you want it. Will you seek *Gott*'s
will alongside me as my wife? Or are you going to leave me
to stumble along without you?"

"Oh, Joseph." His name slipped past her lips, carried on
a sigh. There was only so long a person could resist when
everything she'd ever wanted was offered to her "*Ja*. I will
marry you, if you're truly sure you want me."

"I am sure." The corners of his lips quirked up very
slightly. "Truly sure. Are you? You'd better be. You're not
getting any bargain for yourself, taking me on."

She lifted her own hand to press his closer against her
cheek. "You're talking nonsense, Joseph Hochstedler. Any
woman would be blessed to have such a *gut*, kind, strong
man as you for her husband."

He chuckled, touching the tip of her nose with a gentle
finger. "Like I said, you always add too much credit to my
account. I'll be in debt to you for the rest of my life, I think.
It will be sweet for my heart, though, to have such faithful
kindness in my corner. I must work hard to deserve it, *ja?*"

"*Nee*," she replied with a soft certainty. "*Nee*, Joseph, I
don't think you'll have to work very hard at all."

He leaned down and touched her mouth with his, once,
gently. Firmly. And when he lifted his lips from hers, she
felt as if they'd sealed some sort of promise between them.

Maybe Joseph felt so, too, because his smile broadened
as he looked at her. He put his arms around her shoulders,
pulling her gently into his embrace. Naomi rested her head
against the muscled strength of his chest, hearing the thud
of his heart beating calmly, steadily on.

"You know," his voice rumbled under her cheek. "You
were right. This old barn would make a *wunderbaar* wood-

working shop. When your operation is over and you are well again, we will see to it. Together."

He sounded determined. Naomi closed her eyes, inhaling the sharp scent of pine shavings that always clung to Joseph. Fresh starts, how she loved them. Even if, in the end, they didn't always turn out the way you would hope.

"*Ja*," she whispered against his shirt. "We will fix it up, you and I."

If Gott wills it.

That part she didn't say aloud, but the silent truth hung between them in the air, just the same.

CHAPTER THIRTY-TWO

❧

TWO WEEKS LATER, JOSEPH SHIFTED HIS LONG LEGS in the front seat of the ridiculously small car, wishing he could crack open a window. Being as how the temperature outside was hovering above freezing, and that it was spattering rain, he'd best not. Still, he didn't much care for being in such close quarters with an *Englischer*.

Especially this one.

He shot a wary look at Naomi's friend Eric, who was driving down the highway toward the hospital, darting in and out of traffic like a hummingbird. When Eric glanced back at him, Joseph dropped his gaze to the papers in his lap.

Naomi had explained about her history with this man, how she'd become *gut* friends with his sister, who'd also suffered from heart trouble. From what she'd said, this Eric had cared faithfully for his ailing sister, and that was to his credit. Still, the man was a reporter, and Joseph intended to keep his distance—as best he could anyway.

They'd barely spoken since Eric had picked him up twenty minutes ago, and their silence was strained. Joseph would rather not have called Eric for this ride at all. On their trip to Naomi's doctor's appointment last week, they'd used a different driver because Eric's tiny back seat was too cramped for either of them to ride comfortably. But when Joseph had insisted on meeting with the hospital's financial department alone, Naomi had promptly suggested Eric.

Joseph knew why. She'd hoped he'd balk at asking the *Englisch* reporter, opting for his usual driver. Then she'd try again to convince Joseph to let her come along, since there'd be plenty of room.

That's why he'd decided to suffer through the ride with Eric. It didn't matter who drove him to the hospital today as long as he got the financing for Naomi's operation settled. He was prepared to do whatever it took, but Naomi was still fretting over how much this might cost. He'd rather not argue with her at the hospital in front of the *Englischers*.

She could fuss at him at home all she liked. It would make no difference. He'd gladly give Naomi her own way in everything else from here on, if that's what it took to keep her happy. But this time, just this once, he was putting his foot down.

He thumbed through the papers for the dozenth time. A letter from the bank, detailing Joseph's good credit, some tax papers that gave the estimated value of the farm, a letter from Isaac about his and Naomi's reinstated engagement, just in case there was any question of Joseph's right to assume the responsibility for the costs.

He lingered over that paper, written in Isaac's careful hand, stating that Joseph and Naomi would be married after her operation, if *Gott* spared her. He drew in a deep breath and leaned against the high back of the seat.

At the doctor's appointments, he'd listened closely as the cardiologist explained the test results and the treatment plan. Joseph didn't understand all the details, but apparently this was a routine but complicated surgery, made trickier by Naomi's previous heart problems. The doctor would make no guarantees for the success of the operation, but he'd been awful quick to make a grim guarantee if Naomi didn't have it.

That had settled the matter in Joseph's mind, but Naomi had taken longer to agree, worried about both the cost and the possibility of being permanently disabled.

All Joseph wanted was for Naomi to survive. If her health remained poor after the operation, they'd deal with it together, as man and wife.

Joseph had kept an eye on Naomi as they talked it all through. She said all the right things, but he'd seen little, telling hesitations that worried him.

He knew Naomi loved him. He recognized it in her face, saw his own love for her mirrored back to him whenever she glanced his way. But he also knew that, in spite of everything he'd said, she struggled with the fear of being a burden to him, of not being able to work alongside him or bear him children. If this operation left her ailing, he was going to have his work cut out getting her to go through with their wedding.

He sighed.

"You all right over there?" Eric tossed the question in an offhand way, as a boy might throw a ball to a newcomer in the schoolyard, seeing if the stranger was willing to play.

"*Ja*, I am fine," Joseph responded stiffly, adding belatedly, "Thank you."

"You seem kind of tense. I'm not making you nervous driving this fast, am I?"

Joseph lifted an eyebrow. Nervous? This *Englischer* had never held the reins of a spooky horse while an eighteen-wheeler blew by on a two-lane country road. It took more than fast driving to make Joseph nervous. "*Nee*. You're driving well enough."

Eric drummed his fingers on the steering wheel for a few seconds before speaking again. "Look, if you're waiting for me to apologize for flagging you down that day and telling you off, you're wasting your time. I'm sorry you're mad, but I'm not sorry Naomi's getting the medical attention she needs."

Joseph waited for a second, struggling to choose his reply carefully. He was talking to a reporter, after all. This was no time to muddle up his words.

"I am not angry with you. I believe you spoke out of concern, although you might have picked a better place to do it, maybe." He remembered something, and he shifted to dig into his pocket. "Here is your credit card, with Naomi's apologies for forgetting to return it. I thank you for loaning it to her." He placed the plastic rectangle in the cup holder between their two seats.

"Yeah, well. Naomi's like a sister to me." Eric's fingers clenched around the steering wheel, and Joseph recalled what Naomi had told him, that this Eric had lost his younger sister to her heart trouble sometime back.

Joseph's conscience jabbed him. Maybe this man was a reporter, but he was also a fellow human being, and one who'd shown Naomi a good deal of kindness. The very least Joseph could do was show kindness in return.

He cleared his throat. "I apologize for seeming unfriendly. The truth is, I am uneasy, but not because of your driving. I'll be talking money with the hospital about Naomi's surgery, and such conversations make me *naerfich*."

"Oh." Realization dawned on Eric's face as he maneuvered his small car around a semi. "I can understand that. Is that why you're going to the hospital without her? I wondered."

These *Englischers* sure did like to ask questions. "I don't want her fretting herself over this."

"She would, too." There was an uncomfortable pause before Eric added, "I don't mean to be nosy, but my sister had cardiac problems, too, you know. Hospital stays get expensive even when you have good insurance. Just between you and me, are you going to be able to swing this?"

That was what Joseph was going to the hospital to find out. "I hope. Often hospitals give Plain folk discounts because we pay in cash." And he had the farm to sell, if it came to that.

Which it very likely would.

"Doesn't your church community help you people cover your medical bills?"

Another question. Joseph sighed, trying to hang on to his patience. "They do, *ja*, as they can. Naomi's church back in Kentucky paid for most of her first surgery, along with her brothers. She's uncomfortable asking them to pay for another operation, but she's not technically a member here yet, and anyhow, this is a struggling community with little money to spare. Our bishop has promised to see what help he can pull together, but it likely won't be much. I will find a way to make up the rest of it." He made that promise as much to himself as to Eric.

Eric pulled into the hospital parking lot and parked. "I'm sorry, man. Financial trouble seems a pretty rough blow, especially given everything else that's happened to your family."

Joseph gave his companion a suspicious look, but the man didn't appear to be fishing for information. He seemed genuinely concerned.

"*Gott* will provide what is truly needed," Joseph said quietly. He unlatched the car door. "I thank you for the ride, Eric. I'm not sure how long I will be inside."

"Don't worry about it. Stuff like this takes as long as it takes. Hospitals are usually pretty happy to talk about payments, though, so I doubt you'll have to wait long. I'll be here when you're ready to go home." The *Englischer* pulled out his cell phone and began fiddling with it, his thumbs flying over the screen.

Joseph unfolded himself from the car and shut the door. Clutching his hopeful sheaf of papers, he headed toward the double glass doors leading into the hospital.

A long hour later, he walked back out into the chilly parking lot, feeling as if he'd just done a full day's hard labor. Talking numbers with men in suits wasn't something he was particularly good at, but he'd pulled out his bartering skills and done the best he could.

It hadn't been quite good enough.

The amount the hospital had set for Naomi's procedure had been more money than Joseph could have imagined, almost three times the value he'd been quoted for his farm. After a lot of wrangling and discussion with the hospital management, the price had been dropped by nearly half. It was still a good bit more than the farm's value, though, and that posed an additional problem. Joseph had only come up with one possible solution.

He didn't like it. Naomi would like it even less, which meant he'd best get it all arranged before he went back home.

When he reached the car, Eric's attention was fixed on the phone he'd balanced against the steering wheel. The *Englischer* glanced up as Joseph opened the car door.

"All done?"

"Not quite." Joseph sank into the low-slung seat with a sigh. "Do you have time to make one more stop?"

"Just tell me where you want to go."

Joseph reached into his pocket and produced Mona's card. "I need to go to this office, please."

"You're going to talk with a real estate agent?"

"Ja." He hesitated, then shrugged. He might as well share the worst of it. Folks would know soon enough. "The cost of the operation is more than I'd expected. I need to see about selling my farm. A movie company was interested in it earlier. One of their writers tried to lease it. I got a lawyer to stop that, and they weren't very happy. Well, now they can have the whole place outright, as long as they're willing to pay enough."

Eric whistled. "Oh, I expect they'll pony up the money,

all right. But your family's lived on that place for generations, right? Selling it seems pretty drastic. Are you sure this is what you want to do? Isn't there some other way you could come up with the financing?"

"There is no other way. And *ja*, I am sure."

He was. All his life, he'd loved the old farm, and he'd expected to turn it over to his own son one day. He'd never imagined selling it, much less like this.

Now, though, he'd surrender it gladly to whoever would pay the money needed to make Naomi healthy again. In the end, his decision had been simple.

But although the farm was legally his, his decision wasn't the only one that counted. Knowing what was likely to come of today's meeting, he'd talked it over with Emma and Mirry. Emma's agreement had come instantly over the phone line. Mirry's had been no slower. His sister's face had paled, but she'd nodded grimly and told him to sell the farm, if that's what it took.

Naomi mattered more. To all of them.

"You know what?" Eric said suddenly. "Sit tight for just a minute." He grabbed for his phone, working his fingers furiously over the screen.

Joseph watched him silently, bemused. What was the *Englischer* doing now?

He expected Eric would offer some explanation, but after several long minutes, Eric simply set down the phone, backed up the car, and drove out of the parking lot.

In fact, the younger man didn't speak again during the whole drive back to Johns Mill, although he seemed skittish. He kept tapping the steering wheel and darting uneasy glances in Joseph's direction.

For a few seconds, Joseph wondered over the change, but then he dismissed it from his mind. He'd enough business of his own to tend to. As they passed the county line, Joseph closed his eyes and leaned against the seat, trying to work out how best to explain all this to Mona.

When the car slowed, Joseph opened his eyes—and frowned. Eric hadn't taken him to Mona's office after all. They were pulling into the farm's driveway.

Before he could speak, Eric turned, his blue eyes glittering with excitement. "I know. This isn't where you asked to go. I'll take you to the realty office in a minute, if you still want to go. But first, I'd like to talk to you and Naomi. Okay?"

Joseph couldn't imagine what Eric needed to speak of that wouldn't wait. Still, the man had just done him a favor, flatly refusing to take any payment. "Of course. Please come in."

In the kitchen, Naomi was kneading bread in *Mamm*'s big wooden bowl, three glass loaf pans sitting greased and ready. Miriam sat at the table, a half-finished quilt square in her hand. His sister's welcoming smile faded when Eric trailed Joseph into the kitchen.

"It's all right, Miriam." Naomi spoke before Joseph could. "This is Eric. His sister and I were real *gut* friends."

"Hi." Eric halted just inside the back door, as if he sensed Miriam's fear.

Miriam's cheeks paled. She rose, edging away from the *Englischer* without turning her back on him, like a kitten confronted with an unfamiliar dog.

"*Excuse mich*," she murmured politely, her voice trembling. "I'll just go upstairs." She backed her way to the stairs, then hurried up them. A second later, they heard her door bang shut.

"Sorry," Eric said, shooting a sheepish glance at Joseph. "I think I scared her."

"It's not your fault," Naomi reassured him. "Miriam would be uneasy around any *Englisch* fellow. But it's good for her to see one, I think, even if it does upset her. Still." Naomi cocked her head listening. "Maybe I'd best go upstairs and check on her." She walked to the sink and began washing flour and bits of dough off her fingers.

Joseph cleared his throat. "Miriam will be all right for a few minutes, Naomi. Eric has something he wants to speak to us about."

"Oh?" Naomi's eyes darted between the two men as she dried her hands. "What is it?"

Eric squared his shoulders. "Well, I kind of . . . did something. I hope you aren't going to be mad."

Both Naomi and Joseph looked at him now, puzzled.

"Why would we be angry with you?" Naomi asked finally.

"Because of this." Eric pulled out his phone and ran his fingers deftly across the screen. He handed the device to Naomi, who frowned down at it.

Astonishment and confusion flickered over her face. "I don't understand."

Joseph took the phone from Naomi's fingers and squinted down at the screen. A huge figure with a dollar sign in front of it looked back at him. He glanced at Eric, who was bouncing nervously on his heels.

"It's a fundraising page I set up for Naomi's surgery right before we left the hospital. I know," he hurried on, "I should have asked first, but I wasn't sure you'd agree, and anyhow, I didn't know if it would even amount to anything. But . . . it did. The thing went viral in under thirty seconds, and it's still trending." He turned to Joseph. "I don't know how much they told you the surgery was going to cost, but whatever it is, I'm pretty sure this will end up covering it and then some. I found you another way, man. You won't have to sell your farm to that movie studio after all."

"Joseph!" Naomi frowned at him. "This is why you didn't want me to come with you today, ain't so? You knew I'd never agree to you selling this farm. And to sell it to the people making that awful movie? How could you even consider such a thing?"

He looked down at her troubled face and spoke quietly,

firmly. "It is my farm to sell, Naomi, and you are worth more to me than it is." He turned back to Eric. "I don't understand. You asked people for money? For us?" He glanced back down at the dollar amount on the screen. Eric was right. It was more even than the original fee the hospital had quoted him. Still, Joseph shook his head. "That's very kind of you, but we can't accept it." He held out the phone.

Eric didn't move to take it. Instead, he made a frustrated noise. "You'd accept money from your church, why not from them?"

"Taking money from our own people is different."

"Well, I think you're being narrow-minded. Maybe these people aren't Amish, but they're people with good hearts who feel for you and your family and all you've been through. They can't change what's already happened, but when I gave them a shot at helping you out of this jam, they jumped on it. Obviously. Refresh the screen. I bet it's gone up even more while we've been standing here."

Joseph had no idea how to refresh the screen, and anyway his mind was busy sifting through what Eric had just said.

"Naomi," Eric was saying, "talk to him. Make him see reason."

Naomi looked at him. Her lips firmed, and Joseph waited for her to take Eric's side. Instead, she stepped forward and gently took the phone out of his outstretched hand. She held it out to Eric.

"Joseph isn't comfortable with it. This was very kind of you, Eric, and of them, too. We thank you for it, but we can't accept this money. But"—she turned to Joseph—"we're not selling the farm to those movie people, either."

"Naomi—"

"*Nee*, Joseph. I'll scrimp and pinch until the cows come home, if that's what it takes, but I won't see you lose this place because of me. I just won't."

Eric slowly reached out to accept his phone, but Joseph's eyes were fixed on Naomi. His gaze skimmed her sweet, stubborn face, lingering on the milk-pale cheeks.

Scrimp and pinch.

As the Hochstedler Dairy had faltered and failed, his mother had scrimped and pinched with a vengeance. Determined to help her husband keep his family business, Levonia had stretched every dollar as far as she could and gone without all the little comforts that women treasured.

That's why *Daed* had made the difficult decision to close down the Hochstedler Dairy, the business his family had built by hand, stone by stone. Joseph had seen his father's face when the milk check ran out too early in the month, watching his tired wife mend and scrape, struggling to make it to the next one. Closing the dairy had never been about the money, Joseph realized, not really. It had been about *Mamm*.

Looking at Naomi now, Joseph finally understood his father's decision. In fact, he wondered that *Daed* had held out as long as he had. Joseph knew he couldn't have done it.

Naomi had as much fight in her as *Mamm* had ever had, but she'd never had Levonia's strength. Such a life would wear her down fast and hard. Joseph knew it with a cold, unshakable sureness. Even if the operation was a success, even if everything they were hoping for came to be, it would be so.

He wasn't having it. He'd gladly sell this farm—or anything else he owned—first.

Naomi was watching him. As if she knew his thoughts, she shook her head. "*Nee*, Joseph. We'll have to find another way."

There was no other way. He started to tell her that, then stopped.

Because it wasn't true. There was another way. A strange way, maybe. An *Englischer*'s way, but still.

It was a way.

He cleared his throat. "Explain it to me, the money on your phone. How does this work?" Naomi gasped softly, then pressed her hand over her mouth, her eyes wide.

Eric said, "Sure. It's simple, really." He moved next to Joseph and tapped on his phone, bringing up the screen again.

Joseph listened carefully to Eric's explanation. Afterward, he stood silently, his brow furrowed, trying to think it through as best he could, trying to find some way to square *Englisch* with the Plain.

"The problem is," Joseph said finally, "this is more money than we need, Naomi and I. I don't think it's right to take so much money for just us. We are not the only ones struggling in our community. If this money could be used to help more folks, and everybody only took just what they had to have, then maybe . . . maybe it might be all right."

He had Eric's full attention. "What are you thinking?"

"Well." Joseph's mind scrambled, working to make sense of the dilemma he'd been handed. "I'll have to check with Isaac, for sure, but lots of Plain farmers here in Johns Mill are having to find new ways to make a living. Could be we could use that money to help them do that, to start businesses up that could help the men support their families. Then some good could come out of all this trouble, maybe."

"I don't know." Eric spoke slowly, thoughtfully. "I mean, it's a nice idea and amazingly unselfish, really. But these people donated the money to you, Joseph, to pay for Naomi's surgery and to keep you from selling your family farm. That's how I pitched it. I'm not sure we can ethically use it for something different."

"I'll take some. Enough to pay the hospital's up-front fee and a little to set up a woodworking shop, maybe, big enough to earn a living with. But that's enough for us, and I wouldn't feel right taking more, not when there are other folks with needs, too. Why don't you ask them?" He pointed to the phone in Eric's hand. "You're quick enough with that thing, from what I've seen. Tell 'em what we're thinking and see what they say. If they want their money back, let them take it. But could be they won't."

"Could be." Eric studied him thoughtfully. He shrugged. "Only one way to find out, I guess." He bent over his phone, his thumbs flying over the screen.

Naomi stepped up beside Joseph, tugging his sleeve until he bent down close. "Is this all right with you? Truly?" she whispered in *Deutsch*.

"We'll see what Isaac says, but if he agrees, *ja*. I suppose it is all right."

"And if he doesn't?"

"Then you'll agree to my selling the farm, and we'll do the best we can."

Her brows lowered. "I'll never agree to selling this farm."

He glanced down at her and smiled. "*Ja*, you will. Sooner or later."

She didn't smile back. "*Nee*, I will not. I don't know yet what *Gott*'s will is for me, but I do know one thing. I'll rest easier if you have this place you love to come home to, whatever happens."

Joseph's smile faded, but he dropped the argument. There was no point in it. He'd never find the words to make Naomi understand what he himself knew with a grim certainty.

If he lost her, whether he still owned this farm or not wouldn't matter.

There would be no home for him anywhere then.

CHAPTER THIRTY-THREE

❧

THREE MONTHS LATER, THE HOCHSTEDLER HOUSE was so filled with people that even upstairs in Miriam's bedroom the floor shuddered as the crowd moved about below. Joseph sat on his sister's bed, one arm around her thin shoulders as she cried against his coat.

"I'm sorry," she murmured against the rough fabric. "I'm so sorry, Joseph."

"*Sell is awreit,* Mirry."

"*Nee,* it's not all right." She straightened and scrubbed her eyes with the back of one hand. "I should be downstairs, helping. Your family should be standing by you today of all days, but instead I'm up here, hiding like a coward, no good to you at all."

"Never say that." Joseph tipped up his sister's chin and looked into her reddened eyes. "You've worth to me, Miriam, plenty of it, even if you never step outside this bedroom again."

Miriam gave a broken sigh. "You shouldn't be so kind to me. I've let you down."

"You've let no one down. Now, stop your crying, *ja? Gott* has His purposes, and we must trust Him, even when things don't go as we'd hoped." The bedroom door creaked open behind him. "Anyhow, cheer up. You can stand up with me at my next wedding, just as well."

"Ha!" Naomi walked to the bed, carrying a laden tray of food. "You'd best not make promises you won't be able to keep, Joseph Hochstedler. You'll not be having another wedding anytime soon, not if I have anything to say about it."

Joseph looked up into his new wife's face. Her eyes were sparkling with love and laughter, and a healthy pink drifted over her pretty cheeks. Her deep blue dress was the same shade as Miriam's, the color of the wedding party. They'd all hoped Miriam would find the strength to stand with them through the service, which was why they'd decided to hold it here, in the cleared-out old dairy. But at the last minute, his sister's courage had crumpled.

Naomi smiled at him in that way that always made him catch his breath, then set the tray on the bed and turned to Miriam. "I've got you a taste of all the best dishes, so you're not missing out on a thing. And I promise, later tonight, after everyone goes home, we'll all sit together and talk ourselves silly."

"For a little while," Joseph interjected softly. Naomi caught his eye and flushed prettily.

"For a little while," she agreed.

A short knock on the half-opened door made them turn. Emma, dressed in her own matching blue dress, peeked in, her eyes troubled.

"Joseph and Naomi are wanted downstairs. Let me speak to them a minute, Miriam, and then I'll come sit with you awhile."

"*Nee.*" Miriam shook her head. "I don't want you missing all the fun because of me, Emma. I will be all right up here by myself."

"There's no fun I'd rather have than sitting with my sister after all these long weeks of being away," Emma retorted. "Although if you eat all that chicken casserole before I get back, I'll change my mind, maybe."

Once outside, Emma closed Miriam's door and beckoned Naomi and Joseph a short distance down the hall.

"I'm so sorry," she whispered, "but word of the wedding must have leaked out. There are some reporters outside. The men have lined up across the yard to keep them at a distance. Sam Christner hustled me inside and told me to warn you not to come out." Emma made a face and rubbed her elbow. "He could do with better manners, Samuel could. He almost threw me back in the house when I stepped onto the front porch. That man's strong as an ox and not so much smarter."

Naomi and Joseph exchanged a worried glance.

"*Denki*, Emma," Joseph said. "I'll see to it. Will you stay here with Miriam?"

"Of course," Emma agreed immediately. "I meant what I said. I'd rather sit in there with my sister than be anyplace else in the world. It's like a tonic to me after spending all those weeks at Melvin's. I just wish"—her voice shook—"that *Mamm* and *Daed* and Caleb were here. I miss them so, but I'm thankful that the rest of us can be together." She straightened her shoulders and offered Naomi a tremulous smile. "And I'm grateful that our family's beginning to grow."

She slipped back into Miriam's room and closed the door. Joseph started for the steps, but Naomi closed her fingers around his arm, holding him in place.

"You're not going outside, are you, Joseph?"

"*Ja*, I am."

"What are you going to do?"

"Whatever needs doing," he replied, looking down into her earnest face. She was the prettiest thing, his Naomi, with her light, pretty hair and her delicate little chin. Even better, since her operation two months ago, she'd been gaining strength so rapidly that he'd had a hard time keeping her from overdoing.

He had a feeling that would be a lifelong problem.

"Joseph, what good can come of you getting involved? Sam will keep them down at the road. I know it's wrong of them to come here today, but remember how kind they've been to us, the *Englischers*. So many folks around here have been blessed by that money they gave."

"It wasn't those reporters outside who gave it," he pointed out.

"It was one of the reporters out there who started it," she retorted, jutting out her chin.

Joseph swallowed a laugh. His new *fraw* looked like an aggravated bantam hen. He had a feeling this would be another lifelong problem of his—trying to argue with Naomi without laughing at how cute she was when her feathers were ruffled.

"I'll mind my tongue," he promised. "But I'll not hide inside, either. Not anymore."

"Joseph—"

"Do you trust me, Naomi?"

She broke off, her eyes searching his face. Then she nodded.

"*Ja*," she answered softly. "I do trust you, Joseph."

"*Gut.*"

"But if you're going outside, I'm coming with you."

This time he didn't even try not to laugh. The sound rang against the walls and beams of the hallway and was echoed by laughter from the friends and relatives milling around the house, waiting for dinner to be served.

They walked together down the steps, through the kitchen full of scurrying women who'd volunteered to oversee the wedding dinner on Naomi's behalf. The smells of chicken and stuffing hung richly in the air, and the room was so crowded that they had to thread their way carefully to the door.

"Where are you two going?" Katie Lapp looked up from the table, where she was uncovering a steaming roaster pan full of mashed potatoes. "We're almost ready to serve the first seating. You'll need to take your places soon."

"We will be back in a minute," Joseph assured her.

"All right, but if you're not back in time, I'll give that bell by the door a ring, and you'd best come running. We can't have the bride and groom late for their own wedding supper." Katie turned her attention back to the potatoes, dabbing at her sweaty cheek with her sleeve.

"We'll be back," Joseph repeated. He opened the door and ushered Naomi outside into the fresh air. Then he halted, stopped short by the scene in front of him.

It was disturbingly familiar. Several Plain men were fanned out along the brink of the yard, facing a dozen or so reporters, who were angling cameras in the direction of the house, doing their best to capture photos of the guests.

Joseph's mind flashed back to the day of his parents' funeral, and the happy warmth in his heart chilled. He felt a quick squeeze on his arm and glanced over to find Naomi looking up at him, her gray-green eyes sympathetic.

"It's all right," she whispered. "They will soon be gone again, once this day is done. It is their job to get pictures to sell. They mean no harm, not really. This is nothing to trouble ourselves over, *ja?*"

"They may go away after today, but they'll be back. Ever since news of the movie leaked out, they've been swarming Johns Mill like ants on a cake. This is something we must deal with straight out, Naomi, best we can." He studied the crowd and came to a decision. "I'm going to speak to them. Wait here."

"But, Joseph—"

"Please, Naomi. Just wait here."

He strode across the yard. Samuel Christner was standing in front of the knot of reporters, using his blocky body as a barrier. Sam glanced over his shoulder when Joseph approached. He lifted an eyebrow, nodding toward the man standing off to his right.

"We've had a volunteer," Samuel muttered in *Deutsch*. "Do you want me to send him back to the house?"

Joseph looked, expecting to see one of Naomi's brothers—and then looked again. In his *Englisch* suit, Eric stood out like a sore thumb in the line of Plain men, but he held his place with the same quiet resolution as the others, hands clasped behind him. Eric caught Joseph's eye and nodded a greeting before turning back to face the news crews milling along the roadside.

"Nee." Joseph cleared his throat carefully. "He's a friend, that one, and an invited guest. Let him stand among you if he wants."

"A *gut* friend, to stand against his own like that," Samuel muttered. "Trying to earn his wedding supper, I reckon. You'd best get back to the house, Joseph. You'll only stir 'em up if you stay out here. Take Naomi with you and tell that stubborn sister of yours to keep out of sight, too."

Joseph stared at Sam for a minute, thinking hard. Then he clapped his friend on the shoulder and grinned. "You know, Samuel, you're a sight smarter than my sister gives you credit for."

The man's broad face creased with confusion. *"Vass?"*

Joseph crossed the guarding line of men and walked toward the crowd. The reporters shuffled excitedly, swaying together as they tried to get the clearest picture. They reminded Joseph of birds flocking when the weather turned cold, dipping and moving mindlessly together as one body.

Joseph halted before them and held up his hand. He waited patiently as cameras clicked and whirred, as the men and women called out questions.

How was the wedding, Mr. Hochstedler?
Is Emma here?
Have you spoken to your brother? Was he invited?
Can we get a photo of you and your bride?

Joseph stood silently, hand upraised, waiting them out. While the reporters were still shouting questions, Sheriff Townsend, who'd been standing beside his patrol car, walked over and leaned in close.

"Joseph," he said, "there's nothing I can do about this, long as they stay on the right-of-way. If they ain't on your property and don't cause trouble, they can take all the pictures they want."

"What if they are on my property?" Joseph pitched his voice loud enough to be heard.

The sheriff frowned. "They're not, though."

"They could be." Joseph turned his gaze to the gaggle of reporters, who'd finally gone silent and were listening intently to this exchange. "I would like to invite you—all of you—to come, take a seat at our table and enjoy our wedding meal with us. But—" he added as an excited murmur of disbelief rippled through the crowd. "As you all know, we don't like photographs. So if you accept my invitation, you will have to leave your cameras and cell phones in your vehicles."

"Are you serious?" A tall reporter lowered his camera when Joseph nodded.

"I am serious, *ja*. You are very welcome here, and we are happy to have you as our guests. Just no cameras, please."

"I'm in." The reporter turned and jogged back to his van, and the other reporters quickly followed suit.

"Brilliant," Eric muttered. The *Englischer* had come beside him and was shaking his head as they watched the crowd hurriedly stowing their equipment in vans and cars. "You just took control of the narrative."

"I don't understand what that means."

"It means you're giving them an exclusive that's going to be all over the news tonight, but you're doing it on your turf and on your terms. All just by inviting them to supper. That was a freaking brilliant move, man."

"Not so brilliant," Joseph admitted. "You and Sam gave

me the idea. Anyhow, it's only what I should have done from the first. But never mind. Better late than never, and today's not a day for regrets anyhow. Now, come on. It is almost time to eat."

He led the way across the yard to where Naomi waited by the corner of the house. She smiled up at him.

"I saw. You did *gut*," she whispered as he drew close.

Strange, he thought, how much better he felt whenever Naomi was beside him. Warm and right. Complete. As he looked down into her eyes, he could feel his expression change, shifting into the way he looked at Naomi and Naomi alone. The way, he realized, that he would always look at her.

So this is what marriage is, he thought. Looking at one woman like this for the rest of your life and having her look back at you the same way.

Isaac was right. What man wouldn't want such a blessing?

"Hey!" Angry voices erupted from behind him, and he turned, tucking Naomi behind him. A stocky reporter had his phone angled toward them, snapping pictures.

"Sorry." He flushed defiantly when he caught Joseph's eye. "But the look on your faces right then . . . that was a million-dollar shot."

"I'll ask you to delete that photograph." Joseph spoke quietly. "Please."

"Aw, come on. I'm telling you, it was a sweet shot. Folks are going to love it. I promise I won't take any more, okay?"

"Give me that, Carl." The taller reporter wrenched the phone out of the other man's hand. He scrolled through, muttering, "What's the matter with you? Man invites you into his house on his wedding day, all he asks is for you not to take pictures. *You don't take pictures.* Didn't your mama teach you any manners?" He glared at the rest of the group. "Anybody else need an etiquette lesson?" He waited until they shook their heads, and then he turned back to Joseph.

"Here." He held out the other man's phone. "I deleted the pictures. Go ahead and throw this thing in that horse trough over there if you want to. He deserves it."

"Hey!" the shorter reporter protested.

"Shut up, Carl."

Joseph could feel Naomi watching him, holding her breath as she waited to see what he would do. He offered the phone to its owner. "Go put this in your car, *ja?* You'd best hurry, or you'll miss the first seating for dinner and have to wait for the second."

The shorter man accepted his phone, looking uncomfortable. "So you're . . . uh . . . still okay with me coming inside then?"

"The invitation has not changed. If you don't take pictures, you are welcome here."

"Okay. Thanks," the reporter mumbled, turning toward the row of parked vehicles.

"I'd better go with him." A slender blond woman spoke up with a grim determination in her voice. "Just to make absolutely sure that phone ends up where it's supposed to."

"Sorry, man." The tall reporter held out his hand for Joseph to shake. "It's no excuse for that kind of behavior, but a photo of the two of you, looking at each other like that on your wedding day? It won't really bring a million dollars, but it'll come close enough. The temptation's too much for some folks, I guess."

"I understand." Joseph nodded to Samuel Christner, who'd been watching this interchange with an impassive expression. "Sam, take these folks in and help them find some seats at the table, will you?"

"I will, *ja.* Come on with me, the lot of you."

As the group followed the massive Amish man up the porch steps like a trail of obedient ducklings, Naomi squeezed Joseph's arm.

"You handled that real well," she whispered. She shook

her head. "It's hard to imagine, ain't so? That anybody would pay a lot of money for a photograph of two ordinary Plain folks like us. It makes no sense at all."

Joseph looked down into his wife's sweet face and realized he didn't agree. He understood exactly why people might pay for a photograph of this slim, fair-haired woman in her crisp blue dress, with the pink back in her cheeks and hope and love shining in her eyes.

It wasn't just the beauty in her face, although it was there, for certain sure. But beauty was easy enough to find. *Nee*, it was the gentle strength and the faithful kindness of this small woman that the rest of the darkened world really lacked and hungered for.

He understood that. He ought to. He'd lacked and hungered in his own darkness until Naomi had come to him, bringing a gift he could never begin to deserve.

Herself.

"Vass denksht?" she asked him softly.

What was he thinking? Joseph smiled at her, but he didn't answer out loud.

I think that when I am an old man and my mind stumbles, I'll likely forget many things. But never will I forget this, the way you looked on the day you became my wife. I think that no matter what changes come for us, for the rest of my life, whenever I look at you, I will see you just as you are this minute, today.

He didn't know how to explain that to her. As always, the pretty words, the right words, twinkled maddeningly just beyond his reach. So instead, forgetting the people who might be watching, he leaned down to fit his mouth to hers. As her lips yielded sweetly to his own, Joseph's heart swelled until it crowded his chest and made his breath come short.

"I'll show you." He broke the kiss to whisper the clumsy promise against her lips. "Maybe I can't tell you, but I'll show you, Naomi. Every single day."

She couldn't have known what he meant, but to his surprise, she asked him no questions. She only beamed up at him, her small face flushed and a loving wonder in her eyes. Behind them the kitchen dinner bell began to clang, its raucous song echoing against the spring green hills like a thousand happy bells, calling them in.

ACKNOWLEDGMENTS

This book would never have made it into your hands without the help of some very generous, knowledgeable, and patient people.

My wonderful critique partner and dear friend, author Amy Grochowski, read this story chapter by chapter and helped me polish it to a shine. Thanks, Amy, your thoughtful insights and constant encouragement made all the difference!

A special shout-out to my tell-it-like-it-is beta reader crew: Stacie Boyt, Amanda Boyt, Emily Boyt, and Clarissa Pipes, who helped me drag this story kicking and screaming in the right direction. You ladies are worth your weight in gold!

I'm immeasurably indebted to Anna Mast for serving as my consultant regarding the nuances of the Amish lifestyle. Your good-natured willingness to answer my nosy (and sometimes silly) questions is much appreciated!

I owe additional thanks to Becky Watts for giving me insights into journalistic practices, and to Rand Pressley for answering my questions related to cardiac health. I so appreciate the kind willingness of these folks to share their expertise with me. Any mistakes in these areas are entirely my own.

I'm deeply grateful for my fabulous agent, Jessica Alvarez at Bookends Literary Agency, whose wisdom and vision—

and admirable patience—brought this story to birth. Your awesomeness remains unmatched.

Extra-special thanks to Anne Sowards, Berkley editor extraordinaire, for loving this story, wiping its face, and polishing it up for readers!

Additionally, I can't pass up the opportunity to say thank-you to my talented newsletter and website coordinator (and all-around exceptional human being), author Heather K. Duff.

As always, big love and thanks to my family: my husband, David, and my children, Rebecca (and son-in-love, Kevin), Jackson, Joanna, and Levi, as well as my sister, Leigh Hall—who dealt with my absentmindedness, constant plot rehashing, and quickie dinners while this book was being written.

Finally, to my Lord and Savior, the Author of everything good in my life: I offer this book back to You with a grateful heart.

Ready to find
your next great read?

Let us help.

Visit prh.com/nextread

Penguin
Random
House